Six Days

Other novels by Patrick J. O'Brian include:
The Fallen
Reaper: Book One of the West Baden Murders Trilogy
The Brotherhood
Retribution: Book Two of the West Baden Murders Trilogy
Stolen Time
Sins of the Father: Book Three of the West Baden Murders Trilogy

Current, past, and future projects by the author can be seen
on his website at:
www.pjobooks.com

SIX DAYS

A novel by Patrick J. O'Brian

iUniverse, Inc.
New York Lincoln Shanghai

Six Days

iUniverse, Inc.

For information address:
iUniverse, Inc.
2021 Pine Lake Road, Suite 100
Lincoln, NE 68512
www.iuniverse.com

ISBN: 0-595-33099-1 (pbk)
ISBN: 0-595-66746-5 (cloth)

Printed in the United States of America

Thanks to Nannette Bell, Mark "Otis" Adams, Carol Pyle, Brad Wiemer, James Fullhart, Lesa Fullhart, and Rob "Bobby" Mead for catching my typos before everyone else did.

Additional thanks to Fred Cler, Chris Spencer, and Mike Hill, Ric Oliver, Paul Singleton, Joe Scott, and Brian Lough for input on local details.

Thanks to Chris Kirby, Greg Polk, Mike Fuller, Paul Singleton, Ric Oliver, and Jeff Groves for appearing on the cover.

Special thanks to Jeff Groves for providing detailed information necessary to the story, and for putting up with me more than any one human being should have to.

As always, thanks to Kendrick L. Shadoan at KLS Digital for fantastic work in designing the cover. Work by the cover artist can be seen at:
www.klsdigital.com

CHAPTER 1

▼

Tim Packard felt himself tense as he stepped from an unmarked departmental Caprice, long since removed from his department's regular fleet.

As three officers younger than himself stepped out simultaneously, Packard carefully shut the passenger's side front door to avoid waking local residents in the early morning hour.

He was about to undertake the most dangerous assignment of his career, and the last thing he needed was a mistake. The lives of three young men were in his hands, and he was a green sergeant to his department, heading a new type of task force to his city.

"You three stay here," he ordered the three officers, all dressed in regular street clothes, each armed with their service weapons and a shotgun.

They nodded without saying a word as Packard turned to inspect the area around the house they were about to invade.

Sometimes Packard did things by the book, but there were times he stretched the law to serve the public better. He had two kids and a wife to return to every night, so everything the officer did was to keep them, and their surroundings, that much safer.

Packard had lived in Muncie, Indiana, his entire life, so when the new police chief asked if he wanted to lead a task force aimed at taking gangs and drugs off the streets of his city, the new sergeant jumped at the opportunity.

Walking down an alley to inspect the building they were about to enter, Packard took in the sights along Seymour Avenue, wishing the city would hurry up and tear down the condemned buildings all around him. Recent factory closings had cut the city's population significantly as people transferred, or left to find jobs elsewhere. Empty buildings seemed to be abundant on the south end of town.

The city never did anything quickly, and he blamed that on politics.

In this particular building, bricks had fallen in chunks, windows were cracked or broken, and the awning above the back entrance had collapsed, blocking the doorway.

Holding his shotgun to one side, the sergeant felt along the brick, making certain the building would hold up to their invasion if a door or two got kicked in. He felt a bit warm in his black leather jacket that reached past his waist, but not because of the April weather.

In fact, the entire spring had been mired in unusually cold weather. Packard's warm feeling came from nerves, and the fact he was about to figuratively put his life on the line for little more than information.

His career choice involved some degree of danger, even when he wasn't at work. Some people required little motivation to harm police officers and their families. A grudge, or cash payment, was often enough.

No matter what, he had a reputation to uphold. When people on his department thought of his name, they knew Tim Packard was someone who got things done. In fact, the new police chief used that line on him in January when he asked the rookie sergeant to start the new task force.

Packard looked closely at the back doorway, which was little more than splintered wood and bricks stacked upon steel rails that had collapsed under stress. The door itself leaned awkwardly to one side, off its hinges. It appeared barricaded with boards and more wood, and likely had furniture behind it to keep unwanted visitors away.

Under the overcast sky he spied overgrown weeds, cracked pavement, and trash all around him on the surrounding properties. Everything from discarded needles to old fast food bags lay strewn across the yards, some old, some fresh.

All morning he had kept a strong front for his troops, because they were new to him, and vice versa. So long as they believed he was in complete control, and could do no wrong, they would follow and obey. Packard had trained them to survive outside of an investigative office or patrol car, but what they made of themselves as cops was up to them.

Feeling his stomach tense, then shudder, he vomited along the side of the building, assured his fellow officers didn't see his moment of weakness.

He had sat silently through an early breakfast with them, remaining quiet and stoic as he usually did. After treating, he ran through their plan one last time, then drove them to this spot.

Feeling his mouth with the back of his closed fist, Packard swallowed the few lingering chunks in his throat as he collected himself, staring into a shard of detached glass leaning against the old building.

His blue eyes stared through glasses, which he removed momentarily to wipe clean of sweat beads lining the inside lenses. He had grown in a thick reddish beard to accompany his mustache for his special assignment, because he had little more than a fringe atop his head, with tufts of red hair scattered along his scalp.

Leaning one hand against the building, Packard steadied himself, and his nerves, before daring to look inside one of the damaged windows. Though covered in grime and soot from years of neglect, the windows allowed the sergeant a peek inside.

From his vantage point Packard saw little but garbage strewn inside, then the slightest of movement.

If his informant was correct, there were several local drug dealers sleeping off their highs from the night before.

Part of the reason Packard's new task force was created stemmed from local drug dealers getting involved with gangs, then helping traffic drugs to the north, including Gary and Chicago. From there, they had been rumored to be using Lake Michigan to move the drugs to other areas, despite the Coast Guard increasing their patrols of the lake.

Packard wanted to squeeze these dealers for information to find the bigger dealers and gangs. He was about to encounter what he called small fish, but even small fish sometimes carried big guns.

"You okay?" Clay Branson asked quietly, walking along the side of the building, as Packard finished looking into the window.

"What did I tell you?" Packard asked the rhetorical question in a hushed voice.

"I know, but I got worried," Clay replied.

"If I was in trouble, you would have heard gunshots," Packard said sternly. "Now let's get back there before we wake up everyone in the neighborhood."

Clay's cousin, Mitch Branson, and Ed Sorrell comprised the rest of Packard's team. They were young, but all three were raised in the south end of the city, meaning they knew how to take care of themselves, and each other.

All three seemed night and day in personality to Packard, but gelled to form an interesting team, virtually able to read one another's thoughts in any given situation.

Packard followed Clay up to their car, looking cautiously around because his younger officers didn't always stay aware of their surroundings. Sometimes he felt like a father figure to them, but he maintained a wary relationship. As their supervisor, he could never allow himself to become too chummy with the three, or he risked losing their respect, and their attention.

He trusted Clay, because the younger officer was his blue chip prospect, but he was still digging into the man's past, which proved somewhat elusive. Until he knew more about the officer, outside of his work record, he refused to show Clay more trust than he did the other two officers.

Looking at the front of the building, which had seen better days, Packard pumped his shotgun, glanced at the other three men with him, and marched toward the weakened structure.

With one swift kick, the sergeant sent the door swinging inside the building, startling two residents sleeping downstairs amongst the trash.

One immediately reached for something beside his makeshift bunk, but one of the officers aimed his shotgun threateningly.

"Don't," Ed Sorrell said simply with a negative shake of his head.

Thinking better of reaching for anything, the skinny dealer simply waited for orders from the armed men surrounding him.

Just enough light made its way inside that the officers could see the two drug dealers lying on the floor, startled by the sudden appearance of four armed men. Packard aimed his shotgun down toward one of the men, then freed one hand to reach inside his jacket to pull out a slip of paper.

"It's not your lucky day," he said to the junkie dealer he knew as Squeaky, mainly because the man ratted out his fellow criminals to avoid jail time.

"What the fuck?" Squeaky asked, his eyes widening from fear, or from the effects of the drugs the night before.

Packard displayed a sheet of paper to the dealer, knowing all too well the man was incapable of reading. In his hand he actually held an old court summons he had dug out of his files for just such a purpose.

"This gives me permission to search these premises, and seize anything I find here as evidence of your wrongdoing," Packard said, moving his jacket aside so the badge dangling from his neck showed in the dim lighting.

Squeaky could say nothing as his shoulders slumped and he stared at the ground.

Smiling inwardly, Packard knew he was about to get what he wanted.

"Boys, detain our friend over there while I have a talk with ol' Squeak here," the sergeant said, heading for the front door. "And one of you see what you can find in this dump."

By that, Packard meant for one of the three to discover any possible evidence in the piles of discarded trash and narcotics.

Clay indicated with a nod he would take charge of the search, because he usually took the initiative when Packard wasn't around.

In the meantime, Packard led his unwitting suspect outside to the front concrete steps. The morning sun glowed red in the distance, because the dawn was still breaking.

He took a seat along the dilapidated concrete steps, setting the shotgun to his safe side, away from his suspect.

Reaching inside his jacket, Packard pulled out a pack of cigarettes, quickly offering one to Squeaky, which the man accepted, before lighting one up. His wife, a reformed smoker, was always on him about quitting, which he promised he would before the year was up. As it was, he still needed a smoke to jumpstart his morning.

"Tell me what the boys are going to find in there," Packard casually ordered his newfound snitch.

Squeaky shot him a questioning look as the sergeant drew on his cigarette.

"More important, Squeak, tell me who you're moving drugs for."

"I don't know nothin', man."

Packard shook his head negatively. They always played hard to get so needlessly.

"I know you've had the grand tour of our jail facilities several times," Packard noted. "One more time and you're probably spending some time down in Pendleton, aren't you?"

Pendleton housed a state prison.

"I dunno, man."

"Well," Packard said with a shrug. "I keep hearing about you moving merchandise for Julio Morales and his crew."

Squeaky looked away, indicating to Packard he was hitting close to home with his statement.

Packard took a final drag from his cigarette before flicking it away as he exhaled into the morning breeze.

"I'm betting your buddy in there gives me some information, and if he talks first, he walks and you get sold down the river with whoever else I bring down."

As though on cue, Clay appeared at the doorway, holding several plastic bags, each containing specific drugs marketable on the streets. The younger officer held them up momentarily for Packard to inspect before returning to the building's interior.

"Wow, that's a pretty good collection," Packard said.

He took up the shotgun, emptying it of all cartridges as he waited for an answer. Seldom did Packard speak more than necessary, and he already felt as though he was being overly patient with this suspect.

Waiting pensively while Squeaky pondered his future, the sergeant stared across the street toward other old buildings, then to the Radisson Hotel located very close to a bad part of town. The hotel itself was almost a work of art, with dining facilities and ball rooms for receptions and rented gatherings.

"And if I talk?" Squeaky asked of the sergeant reluctantly.

Packard sat silently a moment.

"You tell me what you know, and I leave you here."

Squeaky knew the system well enough that his options were openly apparent. He believed Packard held a search warrant or he wouldn't be sitting outside with the sergeant. Finding the amount of drugs Clay walked outside with, usually meant arrest and several years behind bars if the prosecutor pushed for it and the offender had an arrest record.

Of course Packard had absolutely no *real* leverage whatsoever. He was banking on Squeaky falling for his charade.

"I deliver to a guy by the name of Salas in Fort Wayne," Squeaky admitted, surprising Packard.

The sergeant expected his informant to fall for the name he had dangled to him, but Squeaky apparently felt honesty was the best policy.

"I want to meet this guy," Packard said. "Can you arrange a meeting down here in Muncie?"

"Hey, I gave you the name. You said that's all you wanted."

Again, as though on cue, Clay walked to the doorway holding a paper sack which he tilted to one side so Packard could examine the property inside. Bundles of significant currency lined the bottom of the bag, which gave the sergeant an idea.

"Set that aside," he ordered Clay, knowing the young man would do what he asked without question.

"I need that or I'm a deadman," Squeaky immediately said.

"It seems we need one another," Packard replied. "I've got some cash you need, and you've got someone I want very much to meet."

Put between a rock and a hard place, Squeaky thought a moment as Packard stood, ready to see the progress of his men inside. They were likely toying with the other dealer, overturning the entire place for evidence. Within a few months, the team had already earned the nickname Rough Riders, because arrests were up, and so were the internal affairs reports.

Packard knew his boundaries, and he also knew the new chief didn't mean for him to play nice when confronting dealers and gang bangers. He would stretch the law as far as he could, and knew the chief would bail him out of some of the questionable situations.

"Where do we go from here?" he finally asked his suspect.

"I can get him down here tomorrow," Squeaky said, sweat beginning to bead at his forehead.

Packard looked around him, growing suspicious of his surroundings, particularly since he had no true authorization to be there. The last thing he needed was a curious patrolman stopping by to see why an unmarked car stood outside a notorious drug haunt.

"Let's step inside and talk about the details," he said, taking up his shotgun before following the snitch inside.

*   *   *   *

An hour later, Packard found himself seated at a downtown coffee and bagel shop with Clay, after they left Ed Sorrell and Mitch to clean up the details.

Like much of the old downtown area, the shop was converted from crumbling bricks to a facade of mostly glass that gave the area a modern look. Strangely, they were only several blocks from where they had busted Squeaky that morning, indicating the downtown area was by no means an island from drugs and prostitution.

Still, it was improving.

They planned the meeting for the next morning at the outskirts of town to avoid suspicion from Squeaky's connection.

Packard's group would have secure cover inside an abandoned vegetable stand, which looked like an oversized wood shed. Perfect for surveillance equipment during the transaction, and a surprise arrest after the business was concluded, the area also provided them with cover and easy access to the suspects.

"So what's our plan?" Clay asked, eyeing Packard and the glass of lemonade set before him.

"We watch, we snatch, and hopefully, we move to the next level."

"Next level, huh?"

Packard took a pen out from inside his jacket, then tapped it almost nervously against the table. He felt his right knee bob up and down as the anticipation grew within him. His group was making a difference, and he felt unusually close to putting away some very dirty people.

"You okay?" Clay asked.

"Yeah, fine," Packard answered in short as he often did.

"You're being kind of vague about this. There's no need to be secretive. We're on the same side."

Sometimes Packard had a supervisor mentality that came with the new stripes on his uniform. He liked working on a need to know basis anyhow, but his three officers would never feel like a team if he didn't make them privy to some of the details.

"There isn't much to it," he finally told the younger officer. "Squeaky is going to set up a meeting with Salas, who's a middleman in their operation, and we snag the guy and his bodyguard, or guards, and pump them for information."

"Why do I get the impression this could turn into a Wild West shootout?"

"It won't if you three do your job."

Nodding silently, Clay didn't seem pleased with such a sketchy plan.

"I'll fill you in when I know more," Packard promised.

"Okay."

Clay was Packard's first-round draft pick for his task force, with good reason. He had a sixth sense about him in the form of intuition and keen observations. Of anyone on the entire force, he was the most capable of defending himself from years in the martial arts. Intelligent, powerful, and seasoned enough to stay alive against the worst of what the group might face, Clay would be missed by the midnight patrol shift he left behind.

Thick, and built better than a pit bull, Clay was a good-looking young man who had yet to marry. His dedication to his job and martial arts kept him busy, but Packard worried about him becoming too much like his cousin, or his father.

Clay's father worked for the city police department with a reputation that preceded him. He was a veteran officer who believed in the old ways of busting kneecaps and knocking teeth loose to get answers.

Packard too believed in the old ways, but knew they were no longer practical. He remained caught between a generation gap of officers, walking a fine line.

Like his sergeant, Clay had a receding hairline, but his was in the early stages and barely noticeable. He usually maintained a neutral face that forbid people to read his thoughts and emotions.

Despite Packard getting his way by attaining Clay's services, the officer came with baggage in the form of his cousin and Ed Sorrell, neither of whom would have been in Packard's top ten choices.

In Packard's opinion, Clay was still a bit too soft. There were times he tended to believe what the criminal element told him, but that was his cousin's fault.

Mitch was openly an environmentalist who wanted to do police work for the right reasons.

To help people.

Part of that rubbed off on Clay, which served the general public just fine, but when Packard confronted drug dealers, gangs, and thugs who would harm their own mothers for money, he wanted hardened officers at his side, not green negotiators.

Hard as he tried, the three officers were reluctant to adopt Packard's ideals. He constantly found himself asking the three if they were thinking correctly. They always answered affirmatively, but he sometimes felt they were holding out on him.

"How far can we go with this?" Clay inquired, as though they might be overstepping their bounds.

"You let me worry about that," Packard replied, aiming an index finger at the younger officer.

Clay didn't appear content, but sipped his lemonade anyway. Packard stared momentarily at the younger man, wishing the officer would act more like an obedient dog than an independent cat.

"Are you up to this?" Packard asked.

"Of course," Clay replied with a brief pause. "Why?"

"You always hide your emotions. I never know if you're glad to be part of this force, or you want to turn me in."

Clay finally chuckled to himself.

"I'd never turn you in, Sarge."

"I know that, but I need you committed to me so your tree-hugging cousin and that goofy Sorrell will fall in line."

Packard regretted letting Mitch come aboard, but at least the man was big, and made for a good enforcer when people required some roughing up. Sorrell was a complete waste of space in the sergeant's opinion, and he was a liability because of the stupid things he did that got him in hot water with internal affairs.

Still, the two younger officers refused to join the task force without bringing their bad apple with them.

His hope that Sorrell might wash out had since come and gone, so Packard was stuck with the daunting task of converting all three to his way of thinking unconditionally.

Clay rubbed his face with both hands tiredly as he yawned.

"You've got my support," he finally said. "We're making a difference, so I'm not going to question anything you've done."

"Then you trust me now?"

"Sure, Sarge."

Clay most always called him 'Sarge' instead of using Packard's first name. He was unusually respectful that way.

"Good," Packard said. "Then trust me that we're going to do some good tomorrow."

Clay nodded.

"You need any help?"

"No. I'm going to have a look at the site so I can create a plan."

"Okay. I'll be at city hall if you need me for anything."

"I might later. What are you going to do at city hall?"

"Lift weights with Mitch."

"Good," Packard said with a strange smirk. "Tell that cousin of yours to be ready tomorrow. I don't want him or Sorrell fucking this up."

"Will do," Clay said. "I'll call you after we're done."

He threw a few dollars on the table to cover the tab and a tip before heading for the door.

Packard often thought of his task force as a mixed blessing. It could earn him a commendation, or cost him his job.

Reaching for his wallet, he decided to get started with his plan by visiting the old vegetable stand.

CHAPTER 2

▼

While it held several rooms filled with unused equipment, the basement of city hall also housed the police department's uniform division, computers on which to do their reports, the evidence storage area, locker rooms, and a workout facility.

After an hour of lifting weights and using the stationary bikes, Clay and Mitch decided to call it a day.

While Mitch went ahead to the locker room, Clay lingered a few minutes to chat with some of his pals from the midnight shift about nothing in particular.

He entered the locker room a moment later to a view of his cousin's backside. Though his posterior was larger than most, Mitch had the muscle to back it up, and carried his extra pounds well.

"Wow, a full moon," Clay commented dryly as he pulled off his T-shirt.

"I think I have a pimple back there if you want to pop it for me," Mitch retorted with his usual off-color humor, pulling a towel from his locker without turning around.

Clay paused a moment to take in his cousin's tattoo collection while Mitch was readying himself for a shower.

On the back of his neck Mitch had a barcode tattoo, which was meant to indicate how modern man was watched by big brother, and processed like cattle into categories. He firmly believed the government kept close track of every individual in America.

Since Mitch shaved his head daily, the tattoo was easy to distinguish. If he let it grow out, he would have a full head of blond hair, but he had long since mastered the art of shaving his head, so he continued to do so.

Most of his other tattoos originated from nature or folklore, since he had an inherent love for the planet. His backside was full of contrast between his flesh and the dozens of colors used in more than five works of original art he toted. The colors appeared especially brilliant because his skin was a pasty color from the lack of a tan during the winter months.

He had a tattoo on each arm as well, kept above the elbow to avoid covering them up, since they were hidden by most conventional shirts.

Or uniforms.

Born Russell Christopher Branson, Mitch received his nickname because from a young age he had a thick belly, that, along with his shaved head, made him look a bit like the Michelin Man from television commercials.

Along one arm he had a black tattoo of Christ as he died, crucified on the cross. Below it was some psalm from the Bible that Clay couldn't make out, or remember. Mitch could be preaching about the Lord as a savior one minute, then beat the living tar out of a suspect the next.

"What did Tim say about the meeting tomorrow?" Mitch inquired, still not turning around, and still without the benefit of a towel to cover his pale backside.

"It's a go in the morning," Clay said, knowing no one else was in the locker room.

Clay took a few seconds to examine the full-color tattoo of a sunny hillside along his cousin's back. Mitch was an environmentalist to the core, and sometimes scheduled vacations and personal days around rallies and events that pertained to environmental causes. He had a crush on a singer from Indianapolis who made it big and used her influence to aid worldly issues.

"What's your next tattoo going to be?" Clay inquired.

"I'm thinking about the Partridge Family bus somewhere on my thigh."

"Your ass seems to have some room."

"I'm saving it for a special occasion."

"Like a biker rally to impress a chick?"

Mitch finally slung a towel over one shoulder. He owned a Harley-Davidson motorcycle and occasionally did attend biker rallies when he wasn't busy preserving the world.

"You'll just have to wait and see," Mitch answered, grabbing his soap bar before heading for the shower.

Clay took off his shirt and unzipped his pants, thinking how much Mitch was like a brother to him, rather than a cousin. The two had grown up along the same street, and both knew from childhood they wanted to be cops, but Mitch was influenced by a longtime girlfriend who was a very active environmentalist.

Though the two had long since parted ways, the influence continued to linger with Mitch to the present day. He knew better than to give his spiels to Clay too often, or his cousin threatened to clock him.

As he finished stripping, two other off-duty cops stepped into the locker room, each shooting Clay an uninviting stare, as though he had switched teams in a competitive bowling league.

Saying nothing, they walked away, carrying on their conversation across the locker room.

Ever since the three young officers took up with Packard, it seemed some officers were bitter. Clay figured they were jealous because they weren't invited into the task force. Packard was liked by most everyone on the department, so Clay doubted they were upset with him. Some probably figured the group wasn't doing dangerous police work, and they spent their days screwing around.

Clay knew better.

He constantly found himself in situations where he could be fired upon, or assaulted from behind if his team members failed to back him.

By no means was his job any easier than a patrolman's.

Grabbing his shower items, he joined his cousin in the multiple nozzle shower room that could house almost a dozen people at once if necessary.

"Were you just entered in Dickhead 101?" Mitch asked just above a whisper, referring to the other two officers who had walked in.

"I don't know what their problem is," Clay answered. "The chief starts something good for this city and everyone here has a hard-on for us."

Clay observed his cousin lathering up as the warm water ran down both of their bodies. He had an uneasy feeling about what the next morning would hold for them. Sorrell was nowhere around, and seemed to be on his own more often lately. Packard did little to make him feel welcome in the group, but Clay felt it wasn't his place to monitor his fellow patrolman.

"You and Sorrell been out bangin' any chicks lately?" Clay asked, deciding to probe in a roundabout way.

Mitch had a girlfriend who had lived with him for a time, but that didn't stop him, or Sorrell, who was married with two kids, from occasionally testing different waters sexually.

"We've been keeping to ourselves lately," Mitch said. "You can only give so many sympathy lays in a month's time."

"Yeah, I heard about the domestic dispute case you *resolved* with some TLC last month."

"Sorrell initiated that. I just went along as backup."

Clay smirked as he looked to his cousin. Mitch couldn't help but break out in his usual broad smile, like a child who had done wrong, playing cute.

"This task force stuff is cutting into my rounds," Mitch added.

"That's probably a good thing. You're gonna catch something one of these days, and I'm not going to feel the least bit sorry for you."

Scrubbing the underside of his arms, Mitch looked up to his cousin.

"What are the chances of me burning in hell?"

"Not as good as Sorrell's, but they're still pretty good."

Clay shut his shower nozzle off and stepped outside, snatching his towel from the nearby rack.

"You being serious?" Mitch called as he walked back to the locker room.

Clay simply shrugged without turning around, deciding to let his kin wallow in thought awhile.

CHAPTER 3

▼

Packard met Clay early the next morning at the same house they had raided the day before. He wanted to speak with his right-hand man before the other two officers showed up. Having Clay share his thought process was important to the sergeant.

He sat on the front steps, which were riddled with cracks, and missing chunks of concrete, finishing off a cigarette as the younger officer pulled up in his personal vehicle.

"You ready for this?" Packard asked.

"As much as I can be," Clay answered, struggling momentarily to find a comfortable portion of the stairs to sit on.

"I get the impression you're more concerned about this than usual."

"I am, because we're holding thousands of dollars that belong to drug dealers."

"And, what? You're afraid they'll come after us?"

Clay shook his head.

"No, it's not that. I'm just wondering, Sarge."

He paused momentarily.

"What exactly is the setup? You hand Squeaky the money, he makes a deal, we squeeze Salas and his crew?"

"Basically. I'm not interested in paperwork and arrests. I want to move up the ladder."

Clay sighed to himself with outward concern, and Packard figured his officer was simply thinking too deeply into the situation.

"I was with Squeaky when he contacted Salas. Everything got set up exactly like I wanted it to."

"But this is Salas' cash we're holding, right?"

"Yeah."

"Could Squeaky have negotiated a deal behind your back?"

Packard heard the words, let them sink into his mind, and pondered the situation. If his informant didn't trust him, a likely option was to feed the four cops to Salas and have the man bring more firepower. Then again, Packard thought, Squeaky would be taking a chance because Packard never informed him about the plan's details.

"I don't think negotiating another deal would be in his best interest, and he knows it," Packard said.

Clay sat still, looking into the deteriorating streets in the distance. Packard glanced as well, knowing how beautiful downtown once was. Now overgrown with weeds along the streets, and buildings that held their original paint while their roofs and walls crumbled, parts of the downtown area had fallen into disrepair.

"Why are you second guessing me?" the sergeant decided to ask.

Clay thought a second before answering.

"Because it's my life in your hands. And the lives of two other guys. I know you're a supervisor and I'm supposed to listen without question, but there's a lot we're leaving to chance, Tim."

"You should learn to trust me more," Packard replied. "I've guaranteed there will be no way Squeaky betrays us. Yes, there is the possibility of gunfire, but it won't be a gang firing submachine gun rounds into the building we'll be hiding in."

Clay shrugged.

"Okay. I'll trust you."

"Good. Now that I've earned your trust, shut up and quit asking questions."

Packard stood as he lightly swatted Clay on the arm. He was playing it off, but still wanted Clay to listen to him unconditionally.

After all, he had threatened to have a lone gunman aiming a rifle at Squeaky's head in case the informant had any notions of conducting business any differently.

When it came to protecting his officers, particularly in their current specialized line of work, there was little Packard would not do.

Instinctively, he patted down the left side of his leather jacket to see if his firearm was still nestled within its shoulder holster. Positive it was, he returned his attention to his surroundings, knowing that within an hour's time he would be undertaking the most dangerous sting operation of his career.

His nerves failed him the morning before, and a pile of vomit was likely still sitting to the side of the building they were visiting. The time to get nervous about the sting was not yet at hand, though Packard already questioned how well he would handle containing thugs from a city bigger than his own.

Packard knew he was not an easy man to intimidate. Especially since gaining his stripes, he often put on a game face that revealed nothing about how he felt.

Clay remained seated on the steps, so Packard put a reassuring hand on his shoulder.

"You're thinking too much, buddy," he said to the younger officer.

"Maybe," Clay replied, though he didn't sound convinced. "You haven't steered us wrong yet, Sarge."

If anything ever went wrong in one of their scenarios, Packard planned to take the blame. He did things that weren't always by the book, and sometimes found himself in situations that bordered on illegal. Having his fellow officers take any blame for actions he left them ignorant of was purely immoral in his opinion.

Clay finally stood, but he turned around, staring at the parking lot of the Hotel Radisson.

"What is it?" Packard asked.

"Seems like a lot of high-priced cars over there," Clay observed aloud. "They must be having some big convention."

Packard squinted in the early daylight through his glasses at the lot. He remembered hearing something about an international fair at the Horizon Center across the street, but the details eluded him.

"It can't be that important," he figured aloud.

*   *   *   *

Less than two blocks away, Ben Haddle walked beside an entourage of almost a dozen people, most being from Thailand for an international gathering of Asian countries in Muncie as part of a festival put on by the university.

Several chief ambassadors, including an assistant to Thailand's national head of security, were present for the festival. This particular group had two purposes for visiting the United States, and for bringing so many people in its party.

Haddle worked for the Delaware County Police, but this was an opportunity for some easy overtime. A young sergeant on the midnight shift, he was only one of two people who requested to work this particular detail.

Walking along the hallway with the group, he wore his uniform as a deterrence to anyone thinking about harassing the group, or interfering with the upcoming festivities. Basically, Haddle's assignment was to get the group from one destination to another without incident, or harm.

He walked beside Thapana Noipa, who was one of several officers sent with the group from Thailand to retrieve a prisoner held in the local Delaware County Jail. Haddle kept vigilant watch over the group he guarded, but took a moment from time to time to ask Noipa questions about the terrorist his jail had housed for over a month.

"Are you in charge of the extrication?" he asked Noipa, who spoke fluent English as it turned out.

"I am."

The group was currently walking along a hallway in the Horizon Center, across from the Hotel Radisson, heading toward a meeting room where they would be briefed about their stay in Muncie, and about Ball State University's program. Noipa was there simply for the extrication of a Thailand-based terrorist who had been arrested on American soil a few months prior on conspiracy charges to blow up a full basketball arena on the college campus.

Why Muncie? Haddle originally thought.

He soon discovered Tien Zhang was a part of a terrorist organization for hire, and his group was split up to destroy parts of the Midwest in small, unsuspecting areas. Links to major terrorist groups in the Middle East, including remaining regiments from Saddam Hussein and al-Qaeda, motivated sister groups, but Zhang's was known to be much more than a cheap knock off of any organization.

For months the man had been held in federal prison in Washington, questioned by the FBI, but now he was back simply for the extradition. Some authorities figured the Bureau had worked a deal with Thailand officials to take custody of the man simply to torture him for information, since he provided little useful intelligence for the agents.

A Muncie agent who formerly worked with the Bureau's Washington branch was part of the interrogating group, which explained, in part, why the terrorist returned to Muncie a few days prior, for the deportation to his homeland.

As the group filed into the meeting room, Noipa waited outside with Haddle, appearing prepared to answer any questions the local officer had.

"Has your department worked out the details of the extrication from your end?" he asked Haddle.

"I believe the sheriff has, yes."

"Good. This doesn't need to be a big production. Zhang does not require any further attention to aid his cause."

"We'll be glad to be rid of him, trust me."

Noipa wore a pressed suit, and Haddle took him as a man bred of military. He walked rigidly, and despite his olive skin, seemed highly accustomed to American customs.

"I hate to reveal my ignorance here, but what exactly did Zhang do in your country to become public enemy number one?"

"What he did had nothing to do with my country, except that we housed his group innocently while he blew up families in Israel, and murdered two ambassadors in Afghanistan, then sent suicide bombers into China. That was just for starters. Authorities have linked almost seven-hundred deaths to his faction."

Haddle never had direct contact with the terrorist, but knew the man kept to himself, and was kept separate from the other prisoners. The sergeant seldom mingled with the jailers, and when he did visit the jail, his stays were often brief. He usually dropped off new prisoners and left without saying more than a few words to his fellow county employees.

"When Zhang is returned to your country, what will happen to him?" Haddle asked.

"He will be put on trial, then executed."

Noipa sounded assured that was how things would go, because his country probably didn't have all of the loopholes the American court system used to save defendants from sure death and long prison sentences.

"Is there overwhelming proof of his crimes?"

"In my country, we do not require absolute proof, but yes, there are witnesses to his crimes, and former members of his clan who have informed us of his activities and plans."

"If he went to trial here, he'd probably buy a topnotch lawyer and go free."

"That is why your leaders have the common sense to let us have him back," Noipa said without a display of emotion.

Haddle nodded affirmatively.

The two men waited a few more minutes as the introductory speeches occurred beside them within the conference room. A few minutes later, the group left the room to move downstairs before heading to their hotel rooms. They would all freshen up and prepare for the grand orientation on the Ball State University campus.

Taking his usual place beside the defense minister's assistant, Haddle hugged the inside wall as Noipa fell in behind him. Similar to a presidential entourage, the group moved along like a group of marching ants, heading to their destination.

Without warning, Haddle heard a boom, then felt something sting his chest like a knife piercing his skin. The sergeant felt his back slam into the wall as the defense minister's assistant collapsed beside him, his head appearing like a busted strawberry pie.

What the hell's happening? Haddle asked himself, looking down at his chest as a thin stream of red emerged from the left side.

*   *   *   *

Packard perked up like a wild deer when the shot from a high-powered rifle echoed through the city blocks around him. Clay flinched, taking notice as well, but waited for a response from his sergeant before speaking or moving.

Following the gunshot, came a sound of cracking glass, giving Packard an indication of where the shot originated.

"This way," he said, taking up a sprint toward the hotel with Clay close behind.

They were only a few short blocks from the hotel with little except streets between them and the hotel. Packard crossed through the hotel's parking lot, looking attentively for signs of a bullet hole while defensively looking for someone with a gun.

If a mad marksman was in the area, he probably held no reservations about shooting snoopy cops. As he reached High Street, which divided the Hotel Radisson and the Horizon Center, Packard looked up to the second story of the Horizon Center across the street and spied a bullet hole in the window with cobwebbed glass surrounding it.

Though not a forensic expert, Packard quickly deduced the bullet had to have come from the hotel across the street. He had no idea what floor, or from what gun, but he knew the gunman was likely still inside the hotel.

"Check the hotel for a gunman," he ordered Clay. "And be careful."

Clay nodded before darting toward the hotel's front doors while his sergeant ran across the street, dodging one moving car before finding the entrance doors to the building.

After flinging open the front door, Packard ran to the nearby stairs leading to the second floor. He was familiar with the building after several tours when it first opened, and from bringing his children to the neighboring Children's Museum.

Somewhat winded, he reached the top of the stairs, finding a group of people standing over two fallen patrons. Glancing at the first, Packard noticed little left of the man's head, because anything above the lower jaw was obviously splintered by the fired bullet. A bloody mix of flesh and gray brain matter lined the floor nearby, so Packard turned his attention to the other victim.

Immediately, he recognized his friend from the county police department with whom he had taken several classes, and knew very well because Ben Haddle had once supervised the jail for a short period of time.

They had even attended the same police academy class in Plainfield years prior. After rooming together, the two graduated, returned to the Muncie area, and worked several traffic scenes and cases together over the years.

Though not close friends, the two had maintained a working relationship. Occasionally they went out for beers or shot pool on weekends after work.

"Ben," he muttered, dropping to his old friend's side where one of the building managers had already begun applying a towel to his chest wound, holding it firmly with pressure.

Haddle said nothing because his breathing appeared labored and heaved, as though he was about to vomit. Packard took hold of his friend's hand, suspecting the worst, even though EMS personnel were stationed only a few blocks away.

"Has someone called 911?" he asked the group in general.

Several nodded or gave affirming answers, but Packard saw the blood continuing to ooze past the makeshift dressings on his friend's chest.

"Call them back and make sure they have police on the way," he ordered a woman from the building's staff.

She left immediately to comply.

Haddle looked at him, trying to speak, but he was already too weak, or the internal bleeding kept him from uttering anything aloud. Packard clasped his hand a bit tighter.

"Hang in there, Ben."

The sergeant wanted to look around for details, to know why someone had shot at his friend, or someone else in the room. Still, he focused on his dying friend, knowing the answers might come later, hoping Clay found the person responsible.

Packard wanted to know Clay was safe, but neither man had a radio with them. They had left the radios in their vehicles for later use at the sting.

Shit, the sergeant thought to himself, knowing the sting was meant to go down without a hitch, and he still had the money Squeaky needed to give Salas at the specified location.

Everything around him suddenly felt like it was falling apart, but Packard focused on Haddle, hoping for a miracle.

"It's cold," his fellow sergeant finally muttered through labored breaths and chattering teeth.

"Stay still, Ben," Packard said, looking to make certain the helpful civilian was applying enough pressure to the wound.

"Tell Stacy...tell her I love her."

"I will," Packard promised. "Don't talk. The paramedics are coming," Packard said, hearing the sirens in the distance, thinking how cliche it seemed that Haddle asked him to give his wife such a message as he was dying.

Then again, he figured, what else could people request during their last few minutes of life?

Packard felt his friend's grasp losing its strength, then wondered how much life Haddle had left. His thoughts quickly wandered to Clay, and what his protégé might be doing.

*   *   *   *

Upon entering the front door of the hotel, Clay immediately crossed a lobby floor, spying the beautiful furniture adorning it as he approached the front desk. He found a young woman and man behind the desk, and decided to confront them about the hotel's layout, rather than randomly run through the building with a dim hope of discovering the marksman.

To this point he had no idea whether he was dealing with kids firing a weapon as an act of vandalism, or someone aiming to assassinate another human being. His gut feeling told him the latter was the probability, so he decided to exercise caution.

"Hello," he said to neither hotel clerk in particular, showing his badge. "I need to know every single exit to this building along the first floor, immediately."

Both shot one another strange looks, but the young man spoke first.

"There's the two main entrances, and three doors that are exit points only."

Clay thought a moment about how hopeless the situation appeared, but quickly gathered his wits.

"Show me the alternate exits," he ordered the young man. "And you," he said to the young lady, "keep an eye on every single person that exits those front entrances. Especially if they're carrying any kind of luggage or cases."

"Okay," she said, the confusion showing in her face.

Clay followed the young receptionist as he led the way toward the alternate exit doors.

"The last is in the restaurant area," he noted, leading Clay the other way.

"I doubt he'll try that one," the officer said. "Just show me the other two, and we'll see what we find."

Briskly walking toward the back of the building, the hotel clerk appeared a bit nervous because his fingers kept bending as though he was trying to revive circulation in them.

"Can I ask what we're looking for?" he finally asked.

"A shot was fired across the street from somewhere in your hotel," Clay said, feeling relatively positive his statement was accurate. "I believe the gunman is about to flee, and I need to find him if possible."

"Was anyone hurt?"

"I don't know."

"Could I get shot?"

"I won't let that happen," Clay promised.

The young man reached the first door in the back of the building that led to an alley as an emergency escape. Clay doubted the gunman would use such a door because the alarm system would give away his location through the audible alarm, or a computerized tracking device that indicated which exit was breached.

"Where's the other one?"

"This way," the hotel employee replied, taking him down several hallways before finding the second door, which also had an alarm, creating more complication for Clay.

He thought a moment about the positions of the elevators, realizing any of the exits were easily reached. Of course, nothing said the gunman was definitely in the hotel, except for Packard's voiced opinion, and if he was, the gunman might already have a room and flee later in the morning.

Clay groaned inwardly.

"The other exit is in the restaurant?" he asked for verification.

"Yes."

"It's closed, right?"

"It is."

"Good. Keep it closed and keep an eye on the front entrances."

Hesitating momentarily, the clerk seemed to want something.

"What is it?" Clay asked.

"I can't stay and help?"

"No," Clay replied sternly. "Now get up there and help by watching for anyone weird walking by."

As the man left, Clay looked for a good vantage point where he could monitor both doors and have a quick response time if the gunman appeared. Trying to watch both doors and every set of stairs and elevators was nearly impossible, so he reached to the left side of his waist, feeling his firearm secured by its holster.

His fellow officers liked to pick on him for being left-handed, and occasionally compared him to Sorrell, which didn't sit well with Clay. Sorrell sometimes acted as goofy as a pet raccoon, but the cousins made it a point to take care of him and stick up for the man when others decided to run his name through the mud.

Thinking of his current dilemma, Clay decided his time might be better spent lying in wait outside the hotel at a corner where the two back exits were visible, but getting to them meant leaving through the front, or setting off the alarms.

Pausing a moment, Clay looked to the stairs behind him, then to the hallway that led to either exit door, though one was completely out of sight.

He decided what he wanted to do, then headed for the front doors, realizing he was probably wasting his time inside the building.

*   *   *   *

Packard had taken time to step outside for a smoke as the building was secured by his fellow city police officers. He felt no desire to be around the two bodies upstairs, and the coroner's office was just beginning the arduous task of investigating the scene.

Flicking his cigarette into the street, the sergeant yanked open a front door, deciding to learn what information he could about the shooting before he met with his own officers.

Taking a deliberately slow walk up the stairs, he spied several detectives from his own department, and one from the county, speaking with the remaining visitors in conference rooms. With both bodies still present, and pool of blood and brain matter lying on the floor, the police had led the Thailand natives and Horizon Center employees to another hallway with several conference rooms. There, they conducted interviews with the witnesses.

He noticed Scott Hahn from the coroner's office photographing the scene. He had the grizzly task of pronouncing both men dead, but he was seasoned enough that the organic matter atop the carpet failed to phase him.

Packard gave him a quick wave, though it wasn't heartfelt.

Seeing the body of his friend mentally wounded Packard a little more, mostly because he knew the county officer's family would hear the tragic news within the hour.

Thinking of his own wife and kids, Packard hurt, just imaging one of his officers appearing at his front door, head hung low, or holding back emotion, informing Sarah that he had been killed in the line of duty.

Packard took precautions to ensure he came home every night from work, but Haddle was conscious of his every move, too. Some situations are beyond man's control, Packard decided.

Whether his supervisors wanted him assisting on the case or not, he intended to find the identity of Haddle's killer. Before the crime scene completely filled up with investigators, supervisors, and scene technicians, Packard wanted to make his mark and assure everyone he was going to be an intricate part of the case.

He walked into the first conference room, drawing a stare from an investigator as he prodded a witness for information. Ignoring the stare, Packard settled into a chair along one corner as the hotel employee explained what occurred less than half an hour prior.

Though he hated to discriminate against any minorities, Packard didn't want to hear a narrative from one of the Thailand visitors, fearing their language might be too broken to understand.

Observing as the female witness, apparently somewhat shaken up, sat at the edge of a conference table opposite the detective, Packard heard low murmurs from outside. Most of the witnesses probably felt somewhat insecure standing in the hallway where two deaths had just occurred, despite the growing police protection around them.

"We were walking along the hallway with the group when I heard a shot, then the noise of cracking glass," the woman began.

She looked young to Packard, but most of the staff at the Horizon Center was youthful and energetic. They had to be just to keep up with the ever-changing building. In the winter a skating rink took up the back lot, and all year round they were constantly having to put on fashion shows, dinners, and plays.

Writing at a furious pace, the detective looked up to the witness, then to Packard, as though inviting the sergeant to leave. Though not officially an investigator, Packard decided to use his rank to bully himself into the case as far as his supervisors allowed him to.

On crime scenes, a fine line of jurisdiction existed between ranking officers and investigators, though the detectives usually took the lead.

"What happened after you heard the noise?" the investigator asked.

"The police officer stumbled into me, knocking me off-balance. I hit the wall, but kept my footing. It was then I noticed the defense minister's assistant falling to the floor, except he was..."

"It's okay," the detective encouraged, allowing her to take her time.

Packard noticed she was close to tears from the traumatic situation. Nothing she said during the course of the interview was going to shock him, but he decided to listen.

"When I looked down at the man, he…was missing his head. Or at least half of it."

"Did you see anyone outside?" the detective asked.

"No. It all happened so fast."

"Did you notice anyone strange inside the building this morning?" the sergeant decided to ask, wanting that one particular question answered before he departed.

"No. We opened exclusively for this meeting," the young woman replied, looking to Packard, failing to notice the dirty stare the sergeant received from the investigator. "No one else was inside the building except our people and the Thailand visitors."

"Thank you," Packard said.

Deciding he had heard enough, and not wanting to badger the witness any further, Packard stood to leave, wondering how his fellow task force member had fared.

As he ignored the other people standing around, and in particular the members of his own department, Packard briskly took the stairs down and found himself pushing his way through the glass exit doors momentarily.

Packard immediately looked across the street, feeling the morning breeze tickle his chin. He spied a nearby patrol car, remembering the transaction he was supposed to take part in within the half hour. The sergeant opened the passenger side door, using the radio to raise Ed Sorrell, who usually kept his radio with him.

"At least he does something right," Packard muttered as he scooped up the microphone.

He used Sorrell's unit number to contact him over the radio.

"Go ahead," Sorrell said in reply.

"Ed, I need you to Signal-8 with me at the Hotel Radisson, and bring Mitch with you."

"Clear," Sorrell replied.

Packard replaced the microphone before crossing the street to the hotel itself. He avoided the flock of squad cars that looked like islands in a bay lining the street. With Clay nowhere in sight, the sergeant opened the front door to the hotel, then crossed the lobby floor with a purpose.

Both employees at the desk seemed to take notice of the badge hanging from a chain around his neck, but appeared as though they had expected him.

"Have you seen a plainclothes police officer within the past hour?" Packard asked as he approached the desk.

Both nodded.

"He had me show him the exit doors," the young man added.

"Where is he now?"

"He left out the front doors about twenty minutes ago, and we haven't seen him since."

Packard nodded slowly, trying to imagine where Clay might have gone.

"Have you seen anyone strange exit the hotel?" he asked.

"Just a few families," the woman answered. "It's been a really slow morning."

"Okay, thanks," Packard said, starting toward the front door.

He stepped outside, looked around him, and fished inside his jacket for a cigarette. His number one task force member was missing, and he had yet to decide how to handle the situation with Squeaky, especially since money and lives were on the line.

"Where are you Clay?" he asked himself before lighting up.

*   *   *   *

Around the back of the hotel, Clay patiently waited on a second story fire escape along a building adjacent to the hotel. He knew there was a flock of patrol cars out front, and the gunman had likely hesitated, perhaps deciding his best course of escape from inside.

Remaining quiet atop the rusty fire escape proved no easy task, but Clay's conditioning allowed him to squat for a good viewpoint of either rear side of the hotel. His position also provided him ample opportunity to pounce if he spied someone exiting the hotel through an emergency exit.

Armed only with his standard firearm, Clay had no way of communicating with Packard or the others, though he shared his sergeant's fears about missing the drug transaction within the hour.

Missing it completely would get Squeaky injured, killed, or hunted by Salas' squad. Failing to show up with money was the one sure way to put the informant in jeopardy, and Packard still had the cash hidden at an undisclosed location.

Clay had about decided to return to the front of the hotel when a window along the second story slid open and a foot cautiously slipped out. Frozen momentarily in awe that his perseverance may have paid off, Clay watched more of the leg emerge from the window, then ducked behind a partition on the fire escape that hid him from view.

Listening intently, Clay heard the person shift through the window, then hesitate before jumping atop a garbage bin below.

Like a cat, the cop threw himself on the fire escape ladder, riding it down to the ground, coming face to face with his new adversary in an instant.

Carrying a case, the man seemed to know who Clay was, but he didn't look the least bit intimidated. Instead of immediately fleeing, the olive-skinned man, who appeared Oriental, adopted a defensive stance reminiscent of the martial arts.

"I take it this is an admission of guilt," Clay noted aloud before a foot came flying at his head.

Ducking the sidekick, Clay threw a left fist, but his new adversary blocked it as he dropped the case to the concrete.

Several punches and blocks ensued on both ends as Clay discovered his skills were virtually mirrored by the foreigner's. He immediately decided this man was from Thailand, and probably had a beef with the group touring the Horizon Center across the street.

Clay swung a roundhouse kick, missing high as his adversary ducked, but blocked several fists in succession with hands that moved like lightning. The Oriental man had apparently not expected an American adversary to put up much of a fight, especially where martial arts were concerned.

With a lunge, the Oriental man lifted his leg, intending to bring it down upon Clay with a scissor-like motion, but Clay caught it, launching a fist into the man's face before the second leg swung up, clipping him in the thigh before he was able to fully move aside.

Barely phased by the move, Clay threw a kick into the man's face, then launched both fists into his adversary's chest as the man stood. As though in shock, the man looked up from the ground at Clay. He was likely unaccustomed to being defeated in hand-to-hand combat, but he had no idea just how proficient Clay was in the martial arts.

Telling Packard and his fellow officers he was proficient in several forms of martial arts satisfied their curiosity, but Clay's training went far beyond what he ever stated.

Outdone, and sent to the ground in a heap, the Asian man thought better of his situation, taking up his briefcase as he darted away from the officer. The alley led to the parking lot of the hotel or a few different streets along the side.

Clay took chase as Packard rounded the corner of the alley, but the Oriental man saw the sergeant first. He propelled himself from the sprint into the air, striking Packard in the face with his right foot, knocking him to the ground.

Landing hard, Packard had never seen the foot coming, obviously rounding the corner from the sounds of combat.

"You okay?" Clay asked quickly, stopping just a few seconds from chasing his newfound adversary.

"Yeah, fine," Packard said, looking stunned, but okay.

"He's the shooter," Clay said as he took chase once more, prompting the sergeant to regain his footing quickly.

Barely able to look behind him, Clay saw Packard dart in another direction, probably to get a patrol car because he was unable to catch up.

In the meantime, the assassin had gained quite a lead on Clay, partly because he was smaller and quicker, but also because Clay took time to check on his sergeant.

The two men sprinted through several streets devoid of traffic, heading east toward residential areas, and in particular, the area Packard's Rough Riders had raided the prior morning.

Though in good shape, Clay quickly discovered he was incapable of catching the smaller man unless the shooter grew fatigued momentarily. Even the case failed to slow the gunman down, but Clay's thick muscles were no comparison to the Asian man's thin frame.

"Damn it," Clay muttered as the Oriental man leapt a fence into neighborhood yards.

Clay quickly made the leap as well, but with abandoned houses, garages, and plant life everywhere, he felt certain he would lose the assailant to a hiding spot.

Losing him meant putting himself in danger, Clay decided, keeping the Oriental man in view. He still had no proof of what the man had done, but assumed it was murder because of the police cars scouring the scene.

Half a block ahead, the man ducked down an alley, behind a thicket of bushes. By the time Clay reached the area, he failed to see the man anywhere, because the alley led to several other paths, and a few overgrown yards that harbored thick bushes.

Stopping in the center of a crossroad of alleys, Clay quickly decided he was at risk if he stood there much longer. An assassin would probably hold few reservations about sniping a nosy cop at close distance if he had murdered foreign ambassadors.

Possibly saving Clay from a bullet to the head, Packard pulled up in a marked vehicle, jumped out, and looked in every direction, despite spying Clay immediately.

"Where did he go?" the sergeant finally asked.

"I don't know. He took off down this alley and I haven't seen him since."

"Did you get a good look at him?"

"Very good."

Packard nodded, though apparently disappointed they lost the man.

"What happened?" Clay inquired.

"He killed the defense minister's assistant and a friend of mine from the county police."

"Who?" Clay asked, shocked by the notion someone targeted a local cop.

"Haddle."

Rubbing his head with both hands, the younger officer wondered what their next action needed to be.

"We need to get back to the hotel," Packard said. "Ed's meeting us there with your cousin, and we've got to finish this business with Squeaky and Salas."

"We can't just leave the crime scene, can we?"

"They were giving me the cold shoulder," Packard replied. "We'll sort out who needs what later, because right now, we need to get to the south end of town or our day is going to get a lot worse."

"Okay," Clay said, able to tell his sergeant hurt from the death of his friend, even if Packard tried to hide it. "Lead the way, Sarge."

*   *   *   *

During the trip to the old vegetable market along South Madison Street, Packard thought of little else except his friend's death.

He looked blankly out to the fields as they neared the abandoned market. It was technically for sale, but in its rickety condition, it seemed unlikely any buyers were going to emerge.

"We're here, Sarge," Sorrell said from the driver's seat as he pulled into a nearby lot.

Packard refused to reply, but plucked his shotgun from the floor. He looked it over, satisfied it was ready for action, though he knew he was nowhere near prepared mentally.

"Let Clay park the car behind the church over there," Packard said, thumbing toward the church and government housing units behind them.

He then turned to address Clay personally.

"I want you to take up the rear and hide in the bushes."

"Clear," Clay answered.

Taking a moment to gather their weapons and bulletproof vests from the car, the officers all slid the vests over their shirts. Packard removed and replaced his jacket after strapping his vest to a snug fit.

"Everyone locked and loaded?" he asked the group, receiving positive nods from everyone around the car.

Currently the group stood in the center of an overgrown lot that once housed a floral vendor shop, which was little more than a shack if Packard remembered correctly. Smells drifted from the industrial center just north of the group, including those of rubber, plastic, and metal being produced.

"Mitch, you and Ed clear the area around and inside the building to make sure we don't have any homeless people or kids in harm's way," Packard ordered. "Once you get inside, stay there. I don't want anyone seeing us out here if it can be helped."

As the two left to carry out their orders, Packard turned to Clay.

"When we get settled inside, pick a post where you can see everything, and if you see anything strange, radio me."

Clay nodded affirmatively.

Registering what his officer said, Packard moved around to the back of the car, opening the trunk to grab the briefcase from its confines. Squeaky was supposed to walk to the designated exchange area early, grab the case from the front of the building, then conduct the meeting as planned.

If all went well, Salas might provide them with valuable information about the local gangs and dealers.

"Once we're inside that building, we can't get out very easily," Packard noted. "And it won't provide us much cover if bullets start flying our way."

"I got it, Sarge."

Packard looked to his shotgun, then the building very slowly, his mind wandering to the events and death his eyes had already taken in that morning.

"You okay?" Clay asked again, apparently sensing Packard's thoughts.

"Yeah. Just watch our backs."

Packard trudged off toward the deteriorating building as Clay stepped into the car, ready to hide it so no one passing along the road, or the incoming drug dealers, would be able to spot it.

Using the single unlocked access door to the shack, Packard stepped inside, finding it a bit darker than he wanted. If he wished for more lighting, he would have to open the few shutters in the back of the hut. Opening anything facing the parking area might serve to get the group spotted, or take away what precious little cover they found.

Very little remained inside the building. A handful of fruit crates sat idly atop the dusty coating on the floor, while sunlight streamed through a few holes in the roof. The entire place smelled musty, somewhat like the few farms Packard had visited in his younger days.

The building had never been secured as much as Packard thought it needed to be. With loose boards, a roof on the verge of collapse, and rusted pieces of equipment inside the building, the sergeant thought it unsafe. Naturally, there was probably no responsible owner locally, or some out-of-state bank had repossessed the property, then left it to its own demise.

Suddenly Packard didn't feel so secure inside the building, the knowledge of his friend being gunned down in a state-of-the-art facility weighing on his mind.

"Not much cover in here," Mitch pointed out.

"I noticed," Packard replied. "If everything goes well, we won't need a bit of cover anyhow."

Sorrell started to say something, but Packard shot him a glare. The sergeant made no secret about the fact he didn't want Sorrell on his team, so the officer turned away, rather than say something he might regret.

Instead of dwelling on the morning's events, Packard turned to see several posts holding up the building, but they were nowhere near the thickness of an adult human body.

Very little cover.

"Ed, check out back and see if there are any boards or old tables we might use for cover," Packard ordered.

Without a word, or any hesitation, Sorrell used the building's single doorway to head outside.

"I don't know what you and Clay see in him," Packard muttered to Mitch.

"He's like the little brother you feel obligated to protect," Mitch replied.

"How on earth he made the hiring list, I'll never know."

Mitch examined the environment by rubbing the old wooden walls, accidentally knocking a chunk of rotting wood loose, catching it in midair.

"Nice," he commented sarcastically.

Packard had reservations about the sting operation, but Sorrell returned momentarily with some old, broken tables, and Squeaky right behind him.

Backing out was no longer an option.

Sorrell left the tables just outside the door, stepping inside with a sour look across his face. Obviously he felt displeased about seeing Squeaky so early, especially since their snitch had likely walked from town.

And he was fifteen minutes early.

All three officers shot one another quizzical looks, knowing snitches, especially Squeaky, were never early to something involving cops.

"What brings you here so quick?" Packard inquired, making his scepticism obvious with a raised eyebrow.

"I'm the one risking his life here. Salas won't think twice 'bout shootin' no holes in me," Squeaky said somewhat nervously.

"You wouldn't be thinking about selling us out to Salas, would you?" Packard asked.

"Not me," Squeaky answered with a quivering voice and sweat beading along his forehead. "No way."

Looking to his two officers, the sergeant noticed they appeared discontent with the situation. To say the least, they didn't appear to trust Squeaky.

"Sarge, this is Clay," Packard heard over his radio.

"Go ahead," Packard said, lifting his radio from where it was clipped to his belt.

"We've got a limo coming down the road, and it doesn't look like one of the local rental jobs."

Everyone around him seemed to tense, and Packard knew without a doubt his hand was being forced. He struggled, but maintained his composure, deciding to get what few details Clay could provide before the impending transaction took place.

"How far out?" he asked.

"Not quite a mile. You've got about thirty seconds to get ready."

"You," Packard said, thrusting the briefcase into Squeaky's hands. "Get out there and make it good."

Squeaky nodded, though he seemed shaken about something. As he darted out the door, Packard turned to Sorrell.

"Get those tables inside here, and set them against the front wall."

Packard looked around him, but saw little hope. Everything was happening too fast, and too far out of his control.

"I don't like this one bit," he said as his two officers knelt down with him behind the tables Sorrell had just brought inside and laid against the wall to provide them with somewhat of a protective barricade.

"This isn't going to stop anything more than a BB," Mitch said pessimistically.

Tragically, Packard knew his officer was correct, so he hoped no gunplay ensued. If Squeaky had done his job correctly, Salas would bring minimal protection with him, then easily fall prey to the officers hiding inside the old fruit shop.

"Keep quiet you two," Packard said just above a whisper as the limousine pulled into the dirt lot. "Have those shotguns ready while I monitor the radio."

Through small holes in the wall the officers watched as the limo stirred up dust in the front lot as it came to a stop. A moment later, two bodyguards stepped out, looked around the entire area cautiously, then opened the last door to the vehicle.

Packard sucked in a breath as he witnessed Salas step from the vehicle.

Wearing sunglasses, even in the dim morning light, he oozed confidence with his expensive, pressed suit and his fair skin. He owned a full head of hair that made the sergeant green with envy, but it was the man's smirk and open cockiness that irritated Packard.

With an almost unseen wave of two fingers, Salas set his henchmen in motion as he slipped into the comforts of the limo once more, never uttering a single word.

Squeaky stepped forward, as though to say something to Salas before he ducked out of sight, but the henchmen reached inside their sport coats.

As though in slow motion, the two bodyguards pulled out a shotgun and a Mac-10 submachine gun respectively, the first shooting a hole through the informant as the second snatched the briefcase from Squeaky's dead, falling body.

Packard's eyes widened in shock, then fear, as the two men aimed toward the building, instantly confirming the sergeant's fear that Squeaky had sold them out to save his own skin. Squeaky's plan backfired as Salas opted to kill him to ensure the informant never testified against him to anyone, then turned on the cops Squeaky had obviously told him about.

Cops he knew were hiding in the building, according to the plan.

"Fuck!" Packard exclaimed as he ducked as low to the ground behind the barricade as humanly possible.

Little room existed behind the tables for three men to take cover safely. Packard felt the other two officers kick him accidentally as they all squirmed for cover while bullets flew overhead, easily piercing the frail wood of the old shack.

To rise and return fire meant certain death, or severe injury, and the table was keeping the bullets from hitting anything vital, so far.

Packard fought to keep his eyes open as more light streams appeared above him from the bullets, making Swiss cheese out of the building's wall. Noise from the two different weapons prevented radio contact by ensuring no one heard the radio, or dared to transmit.

Wood splintered as chips and sawdust debris pelted his backside while the sergeant struggled to ready his shotgun in case the opportunity to use it arrived.

A momentary lapse in gunfire finally came, and Sorrell jumped to his feet first, quickly aiming his gun toward the limo outside, now plainly in view through the gaping holes in the shack's facade.

Before he fired a shot, however, Sorrell was struck by a bullet somewhere in the chest, grunted aloud, and flew backward into the center of the room.

Packard and Mitch had begun standing, but quickly ducked behind the table again after seeing Sorrell's misfortune.

"Ed?" Mitch cried aloud. "You okay?"

A strange groan was the only reply, but Packard quickly spied Sorrell rolling to one side, indicating he still had some life in him. Perhaps his vest had absorbed enough of the bullet to prevent damage to any vital areas.

Checking on Sorrell required crossing part of the dusty floor, and Packard knew the danger was too great. He had no desire to take a bullet when waiting just a moment more would probably suffice.

"Where are you, Clay?" he muttered under his breath.

Apparently the henchmen outside had taken a moment to reload their weapons, but one probably had a pistol of some sort to take a quick shot at Sorrell. Packard wondered why Clay was taking so long to respond to the gunfire, knowing all too well the young officer had courage aplenty.

Setting the shotgun down beside his knees, Packard reached into his jacket, pulling out his service weapon. He placed his hands atop the table without looking up, and fired four consecutive shots toward where he believed Salas and his bodyguards were.

If nothing else, he hoped to make a mark on the car to know he got a piece of something. Without a visible target, Packard had no idea if they were ducking for cover or casually finishing the reloading of their weapons.

Breathing deeply, nervously, the sergeant heard little else until a shot rang out from behind the building, indicating Clay had finally arrived.

A grunt emitted from one of the henchmen, and as Packard finally dared to peek above the table providing cover, he saw one of the men clutch his shoulder and whirl around, striking the car solidly.

Immediately thinking better of the situation, probably because Clay remained hidden from view, the second bodyguard opened the limo's door, quickly shoved his colleague inside, then jumped in behind him.

"About time," Packard said, rising from his position, firing several shots at the limousine, which turned out to be bulletproof.

It sped out of the dusty lot, heading south where any number of highways provided possible escape routes.

Clay emerged from the side of the building as the sergeant turned to check on Sorrell, who was already being attended to by Mitch. Packard, followed by Clay, darted over to Sorrell, kneeling beside him.

"The vest took the shot," Mitch reported. "Ed's just going to be sore a few days."

All three men helped Sorrell out of the vest, discovering a red welt along his rib cage on the right side.

"You're either really brave, or really stupid," Packard told the young officer. "I'm leaning toward the latter, but I appreciate the effort."

Packard stood to survey the damage, listening to the conversation as he examined the hundreds of holes along the front wall, several having made their way through the tables acting as barricades.

"Uh, I think he's showing me some respect," he heard Sorrell utter to the other two officers.

"It's about as close as you'll get to a compliment from him," Clay replied. "You'd better enjoy it."

Ordinarily Packard might have smirked to himself, but his thoughts quickly turned to the dead body lying in the dusty parking lot out front, and who might have witnessed, or heard, the events that just transpired. He had only seconds to decide what course of action he wanted to take, because technically he was violating departmental policy by setting up such a risky sting operation without any legal or departmental consent, much less any paperwork.

"Get him up," he quickly ordered Clay and Mitch.

Both gave him strange stares, like puppies unjustly being scolded.

"Clay, get the car," Packard further ordered. "Mitch, get the body outside. We've gotta get rid of it."

Now all three shot him incredulous expressions.

"We have no legal grounds for being here," Packard quickly explained, "and I have no way of saving our asses if I get a call to the chief's office."

"But it's, uh, a homicide," Sorrell argued.

Packard felt his face flush red. He didn't have time for debate or insubordination.

"*We* didn't kill him, and if we don't get him out of here, *right now*, we'll be crucified by a lot of people who are pissed at us for having this assignment."

He looked at each of them with an intentionally hard stare.

"Got it?"

Clay responded first, which Packard half expected, as he headed for the door to fetch the car. Mitch and Sorrell walked toward the front door, with Packard following close behind. He felt a need to monitor their every move to ensure his group found a tolerable solution to their quandary.

With little traffic going by, the group had been fortunate no one stopped, or apparently witnessed the shooting. If they had, they probably went to a safer area to dial 911.

"Pick him up," Packard said of Squeaky's corpse, littered with holes from the shotgun's pellets.

Blood oozed from almost everywhere in his body, but not in significant proportions. Clay quickly pulled the car into the lot, blocking the view of their activities from the street as Sorrell and Mitch loaded the body into the trunk. Packard momentarily left them alone to ensure no evidence of their presence was left inside the building.

He discovered everything they had brought was collected, meaning they were safe for the moment. Turning on his radio, Packard scanned for county and city police traffic, but heard nothing reported, other than routine traffic stops and a domestic disturbance.

"Good," he commented to himself.

If the city had been dispatched, he would have heard several sirens, because officers never went to dangerous scenes alone. Usually several, if not all cars on duty, sped to any scene where officers might be in danger.

"I can't believe we're doing this," Mitch said as they climbed into the car.

"Hey, plans change," Packard said with a harsh tone from the passenger's seat as Clay pulled away from the lot. "He's the one who fucked us by ratting us out to Salas."

"Then he had it coming," Sorrell said.

"That's the first smart thing you've said all day, Ed."

Packard looked behind him, seeing the piles of wooden debris at the front of the building. Anyone bothering to look close enough at the building would know what had transpired by the holes left in the walls. The sergeant just hoped they failed to figure out anything more.

"Where are we going?" Clay asked.

"Head north toward Eaton. There's an old quarry up there."

"But it's shallow," Mitch noted, apparently knowing the area. "They'll find the body in no time."

"That's the idea," Packard said. "As long as we get rid of this body cleanly, I think we can nail Salas at a later date, after they find it."

Everyone remained eerily silent a moment as the sights of the city flew past Packard's window. Never in his wildest dreams did he imagine his tenure as the head of a task force might lead to the actions he was now forced to take.

He sat back in his seat, sighed, and watched the buildings blur past, thankful to be alive after hundreds of bullets flew in his direction, none so much as grazing him.

*   *   *   *

As if his morning wasn't bad enough, Clay discovered his afternoon had potential to be far worse.

Not only had he and Packard been admonished by their department, and neighboring departments, for leaving the crime scene, they had no good reason for being gone as long as they were.

Packard covered them by saying they were looking for the assassin in the downtown area, but when questioned why he didn't call for assistance, even Packard failed to give a solid reason. He simply said he figured all available units were already at the hotel.

Leaving the difficult task of covering up what really happened to his sergeant, Clay found himself seated inside the local FBI branch, which housed two local agents. He found himself wondering if being assigned to the Muncie branch served as some form of punishment, or if agents actually requested the location.

The office was nothing like people saw on TV shows. Housed in the same complex as a local restaurant and an attorney's office, the suite had no secretary, no director, and no mammoth conference room.

Only three offices, and two agents.

One of which was on vacation.

"Vic Perry," an agent introduced himself, offering his hand to Clay, as he stepped from one of the offices.

A tall, thick man, Perry wore a dark sport coat with light slacks. He seemed confident, but not full of himself by the way he walked and spoke. His dark hair showed specks of gray, indicating he was at least Packard's age.

"Clay Branson, sir," Clay responded, shaking the agent's hand.

"Just call me Vic, son."

With thick shoulders and a face showing few age marks, Clay took the man to be nowhere near the retirement age his real father was. Wearing a serious expression, Perry seemed to be all business.

"Let's step into my humble office, shall we?" Perry offered, waving Clay into the cozy office housing little more than a desk and two filing cabinets.

No personal photos were visible, and Clay found no sign of trinkets or awards anywhere on the desk or walls.

Perry seated himself behind the desk as Clay settled in front of several printouts atop the man's desk showing various faces the cop assumed were trouble from overseas.

Most had olive skin like the man he confronted that morning, and several had lists of crimes and violations far longer than the names Clay knew he would never pronounce correctly.

"I heard you met our assassin face to face," Perry said. "Before you is a compilation of known terrorists and international criminals from Thailand. It seems the defense minister has a number of people who don't like him too well, so today's shooting was likely a message."

"So it seems," Clay said slowly, thumbing through the photos.

Staring at the faces, he hated the thought of being racist, but they all seemed to look somewhat alike, especially for someone unaccustomed to seeing Asian people. He had spent time overseas, but that was a decade ago, and it was in Japan.

Not Thailand.

His cousin had dated an Asian girl, but she was from Korea according to Mitch. At least she spoke fluent English and attended the university, but Clay wasn't even sure he would recognize her if he saw her again.

"It's none of my business," Perry said, distracting Clay momentarily from the pictures, "but what exactly happened today?"

"You were down there, weren't you?"

"Well, sure, but I mean to ask what happened with your group?"

Clay thought a moment, deciding how best to tapdance around the subject.

"Like Tim said, we went searching for the assassin after I confronted him in the alley."

"Two things bother me," Perry said, carefully cupping his chin with one hand. "One, how did you happen to be in the area to begin with, and two, why did it take you almost two hours after you left to come back to the original scene?"

Not liking the tone of the FBI agent one bit, Clay decided to side with his sergeant and let Packard deal with everything.

"You'll have to take that up with my sergeant, Agent Perry. He was in charge, so anything I say might be out of context."

Perry sat silently a moment, then grunted to himself, apparently deciding not to push the issue any further.

"You've referred to your sergeant by first name and rank," Perry pointed out. "Are you guys a tightknit group?"

Clay looked up from the pictures, intentionally giving the agent a less than pleased stare. He originally thought he was going to assist by picking out the shooter, but now he felt as though he was being interrogated on a different level.

"We're not a brotherhood like DEA guys or anything," Clay replied, looking back to the photos. "Our task force is something new to all of us."

"I see," Perry said, standing up. "I'm going to make some coffee. Want some?"

"No thanks," Clay replied, diligently studying the faces laid before him.

As the agent left to fix coffee, Clay studied the faces from the top of the page to the bottom. He flipped the pages twice more before finding a countenance that looked abundantly familiar.

"This one," he said to Perry when the agent returned, pointing to the face.

"You picked one hell of a man to mess with," Perry said, sipping his coffee as he slid into his seat, eyes transfixed on the photo in question. "He runs with a group of international terrorists who specialize in silent assassination."

"He wasn't very silent this morning."

"They also like to make statements," Perry said with a worrisome expression.

"What?"

"I'd be willing to lay odds why he's here, and I'll bet he's not alone, either."

Clay stared at the steaming cup of coffee atop the agent's desk, wondering just what he had drawn himself and his group into. By doing the right thing, and contributing to what now felt like the wrong thing, Clay had placed his rookie sergeant's job, and task force, into considerable danger.

"You still with me?" Perry asked, regaining the young officer's attention.

"Yeah," Clay answered, his head still filled with negative thoughts. "What's so bad about this guy?"

Perry swung the book of photos around to face him, pointing to the photo of the man before typing the name into the computer.

"Charoen Punnim is an international terrorist linked with a group called the Koda. He usually works in conjunction with a brother and sister team of Wichai and Issaree Khumpa. They're trained in martial arts, military weaponry, and nearly every type of specialized military tactic you could imagine. They're also on several Top 10 lists for domestic and international bombings and assassinations."

Clay digested the thought.

"Not a nice bunch then?"

"Not in the least."

"Are they for hire?"

"Typically they work for a cause. Not that they don't get paid, but it usually takes some kind of motive to bring them to your town."

For a moment, Clay took time to think about how close he had come to stopping a wanted terrorist, and how other lives might be lost because he failed to.

"Too bad they're not suicide bombers," he finally said.

"That is a shame."

"So now that we know who they are, what would bring them to our city?" Clay felt compelled to ask.

Perry took in a deep breath, leaning back in his chair. His mouth formed a crooked frown as his brown eyes studied the officer momentarily.

"What I fear the most is that the assassination of the defense minister's right-hand man might have been a setup to something else."

"Why's that?"

"Because they would never touch an assassination like that without a good reason. If they do a political hit, it's usually a public figure or a high-ranking government official. I can't see much motive in this."

Clay stood, deciding it was time to go. He wanted to speak with Packard to see what the task force was doing next.

"I'll leave you alone, Agent Perry. I imagine you have quite a bit of work ahead of you."

"Definitely," Perry sighed. "I have a feeling we'll be assembling some kind of task force to be looking for our assassin."

Clay gave a quick half wave.

"Good luck," he said as he walked out of the office.

If he was lucky, his work and life might return to normal by the next day, assuming Packard smoothed things out with everyone questioning their whereabouts that morning.

Clay's luck was seldom that good.

*   *   *   *

Packard kicked the door closed behind him as he carried in a bag of groceries for that evening's supper at his wife's request.

Married just over twelve years, Packard had met Sarah several years after most people had given up on him ever tying the knot. Their marriage was somewhat typical in that it wasn't perfect, but it wasn't miserable either.

Because she was a veteran nurse in the trauma unit at the hospital, Sarah had seen most every gory thing a person might see over the years. He had little trouble speaking to her about his job, because few things phased his wife.

He walked through the unusually clean living room, into the kitchen, placing the sack on the island counter, seeing no one around. Being late in the afternoon, he expected the kids to be outside playing, or watching something on television. Sarah's car was outside, so he figured they were around somewhere.

Rays from the afternoon sun streamed in through the sliding glass doors of the kitchen that led into the back yard. Several stained glass ornaments threw various rainbow colors atop the counter. Packard stared a moment as the colors spun like a baby mobile, dancing atop the tusk color of the counter top.

As he started unloading the grocery sack, the cop began thinking about how things were different with the task force. Since becoming a sergeant he talked less with his wife about his job, not so much to protect her, but because he found himself being less ethical than before.

He finished, then crumpled the paper sack as a warm body eased up to him from behind. Turning, Packard received a quick kiss from his wife, noticing her conservatively short hairstyle had received a fresh trim.

"You smell like smoke," she said, moving over to the groceries, apparently ready to start the pot roast she had planned.

"Nice to see you too," he commented, slightly taken aback.

Being married to a reformed smoker was pure hell, because he lacked her resolve to quit, like she had several years prior, when their second child was on the way. Not that he hadn't tried, but after three serious failed efforts, Packard gave up.

Until three days ago when he promised to give it one last try.

"I thought you were going to buy the patch," his wife said of the nicotine patch designed to help smokers kick the habit.

"I *did* buy it, but today wasn't the day to start," he said in his best disgruntled tone.

"Things not go so well?"

"We had a Thailand visitor assassinated, and with him, one of my old buddies got killed," Packard said, taking off his jacket, hanging it over a chair.

"I'm sorry," Sarah said, leaving her cooking chores to wrap her arms around him, kissing the back of his neck. "We heard about it at work, but I didn't realize you knew him."

"We used to run around before you and I were married. He was always someone I could count on when I needed backup, or even someone to ask advice from."

Telling her about the rest of his day was out of the question. Sarah was not like some police wives who would be hysterical with fear for his safety if he informed her he was shot at, but telling her about that meant telling her about why he was at the abandoned fruit stand in the first place.

Packard refused to incriminate himself, even to his wife. He knew how easily informants loosened their lips for the right price, or when opportunities to brag came about. Women, on the other hand, innocently gossiped about tidbits of information that came back to haunt their loved ones.

Or so the sergeant believed.

"You going to be okay?" Sarah asked, removing her hands from around his waist to return to fixing dinner.

"I will be," he answered, plucking a beer from the bottom of their refrigerator after opening the door.

He popped the top and took a long gulp, feeling the beverage slide down his throat, quenching his thirst from being outside all afternoon. After returning to the scene, he had assisted the detectives by sorting witnesses, then found himself being interrogated about his two-hour disappearance.

His day was full of holes.

Sarah made up for the qualities he lacked. She had a sense of humor, spoke fluently, and often, and preferred going out in public while he enjoyed the quiet sanctity of his own house.

He looked at her conservatively short blonde hair momentarily, thinking how his hands had run through it a few days ago when they last made love. With the children in school, and their schedules varying by the week, the couple seldom had more than an hour or two alone at a time.

"Where are the kids?" he finally asked.

"Nicole is at a friend's house, and Ryan is upstairs cleaning his room."

Packard smirked. His son of five years was learning several of life's harder lessons, most of which entailed responsibility.

He was about to check on his son when the phone rang from the wall beside him.

"Hello," he answered casually.

"Sarge, it's Clay."

Packard exhaled through his nose, turning away from his wife as she busied herself in packing the roast.

"What's going on?"

"I just got done visiting our local FBI agent," Clay revealed. "It seems our assassin is an international terrorist."

"What?" Packard asked, somewhat stunned, glancing to make certain he hadn't attracted Sarah's attention.

He hadn't.

"He didn't tell me much, but this guy usually runs with a few other bad guys, and they don't do anything in a subtle way."

Packard rolled his eyes.

"Great."

Clay paused before speaking again.

"What's our role in all this?"

"Right now, nothing. Everyone was just running around up there without a clue."

"Okay. Just let me know if we get any action, Sarge."

"You'll be the first," Packard promised.

A moment later Packard hung up the phone, turning as his wife placed the roast in the oven.

"Was that your adopted son?" she inquired.

"As a matter of fact, it was."

Sarah seemed to think Packard treated his three task force members like his own children, and though he didn't try being a father figure, he supposed in some aspects he was.

"What did Clay want?" she asked.

"He just wanted to know if we had anything else to do with the assassination cleanup."

A strange look crossed his wife's face.

"Why would you?"

"We were the first officers there this morning," Packard said, hoping Sarah didn't pry any further.

She seemed to busy herself with the side dishes, so he left the room before she came up with more questions for him. Packard had enough problems to deal with as the beginning of a headache pounded inside his cranium.

Something about losing a friend caused him to feel a bit insecure about being a family man, as though the realization that death might come for him any day suddenly seemed possible.

He began climbing the stairs to see how his son was faring with the room cleaning.

*   *   *   *

Later that evening, Packard sat on the couch with his daughter beside him and his son at his feet. Their difference in age made things miserable for Nicole, who was eleven. Ryan was nearing the end of his kindergarten year, but still found time to annoy his older sister.

Ryan showed absolutely no desire to do anything except police work, as though no other career existed when the topic arose. At five, he was still impressionable, and had no idea of just what his father's job entailed, but there would come a day when television documentaries and talks with his father might bring light to what cops actually did.

They had half an hour before the good shows came on, so the Packard family spent some time talking, flipping through channels, and waiting for the pizza Sarah ordered to arrive.

Living in the city had its advantages, but Packard had left the south end of town for greener pastures. Though the school systems were rumored to be better in the surrounding townships, Packard and Sarah opted to stay in town for the convenience of local stores. Both had short trips to work, and everything they needed was nearby.

"Have you got the check wrote out?" Packard asked his wife as she passed through the living room, speaking of the ordered pizza.

"Yes, dear," she answered in short, disappearing into the kitchen.

Beside him, Packard's daughter, Nicole, stared at the television momentarily, saying little. Though he never meant to, Packard acted tense around his children when he had bad days at work. They seemed to sense when he kept to himself was typically a good time to leave him alone.

Tonight he wanted to change that, and at least pretend his mind wasn't in a hundred other places.

"How's school, kiddo?" he asked Nicole.

"It's okay."

Packard changed the channel to a local news station where a major traffic wreck was being covered. He took some comfort in knowing he wasn't the only miserable person in the state of Indiana.

For the past two years Nicole had received a reasonably large reward for getting straight A's in her classes, now that grades actually counted for something. She did well in her elementary classes, but Packard never put much stock in those grades. He wanted her to excel when the grades started counting toward college and scholarships.

"Have you decided what you want this year if you get good grades?"

"I think you mean *when* I get good grades," Nicole corrected, obviously expecting nothing less of herself. "I think I want to go to Great Realms."

"I see," Packard replied, knowing it had been a few years since the family went to a theme park of any kind.

Ryan was too little to ride anything the last time they traveled as a family, so Packard rather liked the idea.

Great Realms had themes based on various periods of time, picking out the most interesting aspects of the eras. Themes spanned from the Old West to a science fiction area where all of the kiddie rides were located.

Most of the rides were standard, ranging from roller coasters to bumper cars. Food was overpriced, walking around the park exhausted an average person, and the sun usually gave most people a sunburn. Of course it often rained on the days Packard attended the park in his younger days, as though to spite him.

"Can we go?"

Packard shook his head affirmatively in thought.

"Yeah. We can go if you keep your grades up."

Nicole's face lit up. Though Packard hated traveling, there was little he wouldn't do for his kids. He held high hopes for his daughter because she already knew more about the Internet than he planned to ever learn, and her teachers always commented how gifted she was in several different areas.

The world would be her oyster, no matter what she decided to do with her life.

Ryan, on the other hand, was the wild child. Adventurous, rash, and extremely observant, he worried Packard. The sergeant doubted his son had enough of an attention span to succeed in school. Perhaps Ryan was destined to settle down before he reached his official schooling years, but Packard was not optimistic.

Nicole had strawberry blonde hair, which he considered a perfect mix from her parents. She also possessed a face full of freckles and a smile that came easier than butter melting in a microwave.

Packard wrapped one arm around his daughter as a graphic came across the television screen displaying the words "Muncie" and "assassination" in succession.

He watched as a reporter reviewed the story about the assassination of the defense minister's assistant with casual interest, wondering if he or his officers might be in the footage background.

They weren't.

When the reporter sent it back to the studio for a related story, the sergeant perked from his seated position as he leaned forward.

"A terrorist group known only as the Koda has taken responsibility for the shooting," the man dressed in a black suit reported. "They've demanded the release of fellow terrorist Tien Zhang from the Delaware County Jail, claiming the assassination will be just the beginning of their actions in Muncie."

"Oh, shit," Packard muttered under his breath.

"Authorities have yet to comment," the reporter continued, "despite the fact one of their own county officers was killed in the assassination. One officer reportedly had an altercation with the assassin, but the terrorist, identified as Charoen Punnim, escaped."

Packard shifted again, listening to the reporter.

"Zhang is scheduled for extradition in six days to Thailand where he will stand trial for crimes perpetrated within his own country. It is suspected the terrorists will issue a six-day time limit for the release of their colleague."

Before the sergeant even thought about making a call to the supervisor on duty, his pager vibrated at his side, causing him to groan dismally before standing to use the phone.

He suspected his bad day was about to get drastically worse.

CHAPTER 4

▼

Half an hour later Packard found himself outside city hall, measuring up the task force he was informed about from one of his department's deputy chiefs. So far the force included a detective from his department, one of the deputy chiefs, a county investigator, FBI Agent Vic Perry, and Packard.

He suspected the county EMS service would send a representative, along with the Muncie Fire Department, but he had yet to see anyone from their agencies.

Finishing off what might be his last cigarette ever, Packard tossed it down the chute of the outside ashtray, exhaling into the night air as he did so. He vowed to start using the patch in the morning, and if he didn't, Sarah probably planned on leaving him.

Or at the very least denying him sex for a month or more.

Stepping into a conference room on the second floor, right beside the police chief's office, Packard discovered everyone else sitting around an oblong table, including a sergeant from the Redkey post of the state police.

An odor of fresh coffee overtook the room, and through the large tinted window Packard saw several city lights below from the parking lot.

He took a seat, then saw Tom Lyons from the fire department walk inside with Don Brindle, a captain from the county EMS. Lyons had recently taken the arson and fire investigator job, and he was a buddy of Packard's younger brother.

"Hi, Tim," he said, sitting beside Packard.

"What's new, Tom?"

"Nothing much until the news came on."

It seemed no one knew about the demands of the terrorists until they were displayed on the news for everyone to see. The terrorists had gone straight to the news channels to ensure their message reached a mass audience.

"You know anything about all this?" Lyons asked.

"You could say I met the terrorists this morning," Packard replied. "The officer they killed was an old buddy of mine."

Lyons' face displayed his surprise and sympathy, all at once.

"Sorry to hear that."

"Me too."

Randy Ellison, the Director of County Emergency Services, walked into the room, prompting Vic Perry to stand and join him at the head of the table.

"Oh, swell," Lyons said sarcastically.

None of the emergency medical technicians liked Ellison because he was a former EMT from another county who worked only a year or two before taking an administrative position across the state, before eventually returning to his home area.

Most considered him a sellout who bluffed his way through situations to attain higher positions. They seemed to think he was incapable of doing their jobs, much less directing emergency preplanning for the entire county.

"You guys and your hard-on for him," Packard said, shaking his head.

"Try having your boss up his ass and see how fun your life is," Lyons warned.

Packard shrugged.

Perry gave a look around the room, indicating he was ready to begin, since he was apparently the only one who knew anything about the terrorists they were dealing with.

"I'm not sure I know much more than everyone else in this room," the agent began, "but I do know these terrorists aren't bluffing, which is going to make our lives miserable until they're caught, or they leave."

Everyone had been briefed in short before the official meeting, so they all knew about the demands of the terrorists.

"Do they really expect us to release a prisoner because they demand it?" the state police sergeant asked.

"They probably don't care," Perry replied. "If we release Zhang, they win. If we don't, they get to destroy half our city and bolster their list of accomplishments."

Lyons shifted in his chair beside Packard.

"What kind of actions should we expect?" the firefighter asked.

"Everything from random assassinations to bombings. These people are extremely resourceful, and they have no conscience. They've been trained by descendants of the Japanese samurai, and even some of our former special forces."

Packard looked around, registering the infuriated expressions on everyone else's faces.

"That's impossible," one officer said. "Why would our own people train these bastards?"

"We don't all put patriotism above green paper," Perry answered. "We have people moving overseas all the time to train third world nations. Half the time they probably don't even know exactly who they're training, and probably don't care so long as they get deposits in their bank accounts."

Everyone stewed a moment, taking in the fact their own soldiers may have contributed to terrorists now assaulting their city.

"So what do we do?" Packard decided to ask.

"We've interviewed the hotel staff," Perry revealed. "They said they never saw any Oriental men that morning, and that your department is in the process of interviewing the rest of the afternoon and midnight staff as we speak. We're also analyzing the bullet that killed the defense minister's assistant, Mr. Traisorat. Right now we can only play the waiting game and see where they strike next, but you all need to be aware of who these people are, and what they're capable of."

"And what exactly is that?" the deputy chief asked.

"Almost anything," Perry said, sliding folders across the table for each person. "If we're going to be a task force, and try stopping these people, you need to know their history."

Packard opened the folder, leafing through the accomplishments of the group, which appeared very much along the lines of what Clay learned from Perry that afternoon. Little surprised him at this point.

"Each of your department heads will receive one of these packets," Perry said. "From there, they can decide how best to contribute by using their resources to the fullest. I'm not going to pretend to know your personnel, so I'm not going to make suggestions until I talk with them in the morning."

"What exactly is our role then?" the county investigator asked.

"You are the people who know this city the best. I want all of you to start brainstorming places these thugs might hide. They're going to know their ugly mugs will be all over the news tomorrow, and they've probably planned this for months, so they'll be holed up deep."

Thinking of sparsely populated places, Packard wrote a few down as he thought of them, ignoring whatever Perry said next.

He put most of what Perry and Ellison said out of his mind as he leafed through the papers in the folder, thinking about his morning. If he had been a bit quicker, he might have aided Clay in capturing the assassin and the terrorists might have left altogether.

Shifting his stance, Perry looked ready to end the meeting. He looked around the room, regaining Packard's full attention as the sergeant placed the folder on the table to listen.

"The President himself has been informed of the events this morning," Perry said. "I have little doubt other government agencies will be joining us in the search for these terrorists, but all of you here are the backbone of this operation. You know the streets, the buildings, the people. I know as a new person to the area, I can't hope to do this without all of you. I'm not exaggerating, and I'm not sucking up to all of you. Without all of you putting your best effort forward, I fear for the safety of this city."

Soon enough, the meeting was over, and Packard found himself standing outside the conference room with his deputy chief, waiting to see what the man had to say. He stood by the state trooper a moment, discussing something about a district change, which had nothing to do with the problem at hand.

Typical, Packard thought, that his department's brass shrugged off matters at hand to discuss irrelevant issues.

"Tim," the deputy chief said after his conversation, finally turning around.

"What can I do for you, Chief?"

Before the man was able to provide an answer, Perry stepped into the hallway, away from the stragglers.

"We have a special assignment for you, Tim," the agent said.

Packard figured there was a reason he was invited to the meeting, so he folded his arms, waiting to hear it.

"It seems one of our identified terrorists has a habit," Perry stated. "He tends to stick to the upper-class drugs like heroin and several rare opiates."

Packard let his arms fall to his sides as he displayed the most discontent face possible. His job was to track down junkies and dealers on the lowest possible level, in the deepest of holes. His mission was to eradicate scum from the streets of his city.

Not chase down dealers the rich and powerful visited.

"What you're asking is something I'm not even familiar with," he said. "I've just begun scratching the surface with pot dealers and small amounts of crack. If you're asking what I think you're asking, it's beyond my reach at this moment."

"Then get it within reach," the deputy chief ordered. "You're a man who gets things done, Tim. That's why we picked you for the job."

"I take it we're pretty desperate if you've got me pursuing this avenue," Packard said.

"They hide anywhere, they strike anywhere," Perry said, putting it in simple terms. "We need to do everything possible to find them before the citizens of Muncie realize what's here to visit them."

Packard looked to the ceiling, thinking what a challenge he was in for. Roughing up junkies and smalltime dealers was one thing, but discovering and extracting information from the dealers his deputy chief and Perry spoke of was a completely different feat.

"How bad can it get?" he asked the agent.

"*Very*," was the reply. "They have vivid imaginations, and they aren't afraid to use them. I need you to see if any Asians have visited the local dealers, and if so, we need to set up a sting immediately."

"I'll get the boys on it."

"We need two of your officers for something else," the deputy chief said, almost as an afterthought.

Packard felt his eyebrow raise as he gave a perplexed look. Breaking up his team was not something he bargained for.

"Two of them need to work in conjunction with the task force to guard the remainder of the Thailand group while they're here."

Packard rolled his eyes as he repressed a sigh.

"Why *my* guys?"

"It's not just your people, Tim. We've got guys from the county and state assisting us, and you should be able to function with just one of your men assisting you."

Not very well, Packard thought, wondering which of the three was best suited to help him knock around a few heads. To get answers as quickly as his task force wanted, force would likely be necessary.

"Are you clear on what we need?" Perry asked.

"Crystal."

Packard thought about the danger of going into this situation blind. The one thing the task force had on its side was an element of surprise. They knew who the terrorists were, but the three Asians had no idea the police had obtained so much information.

"Can I ask one favor?" Packard dared ask.

"What?" Perry replied, since he was being addressed.

"I know you're going to release their photos and information for the public good, but can you hold off twenty-four hours to give me a head start with the local dealers? I might just turn something up before the Koda knows we're onto them."

Perry shook his head negatively.

"If these three start killing people and word gets out that we sat on vital information, none of us will have our jobs, Tim."

Packard understood, bobbing his head like a scolded puppy.

"Okay. Then I guess I'll just do what I can."

"Good luck, Tim."

I'll need it, Packard thought as he walked away.

He stepped outside a moment later, fishing for one final cigarette as he tossed the remainder of his pack into a nearby trash can, determined to keep his word to his wife, even during one of the most stressful times in his life.

Unlike everyone else, he wondered if the group was simply exaggerating the danger the terrorists posed. After all, what lengths were they willing to go to for an unrealistic plan? And what damage could they do in a mere six days?

Packard stepped into his car, determined to help find them, just to get his life back to normal, if nothing else. He had his own agenda to return to when this was all finished.

CHAPTER 5

▼

In a manner of speaking Packard found two of his three men turning on him, mostly because the third wasn't present when he spoke with Clay and Mitch the next morning.

When he informed them he needed to investigate the drug angle concerning the terrorists, and was allowed to take only one of them along, they voted to stay together to guard the Thailand visitors.

Though he wasn't thrilled about the notion of Sorrell riding with him, Packard took it in good stride, ordering his men to report to Vic Perry immediately.

He currently found himself riding beside Sorrell in a departmental unmarked car, heading toward the campus area to visit a young man Mitch had arrested a month earlier for distributing crack cocaine and heroin to dealers who, in turn, sold to the freshman population on campus.

Being new to the drug task force, Mitch took a piece of evidence with him when they left the man's shop after investigating without a warrant. It might have gone forever undetected, but the shop had cameras, and Mitch barely escaped the incident without suspension or another form of punishment.

"Am I, uh, allowed to ask what we're doing?" Sorrell questioned, looking to his sergeant at a red light.

"Just keep your eyes on the road," Packard said. "We're going to check on a previous client of ours."

Sorrell simply nodded to himself as Packard leafed through a file about Sam Lauffer, a skinny white kid, typically keeping his hair colored from somewhere in the rainbow spectrum. He looked like a chemotherapy patient in the latter stages because he lacked any muscle definition, and his arms were often traced with needle marks.

Lauffer was constantly being picked up for lesser charges, but always had money to get himself out of jail, and apparently keep himself out of prison.

"You seem a little grumpier than usual, Sarge," Sorrell commented as the light turned green. "Any particular reason?"

Not wearing his jacket at the moment, Packard simply rolled up his left sleeve, revealing the nicotine patch he had placed there that morning.

"Oh," Sorrell said with a mischievous grin, obviously recognizing what the patch was.

"Not another word about it," Packard warned.

He sat silently a moment, figuring Sorrell was itching to talk. He always itched to converse with other people. Often he stuttered around people in power from sheer nervousness. Packard once thought the man was slow of mind, but Clay and Mitch said he got nervous around people he didn't know.

On the street, he was in control, so Sorrell appeared normal in front of the city's populace. Packard had witnessed this in person.

There were a few advantages to having Sorrell around. He had some law enforcement experience, equaling Clay and Mitch. Naturally powerful, Sorrell had spent half of his childhood growing up at his grandparents' farm, doing chores. He seldom complained, hardly ever questioned Packard's logic, and had a knack for physically restraining people better than anyone Packard had ever witnessed.

Instead of waiting for the younger officer to talk about one of his unusual topics, like how gorgeous high school girls at the basketball games were, Packard decided to have some fun.

"So is the rumor about you shooting a cat true?" the sergeant asked, knowing already that it was, but wanting to hear his officer's version.

"Well, uh, it wasn't really much of anything," Sorrell said, trying to play it off.

"Did it attack you?"

"Well, no," the younger cop replied, letting the notion dangle.

Packard waited patiently until Sorrell mustered enough courage to tell the tale.

"I was on patrol with Fisk," Sorrell began. "We got a call about a peeping tom who had been badgering the neighborhood lately. Well, we, uh, got to the house."

Sorrell paused a moment to belch to himself. He had been drinking soda pop all morning, which likely gave him excess gas.

"So we get to the house and the resident tells us she just saw him take off through the back yard. I start after him, but it's dark as can be, so, uh, I pulled my flashlight out and ran down the alley behind the house."

Packard chuckled to himself, figuring he knew where this was going.

"You know in horror movies how cops always let their guard down after a cat jumps out from a trash can, then they get jumped by the person they're chasing?" Sorrell inquired.

"Sure," Packard agreed.

"Well, I decided not to wait when I heard a few cans rattle beside me, and drew my gun. Well, uh, the next thing I know I see a streak coming toward me, so I fire instinctively and hear a thud at my feet."

Sighing to himself, Packard shook his head.

"So, in a manner of speaking, you killed a cat in self-defense?"

Sorrell's face flushed red, but he didn't answer.

A moment passed without either saying a word as they entered the edge of campus.

"You know, most people, uh, get commendations when they're shot in the line of duty," Sorrell noted, breaking the silence.

Packard wondered where this statement was coming from. They both knew exposing the events from the prior morning only served to discredit their group, and likely end its existence.

"What are you getting at, Ed?"

"Just that I'm willing to take one for the team, and put duty in front of glory."

Packard swallowed the thought, respecting Sorrell just a bit more.

"I know I haven't made you feel perfectly welcome, but you've got a reputation, Ed. I appreciate you taking a bullet yesterday, and I especially appreciate you keeping quiet about it, but I'm just not comfortable working around you yet."

"You're stuck with me for a few days. Maybe that can change."

"Maybe," Packard replied neutrally as Sorrell turned in the direction the sergeant pointed.

Sorrell parked the car behind an apartment building owned and occupied by one individual, solely as a cover for what really went on. Packard noticed several more cars than usual parked outside the building. This prompted him to believe Lauffer had clients inside the building, or perhaps he decided to rent out several units, since his cover was now common knowledge among local police drug units.

"So you're basing your reservations about working with me entirely on rumors?" Sorrell asked as they stepped from the car.

"We'll talk about this afterward," Packard said, nodding his head toward the building. "We've got business to conduct."

As Packard stepped into the ground level of the apartment building, his nostrils detected incense burning from at least one nearby room. Though not quite in ruins, the building's upkeep was immediately questioned by the sergeant.

"You'd think he could afford a maid," Sorrell commented.

"I doubt the local clientele care too much," Packard replied as he headed toward the mailboxes.

Reading through the names of the building's occupants, he found one box blank, which he cross-referenced with the doorbells at the front door. He quickly discovered the suite on the top floor, which comprised the entire level, was shrouded in mystery because no named occupant lived there.

"Upstairs," he informed Sorrell, leading the way.

The suite offered the best view of the parking lot and street below, and housed security cameras outside the building. It likely contained a panic room, and probably held all sorts of ledgers, if not illegal drugs.

Packard reached the top floor first, stopped by a metal security door that was impenetrable, short of a key or coded combination.

"Nice," he said of the system, though disgruntled he needed to contact the resident instead of using the element of surprise.

Sorrell pointed to a small box mounted to the wall beside them.

"Speaker."

Packard decided what he wanted to do.

"Check the cars in the lot downstairs and confirm which one belongs to Lauffer," Packard ordered. "When you confirm he's here, yell up the stairs to me, then call for Barnes to bring his dog out here."

Jim Barnes was the K-9 officer who typically worked the morning shift and had one of three departmental dogs capable of detecting the presence of drugs.

"Okay," Sorrell replied before heading downstairs.

Packard found himself counting on Sorrell for the first time as he pressed the talk button on the console.

"Sam Lauffer, this is Tim Packard from the Muncie Police. I need to speak with you."

No answer.

Packard waited about thirty seconds before trying again.

He pressed the button, then leaned close to the box, as though keeping it strictly between them, since the camera above filmed his every move.

"You can talk with me, or you can talk with the K-9 officer pulling up downstairs."

A few seconds passed.

"You can't just harass people at random," came the reply through the speaker.

"I'm not," Packard answered, using his prepared alibi. "It just so happens a drug suspect ran through here and ditched a stash. I'm having the K-9 officer and his dog look for the stash, and I'm wanting to talk to you as a potential witness."

Packard waited patiently, figuring Lauffer wasn't going to talk to him willingly.

"I haven't seen a thing all morning," the voice answered in short.

"It'd be a shame if that drug dog picked up something in or around your car down there."

"He won't."

Chuckling loud enough that it carried through the speaker, Packard savored his next statement before even speaking it.

"Oh, I'm pretty sure we'll find *something* down there. Now you can either have a friendly chat with me for a few minutes, or we can have this talk down the road."

Packard sensed hesitation in the air, then peeked out a nearby window at the stairwell, watching Barnes pull up, then Sorrell meet up with him to explain the situation.

Sorrell had come through for him.

"Well?" Packard urged through the microphone.

He heard a buzz disabling the door's magnetic lock, then looked out to Sorrell, called the officer's name, then slid his thumb across his throat, indicating he no longer needed Barnes there.

Sorrell nodded, and by the confused look on Barnes' face, Packard knew Sorrell had done right a second time.

Letting himself in through the security door, Packard found himself face to face with Lauffer, who appeared to be in horrific shape. If not for the sleeveless shirt with numerous tears in it, Packard suspected he might be seeing the man's rib cage in full view. To this point, the sergeant had no idea whether or not Lauffer sampled his own wares, because the two men had never met, but Packard heavily suspected the dealer had an addiction to one of the heavier drugs on the market.

Bad for business in a few senses.

One, his health appeared in serious jeopardy, and two, distributers didn't want anyone on their marketing staff hurting business by consistently being stoned.

Packard stepped in without hesitation, taking out his wallet and letting it fall open to display his badge in one casual motion.

"What do you want from me?" Lauffer asked, his head never quite sitting still, while his hands nervously rubbed and scratched areas of his chest and opposite arms.

"I want to be your new best friend," Packard replied without producing so much as a grin. "What I really need from you is information, and word is you're the man I need to start with."

Lauffer returned a sour look.

"And what's in it for me, other than not getting my car sniffed?"

"I leave you alone. If you haven't heard, I head up the new gang and drug task force. Being my buddy has its advantages."

Showing little emotion, Lauffer simply stared off in several different directions a few seconds at a time.

"I've heard. What do you want to know, so I can get back to business?"

Packard felt a bit impressed that his name was traveling through the drug circles so quickly. Word spread among such communities even quicker than he anticipated.

If he was lucky, his local notoriety might land him some timely answers.

"I need to know if you've had any Asian buyers the past few weeks," Packard said plainly.

Lauffer stopped his nervous actions momentarily to shoot the sergeant a strange stare, as though his time was being wasted.

"That's it?"

"Yes."

"No," Lauffer answered, beginning to pick up magazines and place them in a different area of his loft, as though cleaning house.

Packard felt his face flush a bit. He was in no mood to play games with a dealer junkie, and his time grew more precious by the second.

"I'm not asking just to pass the time," Packard said with obvious displeasure. "The man I'm talking about is a threat to our entire city."

"And why should I care?"

Packard felt his muscles tense. Talking to some of these people sometimes proved futile because their only concern was the amount of cash in their wallets. At the moment he wanted nothing more than to throw this piece of trash against the wall and beat him senseless until he understood the severity of the problem, but experience prevented his temper from getting the better of him.

"You should care because they were involved in the assassination of a foreign ambassador yesterday. If this man comes to you or any of your associates, and we find out about it, you're not looking at run of the mill drug charges. You'd be looking at felony charges ranging from selling and distributing to aiding an international terrorist."

Packard paused, clearing his throat.

"As I stated before, you help me, I leave you the fuck alone."

Lauffer stopped cleaning his suite momentarily, opting to think on his situation a moment.

"Am I supposed to hunt down this mysterious Asian man for you?"

"No. Just use your contacts and see if they've had any Asian customers lately. He'll stick to high-end drugs, and if he hasn't already, he'll contact one of your constituents."

Apparently weighing his options, and not knowing Packard had already sent Barnes on his way, Lauffer made the only realistic decision.

"Fine. I'll help you track him as long as I don't have to see you again."

Packard pulled out a business card with his contact phone numbers and handed it to the skinny dealer.

"Find him, and I'll make sure your life runs smoothly as long as I'm at the helm of the drug task force."

Lauffer nodded.

"Okay. If I find anything I'll be in touch."

CHAPTER 6

▼

Laura Embree watched a normal day at work unfold within the building five attorneys shared as a conglomerate, focusing on accident claims.

As a secretary, she did far more than answer phones. There were meetings to set, complaints to settle, lunches to order, prosecuting attorneys to speak with, papers to file, and sexual harassment from incoming clients to avoid.

Being single only compounded her problems with men of all ages hitting on her, but she absolutely despised their corny lines, trying to lure her on a date, then to bed.

At the same time, no man seemed compatible enough to call a boyfriend, and Laura's definition of a relationship was seeing someone on a third date. Her work often kept her into the evening, leaving her little time for a social life.

She made good money, lived in a nice neighborhood, and stored ambitious ideas for vacations, hoping to find the time to take one.

"I'm going out for some burgers," George Buckley said as he walked by her desk with a stack of folders nestled in one arm. "Need anything?"

"No thanks," Laura replied.

Buckley remained one of the few people in the office Laura trusted and respected. She had never dated him, and he never made comments about how nice she looked, or tried asking her out on dates.

"Are you running more errands for Reese?" she asked as he leaned over her desk casually.

"Of course."

Buckley worked as a paralegal while attending classes at Ball State University. In another year he planned to have a degree in criminal justice, then move toward the next step in his journey to become an attorney.

"What's going on with you today?" Buckley inquired.

"Nothing much."

"Same here. I finally got a weekend off so Jenny and I can visit our friends in Indy."

With things currently slow at the office, Laura stood to join Buckley at a window overlooking the parking lot below.

Currently under renovation, the two levels below their building were under construction, and completely vacated for a few weeks. Much of the downtown area was being redone to lure restaurants and small business owners back to the old center of the city.

Though breezy outside, the sun was shining, leaving an intense glare from the few cars parked in the lot below. Being downtown, they were several blocks from city hall, the headquarters fire station, both political offices for republicans and democrats, and the Radisson Hotel, where an assassin had reportedly fired a deadly shot the morning prior.

"I feel like a prisoner up here sometimes," Laura admitted. "At least you get to run errands, but I'm up here dealing with all the crappy complaints, virtually chained to my desk."

"But you make more than I do," Buckley reminded her.

His smooth features and easy smile always reassured her there were good people in the world, but his type always moved on, leaving behind the assholes and complainers with her.

"Sure you don't want me to pick something up for you?" he asked.

"You kidding? You'd blow my one chance to get out of here for an hour if you got my lunch."

"Okay," Buckley said with a grin, turning to leave. "Don't say I never offered."

Laura warmed a bit inside, knowing her brush with the young paralegal would help her maintain her composure that much longer. As she turned to watch him leave, and in particular, take a look at his shapely posterior, she saw him awkwardly strike against the wall on her right, as though something invisible had shoved him against it.

Offices lined the hallway between herself and Buckley, and as an Asian man rounded the corner, carrying a silenced pistol, Laura knew what had happened to her friend, though she had no idea why.

Buckley's body slumped to the floor in a heap as the Asian man, followed by a lady clad in black leather, both wearing sunglasses, made their way calmly onto the floor with a purpose.

To kill everyone in sight.

Laura knew this, and before they spied her, she ducked behind her desk, peeking out through a crack between the desktop and one of the support legs.

A few people crossed the hallway to other offices, completely unsuspecting, and were gunned down in cold blood before even spying their attackers.

Arms flailing, blood spurting from their injuries, the people fell to the ground with strange expressions, as though being shoved from cliffs.

Breathing heavily in shock, Laura covered her mouth to keep from screaming as the people she worked with every day of her life were murdered before her eyes. Like something out of a science fiction movie, the assailants were dark, cold, and calculating. They had an agenda, and preparation ensured nothing short of armed protection was standing in their way.

Laura knew her building had no guards, no cameras, and no security system activated during the day. She had the only realistic chance of dialing 911, forcing a police response, but her phone was atop the desk, and by the time she reached it, everyone in the office would likely be dead.

No, Laura decided, she needed to stay put and save herself, so there was at least one witness to the crime. She closed her eyes, hoping for an optimistic outcome, but she opened them to see the female gunman firing a shot into the last office on the left, likely killing her boss, Michael Reese.

A quick, audible, painful groan escaped the office, then silence, except for the footsteps coming toward her from the hallway.

Closing her eyes once more, Laura prayed the two were finished with the business of randomly murdering her coworkers, and might just leave. She breathed in deeply, then opened her eyes, seeing nothing except a few bodies lying motionless down the hall, blood pooling from their open wounds.

She wanted to cry out, to mourn their loss, to scream for help, but sensibility forbid her from doing so. Hearing nothing for a moment, she turned around from her crouched position beneath the desk, finding the Asian man knelt at the front of the desk, pointing his silenced weapon at her head.

Laura gasped as the weapon fired a lethal shot.

*   *   *   *

Packard found himself climbing the winding staircase to the third floor of the business building, squeezing past several uniformed officers after news of the massacre came across the scanner as discreetly as possible.

Details were sketchy because city detectives didn't want eavesdroppers of their radio traffic knowing eleven people were dead inside a law firm. Packard suspected what he was about to see because Vic Perry was involved, and most of the task force already knew about the incident.

"Is it starting?" Sorrell had asked on the way to the building.

"I'm afraid it is," Packard replied.

He left Sorrell outside to fish for details from the officers and anyone from the coroner's office, more or less to keep the young officer from being in the way.

As he rounded the last corner, carefully stepping into the third story office, Packard found his path impeded by Perry himself as the FBI agent and two detectives stood at the end of the hallway, short of the starting line of the murderous race.

"What do we have?" Packard asked of the agent, watching as Scott Hahn from the coroner's office, and one of his associates, carefully photographed the scene, and in particular, the bodies.

"We have eleven people dead," Perry replied. "All by gunshots to the head or chest. We let Hahn go in first to verify there were none living."

Hahn had worked as an emergency medical technician for years before joining the coroner's staff and the city fire department.

"Is our Thailand connection responsible?"

"It appears so. We don't have any witnesses, and they didn't have a camera system of any kind."

Naturally, Packard figured, since they didn't really have much of anything worth stealing.

One of the detectives standing beside Packard was Rick Allen, one of two forensic specialists for the city police department. Packard figured he and Perry would comb through the corpses and rooms for any physical evidence left behind.

Even from his limited vantage point Packard spied blood soaking into the carpet, still fresh enough to leave a glimmer from the fluorescent lights above. The harrowing thought that eleven families were about to learn of a personal tragedy ran through his mind.

"Who found this mess?" Packard asked.

"A potential client who's probably taking his business elsewhere," Perry replied.

"That's nice to say," Packard said with obvious displeasure.

"But true."

Packard waited about fifteen minutes for the coroner's staff to finish their investigation and analysis, since everyone on the floor was presumed dead. Typically no one except the crime scene technicians were allowed around victims of homicide, and with so many victims, the sergeant doubted he would see much of anything until Rick Allen completed a very thorough examination of the entire floor.

Sorrell returned to his side as Hahn walked past the group with his gear stuffed in a pack strung along one shoulder. He wore a disheartened expression, as though the senseless murders were almost too much for the most hardened of veterans to bear. Working as a professional firefighter probably gave the man experience in death from auto crashes and DOA calls, but nothing like intentional mass murders of innocent people.

"I think you're going to be part of our task force before this is over," Packard commented as the deputy coroner walked past.

Hahn shook his head negatively, loosening the part in his blond hair.

"Fuck. We don't even have this many slabs at the morgue, Tim."

"How's it look?"

"I've never seen so many blank stares in my life. These people had no idea what was coming."

Often the coroner staff joked at death scenes to alleviate the fact they were standing over a person once walking and talking like themselves. There was no sense of humor, even morbid, about this crime scene.

Sorrell stood silently beside them. If he had found anything new downstairs, he wasn't reporting it. Typically the young officer didn't hesitate if there was something interesting to say.

"Is this your terrorist group I keep hearing about?" Hahn inquired.

"So it seems," Packard answered.

Perry stood close by, and didn't seem phased by them speaking openly about any part of the incident, almost as though he wanted to be privy to the information.

"You might as well include Scott in the task force," Packard suggested to the agent. "He handles most of the cases, so he'll have information about any deaths for us."

Perry nodded in thought.

"And I suspect we'll be seeing more deaths before this is all over."

"Is the city even *considering* letting their buddy out of jail?" Hahn inquired.

"Not at this point, and I doubt ever," Perry answered. "What kind of message would they send if we just set international terrorists free?"

Packard looked down the hallway at the carnage.

"What kind of message will we send if we let scores of innocent people die instead?"

Silence.

"Are you done in there?" Perry asked Hahn before negativity consumed them all.

"Not quite, but you guys are welcome to join me."

Relations between the coroner's office and local police were currently better than in the past. Small turf wars had erupted over who had jurisdiction, and in an ideal world, the two forces worked in conjunction.

Some progress had been made to patch their questionable relationship, but tense moments occasionally arose. Packard knew the problems were mostly attributed to his department's brass, but with the administration change, things seemed better all around.

"We need to figure out what happened in there," Perry stated. "I just hope we can find something that leads us to them."

Packard nodded, knowing he was no good to them, because the fewer people trampling on a crime scene, the better.

"I'm not sure where we're going, but I'm taking Ed with me," he informed Perry. "If you find anything significant, give me a holler, eh?"

"Will do," the agent replied before turning to explore the bloodied third floor.

A moment later Sorrell followed Packard down the last flight of stairs toward the front door. He had remained unusually quiet upstairs.

"Are the rumors about that Perry guy true?" the younger officer asked.

"What's that?"

"I heard something about him, uh, getting his partner killed."

Packard cleared his throat, stepping outside. His hand instinctively reached for the left pocket along his chest, but he caught himself before Sorrell noticed.

"What I heard was his partner got caught in an arrest gone bad. Perry went to the car to call for backup after the fact, and his partner got killed by their perp's brother. If Perry had stayed in the building, nothing ever would have gone wrong."

"So, one mistake and he's forced to work up here?"

"Something like that."

Packard opened the driver's side door before Sorrell conjured up any notions of driving. Preferring to drive himself anyway, the sergeant refused to trust Sorrell with anything more than menial chores at the moment.

"I guess he tried putting it behind him," Packard continued once he was nestled in the driver's seat. "He probably figures no one knows about his past. He's got some sort of small ministry in the Daleville area."

"Who doesn't? There's like a hundred churches down there."

"Well, Perry probably figured he'd just be part of the mix and blend in."

Starting the car, Packard wondered how Clay and Mitch were getting by on their own. He planned on calling Clay later to check.

*   *   *   *

Clay stepped onto the front porch of a cabin just outside city limits along the reservoir. He hated the location because they were trapped by water on one side, and the road behind them was little more than a dead end.

If someone meant harm to the remainder of the Thailand visitors, they would probably get the job done.

Currently, Clay and his cousin were the only two officers guarding five members of the Thailand party. Knowing none of their names, the officer had little desire to get to know them. They were part of his job, and though he tried being hospitable, he was not a butler. They were cozy inside with both American and their native cuisine, along with almost every type of beverage available.

Books, television, a computer, and their own business at hand were their only forms of entertainment, but none of the five seemed upset. It was as though they knew their lives were in potential danger if they stayed in the public eye.

With five different bedrooms, the cabin was a single story, but half the length of a football field to give occupants plenty of space. Clay wasn't exactly sure how the combined task force obtained such property for his particular assignment, but he didn't much care.

Staring toward the trees in front, Clay was able to see across the road, and into the neighboring yards in any direction. With no neighbors closer than a half mile away, he felt secure about his chances of defending against any obvious unauthorized visitations. Grunting to himself, Clay strolled around the side of the cabin, along the wooden wraparound walkway. His hand glided along the railing as his feet slowly stepped in front of one another while his eyes scanned every direction for trouble.

Most officers shrugged off such duty as unnecessary precaution, but Clay took it seriously. If they were willing to kill with a long-range rifle once, little would stop them a second time.

As he reached the back of the cabin with a view overlooking the calm water, Clay's cellular phone rang at his side.

Scooping it up, he flipped it open to answer it.

"Hi, Sarge," he said, recognizing Packard's number from the Caller ID function.

"Clay, I have some bad news."

"I'm stuck here the rest of the week?"

"No, eleven people were just murdered inside an office building."

Clay felt his body grow numb, followed by a cold chill.

"How?" he asked hesitantly.

"They were gunned down by our terrorists."

"Holy shit. Any survivors?"

"No."

Looking out to the water, he felt unsure of what to say or ask next.

"That's terrible," he simply said. "Are there any leads?"

"Not yet. Vic Perry and our techs are looking through the scene as we speak."

Clay waited a few seconds to see why Packard had called. He figured his sergeant was about to reveal the reason, since he was a man of few words.

"Have you been observing our guests?" Packard finally asked.

"Not much. They've been keeping to themselves in different rooms."

"Okay. That murder scene is going to be on the news pretty soon, if not already. When they see the segment, and I do mean *when*, watch their reactions. See if you can get some kind of feedback."

"I take it you don't trust all of our guests?"

"Someone scouted our city long before our assassins arrived. According to Perry, our gunman was in another country as recent as a week ago."

Clay looked up to the sunny sky in thought.

"That doesn't mean one of his partners didn't do the research."

"They're a pack. It doesn't feel right that they'd split up."

"They're in a business. It's not like they're family."

"Two of them are, and our gunmen wasn't one of them."

Sighing, Clay realized there was no arguing with his supervisor. Packard knew only what Perry told him, and Clay knew only what Packard told him. Even with his limited knowledge of the events and the Koda, the young officer had deduced several things. He refused to picture cold-blooded killers hanging out together like family when they weren't shooting or stabbing people.

"Standing here arguing about this isn't going to help us find them," Clay said. "And keeping me and Mitch out here is just plain stupid."

"I have nothing in that. You're out there until the front office says I get you back."

"Great," Clay said sarcastically. "How are things going with Ed?"

"Oh, I really appreciate you two voting to stick me with him like I'm the outcast on a reality show," Packard said with an equally cynic tone.

"You're welcome, but that doesn't answer my question."

Packard paused on the other end as though someone in particular was standing nearby.

"I can't answer your question. I'll call you later."

"Okay. Bye."

Clay replaced his cellular phone to its clip along his belt as his cousin opened the back door, joining him on the deck.

"We have a small problem," Mitch reported.

"What's that?"

"Two of our guests are in a heated debate."

"We have five rooms in there. Why can't they just keep their hands to themselves?"

Mitch's eyebrows raised, giving Clay the impression he was genuinely concerned about the incident happening inside.

"One tried to tell the other to shut up when I approached them."

"You mean like we tell Ed to shut up, or he really meant it?"

Mitch grew openly impatient with his cousin's line of questioning.

"Like he meant it. I don't understand a word of Thailandese, or whatever they speak, but I read their gestures."

Clay groaned to himself.

He wanted to see what his cousin was talking about in person, but subtly enough that their guests didn't realize he was observing them.

"Which room?" he asked Mitch.

"On the east end."

Without another word, Clay stepped inside with his cousin close behind. After motioning for Mitch to stay out of sight, Clay carefully stepped to the end of one hallway, listening to the ensuing argument inside the room.

Like Mitch, he failed to understand one word of what the two men said on the other side of the open door, but he felt certain their discussion related to the assassination at the Horizon Center.

If that proved true, he needed to know exactly what they were talking about, and only Packard had access to the resources he needed.

Through Perry, more than likely.

Figuring the longer he waited, the more interesting conversation he would miss, Clay turned to call his sergeant back. Though highly immoral, he wanted to request surveillance, and especially recording equipment. A translator could be hired to interpret their conversations later, and if it proved useful, the findings might add to their investigation.

He just hoped he wasn't too late.

CHAPTER 7

▼

"Who am I looking at?" Packard asked Perry the next morning as they sat inside a Ball State University office within the new Arts and Journalism building along McKinley Avenue.

A brand new building with a terrace in front for eating, and a food court complete with dozens of tables along the first floor, the upper levels housed the offices of various professors and faculty.

Professor Michael Saunders taught at the university, but spent six years of his life overseas after graduating college. Fluent in Japanese, Taiwanese, and two forms of Chinese, Saunders occasionally found himself summoned by the police and the FBI to assist on cases needing a translator.

Packard already knew this because Perry had given him a quick briefing on the way to the man's office.

"You're looking at Lersak Puthachat, one of the leading ambassadors from Thailand," Perry answered. "He's tied with an umbilical cord to the president over there. It's been rumored for years that he's on the take, just waiting for an opportunity to make his own fortune by backstabbing the people he works for."

"Why do I feel like you're bringing me in way over my head?"

"Because I probably am."

Packard forced a grin as though he was signing his own death warrant.

"Who's the other guy?"

"He's an aide to the president," Perry said. "I forget his name, but it's on our guest list."

"Is he anyone special?"

"Not really. The president over there has a rotation of aides who travel on his behalf as diplomats. Don't worry, I'm having my contacts research him as we speak, but I'm hoping we find out something about his character right here."

Saunders simply sat back, studying the tape as the two law enforcement officers conversed. He seemed engrossed in the tape, and his face occasionally registered shock at what they said.

After Clay's request, Packard wasted little time in wire tapping the safe house, which proved quite a task, because Perry hurried to get technicians from the Indianapolis FBI office to act as phone men, installing phone lines, recording devices, and video cameras, in each room.

Though nothing they recorded was admissible in a court of law, the officers weren't actually positive there was any wrong doing in the first place, and if there was, the Thailand guests were protected by their status. The worst punishment they faced was being returned to their country earlier than they planned.

"They seem to feel safe speaking in their native tongue," Saunders reported.

"Anything significant?" Perry inquired.

"Yes, but I think you'll want to hear the *whole* gist of this conversation."

Saunders had listened to three hours worth of tape by now, and had nothing to report. Most of their conversations were trivial, wondering about the assassination, and when they might be allowed to return home. A few questioned if they were potential targets of the group since they had spoken against the Koda in their homeland.

He had kept both Packard and Perry informed of his findings, but the past ten minutes or so had remained exceptionally quiet.

Engrossed, perhaps.

From intermittently viewing the video, Packard figured the two initial arguers had caught on to Perry's surveillance, but after the three-hour span, they apparently decided to speak privately in the east room once more.

By this time Clay and Mitch had been relieved by two county officers, so Packard had no inside source to tell him what led up to this conversation.

"The one is very concerned the Koda are coming after them," Saunders finally reported, speaking of the presidential aide. "He mentioned something about hiding something from them, and their true purpose for being here."

Packard watched as Perry raised a suspicious eyebrow. He couldn't read exactly what the agent was thinking, but he could almost see the rush of thoughts coursing through the man's mind.

"I wonder if they're on to the recording devices," Perry finally said.

"That doesn't make sense," Packard replied. "If they thought we were recording them, why talk at all, much less implicate yourself as being tied in with the Koda?"

Saunders cleared his throat.

"They didn't exactly implicate themselves," he said, teetering his hand to show the words were minced enough that it was difficult to decipher the context.

"Your boys didn't make it obvious they were eavesdropping the first time around, did they?" Perry inquired.

Packard shook his head negatively.

"They're smarter than that."

Feeling sweat bead along his forehead from the excitement of the breakthrough, Packard removed his glasses momentarily to wipe the steamy buildup from inside the lenses.

"Did they say anything else important?" he asked Saunders.

All three men watched the videotape as the two men stood up and left the east room.

"The one seems to think they're going to get caught for something," Saunders said. "Apparently their reasons for coming over here aren't all they seem."

"So the extradition is a coverup?" Perry asked.

"I wouldn't go that far, but they're taking advantage of it, and they have something that the Koda apparently wants."

Perry's face registered his confusion.

"Have something," he murmured slowly. "They can't have it on their persons or it would have been detected at any number of places already."

"If that's the case, they have a contact here in the States," Packard decided aloud. "And if that's so, this whole plan of the Koda's has been in place since the news of Zhang's extradition came about."

Everyone in the room seemed to feel a black cloud move over them. Just as they were finding answers, the questions got bigger.

*　　*　　*　　*

Sorrell felt a sense of pride because his sergeant had finally seen fit to let him do some investigating on his own.

Granted, checking out leads with local drug dealers wasn't his idea of excitement, and Packard had made certain to tell him to stick to the low level people, but the young officer was getting experiences he otherwise might never have.

His department's criminal investigations division was little more than a boy's club to him. Sorrell figured it was who you knew, and not an individual's talent level that got him or her into investigative work. He didn't fit their profile, and he wasn't a conformist, so he remained in the patrol division until Packard recruited him through Clay and Mitch.

Sorrell had never been on the new chief's good side, which also held him back, but now things were starting to look up.

If not for Clay and Mitch, he might never have gotten his chance to leave the patrol division. All three grew up together in the city's south end, idolizing Clay's father, who patrolled the streets of Muncie on a regular basis.

Things were different back then, when cops knocked out teeth and beat information out of suspects without anyone caring. Civil rights had come a long way, but Sorrell figured they set police officers back, letting big crime filter through more than ever.

Sorrell's father died just before he entered junior high, so he spent a great deal of time on the farm with his grandparents. Teased throughout his teenage years about being a country boy, he withdrew from social functions, turning more of his attention to his friends.

He eventually tested for the police department, missing only one question on the written exam. He mustered enough courage to sound proficient and confident during the interview process, though he questioned his ability to handle the profession if he got the job. Sorrell finished one spot ahead of Mitch on the recruit list, and two behind Clay, who had gone through his second testing process.

Within a few months all three landed jobs, experiencing rookie mistakes and lessons together. They bounced between midnight and afternoon shifts, occasionally getting separated, but eventually gained enough seniority to have a little say about where they wanted to work.

Then came the task force.

Already he had checked with three known dealers that morning, but no one reported seeing any Oriental customers the past month.

He pulled up to a dilapidated parking lot, found a spot to park the unmarked departmental car, and snatched his cellular phone from the seat beside him. Pressing a button to dial a stored number, Sorrell stepped from the car, looking around the area to see if anyone else was around.

They weren't.

"What's up, Ed?" he heard Clay answer from the other end.

"Oh, I'm just here at Kirby and Hackley," he answered, giving the cross streets of his location.

"You're not by yourself in that area, are you?"

"Well, uh, yeah."

Clay's voice sounded strange over the cellular connection, but the wind blowing into the phone made it difficult for Sorrell to hear anyhow.

"What the fuck is Tim thinking?"

"He wanted me to check some of the local dealers out. He thought that Thailand guy might make a buy."

Silence crossed the line a few seconds.

"I'm heading that way," Clay finally said.

"I'll be okay," Sorrell said defensively, and quickly.

He didn't like being monitored by his protective friends all the time.

"We're grabbing a bite to eat, remember?" Clay asked. "Isn't that why you called?"

"I guess it is," Sorrell replied. "We could just meet."

"Nope. I'll see you there in a few."

Clay severed the call before Sorrell was able to further object.

He shook his head as he crossed the street toward the corner market that served more than just groceries if a person was inquisitive enough to ask. Packard had tagged it a problem child when their task force initially formed, but time constraints and other roadblocks had kept them from checking deeper into it.

The time for subtlety had passed, Sorrell decided, monitoring his surroundings as he stepped onto the opposite sidewalk from his car. Another building had been converted into a church, which he found ironic near a narcotics dealership. A hair salon prospered nearby, while across the street cobwebs stretched their strands lazily across the front display window. With only the old cashier's counter and a three-legged chair remaining inside, the building's exterior showed less promise with chipping paint and several bullet holes.

One problem with approaching all of the local dealers, especially for a first contact, was that the group risked making too many allies. When the terrorist situation passed, they would return to their normal job description, which consisted of busting dealers. Only a few were needed as informants to work their way to the top.

Sorrell doubted his visit to this particular pair of thugs was going to prove worthwhile, but the task force had made no good contacts on the south end of town. While Packard figured Punnim, their assassin with a drug habit, was likely going to buy drugs in the campus area, Sorrell wanted a contact in the low end anyhow.

Even if his sergeant didn't want informants in the hood, Sorrell figured having a few personal contacts of his own might be beneficial.

Drawing stares from a few of the local residents, the officer crossed the street anyway. Wearing jeans, a golf shirt, and a form of hiking boots, Sorrell truly looked out of place in a predominantly black neighborhood.

Muncie's south end was divided into sectors by race, gross family income, and proximity to workplaces. No form of riches or royalty existed in that part of town, and when people made enough money, they moved to the northwest end of town where business prospered and convenience was everywhere.

Or they moved out of town to the surrounding county roads.

Few new businesses dared to lease buildings in the south end, but with the renovation of the downtown area, residents hoped the benefits might trickle their way.

Stepping into the corner market, Sorrell felt his body pierced by several cold stares from behind a counter. Though he wore no outward signs indicating he was an officer of the law, the two black men behind the counter seemed to know.

They always knew.

Despite his build, and attire suggesting he was a laborer, probably in construction, Sorrell was just out of place in such a neighborhood.

"Can we help you?" the first man asked without any hint of friendliness.

Deciding his charade was up before it began, Sorrell reached for his holstered gun and badge, laying them both on the counter, though not out of his immediate reach.

"I'd like to know if you've had any Asian customers in here," he said slowly, with more assuredness in his voice than usual. "And that counts for both of your clientele."

Both gave him irritated looks, as though insulted he had audacity enough to just walk into their place of business and ask such a thing.

"Whatchu think this is?" the second asked. "You can't just come in here all Johnny Law and think we gonna tell you every-ting you wanna know."

"This is the first time I've met the both of you," Sorrell said. "It can be the last, or I can arrange it so we're a permanent fixture around your store."

Neither seemed shaken, nor impressed. Sorrell tried to measure their demeanor, and it was growing toward borderline hostile.

He didn't have Packard's experience talking necessary information out of people, and since he was outnumbered, physically aggressive tactics were a risk.

"I'm not asking for my health," Sorrell said. "The man I'm talking about is a risk to all of us, including yourselves if you're selling to him."

"We ain't sellin' shit," the first man insisted, a comb sticking out from his thick fro.

"I'm not asking what you're selling, and I don't give two shits," Sorrell retorted. "I just want to know if you've had *any* Oriental customers the last few weeks. Period."

Each gave the other a strange look, as though questioning whether or not to reveal something to the officer standing before them, being unusually forward in his approach.

"You have, *haven't* you?" Sorrell asked, deciding not to wait for them to change their minds.

Before either muttered another word, the door opened, revealing a young, short man with Oriental features. Upon seeing Sorrell standing there with the two black men, and the gun and badge laid upon the counter top, his eyes widened just before he dashed out the door.

"Shit!" Sorrell muttered to himself, collecting his items before taking chase.

He reached the cool air outside, finding the Asian man had jumped into a foreign-made car of some sort. As the car sped off in a westerly direction, Sorrell hopped into the unmarked car, ready to take chase.

"Damn it!" he berated himself for not being quicker out the door, and for not getting the pertinent information sooner.

$$*\qquad*\qquad*\qquad*$$

Clay jumped out of his personal vehicle to find his sometimes partner slamming the door shut from inside the unmarked city car. Unsure of what was transpiring, but knowing Sorrell would never take off without a good reason when they were scheduled to meet, he sprinted to the passenger's side, yanking the door open without hesitation.

"What the fuck's going on?" Clay asked Sorrell, who was fumbling the keys, trying to start the car hurriedly.

Sorrell didn't answer immediately, but finally started the car, then threw it into drive, beginning a pursuit.

"An Oriental guy showed up as I was interviewing the two men in the store, Clay. He saw me and bolted."

"Is he our guy?"

"I don't know. I didn't see him real good."

Sorrell kept the man's import car within their sight, allowing him to close the gap, since he knew the city streets better.

"What color was his skin?"

"I don't know," Sorrell insisted, apparently growing agitated that he was being questioned while trying to focus on the pursuit. "I just know he had slanted eyes."

Clay ignored the slightly racist remark, trying not to distract Sorrell, since the man had recently had one of his incidents he attributed to bad luck. The cat incident was one thing, but Sorrell smashed a person's chained dog into an electrical pole in a pursuit, despite the department's mixed policy about how long to pursue suspects.

"You sure we should be doing this?" Clay questioned.

"No, but I don't see where we have much choice," Sorrell replied, taking a sharp right turn as he closed in on the other vehicle.

Sorrell had taken several driving courses in Plainfield since the dog incident, mostly to subside departmental fears that he might create more public incidents for them. Clay felt confident in the man's driving ability, since Sorrell raced go-carts and smaller stock race cars in his teenage years. Of course, he had also participated in demolition derbies as well.

"You want to call this in?" Sorrell asked, his eyes glued to the road as the Oriental man cut down several alleys in an attempt to lose his pursuers.

Clay thought a moment. They were not in a marked patrol car, so they needed legitimacy to their pursuit, especially since the man had done nothing wrong, in fact, except for traffic infractions. Speeding and public endangerment immediately came to mind.

Flipping down his visor, which held a small blue and red light bar attachment, Clay flipped it on before calling into their patrol division for a marked car to join them in a pursuit.

"Boy is this going to be a blast to explain," he complained to Sorrell.

"You're telling me," his fellow officer replied, passing a trash can so close that the mirror on Clay's side thumped against it.

Racing blindly through alleys, Sorrell had Clay literally on the edge of his seat. Measuring the value of his own life versus the need to find a lead that might help them save dozens of others, he decided not to intervene with Sorrell's methods.

By now, four marked units had radioed that they were on their way, and Clay did his best to keep them informed about their location, but it seemed as though their quarry overheard everything he said, changing direction after every radio transmission.

"Damn him," Clay muttered.

"Don't worry," Sorrell said confidently. "He's going to hit a dead end before too long."

Watching helplessly, Clay spied the car ahead of them nearly barrel into a couple crossing the street toward a small church, probably for some afternoon supper, or a bazaar.

"Goddamn him," Clay muttered as the driver barely missed the older couple, not slowing or deviating one bit from his course.

Both cars traveled uphill a moment, launching over a cross section several feet in the air before landing hard on crumbling concrete. Sticking with the alleys was dangerous in Clay's opinion, and he decided it was time to do something drastic, especially with no patrol units in sight.

"Take him out, no matter what it takes," he told Sorrell, who had maneuvered their vehicle directly behind the reckless criminal.

"You're giving me permission to initiate a wreck?"

"Yeah."

"And you're going to tell the chief it was your idea when we get called into his office?" Sorrell questioned, never removing his eyes from the car directly ahead of them.

"If this is who I think it is, we'll be heralded as heroes, and won't have to worry about it."

Clay spied traces of a grin reach the corner of Sorrell's lips before the officer applied more pressure on the gas pedal, closing the narrow gap between the two cars.

Under no circumstances were Muncie officers allowed to use the technique Clay suggested, known as pit stopping. With the regular patrol cars, which ironically had ramming bars on the front, there was little danger of failure, but they were in a Ford Taurus, commonly used by detectives and officers on special details.

Sorrell waited until they were in a more open area, without buildings directly on either side, before ramming the corner of the car ahead of them. His action sent it into an uncontrolled, though predictable, tailspin that landed it against an industrial dumping bin behind a small factory somewhat east of where they originally began the chase.

Unfortunately the side not pinned against the metal bin had collided with Sorrell's side of the car hard enough to set off the airbag on his side. Clay's left side smashed Sorrell against the dented door, forcing a painful yell from his temporary partner.

"You okay?" Clay asked quickly as he undid his seatbelt.

"Yeah," Sorrell replied. "My hand is pinned between the door and the seat," he added, trying to tug it loose to no avail.

Spying their suspect climbing from the back of his own car, where the window has shattered upon impact, Clay felt unsure of what to do. Sorrell apparently read his thoughts, though his arm was hopelessly stuck until help arrived.

"Go kick his ass," the officer said, giving Clay the permission he wanted.

Clambering from the car, Clay took chase. Several factory workers stepped outside, likely hearing the crash from their posts, so Clay insisted they call 911 and ask for both the police and fire departments because a man was injured in one of the cars.

Probably hoping to lose Clay early in the chase, the Oriental man darted into the factory, dodging pieces of machinery and workers as the young officer nimbly followed.

"Stop! Police!" Clay decided to yell while he had witnesses surrounding him.

He learned early in his career to identify himself as an officer of the law whenever necessary, because attorneys often tried getting their clients off the hook by stating the guilty party had no idea if actual police officers were pursuing them.

Even if he had his firearm with him, using it in such a crowded facility would be a risky, stupid idea. Nothing set in panic within public places more than a firearm or a bomb. Considering he simply planned on meeting Sorrell for lunch and maybe some basic research, he didn't wear his firearm. Instead, it sat in his own car underneath the seat where it did him no good whatsoever.

Though young and quick, the Asian man was unable to shake Clay because the officer's rigorous workout routine kept him in ideal shape all year round.

Realizing his chances of escape were slim along the first floor, the man darted up a staircase to the second floor, which housed several heavy machines and the major electrical supply for the several buildings that comprised the factory.

Thinking he finally had his man, Clay followed closely, about to tackle the smaller man, but a sudden straight kick at the center of the staircase sent him falling back toward the unforgiving concrete of the floor below.

Catching himself with a railing before any damage was done, Clay quickly took up the pursuit, once again having to make up ground.

Most of the second level was wide open, leaving the officer little option but to dead sprint across the dusty floor after the Oriental man who was quickly running out of places to hide.

He dodged a few workers and a few crates before finding himself at another set of stairs, this time leading to the roof.

Hoping Sorrell wasn't seriously injured, and help was on the way, Clay dashed up the stairs behind the man. He reached the roof level through an open doorway, finding the door swinging back toward him as soon as his feet touched the tar surface of the factory's roof.

Evading the door, Clay finally found himself standing toe to toe with Sorrell's suspect, but this man looked nothing like the assassin he'd confronted just days before. In fact, he was college age, making him too young to be any of the terrorists.

Still, he ran, and more importantly, put lives in danger, so Clay needed to bring him in.

Quickly observing the area, Clay realized they were virtually a full two stories above the unforgiving concrete of a parking lot, penned within a square of guard rails about the size of a large living room. Outside of these boundaries sat an air-conditioning unit and a one-story drop to a storage shed off the side of the building.

Without a word, the man assumed a defensive martial arts stance, but it was no stance Clay knew of, which meant it was a feign to throw him off.

"Uh-huh," he murmured skeptically to himself, assuming an actual stance from his own training.

Since he was blocking the door, Clay knew the man had only two options.

Fight, or run.

There was no chance this kid knew Clay's background, and dashing off the side of the building was likely a painful option, so he took a swing at the officer, determined not to be taken into custody.

Clay blocked the punch, returning a hard jab into the younger man's ribs with his opposite hand.

Clutching his ribs as he backed away, the Oriental man apparently realized his bluff had failed. He shot Clay an unfriendly look as the officer backed off, deciding to try diplomacy once again.

"Give yourself up and I won't have to hurt you."

Somehow his words backfired as another fist flew his way. Clay sidestepped the punch, caught the younger man's arm, and made a split second decision not to break it over his shoulder. Instead, he used both hands to take hold of the arm before flipping the younger man over his shoulder, landing him hard against the rooftop.

Being far more compassionate now than in his younger years, Clay refrained from simply punching him in the face or kicking in a rib. His years of training in the martial arts, and especially the discipline instilled from his instructor, gave him the patience to give this man a chance to end their conflict peacefully.

"You done?" he simply asked.

Instead of answering, the man launched his free fist toward Clay's groin, but the officer caught it, then launched his own fist toward the man's head, but the younger man rolled to one side, nearly causing Clay to impact his fist with the roof.

Stopping short of harming himself, Clay realized the Asian probably had at least a little bit of skill in self-defense, as he evasively stood, hurling a fury of fists and feet toward Clay. This caused the officer to dodge, back away, and think of a new attack approach, which varied every second.

Clay avoided punches by swaying his head, his torso, and his feet in sync with the occasional low kick until he was backed close to one of the guard rails. Instinctively, and without any thought that he might be endangering himself, Clay turned to charge the rail, using it to propel himself backwards in the air toward his assailant, swinging his leg forcefully toward the man's head.

Blood spurted from the man's mouth as the sport boot contacted his jaw, crushing skin against teeth.

Clay landed on his feet as the Asian man reeled, trying to regain his composure and balance. He wasted little time in launching a straight-kick toward Clay's head, but the officer was already in the air, doing a back flip toward the rails as well as any local gymnast. Much like an accomplished gymnast, he grasped the rails in midair, balancing himself into the air with straight arms until his adversary came closer.

Two stories below, a dangerously hard surface threatened to cripple or kill Clay if he was careless enough to fall. Years of training had provided him with confidence and enough physical ability that he had no fear of the situation at hand.

Even if the sacrifices left him lonely in life sometimes.

Using raw strength from his arms, Clay twisted himself from the rails toward his charging enemy, swinging his buckled legs somewhat like a helicopter propeller. The spinning appendages worked like weapons, striking the man in the face before he could muster an offensive move.

Landing catlike, Clay assumed another martial arts stance, using one hand to signal his opponent to bring another charge, if he dared.

He did, but a straight punch to the jaw, followed by a roundhouse kick to the sternum, floored his adversary. Reaching instinctively for his handcuffs, Clay grimaced when he remembered they were half a city away with his gun.

"Hey!" he called in the doorway for any of the factory workers who might be within an earshot, since most of them were probably curious about the chase just occurring in their workplace.

Hearing nothing in return, he peeked inside the door, seeing no one within his line of sight.

"Shit," he muttered, turning to find his adversary gone from the spot where he had just left him lying atop the roof.

Now he was leaping off the roof to the storage shed, only one story below, creating another pursuit for Clay, which was the last thing the officer wanted. Another pursuit would inevitably place him in another battle, and there was no telling where help might be, or when it might arrive.

Clay heaved a quick sigh, looked to the edge of the roof where the storage shed waited below, then ran toward the ledge, leaping over the rail to the surface below, sensing his landing was going to be rough. His training was helpful in landing from higher elevations, but wasn't always good enough to keep him from attaining nagging injuries.

He doubted the pursuit was worth the effort, but Clay didn't believe in starting anything he couldn't finish.

Even if it made for a long day.

*   *   *   *

Packard walked with Perry along McKinley Avenue toward the parking lot where their cars were parked. Having police markings, or at least the right license plate, made parking much easier when necessary.

If they hadn't been able to use the faculty lot, they might have been forced to park where students and visitors parked, almost half a mile away in the closest lot or side street.

"Sitting up there with Mike isn't going to make the answers come any quicker," Perry informed Packard. "He'll call if something important comes up."

"I just feel a need to know, because I'm sure these Koda bastards are just getting started."

"I agree, but we're finding a few answers," Perry said, flapping a manilla folder in one hand like a fan.

Packard gave a questioning look.

"The rifle used to assassinate your buddy and Traisorat was no ordinary gun," Perry said with a quirky smile that seemed to indicate such a piece of evidence was in their favor. "It turns out the gun is an experimental model called the

ATP-16, and it's been on the Asian black market for about six months now, even though it's not in mass production."

Perry reached into his car for the bottle of lemonade he had purchased earlier, taking a drink before he continued his narrative.

"This weapon is based on the Russian SVD Dragunov sniper rifle. The new design allows the gun to be broken down better, which allows for easier transport. And it's lighter, with almost five-hundred more meters of killing distance."

Packard grunted to himself.

"How many of these guns are there?"

"Maybe two dozen."

Packard stopped at his own car, leaning an elbow atop the hood as their conversation continued.

"And people can just bring these weapons on commercial flights, or what?"

Perry let a smirk slip.

"No, but it takes some special licensing and permits to have possession of such a weapon, much less own it."

"How does this help us?"

"My agency knows the circles of people these guns travel with," Perry revealed. "It's only a matter of time before we trace where it came from and begin putting this whole mess together. I'm guessing whatever our two guests are talking about hiding from the Koda is important to all parties involved, and that it might have something to do with the ATP-16."

"I don't know," Packard said skeptically. "It doesn't add up."

"What doesn't?"

"I agree that they aren't here to break Zhang out of jail, but why are they threatening terrorist acts on the city if all they really want is something a few of the Thailand guests have?"

Perry shrugged.

"I think the terrorist acts are a message to hand that something over, or suffer the consequences."

"All the more reason for us to stick around and wait for answers," Packard insisted.

"No, no," Perry said. "You and I are taking a break, giving Mike some space, and then giving him a break."

Packard disagreed, but it was Perry's call. As the agent walked away, Packard stepped into his car, wondering how Sorrell was coming along with the things on his list.

*   *   *   *

Running the length of the factory was not what Clay had planned for when he told Sorrell he wanted to meet with him.

Mitch asked him to grab an early lunch, but Clay declined, stating it was rude to leave Sorrell to his own devices.

Oh, heavens no, Clay thought sarcastically, chasing a worthless suspect through an industrial area with no backup is much more fun.

In front of him by almost five car lengths, the suspect had never let up, and now he was nearing the building's corner, which led into traffic, then the local neighborhood. There, houses, alleys, and trees would provide all the cover the Asian man needed to elude a tardy police force if Clay lost him.

Suddenly two things crossed his mind about the suspect. One, why was the man so desperate to escape, considering he was never caught perpetrating a crime? Two, what if Sorrell's explanation of what happened wasn't fully accurate.

Regardless, he decided, the man had nearly run down several people from his poor driving skills alone. He needed to be stopped.

Clay watched helplessly as the man reached the edge of the building, suddenly falling hard to the ground as though he had struck an invisible wall. After falling, the man skidded across the concrete roughly.

Not slowing for one second, Clay quickly realized the reason for the man's sudden collapse.

After moving around the corner, Mitch stood over the victim of his large fist, making certain the Oriental man was no longer conscious.

"Nice one, cuz," Clay said.

"I heard you might be in need of an assist."

"You heard right. I don't suppose you checked on Ed?"

Mitch shook his head solemnly.

"The fire department had to amputate his hand."

"Oh, shit," Clay muttered, feeling a sense of shock shoot through his body.

Why had he left Sorrell in such bad shape? Why had Sorrell urged him to pursue the suspect if he was in such horrific condition?

"I'm just fuckin' with ya," Mitch said, giving his cousin a playful punch in the shoulder. "They got him out, and one of the boys took him to the hospital to get checked out."

"But his arm's okay?"

"I think so. It got pinched a little bit, but nothing looked broke."

Mitch pulled out his handcuffs, which he happened to have with him, since he had his complete gun belt. Kneeling down, he aggressively cuffed the suspect.

"You're such a prick sometimes," Clay informed him.

"Why?" Mitch asked without looking up from the business at hand.

"Lying to me about Ed. He could have bled out for all I knew."

Mitch chuckled.

"You're way too serious, cousin," he replied, standing as he yanked their suspect up with him to his feet. "And you might want to start carrying your gun with you, so you don't have to do a two-mile run again."

Clay faked a laugh with a half sneer.

"Fuck you."

CHAPTER 8

▼

Delaware County police officer Jack Garver worked on a crossword puzzle in his patrol car behind the wrought iron gate in the front of the Muncie water company. Currently off-duty from his regular patrol shift at the county police department, Garver made good money at one of the most boring second jobs a cop could ask for.

No one to talk to.

No rounds to make.

No way to leave, even for a dinner break.

Diminishing light to read or do crosswords by.

"Four-letter word for helpless," he said to himself, tapping his pencil against the heavily creased newspaper. "Starts with 'w'."

If he had his way, Garver would be at home checking on his horses like he often did on patrol. After almost thirty years on the force, he felt entitled to keep occasional tabs on his farm, but he sometimes visited his old high school friend who owned a convenience store. Then there was his favorite family restaurant, and the coffee shop he liked.

Sometimes his shifts ended before he even knew it. Unlike his shifts, however, there was no leaving the front gate of the water company unguarded. Not that anyone ever seemed to be around, but after the terrorist attacks in New York, the utility company made certain their water was guarded around the clock against the possibility of toxins or chemical contaminants from an outside source.

Sitting in his patrol car with the heat turned on low, the county officer glanced in the mirror, seeing the wrinkles in his forehead appear more prominent than ever. With a receding hairline and three divorces behind him, Garver had wasted little time in pursuing the affection of another woman he met in a pub three weeks prior.

On duty no less.

He considered her perfect, but to this point she had failed to show she felt the same way. They both loved horses, they were both divorced, and neither had kids still living at home. Garver envisioned them riding off into the sunset every night on horseback, and after she spent the night at his place the night they met, he figured something good had literally come to his doorstep.

With dusk creeping over the horizon, the county officer turned on the two overhead lights beside his rearview mirror. He decided to flip through the rest of the newspaper before engrossing himself in more crossword puzzles.

Reading the headlines about terrorist activity in Muncie, Garver found himself compelled to question how legitimate these overseas terrorists were in extracting their comrade from jail. In his day, he never had to deal with terrorism. Domestic brawls, disorderly drunks, and the occasional homicide were all he ever dealt with.

His department ran the jail, and he knew there was no chance of them actually breaking him out, or their threats prompting his release. Their sheriff would stand against any demands they made, because caving in was no option. He said as much in several key meetings, that even if a hundred people died from their terrorist activities, the man would never be released, short of extradition back to his own country.

Of course, the sheriff also stressed capturing the terrorists before any further damage was done, was his department's new top priority.

Garver himself hadn't changed his routine. International terrorists weren't going to simply walk around in public, unless perhaps they blended in with the campus crowd. Even then, that became the jurisdiction of the Ball State University Police, and he wasn't about to step foot on campus unless absolutely necessary.

Stretching his feet momentarily from his car seat, the county officer happened to look up, spying someone standing at the gate of the utility company.

"Ah, shit," he muttered, pulling the handle to open his door.

Stepping out, Garver sauntered toward the gate, ready to answer a question about directions, or refuse the stranger access to the facility. Strangely, the person wore a hooded sweatshirt, staring toward the ground until the county officer drew close enough to make out details in the low light.

Because he refused to think he was in any danger, Garver kept his hands at his side, rather than near his firearm. When he drew close enough to the stranger, however, and the man lowered his hood, revealing an Oriental face with a sinister smile, he instinctively reached for the gun at his side, but a sharp pain struck him through the back of his chest, piercing his heart.

He gasped as his heart stopped, then collapsed to the ground in a heap, leaving his murderers free run of the water treatment plant.

*   *   *   *

Packard remained at city hall as long as he could tolerate for the interrogation of the new Asian man Clay and Mitch brought in. He refused to answer any questions, but his body language indicated he might have something to do with the terrorists threatening the city.

Perry took charge of the situation, receiving some assistance from the afternoon shift city detectives. They took turns asking questions, but silence was all they ever received as a response.

Paperwork and identification led the investigators to discover he was indeed a college student, and his American-born roommate answered questions freely when Perry asked him to visit the second floor of city hall for questioning.

What they now knew was their prisoner spoke fluent English, did fairly well in his studies, had very little social life, and had involvement in terrorist ideas, if not the executions of anti-American terrorist activities.

Still, he refused to answer any questions.

Packard walked into the new emergency room of Ball Memorial Hospital, wasting no time before asking a nurse where his officer was. While Clay and Mitch went home to sleep before their next guard duty shift, the sergeant was left to tend to Sorrell and ultimately take the man home.

Lit better than most department stores, and surprisingly easy to navigate for staff, patients, and visitors, the new emergency room seemed well worth the millions the hospital invested to create it. While the old emergency room remained a bay to occasionally transport dead bodies from ambulances to the morgue, the new emergency room flourished.

Though the hospital promoted it as a better staffed and equipped emergency department, Packard referred to it as an emergency room as he always had.

Security was heightened in the form of aluminum bay doors for the ambulances, and a centralized security room where officers constantly monitored rooms with potentially dangerous or escape-prone patients. The single entrance from the back of the hospital now allowed officers to view anyone walking into and out of the emergency ward.

Before, people might enter from several different locations, and security officers sometimes found themselves tied to monitoring individual rooms, occasionally utilizing the entire shift's staff, leaving the rest of the hospital vulnerable.

Things were definitely improved after months of inconvenience and countless dollars spent for the modifications.

"You okay?" Packard asked his officer when he found the appropriate room.

The new emergency ward had divisions based on what type of medical care incoming patients required. Sorrell was placed in the least critical area available, since his arm had been pinned in the self-induced car wreck.

"Uh, I'm doing okay," Sorrell replied. "The X rays turned out negative, so they think I might have busted a few blood vessels."

"No torn tendons or anything?" Packard asked, taking a seat beside the cot where Sorrell was seated.

"Nothing like that. It hurts, but I've definitely had worse."

Packard yawned involuntarily from his long day. He desperately wanted to crack their prisoner open like a coconut and see what information spilled out, but Perry and the investigators said if he didn't speak before long, they planned to leave him in an isolated interrogation room by himself until he decided to cooperate.

Strangely, leaving suspects alienated from all human contact, almost to the point of sensory deprivation, seemed the best way to get suspects to crack. Packard knew it from talking to investigators over the years, and trying the technique himself a few times to break drug informants.

"Has the guy said anything yet?" Sorrell inquired.

"Not one word."

"I think he knows something because of the way he ran."

"His roommate told us all sorts of information about him, and the investigators are getting a search warrant to check his portion of their dorm room, since it's technically university property."

Sorrell chuckled.

"Technicalities and red tape."

"You got that right."

A few minutes later the doctors cleared Sorrell to leave, simply telling him to take it easy a few days, and avoid work until he felt better.

"Uh, I don't want to miss work," Sorrell confessed as they walked out to the unmarked departmental car Packard was driving.

"You've had a rough week, Ed," Packard replied, recalling how the man was shot just a few days earlier. "I can handle things."

"I think I can help. If that guy was connected to the terrorists, I, uh, definitely want to track them down."

"Out of revenge for your busted arm?" Packard asked with a chuckle, climbing into the driver's seat.

"Something like that," the younger officer said as he climbed into the opposite seat, forcing a grin.

Sorrell didn't live far from the hospital, but Packard decided to stop at a convenience store on the way, simply to save himself from making a special trip after he dropped the officer off.

"Want a Coke or anything?" he asked Sorrell as he opened his door.

"I'm fine," Sorrell replied as he decided to step out.

Packard left his officer outside as he walked into the convenience store, immediately heading to the back to grab a soda. He picked one out, took it up front, and found himself staring at the packs of cigarettes behind the counter.

Despite the patch, he still had cravings. Maybe it was an oral fixation, or the habit of lighting up, but he missed whatever the clerk said to him the first time, too entranced in the decision running through his mind.

"I wouldn't," Sorrell said with a tone of warning.

His officer had entered the store without him even noticing.

"Wouldn't what?" Packard asked almost defensively, as though the thought of buying cigarettes never crossed his mind.

He quickly slid a dollar and change across the counter to pay for the soda, then led Sorrell outside. Though he might never admit it to Sorrell, or himself, the officer probably saved him from giving in, just days removed from kicking the habit.

"You said you quit because of your wife, right?" Sorrell inquired.

"Yeah. She kept nagging me."

"You don't think she'd know if you started again?"

Packard shrugged almost indifferently, though he was positive Sarah would know.

"My wife just about kicked my ass when she found out I was chewing," Sorrell admitted, speaking of chewing tobacco. "I told her I quit, even though I didn't, and uh, there was probably a pile of discarded chew in my neighbor's yard where I threw it out every night just before I got home."

"You don't chew now, do you?"

"No, because somehow she seemed to know. They always know that stuff, Sarge."

Grinning to himself, Packard concurred with the statement. Wives had a tendency to know when their spouses were doing wrong.

A moment later, he pulled into Sorrell's driveway, putting the car in park.

"You're cleared for time off if you need it," he said to the younger officer.

"No way. I want to work."

Packard nodded in understanding.

"You've got nothing to prove to me. If you change your mind, call me tomorrow. Otherwise, I'll see you after my meeting at city hall in the morning. If we're lucky, I'll know something before the night is through."

Sorrell displayed a poker face, because Packard couldn't quite tell what the man was thinking. He just seemed determined to fit in with the group.

"Then I'll, uh, see you in the morning," Sorrell said as he opened his door.

"I suppose so," Packard said as his officer walked toward the house and he put the car in reverse.

He needed some good news and willpower to get him through the night.

CHAPTER 9

▼

Morning came sooner than expected when Packard received a phone call shortly after midnight regarding a murder at the water plant. Perry saw fit to call him because this was almost certainly the work of the terrorist group.

Sarah, who had complained about not seeing him enough lately, was less than pleased when the phone rang beside the bed, waking them both. She gave him the silent treatment as he dressed to go into the night once again, and he said nothing.

What was there to say?

He approached the scene, parking just off Burlington Avenue on the opposite side of the water treatment plant. Several marked and unmarked city and county police cars formed an artificial gate at the front of the facility, and he spied several vehicles from the water company and health department as well.

Three blocks in either direction were blocked off to civilians because the police presence took up so much room. Patrolmen were left at every conceivable entry point to prevent citizens and any other terrorists from gaining access to the scene.

Walking across the street, Packard found Clay approaching him from within the facility.

"What do we have?" he asked the officer, who he had called before leaving his house.

"A county officer was murdered while guarding the front gate," Clay replied. "They've got Stephens doing his thing, and Perry is with the water company people inside, testing the water supply."

Del Stephens was one of the city department's technicians, capable of dusting for fingerprints, finding forensic clues, and compiling DNA evidence for court.

"Those bastards could have put anything in the water," Packard said. "How long ago did Perry go inside?"

"Just a few minutes ago. Stephens just now cleared the path back there. He said everything else is still off-limits until he's done."

Packard knew too many people trampling through a crime scene only damaged or completely dispelled more evidence.

"I can pretty much guarantee it was our group," Clay noted.

"How's that?"

Leading Packard over to the technician's van, the younger officer pointed out the body just past the vehicle, which had a bladed weapon sticking out the backside, since Garver landed face down in death.

"What's so special about that?" Packard asked, only glancing at the body before turning away.

"The weapon is called a *wakizashi*, or *shoto*," Clay explained. "It's a Japanese short sword dating back to the days of the samurai."

"So it's a message?"

"Loud and clear, I'd say."

A concerned look crossed Clay's face as he studied the sword stuck in the county officer's body.

"What's the matter?" Packard asked.

"Nothing," Clay replied quickly, as though something bothered him, but he didn't want to discuss it.

"Okay."

Stepping around the van, but not past the yellow crime scene tape, the sergeant noticed Stephens at work. He finally stared at the body of Jack Garver lying on the ground. A small pool of blood showed from the back of his shirt where the sword had penetrated from behind. For forensics and investigative purposes, the sword was left in place, and would remain there until the body reached the morgue.

Garver was lying face down, eyes open, obviously taken by surprise.

"He felt no pain," Clay noted.

"That's not much consolation," Packard replied, glad the first arriving officers had shielded the body with a sheet, combined with a few stakes, to create a makeshift lean-to.

Clay seemed to study the sword momentarily from afar.

"How do you know so much about that Japanese stuff anyway?" Packard decided to ask.

"When I was young, my father forced me to attend a martial arts school with a friend of his from Japan."

"Why would he force you to go?"

"Because I needed it," Clay admitted. "I was a bully, and a mean little son-of-a-bitch until the time he sent me. Maybe it was because Dad was gone all the time, or because he was a cop and that gave me the right to break any rule or law I wanted to, but I was lost as a kid."

Packard nodded, knowing Clay's father was still active in their police force, but it suddenly occurred to him the two were never chummy at the training sessions. They spoke, but it seemed Clay usually forced himself to carry on a conversation with the man.

"So now you have discipline, you're honest, and you're a black belt in what, ten forms of martial arts?"

The last part of his statement was meant as a joke, and Clay took it as such, smirking.

"A few, but who's counting?"

Packard paced the asphalt driveway a moment, realizing he was not allowed on the grounds of the crime scene, and refusing to burden Perry when the man obviously had important things to do at the moment.

Instead, he decided to converse with Clay further.

"So here you are in your mid-thirties, and you still aren't hitched, Clay. Why is that?"

Clay shrugged.

"Just haven't found the right girl yet. It was hard to keep a relationship working afternoons and midnights, and now the task force work keeps me busy."

Packard gave a sly grin.

"What's that for?" Clay questioned.

"I manage to keep a marriage with two kids together. I think you should probably be able to find a relationship."

"Considering we're at a death investigation, you sure are focusing on me a lot," Clay complained.

"Well, there isn't much else to do at the moment."

Stephens took a momentary break, walking over to Packard and Clay, who were still involuntary sentries beside his van. The sergeant assumed the technician had done the photography and video work before everyone else arrived.

"What have we got?" Packard asked him.

"He was hit from behind," Stephens answered. "I'm guessing he was distracted at the gate and killed there because there are footsteps in the grass behind his squad car, and a blood trail where they dragged him back from the road."

"Any prints?" Clay asked.

"Nothing on the weapon, so I doubt there's any at all," Stephens answered. "We'll know once we get the body into the morgue. It's about to rain out here, so I don't want to waste too much time moving him."

Packard looked around to the various officers standing around, waiting for further orders. An ambulance sat in the distance with two medical technicians ready to transport the body. He knew the county police were in for a long week, burying two of their own. Line-of-duty deaths were rare in the Muncie area, but the rules were quickly changing.

Because the technician seemed a few pounds heavier by the day, in Packard's opinion, Stephens was probably taking a break because he was tired. With his supervisors and the coroner's office continuing a pointless quarrel over how death scenes were handled, he didn't want to see one single detail missed in this particular case.

"Del, you might want to get that done before it rains," he suggested to the technician, who was leaning against his own van for support as he exhaled heavily from the labors of his job.

Stephens shot him a strange stare, as though wondering why a sergeant from a different division had the audacity to order him around.

"I'm not trying to be a dick," Packard said. "It's just better for everyone if you get your job done so we can move the body."

Stephens nodded, though outwardly unhappy, and left to continue his job.

"Aren't we the picture of solidarity?" Clay asked sarcastically.

"Quite," Packard answered, turning to see Perry emerge from a building toward the rear of the property.

"What's going on?" Perry asked, shaking Packard's hand as he stared at Clay, possibly wondering why the sergeant invited him along.

"Not much. Is our water supply safe?"

"We don't know yet," Perry replied with a concerned look. "I've already asked your chief and his ranking officers to contact the radio and television stations to warn people about drinking or using the water."

"God only knows what they might have put in it," Clay chimed in.

Packard wanted to speak with Perry, but he needed a moment alone with the agent.

"Clay, do me a favor and see if the detectives need help canvassing the area."

From the look his officer returned, Packard knew Clay figured he was being shooed away temporarily. Still, he turned to find the detectives.

"This is getting a bit out of hand," Packard told the agent.

"What are you talking about?"

"I've been doing some thinking, Vic. I'm trying to figure out exactly why we have custody of Zhang when by all rights the men in black should have swiped him up and taken him to Washington to rot."

Perry made it obvious he was upset about the sergeant's line of questioning, or that Packard had been doing independent thinking, but after an audible sigh, he answered.

"He was taken to Washington by my partner, questioned for several months with my partner present, and finally brought back here to be extradited from the area where he was captured."

"But why did it have to be here?"

Perry seemed agitated he was being questioned further, but his lead position on the task force likely shunned him into answering.

"With the group coming here for the university's international exchange, it made sense to further strengthen the relationship between our country and Thailand by having them remove an international terrorist. It allowed them to crack a nut that we couldn't, and showed their countrymen they were no longer tolerating harboring or assisting known terrorist factions."

"And it backfired?"

"Intelligence reported the Koda was planning to break him free in Thailand, which was another reason we wanted him gone."

"Again, a backfire."

Perry soured as thoughts galloped through his mind in Packard's estimation. He looked around momentarily to ensure they were alone.

"My partner was basically left in charge of the entire situation because he's an old terrorism specialist who came here to retire and be with his family."

"And where is your partner?"

"On vacation."

"Well, that's convenient," Packard scoffed, making his displeasure apparent. "Have you tried reaching him?"

"Of course," Perry insisted. "There are several areas of this case I could use his expertise on, but without him I guess we'll have to get by."

"You make it sound like we're in a backyard football game without our star quarterback. There are lives at stake, Vic, and you're telling me your partner isn't answering his phone?"

"Hell, he may be out of the country for all I know."

"Highly unlikely if he was supposed to be here for the prisoner exchange with our guests. If he's the reason we're in this mess, I suggest you find a way to reach him at any cost."

Perry nodded, but the look on his face indicated he had something else weighing on his mind he had yet to reveal.

"What is it?" Packard prompted, since he was already fired up about Perry deceiving him the entire time about certain details.

Perry refused to answer immediately.

"What *is* it?" Packard demanded this time.

"My partner may be in Washington. And he may have Zhang with him."

Packard felt his face flush red from the anger of being deceived twice within the past five minutes.

"What the fuck?" he yelled loud enough that everyone in the area heard him, likely including the civilians behind police barricades three blocks down in any direction. "What in the fuck kind of operation are you running?"

"That's enough," Perry said, pointing a finger right at the sergeant's chest. "I know what I need to know, and I've already told you more than you need to know."

Packard felt his right hand clench into a fist, but he was professional enough to hold himself back from doing anything regrettable.

"I don't know anything except that you've had the rest of us wearing blinders the whole fucking time we've been working on this task force of yours."

By now Clay had overheard a few of his sergeant's outbursts, and started back toward the conversation. Packard spied his officer edging up to him cautiously.

"Everything is being done for the safety of everyone involved," Perry stated.

"So letting these terrorists think Zhang is being held locally, when in fact, he could be hundreds of miles away, is the best thing for our city while they murder half our population by poisoning the water?"

"I don't think Zhang is their real motivation," Perry admitted.

"What do you mean?" Packard asked, sensing another swerve coming his way.

"Mike translated more of those tapes for me, and I discovered what our two guests were talking about that seems so important."

"And that is?"

Perry looked to Clay as though the officer was intruding in business he deserved no part of hearing.

"He's with me," Packard said. "And if it wasn't for him, you wouldn't have that suspect in custody whose been running drug errands for Punnim."

Perry gave an incredulous look, since he had been left out of the loop for a change.

"That's right. On the way over here I phoned my department's investigators and discovered the informant Clay here brought in this afternoon had some vital information for us. We might be able to nail Punnim on a sting operation and bring this whole shitball to close sooner than any of us hoped."

"And you didn't tell me this sooner?" Perry asked, outwardly infuriated.

"Fuck you and the horse you rode in on. After the line of shit you just fed me, you're lucky we're even having this conversation."

Packard paced the ground a few seconds, too angry to decide what he wanted to do next. He wanted to know what information the translator had fed Perry, but he had obviously just one-upped the agent, so he decided what to do next.

"As a matter-of-fact, we're not having this conversation," Packard said. "When you decide to be a team player, give me a call. Until then I'll be conducting my own investigation."

He led Clay away from the scene, since his officer was confused.

"You can't do that!" Perry called, his feathers ruffled.

"Just watch me!"

Clay kept looking behind them, but followed Packard's lead to their vehicles.

"You're not really going to send us flying solo, are you?" he asked.

"I'll do whatever it takes to get this over with. But I doubt the deputy chief is going to let me be a rogue."

"Then why make that kind of threat to Perry?"

"To let him know he can't fuck me around and expect me to sit back and take it. He's been keeping secrets from me and this entire city since this whole investigation began."

"So now what?"

Packard opened his car door, glancing back to the scene.

"We get a good night's sleep and I see about getting you and your crazy cousin back in the morning."

"I hate the idea of keeping you and Ed from bonding," Clay said with a sly grin.

"And I would feel bad if I forgot to liberate you from your assignment in the morning."

"You'd lose sleep wondering how we were doing," Clay playfully warned.

Packard smirked as he slid into his driver's seat.

"I guarantee you I won't lose any sleep tonight," the sergeant answered, starting his car. "And you'd better not either. We have a full day ahead of us tomorrow."

CHAPTER 10

▼

By noon the next day, Packard had accomplished two major victories in his eyes.

One, he had Clay and Mitch off their guard dog assignment. This meant he had their services exclusively to himself once more.

The deputy chief was none too happy with Perry's secretive nature, even wondering outwardly whose side the agent was really on.

His second accomplishment resulted in him working with the detectives that morning to get their suspect to talk. Because they finally formally arrested him, a lawyer was necessary, but Packard had no concern about a future court case, much less upholding the informant's civil rights, because he was after bigger fish.

When presented with the situation, even the court-appointed attorney wasn't very sympathetic with his client's plight.

Packard talked the man into painting a grim picture for his client, and it took little figurative arm twisting to convince the man of exactly what to say. Faced with years and years in prison, or possible deportation with criminal charges, the man reluctantly agreed to help them set up a sting operation to catch Punnim.

Faced with a dilemma because Chang, their new informant, had failed to meet with Punnim the prior afternoon, Packard needed to think of an appropriate cover story. If he didn't, the assassin might shoot Chang on the spot, suspecting he had betrayed him.

Fortunately the arrest was not public knowledge, and Packard made certain it was kept within their little circle, including the public defender. The district attorney had given Packard permission to use Chang in the sting in exchange for leniency when the man went to trial.

Packard had little interest in the Ball State student who had ran drugs to Punnim, who apparently hid his habit from his fellow terrorists. After he was done with the young man, he cared less if Chang rotted in prison, went back to his own country, or was executed the most inhumane way possible.

He found it strange that terrorist groups had their own list of standards and practices to follow. Even as he sat across from Chang on the second floor of city hall, a slew of detectives around him, Packard wondered how he came to meet Punnim in the first place.

"Why would you traffic drugs for Punnim?" he asked Chang, since all of the figurative cards were now on the table.

Chang spoke broken English, and it showed in his previous brief interviews.

"Just for the money."

"And how did you meet him?"

Chang sat across from Packard, isolated from the group in a chair behind a small table.

"He found me…at university."

Behind Packard, a group of detectives and his own three young officers, stood with arms folded, staring daggers into the foreigner even though he was now cooperative. They were as unfeeling as he was about Chang, but despite their hatred over one of their own being murdered in a cowardly fashion, they maintained level heads and a degree of professionalism Packard himself fought every second to display.

Standing from the chair he had been seated in the past fifteen minutes, Packard reached into his jacket pocket, tossing Chang a cellular phone the Asian man seemed to recognize.

"It's yours," Packard said. "You need to call Punnim and say your suppliers were busted by the police and you've been searching for a new seller."

"He won't believe me."

"Maybe not, but you're the only way he knows to get his fix. You'll convince him you've been scouring the city for a new supplier, and now you've found one. You can meet him as soon as your biology class is over."

Chang shot a look of surprise.

"Oh, I know your schedule," Packard assured him. "I've spent my morning studying you and talking to your roommate."

"I have nothing to sell him."

"By the time he knows that, we'll have him," Packard assured the young college student.

Chang looked to his phone, then to Packard, then to the angry mob standing behind the sergeant with arms folded and unfriendly faces staring back. Packard turned the chair around, sat down with his arms across the backrest, and looked to the prisoner.

"Your move."

*　　　*　　　*　　　*

"Something isn't quite adding up," Clay deduced from the passenger's seat as Packard drove them into the campus area.

"What's that?" the sergeant asked.

"Why would Perry be part of a coverup for his partner? It makes no difference whether Zhang is in our custody, or on Mars. The Koda think he's here, and that's what counts."

By now Packard had filled his right-hand officer in about Perry's strange behavior, and the new clue from the translator he never asked the agent about. Clay had only heard part of their conversation the night before, despite Packard clearly remembering how he yelled at the top of his lungs several times.

"I don't know if he's playing double agent games to keep us from spilling the beans on something, or what," Packard said. "I keep getting this feeling they want people to think he's here because they knew something like this was coming, and they didn't want their hands dirty in Washington."

The group had disbanded because they had three hours before Chang was to meet with Punnim. Their plan was worked out, and they planned to meet a full hour before the sting operation to iron out every detail.

"Did everything seem to go smoothly when Chang called Punnim?" Clay inquired.

"It's a little hard telling since they were speaking some form of Chinese," Packard replied. "But, yeah, I guess our boy didn't sweat too badly."

"You heard from Perry?"

"No. And I don't hope to."

Clay sat back as Packard pulled into the university parking lot, hoping he managed to catch Mike Saunders in his office. The sergeant had no idea what office hours the professor kept, and he certainly hoped the instructor provided him with the same information he gave Perry.

"You don't trust Perry at all, do you?" Clay asked as they stepped from the car.

"He seems to know too much. And now he's hiding too much information from the rest of the group."

"Know too much?" Clay prompted as he opened the front door for his sergeant a moment later.

"Like the prototype of that sniper rifle he told me about. Most cops I know can't rattle that kind of information off the top of their heads."

As they waited for the elevator to come down, Clay looked at his sergeant with a perplexed stare.

"What?" Packard asked.

"You quit smoking?"

"I thought you'd never notice."

Clay rolled his eyes as though his sergeant was thinking too highly of himself. Packard, on the other hand, was proud of himself, even if it had been only a few days.

As the door opened, the two officers waited for people to exit the elevator before stepping on.

"You quit? Just like that?" Clay asked with a snap of his fingers.

"I'm on the patch. And your good buddy about caught me cheating last night."

"Ed?"

"Yeah."

Clay chuckled.

"I doubt it would take much to pull a fast one on him."

"He's more intuitive than I originally thought."

"Ah, you're softening up to him, aren't you? Like the father figure he never had."

Packard shot a sour look.

"Fuck you. If it wasn't for you and your cousin, I wouldn't have his bad karma following me around all the time."

After the brief ride up the elevator, the officers waited almost fifteen minutes for Saunders to show up to his scheduled office hours posted just outside his door.

He spied the two when he rounded the corner, and presented Packard with a smile.

"I don't have anything else new if that's what you're here for," Saunders said easily as he unlocked his door.

"I actually need to know what the vital information you gave Perry was," Packard admitted. "He didn't get a chance to tell me specifically last night."

Saunders didn't question Packard any further as he invited the two officers inside.

After taking a seat at his desk, the professor eyed the officers. Neither Packard nor Clay took a seat because Packard had little time to waste.

"Why didn't you just talk to Agent Perry this morning?" Saunders asked curiously.

"He's working a different angle," Packard replied a half truth.

Saunders displayed a poker face, not letting the officers know how he felt about Packard dropping by for information he had already shared once.

"I have reason to believe some of your invited guests are up to no good," the instructor finally stated after a few seconds of silence.

"In cahoots with the Koda?" Packard asked.

"Perhaps to the point that their entire visit is a sham."

"This doesn't sound good," Clay said.

"It's not," Saunders replied, a concerned look scrawled across his face. "Do either of you remember a diamond heist in Chicago about a month ago when they were being transported to a museum for show? They were going to auction soon after that."

Packard thought a few seconds before recalling a brief segment on the news about the incident.

"I remember. What about it?"

"Though they haven't mentioned it specifically, the guests made mention of the diamond shipment they're supposed to receive from the Koda in exchange for money."

"Why would international terrorists care about money?" Clay questioned.

"Even terrorists need to retire," Packard said. "Their god doesn't provide money, and they probably get burned out on charity assassinations and explosions."

Saunders shrugged as they looked his way.

"Vic figured they probably had some big job lined up with that kind of money."

"Like hell," Packard said. "Those diamonds are worth millions to the right buyer, and these guys don't need money for any big job. They have connections for that."

"Then why create havoc all over the city?" Clay asked.

"Because they don't have their money yet," Packard said.

"And the guests are getting cold feet about turning over such funds," Saunders chimed in. "If they return to their country and their president discovers what they've done, they'll likely be executed as traitors because the funds are *not* from their homeland."

"Then where?" Packard asked.

Saunders shrugged.

"They haven't said. I'd be willing to bet it's someone Thailand isn't on good terms with, because everyone involved in this situation stands to lose a lot, except for the Koda."

"So we have all kinds of covert ops behind everyone's back, don't we?" Clay said. "The Koda are probably pissed off that we stashed their contacts in a secure cabin."

Packard turned away from Clay and the instructor momentarily in thought.

"What is it?" Clay asked.

"I'm just thinking anyone guarding them may be in danger if the Koda decide they need to be bold in their mission statement."

"I doubt they'll have to be," Saunders stated.

Both officers turned to look at him.

"From the way they've talked, they seem to think they're going to be walking out of there when the time is right and meeting the Koda."

"What are they waiting for?"

"For a sign," Saunders said with assurance.

"What kind of sign?" Clay asked.

"They haven't said, but it's going to be pretty obvious, and I think it's going to follow the lines of what the Koda have done so far."

Packard sighed to himself, rubbing the smooth front of his forehead with a frustrated hand. He dreaded the thought of what the terrorists had planned, and even worse, that he was powerless to stop them if he failed to catch Punnim in approximately two hours.

"Damn it," he muttered to himself.

*   *   *   *

Before meeting with the other task force members, Packard stopped at the grade school near his home to visit his son a moment. He made no mention of his intentions to Clay, and the young officer never questioned him when he slid into the driver's seat when he returned.

Now, after the meeting, as they waited for Punnim to show up for the drug transaction, Clay sat beside him in their unmarked car monitoring Chang.

"So why did you stop at the school?" he finally asked.

"Did you get antsy waiting for me?"

"No. It's not like you to check on the kids, so I just wondered."

Packard nodded, keeping his eyes on their target. Their car remained hidden behind several metal trash cans at the end of an alley.

"There was something I needed to get from Ryan that I missed this morning."

Clay made a strange face, as though questioning what a father needed from his five-year-old son. They both stared out the front of the car, where Chang waited in his own beat up car, still damaged from the wreck Sorrell intentionally caused.

Packard decided to turn the wrecked car into part of the cover story. Without wheels, it would undoubtedly be difficult to find a new buyer in a city the size of Muncie.

"Any word on the water testing?" Clay inquired.

"Last I heard they hadn't found any contaminants, but they still had a few tests left to run."

Clay sat silently a moment before speaking again.

"Why go through the trouble of killing a police officer if you're not going to do anything to the water?"

Packard shrugged, still watching Chang sitting inside his car.

"Maybe they aren't monsters enough to kill off half the city. Maybe they think just the threat of it is enough."

"Or maybe they want our police force up there guarding the water supply so they can have run of the city."

Grunting to himself, the sergeant didn't like the thought of his own force being duped by terrorists, but to this point his department had done little in the effort to stop them. Though not for a lack of trying, he felt his department had failed by going about things the wrong way. Then again, he wasn't in the front office, and perhaps more was being done than he realized.

They had spread the word quickly about the possible water contamination through every possible resource. With the warning came a moderate form of panic throughout the city. People were losing faith in their protectors, and Packard found no reason to blame them.

He sat back a moment, wondering why Punnim was taking so long to show up. Perhaps he caught wind of their sting operation, or maybe another dealer had come along. There was also the possibility he was unable to escape the attention of his fellow terrorists. It was known from intelligence reports that they disapproved of his taste for narcotics.

All around them, hidden in various buildings, sat five members from the city's SWAT team, plus a sniper from the county. It was technically the team's mission, but Packard had his own idea of how he wanted things handled.

They sat in a decrepit area of the old downtown, not far from the raid Packard's team made several days prior. He didn't like the idea of his informant turning on him, or the fact that the man was shot down in cold blood. The last thing he needed was a reputation for not protecting those he swore to help if they aided him.

"He's coming," both officers heard a transmission over the radio on their tactical channel from the county sniper.

Packard had to imagine the man had an itchy trigger finger after two of his colleagues were murdered. Because of that, he seriously questioned the SWAT team's sergeant for making the decision to include the man on the operation. Then again, he was probably the only qualified sniper within a forty-mile radius.

Their plan was simple and straightforward. Once Punnim drove down the alley, the officers planned to block it off with their armored truck. That left two alleys in which the terrorist might escape, but Packard had parked in one of them, and there were three officers along the first floor of the buildings down the other alley. At a second's notice they were ready and able to block the path of a suspect on foot.

For the moment, everyone needed to simply wait and watch.

And listen.

Packard decided to have Chang wired in case the man dared to backstab the group, or give Punnim an unfair advantage with a warning.

After what happened to Squeaky, he left nothing to chance.

Packard's main job was to listen to the wireless microphone transmissions from across the alley intersection, but if they spoke Taiwanese or Chinese, he had no prayer of understanding them.

He had ordered Chang to speak English if at all possible, short of blowing his cover, and as Punnim pulled up, stepping from his car, he did so.

"I apologize," he said immediately to Punnim. "I had bad day yesterday."

"I don't care," Punnim replied with a cool voice. "My time is limited, so let's get this over with."

Packard heard this through his earphones as Clay stared at him with anticipating eyes. They had no reason to wait for any drug and money transaction because those were the least of the charges waiting to be posted against Punnim.

Picking up his radio, the sergeant stared at the scene ahead of him, deciding to wait for the transaction to take place, simply to have Chang safely out of the way. He watched Punnim hand over the money to Chang, and as the newly-acquired informant went to open his trunk, Packard decided it was the safest place for him to be when all hell broke loose.

"It's a go," Packard said calmly, but firmly, over the radio.

All at once the officers sprung from their various positions identifying themselves with yells. As though Punnim sensed the trap from just the noise of their impending footsteps, he examined his escape options with a quick glance.

With officers blocking the first and second entrances in his view, he opted for the alley where Packard assured everyone the terrorist would fail to escape from if he dared try it.

"Oh, shit," Packard said as he stepped from the car.

Reacting too late, the sergeant was relegated to watching the terrorist leap to the front of his car, then run over the vehicle as though it was an obstacle in an endurance race. With uncanny instincts and catlike quickness, Clay was already initiating the chase ahead of him, which was the last thing Packard wanted.

Not because the sergeant was a glory hog, or feared for his officer's life.

Packard had a specific reason why he wanted to be the one to bring Punnim down, and regardless of what it took, he planned to accomplish his one goal.

With the other officers picking up the chase, but behind from the start, the sergeant quickly followed Clay's lead, making certain to keep Punnim in his sights. Desperation showed in the terrorist's face as he turned to see the young officer closing in. This was likely because the plans of his group hinged on his participation, which included staying free, but his habit had already placed a shadow over their accomplishments. With his capture, their plans were sure to be in jeopardy.

Beyond the block of clustered buildings sat a wide-open area of neglected yards from rundown housing, and a small field between city blocks where a business once stood, only to be demolished like so many parts of the south end.

Following Clay as closely as possible, Packard discovered only a handful of officers emerged from the original sting area. He rounded a corner of the alley before it emerged into a wider area of abandoned houses which stood ready for leveling or some obscure use as city property.

He made the turn, plucking a sheet of paper from his jeans pocket as he did so, letting it fall to the ground before they entered the open spaces where Punnim's escape might become more likely.

Whether the terrorist escaped, was captured, or somehow got a bullet in the head, Packard didn't much care. He had just accomplished phase one of his personal strategy, and there was no going back once the sheet of paper was discovered.

Doing things Perry's way was no longer his way. His first priority was now to cover his own ass, and those of his officers. He no longer trusted the agent, though he had deduced no reasons why the man might turn rogue and betray his own people.

Maybe Perry was truly in the dark by his own partner's hand as he stated. Then where exactly did that leave his partner?

Packard watched Clay follow Punnim into an abandoned house after the terrorist kicked in the boards acting as a front door with little ease. He felt a bit winded, wondering if the SWAT team members behind him felt the same. Even their training failed to match the remarkable shape Clay kept himself in all year round.

Some officers had second jobs.

Clay's was simply to keep himself in perfect health, physically and mentally.

That, among other things, was why Packard drafted him first for the task force.

Packard entered the house, hearing footsteps and clambering upstairs. Something wooden broke with a loud crack as he rounded a corner to the stairwell, hating the fact he was so far behind the action.

He smelled rot and decay from old cans of opened food, now strewn across the floor. It smelled like a dump site, quickly left behind as he took the stairs two at a time. His foot fell through a worn board, ensnaring him between the stairwell and the basement almost twenty feet below if more of the wood gave way.

"Shit," he cursed to himself as he contemplated his situation.

Moving suddenly might send him in a death plummet, but more crashing noises from above caused him to react without thought of consequence, pulling his foot up from the artificial trap. He carefully skirted the edge of the stairway, hoping the rest of the team didn't enter the house, much less rush up the stairs.

Why doesn't Clay just draw his gun and shoot the bastard? Packard wondered to himself as he reached the top of the stairs, hearing no noise.

"Clay?" he asked, cautiously rounding the corner, his own firearm now drawn. No answer.

He entered the next room quickly, his gun held in a ready position, only to find an open window with old greenish draperies blowing inward. Along the floor were piles of leftovers the last homeowners left when the city purchased the house, or kicked them to the curb because the house was an occupational hazard.

Loose clothes, dirty magazines, kitchen utensils, and old posters, among other things, remained in heaps along the floor. The walls had holes where people had kicked them in for fun. Remnants of drug paraphernalia and residue were interspersed among the other junk.

A rusty fire escape remained outside, and the lack of any human presence led him to believe Clay was now in pursuit of Punnim in the wide-open outdoors once again.

"Just shoot him, kid," Packard said, sticking his head out the window, seeing no movement between the sea of buildings leading to the north end of town.

If they reached the downtown area, which housed a good number of people between businesses and restaurants, the chances of Punnim taking a hostage and escaping only grew. Knowing he was out of the chase, Packard walked back to the stairwell, meeting the SWAT team as they entered the house, apparently unaware of the new chain of events.

"Clay's after him," Packard said, nodding in the appropriate direction.

"If your boy doesn't catch him, we're all fucked," the SWAT team sergeant said.

"Yeah," Packard replied solemnly. "I know."

*   *   *   *

Clay found himself pursuing Punnim by himself, with no one else to back him up.

Or interfere.

He dodged old metal trash cans as the terrorist led him between more abandoned houses on the way to the downtown area.

In some ways, Clay preferred being a loner in a job that required men and women to constantly depend upon one another. His extensive training usually told him to leave others out of harm's way while his enhanced senses gave him a distinct advantage over his colleagues and criminals alike.

As he closed the gap between himself and Punnim, Clay felt reasonably certain the man had no firearm, because he never showed any inclination to grab it, even when the cop threw him from wall to wall during their combat inside the abandoned house.

If he had one, perhaps he dared not fire it because of the police presence in the area. Clay considered this as he leapt for Punnim's feet, tripping up the smaller man as they both landed hard on the wooden steps of a front porch to another house.

Clay felt his left shoulder slam against the porch surface as Punnim crashed his knees against the steps, then recovered to run inside the house.

"Damn it," Clay muttered before taking chase once again.

He halted in the living room, seeing several places the terrorist might have run to.

The stairway to his left, the spare bedroom beyond it, the kitchen directly ahead of him, or the bathroom with the door half ajar just ahead to the right.

Listening intently, Clay decided he would have heard the noise from the wooden stairs if Punnim climbed them. They looked old and rickety enough that they weren't going to keep any secrets.

Unlike the last house, this one was devoid of any trash or leftover items. A few parts of the wall looked as though they were being torn apart for renovation because paperbacked insulation and wood studs were exposed in a few areas.

Through the kitchen Clay spied the back door directly ahead of him. An old wooden door with a single pane of glass in the upper half, it was sure to give way if Punnim wanted to exit through the back of the house.

Still, he hadn't tried, leading the officer to surmise he had to be in the spare room to his left. Seeing holes in the wall between the living room and spare room he felt certain Punnim was hiding in, Clay reached for the firearm nestled in his shoulder holster as he found an eyeball peering back at him through one of the holes.

"Freeze!" he ordered, drawing the nine-millimeter issued by his department.

Punnim simply ran around the corner, then up the stairs. He either refused to be taken alive, or felt reasonably certain the cops after him would kill him only as a last resort.

Immediately pursuing, Clay tripped up the terrorist before he reached the top stair, sending him toppling down the main hallway. All around them were the skeletons of what were once bedrooms, now divided only by bare plasterboard and wooden slats.

Punnim regained his footing before stumbling down the hall as Clay calmly walked up the stairs, knowing there was no escape, short of jumping out a window. Even that provided only a hard landing on the ground below.

Before the terrorist decided anything specific about how to deal with the cop pursuing him, Clay reached the top of the stairs, prompting Punnim to turn and stare at him.

"Your options are run, and I shoot you, draw a weapon and I shoot you, or you can just give up," Clay said. "I'm through dealing with you, and I have no need for talk at this point."

Punnim grinned as though he harbored some deep dark secret that gave him absolute freedom no matter what he did.

"You have no desire to fight me?" Punnim asked with a smug stare. "Sato said you lost your will to fight when your wife and son died at his hands."

Stunned, with the past flashing before his eyes, Clay lowered his weapon.

All at once he remembered his hands covered in blood, two bodies at his feet, and a red sunset behind him. Banzai trees loomed outside his kitchen window as a stream flowed beside the hut he had learned to call home.

"Sato is dead," Clay said the only response that might elicit further explanation.

"No, he is quite alive, and he is here with me."

Clay holstered the gun, then struck Punnim without warning, flooring the smaller man. Though a master in the martial arts, the man was not about to fight him. Not while he had a mental advantage. If he truly knew Sato, Punnim also knew Clay was a much better fighter than himself.

"I want to know where he is," Clay said, reaching down to clasp the man's throat. "Or we can pick up where we left off at the hotel."

"You're the reason we're here," Punnim said. "Sato says you're unfinished business."

"Then let's finish it," Clay said, stepping back to draw his firearm once more.

He aimed it directly at Punnim's chest.

"Tell me where to find him, or I'll send him my own message."

"You'll never find him."

"Wrong answer," Clay said, starting to squeeze the trigger as a wooden stair directly behind him creaked.

Instinctively ducking to one side before investigating, Clay heard gunfire, and a bullet lodge in the wood of the door where he had stood just seconds prior.

Sounds of someone charging up the stairs filled his ears as he ducked into the first room to his right. Little cover existed in the skeletal walls, so he ducked behind several thick studs, listening intently for his newfound adversary's next move.

"The diamonds," he heard a gruff voice ask the terrorist, who still sat in a corner atop the stairs.

"I don't have them," Punnim answered, a gun pointed at his head from what Clay saw around the corner as he peeked.

Ominously tall and thick, the man meant business, and appeared almost twice as large as his new captive.

"I have no idea where they are," Punnim sneered as though he had a mental advantage over this man as well.

He apparently knew who the man was, or at least who he was sent by.

"Too bad," the man said, pulling the trigger without a sign of remorse or hesitation.

Punnim's body shuddered, then went limp from the bullet in his forehead.

Reaching behind his backside for his second firearm, Clay drew it, giving him firepower in each hand, then rounded the corner, putting him face to face with the murderer. Dressed in a black suit, with indistinguishable features and sunglasses masking his eyes, the man took notice of the cop. He fired a semiautomatic pistol of some sort almost immediately, causing Clay to dive into the room across the hall, firing shots down the hall and through the thin walls of the decimated house as his body sailed through the air.

Landing hard on one side, Clay saw bullets pierce the wall, coming in his direction, but none of them hit the intended target as the man clopped down the stairs in a hurry.

He rolled to the far wall, avoiding the trajectory of the bullets as they flew over him, hitting further and further up the wall. He now knew for certain the man was on the run, and stood to take chase of a new quarry.

He suspected the gunfire was due to attract his fellow officers, but if they were too far away, he was again the only hope of stopping this new menace.

Already rocked by the words Punnim uttered about a past Clay had struggled for years to put behind him, he barely contemplated who this thug might be. He inquired about the diamonds their visitors spoke of, but Clay had no idea the theft was a private job. Perhaps it wasn't, and this man was hired to bring the diamonds to a secret third party, no matter the cost.

Reaching the bottom of the stairs, Clay dashed out the front of the house with little regard for his own safety, still numbed by the words running through his mind. He found the man jumping into a nearby black sedan, which sped off before the passenger's side door even closed.

Now knowing the man had at least one partner, Clay refused to give up, even as his own officers rounded the corner behind him. He sprinted after the car, knowing the short streets left it little opportunity to cleanly escape.

Knowing both of his guns had magazines less than half spent, he opened fire into the rear of the vehicle, shattering the rear windshield with the first few rounds. Immediately the car swerved toward another side street, which inevitably led to Madison Street if it continued in a straight direction.

Not far from catching the car, Clay stuffed one gun into his backside as he clasped the other with both hands, still in a dead sprint, firing deliberately toward the driver's head. At this point his emotional control was left somewhere in the building two blocks behind him. Clay had little regard for how he stopped this man who attempted to take his life, even at the expense of the driver, who did little more than aid in an attempted murder.

Missing the driver's skull by inches, Clay's second bullet pelted the windshield, causing him to swerve drastically, exposing the right side of the car. Clay quickly changed his mind, aiming for both tires, hitting both consecutively with steady arms and a practiced aim.

Though almost crippled, the car maintained a course toward the heavy traffic of Madison Street. Clay reloaded his firearm for one last stand before the car entered heavy traffic, filled with cars and pedestrians. Shooting at the car now was already dangerous because his aim was toward the busy street, but he felt confident in his shot, and even better about the idea of stopping the two thugs before more innocent people felt their wrath.

Regardless of whether he shot it or not, he was quickly catching up with the car, now crippled on one side. The thought of jumping on the back of the car like cops always did in old television shows crossed his mind, but even with his training and athletic nature, Clay decided it was not in his best interest as the car began swerving onto the next street.

Taking careful aim as the vehicle traveled its last few feet of confined space before swerving sharply into traffic, Clay came to a complete stop, aiming directly at the passenger's head as he etched the license plate number into his mind.

Clay fired just as the man turned to look out the shattered side window, causing the bullet to fly harmlessly through the front windshield, landing against nothing but the concrete of the city streets.

Lowering his firearm, Clay was content to stand there a few seconds to catch his breath. He breathed through his nose deeply a few times, hearing the sounds of footsteps clop rapidly behind him as the rest of the group caught up.

"We'll meet again my friend," Clay assured the passenger silently to himself.

He quickly drew a pad and pen from his back pocket, writing down the license plate number before he forgot.

"Clay!" Packard called as he greeted the officer first, far more out of breath than Clay himself. "What the hell happened?"

Replacing the gun to its holster, the young officer simply turned to his sergeant, then walked past him after placing the sheet of paper with the license plate number in his hand.

"It'll all be in my report," Clay said simply. "Punnim's dead in that house over there," he added with a finger pointing out the direction.

Everyone seemed to be shooting him questionable stares, as though wondering why he was acting so strangely after an adrenaline-pumping moment. He didn't care because he now had other things to worry about.

"What's wrong with him?" he heard someone ask.

"I dunno."

"He all right?"

"What the hell just happened?"

Clay walked away from the people involved in his current life, dwelling on the past, and what the future held if his nemesis was still alive.

CHAPTER 11

▼

Packard read his officer's report and understood every part of it, but he still had to hear it for himself. Four hours after the incident originally occurred, now getting late in the afternoon, he approached the front door of Clay's house just outside city limits.

A long, ranch style home, Clay's house had a large back yard and trees in every direction as boundary markers. Bricks lined the bottom of the house, complementing the beige color of the aluminum siding along the top. A two-bay garage likely remained empty, or full of the officer's belongings, because his sports car remained parked along the blacktopped driveway.

The side facing the road was long, but Clay modified the back when he bought the property, making it nearly as wide because he added on some special room. Packard never received a straight answer about what the room was, exactly, but suspected it might be some sort of workout area for the diligent officer.

He followed the sidewalk up to the front door, unable to see neighbors in any direction. Wondering why Clay preferred so much isolation, he realized suddenly how little he knew about his officer, aside from what Clay's father said of him.

Pushing the doorbell button, Packard received no answer, but suspected Clay was home. He waited a few minutes, then pushed the button again, opening the front door as he did so.

Walking inside, he found an immaculate household capable of shocking anyone from the countless redecorating shows he had seen recently on cable. The living room appeared completely conventional with furniture and a television set, but as Packard walked through the kitchen toward the back area where the added room was placed, he began to see subtle differences in taste.

"Clay?" he called. "You home?"

He has to be, Packard thought. No one just leaves their front door unlocked.

In the kitchen he saw several Oriental decorations, including Japanese porcelain dolls lining several display shelves. The table was set with chopsticks and colorful cloth napkins to one side. A paper decoration of red, white, and tan colors spun, attached to the ceiling by only a string. Packard walked up to touch it, only to be startled when someone spoke from behind him.

"You know breaking and entering is a crime," Clay said from the second door of the kitchen, emerging from the back.

"I just entered," Packard retorted. "I was worried about you."

"Why?"

Packard studied his officer a moment.

Clay leaned casually against the doorway with a towel draped over his shoulder, shirtless, and covered from head to toe with sweat beads. The only piece of clothing he actually wore was a pair of bicycle shorts, which hugged his skin.

He walked to the refrigerator, pulled out a jug of orange juice, and guzzled it a moment before replacing it.

"You left without saying a word, filled out your report without speaking to a soul, including me, and took off. The chief, deputy chief, and Agent Perry would like to have a word with you. Internal affairs may want some of your time as well."

Clay grunted aloud.

"Something happened back there, didn't it?" Packard inquired. "You didn't kill Punnim, so what happened?"

"You read the report, didn't you?"

"You know I did. So you're in the process of arresting Punnim, asking him questions, and this man in black comes from nowhere and starts shooting at you without warning?"

Clay looked almost everywhere in the room except toward his sergeant.

"That's pretty much it."

"Bullshit. I want to know what Punnim said before he was executed. I know there's something more to it than your report says."

Taking a deep breath, Clay hesitated, then walked into the room he had emerged from. Now Packard was certain his officer knew something more than he originally revealed.

Packard followed, finding a room filled with blunt and bladed weapons, a strange decorative chest with Asian writing, and a padded floor. Weapons hung from tiny hooks mounted along several walls, or stood on racks specifically designed to hold them. Swords, sticks, and strange fork-like metallic weapons were among the weapons Packard readily saw.

The walls appeared to be covered in some sort of papery substance. A staircase along the far wall led up to a second level that simply overlooked the room from above like a wrapping balcony.

Most everything in the room appeared to be a beige color with accent colors of red. It seemed very bright, despite only a few overhead fluorescent lights, and seemed larger than it actually was.

In the far corner the sergeant spied a small black table with several pictures and candles lining the surface, as though a shrine of some sort. To either side of it stood a Japanese screen, each of which folded in three different places, able to reveal silhouettes behind them.

"This is where I go when I need time alone, or to find my inner strength," Clay confessed.

"It's impressive," Packard admitted. "You do it yourself?"

Clay nodded.

"It's modeled after the arena my sensei used in Japan."

"You really looked up to him, didn't you?"

"You could say that."

Packard walked around the room a moment, careful not to step on the mats taking up the central portion of the floor. They looked immaculately clean, so he didn't want his dirty footsteps discoloring them.

"What happened out there today?" he asked again, a bit softer in tone this time.

Clay didn't answer in words, but slowly walked across the room to the small table housed in the corner. Several photographs with Clay and a Japanese woman lined the table. A few of them displayed the pair holding a baby, or the child seated between them.

"There are things you don't know about me," Clay revealed to his sergeant. "When I was supposedly away at college for four years, I was away, but much farther than Boston."

"I always wondered how your dad could afford to send you there on what we make."

"It just seemed easier to say I was away, rather than spending four years in Japan."

Packard hesitated a moment.

"How exactly did you end up there?"

"What was originally supposed to be a summer vacation, of sorts, for me over there, training with my instructor while he went to his homeland, ended up being much more. To make a long story short, his niece died, he ended up staying, and I ended up staying with him, marrying a beautiful woman who showed me more than I ever wanted to learn."

Packard picked up one of the pictures, studying it more carefully. Clay appeared happier than he ever recalled seeing the officer. Usually grim, serious, and all business, Clay never smiled like he did in those photos.

"So you stayed, fell in love, had a child," Packard summed up the story, "but something apparently happened."

"My sensei had a school there, and when he returned, making no secret I was his favorite, hardest-working student, there were a few men who took exception to a man of barely twenty years being placed on a pedestal above them."

"And?" Packard asked without any pressure in his voice.

"A man named Sato resented me for becoming my master's number one student. I guess when it was announced I would be taking over the instruction of his classes when I was ready, and he was ready to step down, it pushed Sato over the edge."

Clay hesitated a moment, staring down at the pictures.

"He was always violent with the students, which was why Nosagi wanted him replaced. Hate, contempt, and greed ruled his thoughts and emotions. Nosagi saw the danger, and wanted to steer his students clear of it, but it was too late for Sato. He decided he could do better on his own, but before he struck out to the great world beyond, he challenged me to a duel."

Clay stood silently a moment, the painful past apparently running through his mind.

"Did you accept?"

"No. I knew what he wanted, and it wasn't worth ruining my life by committing murder, or having my own life taken away when I had a family waiting for me. I wanted absolutely nothing to do with his way of life."

Packard took off his glasses, wiping them in his shirt as Clay paused once more. Almost certain he saw glistening moisture in one of Clay's eyes, he didn't want to push the issue.

"Sato decided one way or another he was going to ruin my life, so he took the two things most precious to me in life," Clay finally said. "I held their bodies, covered in blood, in my arms. At that point I had nothing left to live for, so I came back here and made a new life for myself all over again."

"He killed your family just like that?" Packard felt compelled to ask.

"No," Clay admitted. "He had basically demanded on several occasions I move back to the States, and of course I wouldn't. There was a time I hunted for him in Japan, but he was instantly labeled a murderer, and my search was in vain. The police and other agencies looked for him, but never found him. He left the country with his clan, never to be heard from again."

"Until now?"

"Today, at the building, I had Punnim cornered. He told me a reference about Sato murdering my family since I was a coward. I knew right then and there this entire terrorist thing was his doing, and I'm the reason he's brought everything to a head right here in Muncie."

Packard sighed, feeling his officer's pain, but questioning Clay's judgment.

"So you come back here for an intense three-hour workout instead of telling me this, or warning the rest of your family that a mass murderer might walk into their lives?"

"I don't think he's after my family, Sarge. He wants to embarrass me, and make it seem like I'm incapable of protecting my city from scum like him. He'll eventually come to me to finish what we started because he thinks I ruined his life."

"After he's finished murdering hundreds more, no doubt. You can't just lay back and wait, Clay. If we're not pro-active on this, he'll run amuck through the city killing anyone he pleases."

"I know that, and I don't want to hear any of your sanctimonious bullshit, Tim."

Packard was stunned, only able to return a blank stare, because Clay seemed genuinely pissed at him.

"I heard how you miraculously saw Punnim drop a piece of paper, even when I didn't, and boy was I surprised to learn what it said."

"You don't have any idea-"

"Don't I?" Clay asked, cutting his sergeant off. "It was a nice touch having your boy write the note, considering the Thailand language is symbols. Of course any new person to our language would have trouble writing it. And I especially love how you brought Salas back into this piece of shit operation of ours. That's just what we need is the feds poking around until they find that body we dumped a few days back."

"If you're questioning my judgment, don't," Packard said sternly. "The feds will go after Salas, leaving us free to get our agenda completed."

"And exactly what is our agenda?" Clay asked with open sarcasm, which was unbecoming of his character. "I seem to be losing track from day to day what we're trying to accomplish."

"If you were in my shoes, you'd understand," Packard said. "You've got to bend rules to get things done sometimes."

He was getting irritated with Clay, despite the officer's painful throwback to his previous life.

"You know, I'd smack you upside the head right now if I knew you wouldn't beat the shit out of me," he confessed.

Clay stood there a moment, apparently weighing his options.

Finally, he forced an insincere grin, then turned serious once more.

"I want to see the photos of the terrorists that Perry gave you," he finally said. "If I can confirm Sato is actually Wichai Khumpa, the man responsible for the terrorist attacks, I think he can be stopped."

"How?"

"I know how he thinks."

"How can he be the same man? Wouldn't Sato be Japanese?"

"No. My instructor took in many orphans and hard cases like myself, often from different nationalities. He's from Thailand, and he left any conscience he once owned in the country when he left it."

Packard felt uncertain about trusting Clay after the officer's mood swings, but he needed answers just as badly.

"If I show them to you, you're going to forgive me for dropping that note, right?"

"I have a feeling you'll sleep just fine either way, but for the record, I understand what you're trying to get done."

Nodding slowly, the sergeant took up one of the photos again.

"And for the record, I'm sorry. I had no idea about your loss. All these years we all thought you were just too consumed with your work ethic to be bothered in a relationship."

Clay looked him in the eye with a bit of regret in his own.

"It's my own fault. I never told anyone, including my own family. I blamed myself for my wife and son's death. That's something hard to live down."

"Yeah," Packard simply said, looking away. "Give me a minute to get those files from my car."

Even as he walked outside, Packard felt bad for Clay, knowing secrets were capable of tearing the best of men apart. He had his own to harbor now, but if the feds started breathing down Salas's neck, his world was bound to become a better place to live. Salas deserved nothing less than to be gunned down after what he did to Squeaky, and tried to do to four police officers.

Of anyone in his group, Clay should have understood his motivation the most.

Clay's nature wasn't to sulk, or to run off by himself, especially after a big raid or sting. Now Packard understood why, but he needed to make certain the officer was on his side before continuing with his own plans to find the terrorist faction.

He returned to the inside of the house, files in hand, finding his officer guzzling a glass of water. Clay seemed both relieved and disturbed about telling the details of his years overseas. Packard had no idea for so long what motivated Clay and molded him into the man he was, but now he knew some of the factors.

"Here's the file," he said, opening it for his officer.

Clay stared at the photo intently for a few seconds, then angrily as he recognized the face. It had been plastered across the news and Internet for days, so Packard wondered why this was the first time his officer had seen it.

"A little plastic surgery and a change of identity makes you a little harder to find, doesn't it?" Clay questioned the photo, confirming indirectly it was Sato, the man he spoke of.

"I thought he went by his real name."

"He does. Sato was his given name in our clan. He has a sister, too."

"So she's a blood relative?" Packard asked, flipping another folder open, letting Clay see the photograph, poor as it was, of Issaree Khumpa.

Clay stared at the photograph a moment, as though unsure of whether he recognized her or not.

"Have you ever met her?" Packard inquired.

"No," Clay said, staring intently at the photograph.

He drew closer to it, then a look of horrified realization crossed his face.

"Dear God in heaven," he said. "Yes I have."

Packard sensed the urgency in his officer as Clay reached for the phone.

"Who is she?"

"She's Mitch's girlfriend," Clay answered without looking in Packard's direction as he desperately dialed his cousin's phone number.

$$*\qquad*\qquad*\qquad*$$

Mitch heard the phone ring from outside his apartment door as he fished the keys out of his pocket, still walking down the hallway on the second floor.

His morning and afternoon had been spent tracking down leads generated by Chang's further confession after Punnim was murdered. He and Sorrell had been booted from the sting operation at the last minute by the deputy chief, who again cited that Packard didn't need all of his officers all the time.

"Fuck," he said as the phone quit ringing and his voice mail likely picked up the message, if one was being left.

Stopping short of his door, key ring in hand, he instinctively looked toward the knob, finding it out of place. In fact, his entire door was open about three inches toward the inside of his apartment.

Though dressed in plain clothes, his firearm remained at his side. His right hand slid over it, his thumb undoing the latch that secured it in place. He saw no sign of forced entry such as splintered wood or damage to the frame, so someone had picked the lock or used a key.

At this point in his life, no one else had a key except for his cousin, who occasionally fed his fish and iguana when he took vacation outside of Muncie. He suspected Clay was far too busy to be entering his apartment for no good reason.

Keeping his hand over his service weapon, he slowly pushed the door in, wondering if a need to call for backup existed. True, he was living in dangerous times, but a false alarm call for help would bring years of endless teasing and jokes.

No, he decided, stepping inside, hearing a slight thumping noise from his bedroom. Swallowing hard, he stepped carefully, silently, into the living room and kitchen combination, putting himself in a position to safely view his bedroom without being seen or heard by whatever person was rummaging through his belongings.

Noticing who it was, he snapped the latch atop his holster closed once more, gaining the attention of the young lady inside his room, pulling a box down from a shifted ceiling tile.

"Hi, Mitch," she said with an Oriental accent, putting forth a smile.

"It seems I remember you giving me my key back," he said cooly.

She pulled the box down from the ceiling, replacing the tile. It was not a box he recognized. In fact, he had no idea the tiles could be moved from their fixed positions.

"Well, I thought you said we were through," she said, stepping down from the chair she used to reach the ceiling, stepping toward him.

"That's far enough," he said, holding out a foreboding hand.

She stopped short, giving him a pouting look.

"I just wanted to see you."

"I can tell," he said sourly. "Funny, I don't recall us stuffing a box up there, Tia. Or is that your real name?"

"You're being paranoid, Mitch. I thought we left on good terms."

He examined her athletic build from head to toe, recalling the nights of endless sex, and how she left him both exhausted and sore several mornings, as though the act itself was a form of punishment. Extremely pretty and intelligent, Tia had secretive qualities about her he never chose to dig into.

Relationships based on sex and nothing else were his favorite kind, and he usually preferred to keep them that way.

This time, however, that seemed to prove erroneous in his decision making. He looked into her brown eyes, then examined her shapely breasts beneath a tight mock turtleneck, and the muscular legs hidden beneath tight polyester pants. Her black hair flowed beyond her neck, behind a face of smooth features that acted like a chameleon, often displaying only what she wanted others to see.

He refused to fall for it this time.

"You're not going to shoot me, are you?" Tia asked in a seductive voice, inching closer to him with a swagger she used to lead up to intercourse when they were a couple.

Mitch backed away defensively, placing his hand atop his firearm, eyeing the cardboard box behind her.

"What's in that box?" he asked, keeping his attention where it needed to be.

"Nothing you need to worry about," she answered, reaching her left hand up to his chin.

He clasped it, but used his gun hand to do so, failing to duck a swift, perfectly placed side kick to the left side of his head.

Grunting in pain, he stumbled back as his ex-girlfriend went for the box behind her, but he grabbed the waistline along the back of her pants, tugging her to the floor.

She landed hard on her knees, but turned quickly to backhand him across the face. He grunted again to himself, but refused to let go. A kick placed squarely in his gut sent him falling back, discovering the innocent college girl he once dated as something much more sinister. It seemed as though she had extensive training in beating up men because the strikes were not wasted, and they hurt like hell.

Mitch's back slammed into the refrigerator behind him, and as he stood, she hurled the back of his head against the surface, cutting it on the edge of a magnet. Regaining enough of his senses, he punched her across the face, flooring her with the direct hit from his thick arms.

He started toward her to inflict more damage, but she pulled a knife from behind her, waving it dangerously before him.

"I can't say we're parting on good terms after this," he said in his usual light-hearted manner, trying to keep any fear he had of the knife to himself. "If you want to get back with me, this isn't the way American women usually do it."

"I wouldn't touch you again in that way to save my own life. You disgust me to no end."

"Now that's a little harsh," Mitch said, forcing a hurt expression, his right hand edging toward his firearm. "We had some good times."

Tia rolled her eyes.

"We had sex, and I used you. You're so stupid you don't even know who I am now, do you?"

Mitch tensed, his hand stopping short of the gun. He knew from the second he found her in his apartment who she really was, but he tried playing dumb.

"I know who you are, and unless you plan on using that pretty quick, I'm going to arrest you or shoot you."

With an evil grin, Tia glanced behind her, then toward the gun.

"You're not quick enough to reach that before I kick you again."

"I'll take that bet," Mitch said, his fingers clasping the leather of the holster as a foot came flying toward his face.

Anticipating the move, he leaned back, letting the dangerous foot fly by, but before he completed the action of pulling the weapon from its housing, Tia shifted positions and sent her other foot hurling into his abdomen.

He fell back, his arms helplessly flailing as his gun fell to the floor.

Without hesitation, his ex-girlfriend charged him, planting a knee squarely in his face, landing the back of his skull against the wall where he had landed a moment prior.

Barely conscious from the continuous assault, he fell to a prone position on the floor, watching her casually walk to the other room as though perfectly at home in his apartment, her hips swinging beautifully as she strode. Even in a battered state, he still couldn't resist looking at a woman's anatomy.

His primary weakness, almost a sickness, Mitch never stopped analyzing womanly figures.

As he began regaining his senses, thinking about the gun lying only a few feet away, his former girlfriend walked toward him, box now in hand. Before his hand reached the only means of effectively defending himself, she planted her knee in the side of his head, scraping the knife off the ground before placing it against his throat.

"I hate to part like this lover, but I can't have you telling the world who I really am, now can I?"

"I thought we were going to make up," Mitch said, unable to put up any resistance without the risk of his neck being snapped when he rose from the ground.

"Not this time I'm afraid, lover."

He felt the blade press against the side of his throat, endangering his very existence because one slit compromised his carotid artery. From there, blood would seep out uncontrollably until he lost enough that his body went into shock.

Then died.

As though heaven sent, the noise of footsteps quickly coming closer, then stopping at his door, brought him unexpected relief, especially when he saw a pair of familiar shoes at his doorway.

"What the hell?" Ed Sorrell asked from the open door, probably thinking his occasional partner was involved with some kinky sex game.

Barely able to look up, Mitch saw Sorrell wearing a sling to immobilize his injured arm. Dressed in plain clothes, he had a green jacket on that covered his firearm, making it nearly impossible to defend himself, considering his injured arm was the one he needed to accurately fire his service weapon.

Outnumbered, and already possessing what she came for, Tia likely decided to escape the easiest way possible, rather than confront two police officers.

Springing forward before Sorrell understood exactly what the scene before him was, Tia slashed him in the injured shoulder with the knife as she rammed her knee into his groin, sending him to the floor.

Practically crippled from his week of injuries, Sorrell crumpled to the floor, writhing in pain as he groaned aloud.

Mitch reached for his gun, feeling a slight cut along his neck where the knife had been dangerously close a moment before. He jumped to his feet, deciding Sorrell was too incapacitated to join him in the chase.

"Thanks," he said to Sorrell as he darted out the room. "Call 911 when you can!" he called back, darting down the hall.

A moment later, after realizing Tia was nowhere to be found, and likely wouldn't be, even if his colleagues from the city immediately started combing the area, Mitch returned to his room. He found Sorrell seated in his favorite easy chair, a pack of ice sitting atop his groin area.

"Aren't you a sight?" Mitch asked with what little bit of a chuckle he was able to muster.

"Aren't we a pair?" Sorrell countered. "What the hell just happened here?"

Taking a seat across from his partner, Mitch sighed. He heard sirens in the distance, indicating Sorrell had indeed phoned for help.

"It's a long story, Ed. I suggest you keep your seat and rest your balls, because that was my ex-girlfriend, who I believe is one of our terrorists."

"Holy shit."

"Holy shit indeed," Mitch replied, thinking of the consequences for himself and the entire city if he was correct.

*   *   *   *

As Clay drove, Packard wondered exactly what was going on. Mitch hadn't answered his phone, but the sergeant wanted to know how this revelation had slipped past Clay for so long.

He had little fear for Mitch's safety, because Clay explained the two had broken off their relationship months prior. Clay appeared worked up about his cousin's safety, insisting they drive to Mitch's apartment, since neither his cousin nor Sorrell could be reached.

"Hey," he heard Clay ask suddenly from the driver's seat.

He turned, quickly realizing his officer was on the cellular phone with someone. A moment passed before the officer spoke again.

"What? Are you okay?" Clay asked over the phone.

Another moment passed.

"Okay. We're on our way."

Clay severed the call, replacing the cell phone to the clip along his belt.

"What was that?" Packard asked.

"She attacked Mitch."

"Who?"

"Tia, or Issaree, or whatever the fuck you want to call her."

Packard shook his head quickly, trying to figure everything out.

"So where did he even find her?"

"He didn't. She was in his apartment when he got home."

"Why would she come back to his apartment?"

Clay kept his eyes on the road, making a right turn behind another car.

"He said she had some sort of box hidden in the ceiling. She took it down, got the best of him, and took off."

Packard twisted his face as he thought. The image of a man of nearly three-hundred pounds being bested by a woman half his size didn't manifest itself in his mind very easily.

"Got the best of him?" the sergeant finally asked aloud.

"She had a knife. Mitch said she cut Ed, then kneed him in the nuts."

Packard grimaced. Sorrell was on some sort of record pace for police injuries suffered during the course of a week. If he had nine lives, they were quickly running out.

"I take it they're both going to survive?"

"Sounds it."

"And Mitch has no idea what was in that box?"

"No. My guess is it's the diamonds everyone's searching for."

Leaning back in his seat, Packard sighed. Again, another solution had slipped through their fingers. Near misses were plaguing his team, and their misfortune couldn't come at a worse time with so many lives at stake.

He felt lucky the water tests came up negative, because the terrorists might have easily taken out hundreds, maybe thousands, of residents before anyone knew what had occurred.

They were still across town from Mitch's apartment, and Clay seemed to have little regard for traffic laws or other drivers.

"Hey, settle down," Packard ordered the younger officer. "We're still representing the department in this car, and you said it yourself, your cousin is fine."

"Sorry," Clay quickly apologized, immediately adhering to the laws of the road.

Packard sat idly a moment, simply watching the buildings pass by. Times like this, full of stress and apprehension, made him want to light up a cigarette, but he had fought the urge so far. Of all the times for him to try quitting, this was by far the worst.

To take his mind off the subject, he decided to probe further into Clay's mysterious past.

"So, you have all this training overseas with a master of the martial arts," he stated. "All those weapons and everything along your wall, Clay. Are you trained as some sort of ninja or something?"

Cracking the thinnest of smirks, Clay turned to look at his sergeant with a neutral stare before answering.

"No, I'm not a *ninja* or something," he said, mimicking the words Packard had used. "I'm trained extensively in hand-to-hand combat. I can use most any sword, wood-handled weapon, small bladed weapon, or projectile ever constructed for assassination purposes."

"Proficiently?"

"In all, yes."

"So this is why you spend so much time training?"

"Yes," Clay answered, appearing to grow tired of the questions.

"So how does that feel?" Packard asked.

Clay turned to look at him with a perplexed expression.

"How does what feel?"

"You know. Being able to walk down the street knowing you could kill any-one who walks by you. It has to be empowering."

Clay cleared his throat.

"I'm trained much like the feudal assassin warriors in Japan were, but the mentality is nothing like that. We use martial arts as a last defense, and the weapons are more tradition than anything else."

"You're dodging my question, Clay."

"I'm not, because the answer is no, I don't walk down the street picking out people I could maim or kill. In the world I come from, everyone is equally dangerous, so we don't predict anything. I'm not going to take a bullet to the head any better than you, Sarge."

"So you're trained to consider everyone a threat?"

Clay sighed in a disgruntled manner.

"No, I'm trained to think everyone can be equally dangerous. If I thought everyone around me was a threat, I wouldn't have much of a positive outlook on life, would I?"

Packard nodded, deciding not to push Clay for too much information at once. If Clay's link to the Koda was accurate, he needed the young officer's services more than ever. He also wanted his crew back together, banged up as they all were.

Clay waited at a stoplight a moment, staring out to the side. Packard understood his pain if Khumpa murdered his wife and son. It sounded like Clay had lived in something from an old samurai movie, rather than modern-day Japan. With modern technology, the Japanese preferred to be known as innovators, rather than warriors of an age long since dead.

He now understood Clay's respect for tradition, and where his work ethics were formed. Somehow he suspected the new revelation of Khumpa's identity was destined to put his officer in a dangerous path. If Clay let revenge cloud his judgment, Packard would have a difficult time controlling him. He needed the officer doing his job, not chasing after Khumpa in a feud that might get him killed.

When the light turned green, Clay drove forward once more, nearing his cousin's apartment building.

A moment later they were walking up the stairs toward Mitch's apartment.

"You realize we're getting close, don't you?" Clay asked almost distantly as he reached the correct floor.

"Close to what?" Packard asked.

"Six days. At the end of six days the Koda want their demands met, or they claim all hell will break loose."

Clay paused as his sergeant didn't readily answer.

"Right?"

Packard reached the door first, looking in to see his two officers seated in opposite chairs, Sorrell with a bag of ice lying atop his groin.

"Right," he finally said, wondering where Clay's statement was leading.

With a streak of blood across his neck, and bruises randomly placed along his neck and arms where skin actually showed, Mitch looked as though he had been through a bar brawl. Sorrell appeared even worse, with a sling harnessing his dominant arm, the bag of ice in place, and his only useful arm holding up a pink towel to his shoulder. A blood stain emerged from the towel where he had been cut, and his eyes looked up to Packard with a scolded dog appearance.

"You two are a sight," Packard said, shaking his head. "This would be comical if we were in different circumstances."

"How'd she get by both of you?" Clay inquired.

"She beat the fuck out of him, then I got here," Sorrell quickly spoke first. "I thought they were in some kinky sex act, so I didn't react right away."

Mitch shot him a look that equaled daggers.

"You really think I'd do a sex act that required a knife being put to my throat?"

Sorrell shrugged before realizing the action hurt his shoulder. He winced, looking toward the fresh wound.

"I don't know *what* kind of shit you do after that rubber ball in the mouth trick you did with Denise that one time," Sorrell said.

Both Packard and Clay gave Mitch inquisitive looks with raised eyebrows.

"That *was* a secret," Mitch said. "I don't get into kinky stuff."

"What about that time you were in a three-way and started sticking that dildo up-"

"That's enough," Mitch said sternly, cutting Sorrell off before the sentence finished. "Clay and the sergeant don't want to hear about that stuff."

"On the contrary," Packard said. "I'd love to hear about it sometime, but right now we have other things to worry about."

Mitch whacked Sorrell in the arm to ensure his buddy kept his mouth shut.

"Ow!" Sorrell complained.

"Both of you can carry out your sex fantasies later," Packard said. "But first, I want to figure out where our terrorists are going to strike next, or when they might strike."

"I don't know about finding them," Clay said, "but I know where I would start."

All eyes turned to him, including those of his sergeant, who hoped he had the answer to their prayers.

CHAPTER 12

▼

Already late for supper at home, William Branson had decided to put off his few remaining duties at the hospital until Monday when he returned to work. He had a weekend to enjoy, and he was late getting to it.

Being Director of Maintenance at Ball Memorial Hospital kept him busy, but he played hard too. Often he took two or three vacations with his wife to go sailing, horseback riding, mountain climbing, hiking, camping, or any number of other activities that got them out of their mundane lives and the city.

Life was good.

He answered to one boss, who oversaw the maintenance and security departments. He worked a straight Monday through Friday shift with no overtime and a highly dependable crew. His hours were set from seven in the morning until four every afternoon, but most nights he worked later than his schedule showed, never getting paid for the extra time.

Tonight was one of those nights.

He sat in his office behind his desk, playing online euchre with a partner who was costing him the match. Often he played a hand or two before heading out for the evening, long after his morning shift maintenance men, office manager, and secretary went home.

"Ah, you suck," he complained to his partner from a random town anywhere across the country.

He only knew his partner by the anonymous nickname each player was forced to choose when he or she entered the game zone. Unless details were specified in one's profile, people remained mysteries to everyone else using the website.

"Shit," he complained to the unsympathetic computer screen. "Don't lead trump twice if you don't declare trump."

Taking his glasses off momentarily, he wiped them with a clean handkerchief, then replaced them.

Shaking his head, he played out the hand, which he lost. Ultimately losing the hand cost him the game, so he signed off, checking over the paperwork lying atop his desk for anything needing completion before he left for the weekend.

Nothing stuck out.

Both the office manager and secretary worked in an office that shielded his own, which sat further back, mostly out of sight from the main entrance. Along the basement hallway that housed his office sat several maintenance shops. Among them, a carpenter shop, sign shop, mechanical shop, a welding center, and a stock room close to the electrical shop. His crew seldom needed to leave their workplace to find what they needed.

Sitting back a moment, Branson stared at the photographs lining his desk. His wife, Emily, was in one by herself. Another featured them both together in a studio photo, while the one beside it had a composite of their various trips across the world. At the end of the photographic row sat a photograph of his older brother along with his two nephews. All three were in their city police uniforms, the two boys standing behind Clay's father.

His other older brother, Mitch's father, had chosen to work for the city as well, but he worked for the street department, repairing and plowing streets, depending on the season. Only Bill Branson had taken a different path, heading west to attend Purdue University. He earned his engineering degree, took a job in Michigan as a maintenance supervisor at a large car factory, then returned home after interviewing for his current position and accepting the offered position.

All kinds of manuals and guides surrounded him along the bookshelves over his desk as the small window behind him barely let in any daylight, as though he sat in the confines of a prison cell deprived of light. Several scented candles sat at the edge of his filing cabinet, never to be lit, giving off fragrances of the fall harvest and morning dew.

Yawning to himself after a day full of meetings, repairs, and paperwork, Branson looked to the floor where his leather briefcase waited for him. He began the process of shutting down his computer for the weekend, hoping no major disasters brought him back until Monday.

Leaving last had become routine for Branson over the past four years he had held his position. He never wanted the women there by themselves, because although the basement corridors were isolated from the rest of the hospital, they were accessible by anyone who had ambition enough to look for them.

It came as no surprise when he heard the front door to his office open, but as he leaned forward to see who had entered, he saw no one.

Branson stood as he pulled his tie down from around his shoulder where it had gotten lodged during one of his tantrums toward his euchre partner. He patted himself down along his waist, verifying his pager and hospital radio were still clipped to his belt.

Satisfied, he picked up his briefcase from the floor as the light from the main portion of his office was suddenly cut off. He looked up, shocked to find a silenced gun pointed at his head, and the man behind it devoid of any personality or mercy. He instantly recognized the Asian man from several newscasts, but never expected to be confronted by a terrorist.

"Who are you?" he demanded, despite the gun aimed at him.

Wearing a janitorial uniform, the man changed his expression just enough to reveal a sinister, arrogant grin.

"What do you want?" Branson asked, since he was still alive, assuming this man wanted or needed something from him.

"I want your assistance."

"And why should I help you?"

Khumpa looked to the gun, then to his new captive.

"If you refuse, I won't kill you," he said. "I'll kill everyone you care about in life and let you live to regret it."

"I don't believe you."

Khumpa scooped the phone from its receiver.

"Shall we call your dear wife? Emily, is it?"

Feeling his temperature rise, and his blood pound through every vein and artery in his body, Branson clenched a fist, but realized he had no choice. If he refused, he knew full well the terrorist would carry out the threat, and if he helped, he was likely creating harm or death to people all around him.

He doubted Khumpa was planning a prank like they had done at the water treatment facility.

"What do you want?" Branson asked again.

"I want you to give me a tour of your facility. I have some renovation plans in mind."

The sinister grin spread across the rest of his face, sending a sinking feeling into Branson's gut.

*   *   *   *

As he sat in his office, staring at the phone atop his desk, Vic Perry had serious concerns about several issues. His worries included Packard convincing the city police department to let him conduct his own investigation, and his partner's recently deceptive nature about where Zhang was being held.

He understood being discreet was necessary toward the public, but Perry felt rubbed the wrong way because his partner had left him in the dark. George Furnett was nearing retirement, bred from the old-school days of the Bureau, before the FBI was bogged down by their own rules, regulations, and upper management with little or no field experience.

Perry and Furnett had field experience, often sharing a close partnership. While Perry was relegated to the city of Muncie, Furnett chose the location because of family. Perry never looked up to his partner as a father figure, or even a close friend, but he respected Furnett. And lately, his partner had been unusually distant.

A strange sequence of events caused Perry to wonder about his partner's loyalty to the Bureau, because he was not returning calls, and he was nowhere to be found.

Perry had gone so far as to visit the man's house, but no one was around. Divorced for two years now, Furnett lived alone just outside of town. His house appeared as though no one had been there for a week or two.

No fresh tire marks, a stack of mail at the front door, and newspapers forming a small pile at the edge of the driveway left the agent wondering exactly what his partner might have been away doing.

Finished staring at the phone, Perry decided to call his partner's cellular phone for the third time that day, hoping he might finally get a response after days of trying in vain.

"Hello, Vic," he heard a voice say from the other end of the line, startling him so much that it took a few seconds to collect himself.

"George? Where the fuck have you been?"

"Nice to hear from you too," the smooth, educated voice on the other end replied.

Fluent and well-versed enough to make Perry ill, his partner never seemed to screw up when speaking, and had a way of making everyone else who spoke with him feel inferior in the English language.

"What's the matter?" Furnett asked.

"For starters, you cost me my task force command by failing to inform me of your whereabouts, and those of your prisoner."

"You know I've been back and forth to Washington with him."

Perry cleared his throat on purpose.

"But we're on the same side. And we've been partners for how long?"

"Long enough for me to trust you," the smooth voice on the other end answered.

Perry glanced out the window toward city hall, feeling a bitter resentment toward the building and some of the city police.

"I guess I haven't been in touch since I've been in Washington all this week. What the hell is all this crap I'm reading about terrorists?"

Perry gave a quick review of the past week, and how his partner's prisoner was the cause of the attacks.

"Well, I'm back with him now," Furnett said. "Anything I can do to help you get your task force back together?"

"It's still together, but I've got a renegade sergeant from the city police who's gotten his group out of the mix."

"And what's with Punnim's death? Any leads on who killed him?"

"Not particularly. You've gotta figure these guys have lots of enemies."

"Maybe, but they're survivors. You don't become an international terrorist if you can't defend yourself."

Perry returned his attention to the boring office around him.

"He was defenseless because one of the city officers had him on the verge of arrest."

"And he just let some guy walk up and waste him?"

"Not exactly. George, why don't you and I grab a bite to eat so we can catch up on more of this in person?"

"You don't even let a man get settled, do you?"

"Not in times like this."

Furnett paused a moment.

"Okay. Let me get my stuff unpacked, then I'll call you back."

"Great," Perry said with little enthusiasm.

As he hung up the phone, he stared across the street in the other direction, spying the county jail centered between his office and city hall. Something about his partner's recent whereabouts and excuses didn't quite add up. Considering he had the same credentials as Furnett, Perry decided to use them to discover exactly how much time Tien Zhang had spent in the local jail the past few months.

If his hunch was accurate, he planned to bring some interesting dinner conversation to his partner within the hour.

*   *   *   *

Bill Branson felt positive he was being used like a guinea pig for an experiment.

After experiments, most living animals were killed, then thrown in the trash.

He expected little else except a bullet in the head before his body was discarded in the closest isolated room.

So far, Khumpa had left him little else to expect.

He forced the director to show him blueprints of the hospital's first floor, then print them out. Khumpa then ordered Branson to grab his coat, keys, and briefcase. The terrorist double-checked the desk to ensure his prisoner left no clues behind, such as a cellular phone or pager. Branson still had everything with him, but soon found himself handing over his keys, pager, and employee identification card to the terrorist.

Before they left the office, Khumpa demanded Branson circle the areas on the map that indicated the main oxygen supply to the hospital, the electrical intake area, and where the new emergency department stood in relation to both.

Reluctantly, he agreed to share the information. His own life was worth wasting if he thought he might save the countless other lives Khumpa likely planned on taking. He thought of his wife, and his family of cops the terrorist might target if he refused, so he cooperated.

With a nervous gut feeling he was on his way to die, Branson shut off the lights to his office, then locked the door as Khumpa stood behind him. Khumpa held Branson's briefcase and jacket in his other hand. The silenced gun was no longer necessary to force his cooperation, but Branson found it pointed at him at all times.

"Hurry up," Khumpa said as the manager made certain his door was locked.

"Okay, okay," Branson quickly said, assured the door was locked.

Untrusting, and with good reason, the terrorist checked that the door was locked, then indicated with the gun he wanted Branson to start down the basement hallway toward the main stairwell.

"I know you're thinking about running," Khumpa said. "I'm trained with firearms, and I will hit you wherever I choose to if you run."

Branson rounded a few corners, quickly away from the shops and his office, but not the threat following him closely. After business hours, and especially on weekends, the halls seldom saw human visitation because the maintenance personnel were busy on other floors. They repaired all sorts of problems, performed preventive maintenance, and unloaded trucks, among other activities.

No expense was wasted in decorative coverings for the basement walls, ceiling, or floor. Bare as the day they were constructed, the gray walls gave a factory-like impression to anyone who visited the bowels of the hospital. The most colorful thing in the otherwise pure gray hallways was the white coating over the half dozen steam and water lines that ran along the walls and ceiling.

Few people, aside from those who worked in the basement, ever had a need to visit the area.

An initial tingle of joy quickly turned to thoughts of horror when Branson witnessed one of the custodial staff wheeling a basket of soiled linens toward him. Sounds of machinery and exhaust fans drowned out most any noise in the basement, but Khumpa leaned forward, inches from the director's left ear before the janitor spied them.

"One wrong move and *he* dies," Khumpa threatened, again taking the desire to act from Branson.

He refused to have any murder on his conscience for angering Khumpa, even if he was inadvertently assisting in terrorist activities.

Branson simply passed the janitor with a nod and a quick wave, since any speech was sure to be muffled by the ambient noise.

"Very good," Khumpa said with a hint of arrogance. "You obey well."

"Fuck you," Branson said under his breath.

Stopping at an intersection as he was told, Branson watched Khumpa glance around him, as though pondering where the most damage might be done.

"What's that way?" he demanded, looking from Branson to the printed map, apparently not positive which way he was facing.

"It leads to a storage area, and eventually out of the hospital," Branson answered.

"And that way?"

"The main stairwell to the outpatient area, and further down are some maintenance rooms."

Khumpa thought a moment with his shrewd eyebrows raised.

"Take me that way," he said of the second option.

Without hesitation, but an inward sigh of nervousness, Branson led the way. A feeling he was nearing the end of his existence plagued him. He wanted to go home to his wife, Emily, but he wanted her to live more than anything. Khumpa left no openings for attack, and Branson was not trained in any sort of self-defense, despite being in good shape for a man in early middle-age.

He suddenly wished his nephew had given him a few lessons in martial arts. Every Christmas he teased Clay about sharing his secrets of the Orient, but he never meant it. Even so, his extremities moved with nowhere near the quickness of a bullet.

A moment later the two men reached one of the machine rooms, which held various water pumps, an assortment of water and steam pipes, and an air handler that kept various parts of the building in fresh air supply.

"Which key?" Khumpa demanded.

Branson took hold of the set, picking out the correct key from several on the ring. He expected the terrorist to demand a quick education on which keys worked where, but it never came. The assortment of keys wasn't vast, so with a minute or two of trial and error, most anyone would figure out the system, particularly since one master key unlocked every door in the building.

Glancing behind him, the maintenance director saw the gun point toward the ground momentarily. Deciding he was going to die either way, Branson wanted to risk his own life if there was a chance he might stop Khumpa.

Whirling quickly, Branson charged Khumpa, ramming him like a football player, pinning the gun in a downward position. He knew from the news that Khumpa was educated in weaponry and martial arts. Finding out firsthand, Branson felt his grip broken by the terrorist, before a foot swung around, crisply striking him in the jaw.

Hitting the ground and the wall as he tumbled back, Branson watched Khumpa place the gun along his backside before striking the director with his right fist. Immediately realizing he was outdone, Branson still had no regrets. If his hospital was decimated and he made no attempt to stop the terrorist, his credibility would be ruined.

And he would be haunted by his cowardice for the remainder of his life.

"How noble," Khumpa sneered. "Throw another punch if you like. I promise I won't render you unconscious, because I have special plans for you."

Rising quickly to his feet, Branson threw another fist, but the terrorist easily evaded it, keeping the director off-balance enough to whirl him around. Branson felt two consecutive fists bury themselves in his kidneys, then dropped to his knees from the pain.

Groaning in agony, Branson slowly stood, refusing to simply give up, but found the gun pointed at him once again. Khumpa had apparently grown tired of his retaliation.

Khumpa handed him the keys, then Branson unlocked the door after pausing momentarily to show his reluctance. Now he felt positive he was going to die.

"Turn around," Khumpa ordered after the door was unlocked.

Branson felt the gun barrel pressed stiffly into his right kidney as he was shoved into the room. Barely stumbling, he turned to face the terrorist, who pulled out a set of handcuffs from one pocket.

Thank God, Branson thought, praying his life was being spared. Any hope of escape was better than a bullet to the head.

Khumpa examined the room, which Branson already knew by heart. Wrapped pipes carrying water and steam were almost everywhere around them. Most went up through the ceiling, then formed an 'L' shape as they jutted down a cement corridor before disappearing around a corner.

The basement was vast, and this room in particular had lots of square footage when the space around the corner was included. The pipes were all a foot off the ground, leaving clearance for maintenance work underneath them, or room to crawl around the corner to other areas.

A water booster pump unit in the corner was anything but quiet as Khumpa studied the room.

Lit only by a single bulb, the room was dark, hiding the dust carpet lining the floor. Branson had spent countless hours on that floor, usually in long spans. He recalled blowing his nose, seeing dingy remnants for days afterward, in facial tissues.

Branson saw nothing useful in the room except a flashlight, which Khumpa immediately took up and turned on, shining it underneath the large pipes.

"Crawl under there," Khumpa ordered the director.

Considering he was accustomed to crawling in dirty, greasy, dark areas, Branson had no objection to the order, but quickly realized the terrorist was following him at a safe distance.

Now on his back, beneath the insulated pipes, Branson looked up to his captor.

"To that pole," Khumpa answered, ducking several pipes, then lowering himself to a crawl, checking the sturdy nature of the pipes, and a threaded metal rod, all while keeping the gun focused on Branson.

"Come here," he ordered Branson, who moved slowly along the floor, since his back was against the ground, like a mechanic working under a car.

He found both of his hands cuffed around the metal rod and a medium-sized steam pipe, ensuring he had no chance of escape. Even if the rod wasn't there and he only had to contend with the steel pipe carrying three-hundred-sixty degree steam, he risked severe burns to his skin, and creating an environment that would quickly rise in temperature and humidity.

And the room already felt as hot as a sauna from the machines and residual heat generated by the steam pipes.

"Are you wondering why you're alive?" Khumpa asked with a smug look, stuffing the gun into the back of his pants.

"I suppose so," Branson answered, still feeling moderate pain from the scuffle along his face.

His kidneys felt as though they were on fire.

Khumpa grinned arrogantly, stuffing an envelope into Branson's front pocket. He threw the director's jacket and briefcase off to the side, and out of sight from anyone entering the area. No evidence was left to help anyone trace Branson's whereabouts if people started looking. His position allowed him to come and go freely from work without clocking in or out, since he was in a salary position.

"I may need you for further information. Or I may not."

Khumpa shrugged indifferently.

"Either way, you won't survive what I ultimately have in store for your hospital, and when they find your body, that piece of paper will let your precious nephew know it was *me* who murdered his uncle."

Branson knew his expression registered his shock, but it couldn't be helped.

"Clay?"

"Of course."

"But why?"

"Only *he* knows, and to use the hours it would take to explain it to you would certainly be a waste of my time. But only because you'll be dead soon, so you won't be able to retell the tale."

Branson felt almost cliched asking his next question, like the hero at the edge of extinction questioning the ultimate villain about his evil scheme.

"What are you going to do to the hospital?"

"I'm going to render it helpless," Khumpa sneered. "But not before I create a mass-casualty incident that will exterminate hundreds of you pathetic Americans."

"Why?"

Khumpa's confidence turned to a flush, outward hatred.

"Why don't you ask your nephew?" he said gruffly, turning to leave. "In the afterlife."

As he left, the terrorist turned off the only light source in the maintenance room. For all intents and purposes, Branson was left blind from no light, deaf from the incessant humming of the various water pumps, and hopelessly cuffed to a steel bar that refused to hear his plight.

He had no radio, no pager, no keys, and no tools nearby offering any trace of hope.

"I'm fucked," he sighed to himself, glancing around his lonely confines, waiting for his eyes to adjust to the dark setting.

*   *   *   *

Although Clay seemed to vehemently disagree with the plan his sergeant dreamed up, he verbally consented to participate. Even by the recent standards he set for himself as an extremist leader, Packard considered his newest idea the most far-fetched yet.

Without Clay, and the younger officer's permission to help, the plan had no chance of success because it could never begin.

Packard sat behind the steering wheel of a rental car he had held on his personal credit card, while intending to pay cash when he returned it. A ski mask rested between his legs, and as he looked over to Clay, he saw the officer with one between his knees, and a shotgun resting loosely to one side.

"You ready for this?" he asked Clay.

"I don't really have much choice, do I?"

"You do if you have a better idea."

Clay kept the back of his head posted against the seat, but turned it to give Packard an awkward, inquisitive stare.

"Well, I don't, and we need to do something before Sato creates more panic in the city."

"I'm not used to hearing that name yet."

Clay frowned.

"It's been on my mind for ten years, so it's a bit hard to forget."

Packard shifted uncomfortably in his seat. He stared at a car passing along the desolate state road just outside of town. The car was parked in a small overgrown lot so it could easily pull onto the paved road at a moment's notice.

"I can't imagine what you went through over there."

"Then don't," Clay replied with a tone of warning.

Both sat silently a moment.

"If this plan of yours works, I want you to lead Sato straight to me so I can settle things once and for all."

Packard felt grave concern for his officer. He knew nothing about blood feuds with swords and bladed weapons, but Clay had learned a completely different lifestyle overseas. In Packard's opinion, tradition and heartache would easily be thrown aside with a loaded gun and a bullet to Khumpa's head.

He knew if someone murdered either of his children, he would feel the same way. He maintained vigilant watch over his children at all times. Sarah said he was too protective, but Packard considered his children in more danger than most kids, simply because of his profession.

"I don't want you taking this upon yourself," Packard confessed to his officer. "We're a team, and we'll bring these pricks down together."

"I'm not sure you understand," Clay said evenly. "I'm not trying to be some hero, or the Lone Ranger, but I don't want you, Ed, or Mitch getting hurt."

"So you're going to be some action hero and take them all out by yourself?"

"If we get that money, they won't hesitate to come after me."

"That isn't very comforting," Packard squarely admitted. "Dead bodies everywhere isn't going to help our cause, especially if you're one of them."

Packard started reaching for a cigarette, then remembered the fresh patch along his back was supposed to satisfy his cravings. Though it did to some extent, his mind didn't always accept what his body told it.

"I know things were different when you were in Japan, and you probably joined our force for the right reasons, but I can't just let you become a vigilante because of this turn of events," the sergeant said. "I know some of the things I've done since you joined the force don't seem ethical or appropriate."

"Or even legal."

"Yeah, okay, but I'm doing them for the right reasons, ultimately."

Clay shook his head.

"I've played along to this point, but I don't feel any level of high moral fiber when we're dumping dead bodies and planting evidence during pursuits. What's next? A throw-down weapon after we whack some bad guy?"

Packard looked his officer straight in the eyes.

"I'll do whatever it takes to reach my objective."

"And what is your objective? There is no ultimate villain to bring down, and even if there was, there are going to be a hundred replacements waiting in the wings. It's a vicious circle of shit that we deal with, Tim."

"That may be true," Packard conceded, "but when I'm asked to do a job, I finish it the best way I know how. I don't have all the answers, and I don't pretend I'm God, but I guaran-damn-tee you I won't lose sleep at night unless innocent people are killed as the result of something I did."

A moment of silence filled the car.

"Don't even say it," Packard said before Clay uttered any additional words. "Squeaky was not an innocent, and he wasn't clean. I could have busted him dozens of times for things I knew he'd done."

Clay fidgeted with his ski mask momentarily, staring out his window.

"I don't think we're on the same page anymore," he finally said.

"I *know* we're not."

Packard sensed more tension between them than ever before. He needed Clay on his side more than the day they started working together. They had a common goal, but two separate notions about how long their cooperation was necessary.

"Are you willing to throw away your career if you get the chance to do battle with this...Sato?"

"Are you willing to try stopping me?"

Packard thought a second before answering.

"If it means saving you from making a grave mistake, then yes."

Neither had time to take their conversation further because a pair of headlights rounded a bend along the road.

"Time to move," Packard said with a hint of excitement, starting the car.

*   *   *   *

Perry had waited over an hour for his partner to call, but Furnett never phoned. Now the agent debated whether to head home for the night or assemble with the few members remaining in his task force for a meeting about their next plan of action.

His visit to the jail provided little information except that Zhang had been gone for almost a month, apparently transported to Washington by Furnett.

Though the information contradicted what Furnett had told him, it upheld his statement about feeding various information for Perry's own good.

Being in charge of the task force gave him a feeling of purpose again after being shunned by his own people, but Packard took away that feeling, and the trust of a lot of the members, when he left. Still, Perry vowed to carry on, despite the fact his partner had not been completely up front with him on several issues.

Unable to keep himself from harboring negative thoughts about his partner, Perry wanted to be vigilant, but not mistrusting of everyone around him. Furnett had never been anything except dedicated to the Bureau, but as he drew closer to retirement he seemed more disillusioned with what their division had become.

Unlike his partner, Perry had little else in life aside from his work. His wife had left him, his church never really got off the ground, and he had little chance of ever making a name for himself in his profession again.

He decided his time was better spent investigating his current case or getting a bite to eat, rather than waiting for his partner to call back.

Tapping his fingers against the desk, Perry decided he was going home instead.

He stood, but heard footsteps coming down the hallway, and from more than one person. He warily peered around the corner, spying his partner with Zhang in tow.

"Isn't this a pleasant surprise?" he asked when his partner stepped into the office. "I didn't realize you babysat on a personal basis, George."

"I do for a price," Furnett said, producing a smile as his prisoner stood cuffed behind him. "Good to see you, Vic."

Shaking hands, the two agents seemed to disgust Zhang, who turned away with a sour look.

"What have you been doing all day?" Perry's partner asked, looking around the office he probably hadn't seen in almost two weeks.

"Lots of thinking," Perry answered, pausing a moment to look across the street to the jail. "And checking."

"Checking?"

"Yeah," Perry replied, turning to face his partner. "I've been thinking about a few things, including how international terrorists have slipped past our defenses in the last month or two."

"It's not impossible," Furnett reasoned.

"No, but when they're able to smuggle in experimental weapons, I tend to raise questions about their abilities," he said, turning his back to the window once again. "It's almost as though they have some good inside help."

"Now who on earth would help terrorists over here?" Perry listened to his partner ask as he distinctly heard a snap being undone, like that of a latch on a holster.

He knew what was coming, but felt confident in his ability to leave evidence, even if he died. At this point he cared little if he survived his impromptu interrogation of his partner.

"You had your chances to be a hero, Vic, but you fucked up for the last time."

Perry turned around, seeing his partner's firearm pointed at his stomach.

"I knew there had to be a reason the Koda got around town so easily. Their faces are internationally known, so they couldn't have scouted around themselves. And they aren't going to buy weapons off the streets. Someone had to provide them with firepower, reconnaissance, and a place to stay."

"And there's no place safer than jail for some," Furnett admitted. "I'm surprised you put it all together, Vic."

"It wasn't that hard, especially when you conveniently took vacation when all of the shit started flying. Did you even bother taking Zhang to Washington to have the black suits interrogate him?"

"Of course. Him getting caught was never intended," Furnett admitted.

Zhang gave an arrogant grin as he raised his hands, now free of cuffs by the key he held in one of them. Furnett roughly patted the agent down, finding his service weapon, then taking it from the holster along Perry's waistline.

"Why are they here, George?" Perry asked. "Why our city of all places?"

"Khumpa picked the location. He has some kind of lifelong grudge against a local cop here. It's kind of a two-for-one package. They get the money, I get my cut, and everyone leaves happy, except the cop Khumpa wants to kill."

"You'll never get away with it, George, and they'll never be able to leave the country."

"That's where you're wrong as always, Vic. I plan to personally escort my prisoners out of the country with the Bureau's blessing."

"*Prisoners?*"

"Of course. I'll be a hero after I catch the rest of the pack and they're ordered to be extradited back to Thailand. Naturally you won't be around to see any of this, I'm afraid. You've fucked up bigger than ever this time."

Perry felt his skin flush red with anger. In his last few minutes of life or not, he refused to believe his partner was about to better him.

"I've never fucked up, George," he said. "I've spent my entire career covering up everyone else's mistakes and playing lapdog to everyone around me, including you. Maybe Packard was right when he said I wasn't fit to lead the task force. Maybe I've been letting you pull the wool over my eyes for too long. But not anymore. Even if you kill me, you're fucked, George."

"Why's that?" Furnett asked, not lowering the gun.

"Because I just recorded everything you've said and sent it to headquarters via wiretap."

Furnett's face registered surprise and shock, then a grin crossed his lips, indicating he was calling Perry's bluff.

"You're lying."

Perry slowly reached down to the desk, pulling a wire from just underneath the top. He dangled it with a smirk of his own, simply to aggravate his arrogant former partner.

"You son-of-a-bitch," Furnett said, steaming with anger. "I never would have given you credit for figuring out the truth that quick."

"And that's why you failed," Perry said. "You going to kill me now?"

Furnett scowled, raising the gun toward Perry's head.

"As a matter-of-fact, yes."

A silenced gunshot echoed down the hallway, but it wasn't from Furnett's gun. Perry stared in surprise as his partner's face registered shock, then his body slumped to the floor in a heap.

"Plans have changed," Issaree Khumpa said, stepping forward from behind Zhang. "It seems our local contact had become a liability."

Perry swallowed hard, recognizing her, but surprised she arrived alone.

"And I suppose I'm a liability too?"

"No, you're our ticket out of this country when our business is completed."

"You think I'll cooperate?"

"You will if you don't want thousands of innocent people dead."

Perry found a new gun pointed at his head.

"We just need an FBI agent to escort us from the country, then that agent can go as he pleases, because we'll be in our homeland."

Shaking his head, Perry thought otherwise as the young woman severed the tap wire, which had actually done no transmitting whatsoever, then discovered just that as she followed it down the desk.

"Nice try," she commented. "Now are you ready to cooperate, or do more of your citizens have to die to provoke you?"

Sighing, Perry realized he had little choice.

"If you choose not to cooperate, you can die and we can make it seem as though you and your partner killed one another. It wouldn't take much to convince local authorities of such an act, considering all of the turmoil lately."

"If you kill me, how do you expect to leave the country?"

"We're resourceful," Zhang answered. "You're not looking at this in the right way. We're trying to do you a favor."

"I realize you're already up for citizens of the year after so many acts of kindness in our city, but you'll have to forgive my pessimistic nature."

Zhang and Issaree soured at his humor.

"We have no time for this," Issaree said, looking down coldly at the body of Furnett. "Cuff him and let's get moving before someone sees us."

Zhang stepped forward, launching a fist into Perry's abdomen to keep him from getting any ideas of escape, then roughly handcuffed the agent.

"Play along when we leave the building or we kill everyone we encounter," Issaree warned. "You Americans think you're so heroic that you'll do anything to save another life, but you don't even realize how much of your life is wasted trying to please others."

"And murder for profit is a better alternative?" Perry questioned between heaved breaths, his stomach and lungs trying to recover from the punch.

"In the end it doesn't even matter," Issaree said. "We used to think our political agenda would make things right with our God, but now we've decided to make ourselves our number one priority."

Perry shook his head, knowing exactly what she meant.

"So one final job to set yourselves up for life, eh?"

"You could say that. There are parts of this world where we're considered heroes, Agent Perry. We won't live in fear of being shot in the back, or captured by U.N. forces. We'll be rich beyond our wildest dreams in retirement."

"You'll be trapped in some tiny country like fugitives, unable to enjoy what you've earned."

Zhang shot another fist into his gut, sending the helplessly cuffed agent to his knees for his remarks.

"Perhaps we'll bring you along so we can cut off a finger or toe each day, just to count the number of days we're hiding like dogs," Zhang said. "It could just as easily be you lying on the floor in a pool of blood."

At this point Perry didn't much care. Furnett got what he deserved for betraying his own country and people. The Bureau didn't pay much, and their retirement plan hardly matched the countless hours and sacrifices agents made over the years, but recruits never opted to join the Bureau for glory or money.

They did it for the right reasons.

Zhang yanked him to his feet, then waited for the agent to walk on his own so their exit from the building appeared normal. As luck would have it, no one was around anyway to see the agent leave with the terrorists out the back. When he missed a meeting or two, his remaining task force members might grow worried about him.

He felt a sense of role reversal as he was stuffed in the back seat of a car like some federal prisoner heading to prison. As he was being shoved inside, ducking his head to avoid the car's frame, he considered dropping a form of identification, but considered it more risky than simply disappearing. If it fell into the wrong hands, he might jeopardize the terrorists, which in turn jeopardized himself and thousands of other people.

Before leaving the building, the two terrorists made certain to hide Furnett's body in a closet, then searched Perry for weapons and useful items. They took his cellular phone, Bureau identification, his wallet, and holster for later use. They missed his secondary work identification, which he kept hidden, in case the opportunity to drop it arose.

If he didn't fit the part of an agent when he took them through the airport at a later date, he was no use to them.

He absolutely hated being a pawn in their scheme, but unless he found a clever way to escape, he felt certain he was going to be a corpse stuffed inside a closet, or worse, inside a plane's cargo hatch once the Koda had what they wanted.

For now, he simply stared at the city buildings passing by, wondering what these twisted individuals had in store for his city. If only he had stood up to Furnett sooner, or questioned why his partner wanted it publically known Zhang was in their jail, even when he wasn't, Perry might have put a stop to the situation before it even began.

Or he might have died.

Either way, he would not have endangered citizens by involuntarily assisting the Koda as he was at the moment. He silently prayed the sins he was about to commit were forgiven by the time he faced his maker.

Taking a deep breath, the agent began studying where he was going for future reference as dusk overtook the day.

CHAPTER 13

▼

Branson felt sweat run down through his shirt as the dark room seemed to close in around him. His torso felt as though someone had thrown a bucket of water on him, except the sticky combination of sweat and his deodorant made the experience more unpleasant.

His hands and arms were going numb from being elevated so long, and his back was uncomfortably positioned against the floor.

Able to move his legs, even swing them if necessary, the maintenance supervisor found no use for his limited freedom. So long as his arms were bound, he was hopelessly stuck in one spot. Despite his eyes adjusting to the darkness, he saw no means of assistance in the form of tools or supplies.

Hollering for help was forbidden because of Khumpa's threats to murder anyone in the area, and Branson refused to put other lives in jeopardy. Still, he needed to discover exactly what the terrorist had in mind if he hoped to help stop it in any way.

Also, he needed to warn Clay of the imminent danger.

Smelling the oily fumes from the pump in the corner, Branson wiggled along the floor, looking for anything nearby of use to him.

His main problem lay in the fact that he was tied to the threaded metal rod running from the concrete along the floor to the false ceiling above. The rod might have had a weakness where it was mounted above, but Branson's hands were also cuffed along a steam pipe running parallel to the floor, which kept him from scaling the threaded bar to check for weaknesses.

Being tied to crossing bars left him no room to move in either direction along the pipe or the reinforcement beam. Khumpa had thought ahead by confining him in such a way because it allowed him no movement up or laterally to search for an escape or tools to assist him.

Covered by insulation, the steam pipe was hypothetically easier to bust by using a tool because it had a hollow center. Either way, the handcuffs themselves were what needed breaking, or unlocking, to free him.

In vain, he tugged the cuffs against the steel rod, bracing his legs against the other pipes. Nothing happened, as he expected, so he laid still with his back against the ground once more. His hands helplessly rested above him against unyielding steel and padded insulation.

His only hope seemed to be a security guard stopping by inadvertently with a key to unlock the cuffs. The chance of a guard being in the basement area, even during rounds, was slim. Relegated to hopelessness, Branson tried squeezing his hands through the cuffs, but the result was scuffed up skin along his wrists.

He remembered hearing something about dislocating one's thumbs as a means of escape, but didn't feel his threshold for pain was that great, and didn't feel convinced it was a viable plan. Looking at his thumb, Branson felt positive the appendage would still be in the way, even if it was dislocated.

Shifting in his spot along the floor, Branson stared at the pump in the corner, noticing a tool box in front of it. Even with the doors typically locked, it was unusual for his maintenance crew to leave tools in a room where they weren't presently working. Occasionally, however, they left trinkets behind for short periods of time.

"Shit," he commented to himself, realizing the box was too far away from him to be of any use.

He thought about the possibilities of where Khumpa might strike the hospital. Obvious choices were the emergency department, the oxygen supply tanks, transformers, and possibly even the power plant across the street where steam supplied much of the hospital and campus area with power to run their everyday systems.

Branson regretted having to show the terrorist the key points of interest on the map, but Khumpa was destined to figure out where the weak points were anyway. Self-preservation forced the director to share his knowledge, but his chances of escaping to prevent the evil plan from following through, grew slimmer by the minute. He desperately needed to find a way out of the cuffs to warn authorities about what he knew.

Yelling for help was no option. His voice would never carry over the noise of the machinery, and even if someone heard him by some miracle, Branson refused to risk another life if Khumpa saw someone coming to his aid. Any rescuer would be shot on sight, and he figured to be next in such a scenario.

In frustration, he kicked against the short concrete ledge that stepped up to the main floor where the machines continued working. Instead of hitting solid concrete, however, his foot tapped against something that make a clacking sound against the hard surface.

"What?" he questioned aloud.

Kicking a bit more lightly, Branson found the object to be fairly small, probably plastic in nature. Using his feet in unison, he managed to bring the mysterious object toward him over the course of the next minute.

As his knee slowly raised the object close enough for him to see it clearly in the dim lighting, a surge of excitement ran through his body as he recognized the object as a miniature rotary tool with interchangeable heads. Used for cutting, polishing, buffing, and several other uses, depending on the tip used, the rotary tool could easily cut through a handcuff chain if it had the right head.

By some miracle someone had dropped it or left it in the room.

Taking a closer look at the head, Branson noticed it was likely useless to him.

"God, no," he muttered, finding a sanding attachment at the end of the battery-powered device. "I'll be lucky if this thing takes the polish off the chain."

A sarcastic thought of sanding flesh and muscle tissue off his hand being quicker ran through his mind, but he doubted the tool had enough charge left to do much of anything.

He was about to start the job of sanding away at the chains in a futile attempt to escape when a beam of light crossed the floor from someone opening the door to the machine room.

Staring intently toward the light, Branson took a deep breath in anticipation of whether a friend or foe had entered the noisy room.

＊   ＊   ＊   ＊

Packard's plan was simple.

He knew from the documents Perry provided him early in the task force's formation that the foreign diplomat involved in the argument on tape spoke Japanese among several other languages.

Thanks to his four years in Japan, Clay had become fluent in the language, even if he hadn't used it regularly for a decade.

"You sure you're ready for this?" Packard asked his officer.

"As much as I'm ever going to be," Clay answered unemphatically.

"Good," Packard said as he threw the car in drive and let it spit up dirt and gravel as his foot floored the gas pedal.

Though everything occurred in a flash, the plan was flawless in Packard's eyes.

He stopped the car in front of the oncoming vehicle, forcing it to stop in the middle of the desolate road with a squeal emitting from the brakes.

Both he and Clay exited the car simultaneously, drawing their service pistols, both loaded with rubber bullets. At close distances rubber bullets are just as lethal as the real thing, but Packard banked on both Clay and himself taking perfect aims at the bulletproof vests Mitch and Sorrell were wearing as they stepped from the second car, already drawing their own weapons.

Everything hinged on waiting until Sorrell and Mitch took a shift looking after the foreign guests with the task force's blessing. With Perry nowhere to be found, and the force in shambles, they agreed to let Packard's men take a shift watching after the guests, then agreed to allow the guests to be transported to another safe house at the end of the shift because he felt the man in black who shot at Clay probably knew the key players on both sides, and had ideas of taking out the guests, among other people.

While two other officers babysat the remainder of the guests at the new location, Mitch and Sorrell were to take these two over, then head home for the evening.

So the task force thought.

Packard met with little resistance because he had been more accurate than Perry on several key issues, so the force's faith was in his hunches.

Now, Mitch and Sorrell had to act out their parts, then play dead to proceed to the next phase of the plan.

"Stand down!" Mitch ordered the masked intruders, stepping carelessly around the open driver's side door.

He knew better, but Packard had ordered him ahead of time to abandon his standard operating procedure.

Without hesitation, once Mitch cleared the door, Clay opened fire, putting two rounds in his cousin's chest. Pouches under Mitch's shirt, but atop the vest, filled with fake blood, did their job, spurting red liquid forth as Mitch collapsed to the ground. It seemed so realistic to Clay that the officer stared in awe a few seconds as Sorrell took aim from behind the opposite door, firing a few rounds that missed Packard completely, but came a bit too close for the sergeant's taste.

Still, Sorrell was a good aim.

Particularly for a lefty.

I'll never pick on him again, Packard thought as he ducked behind the door of his own vehicle for cover, watching Clay crouch down, then circle the car. From the back seat of the car he read the fear in the eyes of the two Thailand traitors.

They had sold their souls for cash, and soon enough he planned to know their entire plan.

Sorrell turned to defend his position against Clay, exposing his side to Packard, who continued to point his weapon directly at the officer. Both Mitch and Sorrell had worn jackets to cover the armored vests, despite fairly warm temperatures. Packard knew, even without seeing the vest, Sorrell's side was vulnerable because no armor covered parts of the sides. The vests contained several weak areas where only velcro covered the sides of wearers.

Shooting now risked hitting Sorrell in one of those weak spots, possibly causing serious injury, or killing the officer.

He watched and waited until the left-handed officer stepped away from the door, squarely facing him. Squinting his eyes with a questioning look as though asking why his sergeant wasn't shooting him, Sorrell took another step toward the side of the door, keeping his weapon focused on Packard instead of Clay, who had made his way along the side of the second vehicle.

Finally Sorrell pointed his weapon at Clay, firing a round as Clay ducked below the hood. He then turned to face his sergeant head-on, allowing Packard to fire two shots in succession at Sorrell, whirling him around like a villain downed for the last time in an old western as he landed face-first to the ground.

Packard respected Sorrell's endurance and tenacity after a week of bumps and bruises. He had taken off the sling against his doctor's orders when it likely pained him to use the arm, especially to draw a firearm and maneuver it the way he had.

Finally down to the business at hand, Packard helped Clay roughly pull the two Thailand guests from the rear seat of the car, then let Clay begin his interrogation. If all went well, Clay's line of questioning, along with the 'deaths' of two officers would force the two men to spill the beans about where the cash was hidden.

He doubted much resistance was forthcoming, considering the violent display the four officers had just played out.

Packard observed the situation, since he didn't understand one word Clay was speaking in his second tongue.

He recognized fear in the eyes of both men as they quickly scrambled for excuses or begged for their lives to be spared. With cold, hard blue eyes trained to adapt to any situation, Clay stared the two men down, continuing relentlessly with his questioning, raising his voice as needed.

Both men appeared reluctant to reveal any information, shaking their heads doubtfully, looking as though their lives depended on them keeping their secret to themselves. Clay holstered his pistol, slinging the shotgun strapped to his back to a useful position. He quickly pumped the action slide for an audible effect, and received the result Packard wanted.

Just as both men were intently watching Clay, probably about to give in to his demands, a sneeze came from beside Packard's feet. Since he wasn't directly in the interrogation, the sergeant quickly jerked his head to one side, since the ski mask covered his true actions. Neither man looked away from Clay anyway, so Packard kicked Sorrell lightly with the steel toe of his boot in the ribs to let the officer know his accidental sneeze hadn't gone unnoticed.

Sorrell grunted lightly, his face still down in the dead grass, leftover from the winter season.

Packard rolled his eyes slightly, wondering why the officer had chosen to fall head-first onto the ground in the first place.

He returned his attention to Clay, who motioned for Packard to join him. Packard made his way over, noticing one of the Thailand visitors had wet his pants from the experience, indicating Clay had done his job.

Leaning toward his sergeant, Clay reported in English in a hushed voice to avoid the visitors hearing him.

"The money is in a storage locker at the airport."

"Why there?"

"They didn't trust the Koda, and the airport provides a secure exchange point. I guess the Koda weren't too pleased, which is why they sent a message."

Packard thought a moment.

"So these creeps have been in touch with the Koda?"

"Not since the assassination. They're legitimately afraid for their lives."

Packard licked the edge of his lips beneath the ski mask.

"Let's keep them scared, but let's get the location for the money first."

"After I find that out, what do we do with these two?"

"We take them to the new safe house and tell them if they say one word about any of this to the cops they'll have an 'accident' because we have corrupt cops working for us."

Clay grunted to himself.

"Not too far from the truth."

"If it gets us the Koda, I don't care what they, or you, believe."

Clay nodded as though he understood the consequences of going back on their plan. They had come too far to avoid taking chances now. Packard found himself willing to sacrifice his job to stop the terrorists from destroying half of his city, hoping Clay felt the same. As he watched Clay order the two men into the back seat of their car, he wondered if the younger officer's thirst for revenge might compromise everything they had worked for.

✳   ✳   ✳   ✳

Branson scrambled to hide the rotary tool under his legs as the person stepped inside the machine room. Visible only in the form of a silhouette, the figure stood just past the doorway a moment, then stepped inside for the maintenance supervisor to see.

"You behave well," Khumpa said. "No cries for help, and no attempts at escape."

"Considering you've threatened to kill anyone I come in contact with, and I don't have a key to these things, it's hard to do either," Branson answered with an irritated tone.

Khumpa flipped on the light switch, grinning in a sinister manner as he did so.

"Your troubles are almost behind you," he noted. "Or should I say scattered in pieces around you with the remains of your flesh and bones."

He held up a mechanical device Branson assumed was a bomb for verification.

"It seems I can serve two purposes with this device. One, kill you soundly for your dear nephew to find, and two, compromise one of the major elevator shafts in this facility."

Knowing death was closer than ever before, Branson felt his back muscles tense as he tugged against the cuffs binding his hands.

"There are almost thirty elevators in this building. You'll hardly begin to cripple operations here if you do that."

"True, but my primary objective is to kill you and leave enough pieces for your nephew and his police friends to find. That should keep them busy for hours while I'm out recovering my retirement funds from two imbeciles who think they can hold out on me."

"I've never done a thing to you, but you're willing to kill me and hundreds of innocent people just to make a point and create a distraction?"

"Yes."

"How does human life mean so little to you?"

"Because all of my life I've known nothing except compromise, death, and wars with causes. When I finally thought I had found my calling, my family, I learned the hardest lesson of all."

He paused to clench a fist, then held it up for Branson to see.

"Betrayal."

Branson grimaced as Khumpa began looking around the machine room for the correct place to set his bomb.

"I don't suppose you'd be kind enough to tell me where to place this little device, would you?"

"You'll understand if I'm not forthcoming?"

Khumpa grinned.

"Suit yourself. Everything else is in place. Once this is set, I'll leave to carry out my other plan and you can think about how you want to spend the last few hours of your life."

Branson felt his one hope resting under one thigh, but his hopes were fading. He watched helplessly as Khumpa ducked under the pipes, getting on one of the creeper systems Branson's maintenance men used to work under the pipes. Lying on his back, the terrorist navigated himself along the pipes by holding his hands up to the insulated metal rods like a child using monkey bars.

He disappeared around the corner a moment, leaving the maintenance supervisor to wonder just where the bomb was being placed. Branson knew Khumpa had picked the right spot, or close to it, because he had long since memorized the layout of his building.

Able to hear nothing, Branson speculated about what kind of blast the bomb might create. It didn't appear large enough to create a mammoth explosion, but instead of reaching around the corner to bake him, its purpose might be to weaken the structure of the walls, bringing down the elevator shaft and portions of the first floor.

If that happened, the other floors might follow.

After a few minutes passed, Khumpa finally turned the corner, forcing Branson to face him. If not for the overbearing sound of the nearby pumps, the director might have heard squeaks from the creeper.

Once he was clear of the pipe system, Khumpa stood, dusted off his pants, then looked to Branson, who felt his heart thumping inside his chest. A countdown to the end of his life had begun, and he didn't even know how much time remained.

"Soon your troubles will be over," Khumpa stated.

Branson said nothing, simply glaring upward, wishing the terrorist would finally leave. If Khumpa wasn't lying, nothing remained to hold Branson back from freeing himself or taking any opportunities to get help. Chances of random help stopping by seemed slim, but if the door opened again, he was bound to yell at the top of his lungs for assistance.

"Any last requests?" Khumpa asked, apparently trying for a rise from his victim.

"None that you'd honor," Branson said with a degree of disgust.

"Honor is something I gave up a long time ago. Think about the wrongs you've done during your lifetime in your last few hours and know they'll never compare to what your nephew did to me, and what I've done to the world since."

So bitter, so hateful, Branson thought. He wondered what made a man hate mankind so much to create random violence. To kill without giving it a second thought, as though people were animals for him to master and consume at will.

Branson watched as Khumpa silently took his leave, walking up the concrete incline toward the door, careful to lock it behind him. The action further dampened the supervisor's hopes of being rescued, but finally gave him the chance to maneuver the rotary tool toward his mouth once more, so he could place it into his hands.

He hoped somehow the rotary tool might save him, because little else could at this point.

*   *   *   *

Packard found himself at home after the action with Clay and his other two officers earlier that evening.

Mitch and Sorrell were told to keep low profiles, especially when it concerned the Thailand guests. Even the thought of the Koda or secretly local hired hands plagued Packard because everything hinged on the two frightened guests remaining that way. They went to the new hiding spot afraid of everyone around them. So long as it stayed that way, the officers would remain free to track the Koda without fear of being arrested or kicked off the force for actions unbecoming police officers.

He knew where to find the money at the airport, and the amount of cash. He also understood the hesitance by the two guests to hand it over to the Koda. After all, they were on foreign soil, they had betrayed their country, and their lives might be forfeited after handing over the money, assuming they broke free of their protectors long enough to meet with the Koda.

Packard assumed something had happened to trigger the assassination of the defense minister's aide. A meeting with minimal security seemed much more feasible to pull off than the situation they put themselves in. Perhaps they balked at the notion of meeting so quickly after arriving in the States, so Khumpa put pressure on them by assassinating one of their party, to show he could kill any one of them at any given time.

With the kids in bed, Packard sat on his couch flipping through the news channels, seeing little of interest. His feet were propped on the coffee table, which left him in an unusually comfortable lounging position. Though his body was comfortable, his mind raced through the events of the past few days, causing him mental anguish.

"You seem distracted," Sarah said, sitting beside him.

He wrapped his arm around her, pulling her close.

"I've had better weeks," he admitted. "This terrorist thing has been terrible."

"How involved are you?"

"I'm kind of on the outskirts of the whole thing," Packard answered vaguely.

She put her head against his chest as both of them settled into the couch. Using her palm, she rubbed his chest.

"I'm proud of you."

"For what?"

"You're in the middle of a crisis and you've been faithful to quitting smoking."

Packard exhaled a chuckle through his nose.

"How do you know I've been faithful?"

"Because you smell a lot better. I know you have to be under a lot of stress, so I'm extra proud of you."

"Thanks, dear," he said. "I'll confess it hasn't been easy."

Sarah reached for the television set's remote, muting the sound.

"The kids miss you," she said.

Packard rubbed his forehead uncomfortably.

"This will all be over soon and things will be back to normal."

"As in normal before you started your task force?"

Sighing and groaning to himself at the same time, he sensed not only the kids missed him around the house, but his wife as well.

"I promise I'll make time for all of you when this is over. The way things are going, there may not be a task force to go back to."

"Oh?"

"Ah, they've got us guarding the Thailand nationals and running around like sniffing dogs, looking for clues while the terrorists stay two steps ahead of us."

"What's that have to do with your group getting broken up?"

"They keep separating us to do all these tasks when we were doing fine as a unit."

Keeping her head against his chest, Sarah remained silent a moment before speaking again.

"You still giving Ed a hard time?"

"Who said I was?" Packard asked somewhat defensively.

"Clay called for you a few times last week. I pry information out of him sometimes."

"You know, Ed's turning out better than I thought. He follows orders, keeps his mouth shut, sometimes, and takes a lickin' but keeps going."

Sarah often told him he was too judgmental about other people, particularly before he knew them.

"I told you he was a nice kid."

"When did you meet him again?"

"At the Christmas party last year. And he brought his kids out to the picnic last July."

Packard nodded. Sarah was far more attentive than he was. She also had a much better memory for details. He remembered things relevant to his job, and little else most of the time. If not for his wife, he might sometimes forget important birthdays and events.

"Yeah," he said thoughtfully. "Ed's okay."

"But not like your adopted son, is he?" Sarah teased as she sometimes did about Clay.

"I don't know what you're talking about," he said, pretending not to know.

"If you couldn't have landed him, I don't think you would have taken the task force assignment."

Packard grinned with a light groan.

"Now that's a little extreme."

"Is it?"

"Sure, I would have taken the job regardless of who they gave me. I may not have liked it very well, but I wasn't going to pass it up for anything."

Both sat silently a moment, but Packard watched the violence on the news channel happening overseas after a bomb rocked an innocent city, caught in the middle of a vicious religious war.

People threw rocks, cried, searched for loved ones, and sobbed over the bodies of their dead family members and friends, all in the course of thirty seconds. Packard wondered why he was home, instead of preventing such things from occurring in his city. He looked down to his wife, and knew why.

"So, if I start smoking again are you going to leave me?" he asked, almost as a test.

"No, but I'll nag you like never before."

"Oh," he said thoughtfully. "That would be worse."

She slapped him on the arm, drawing a cry of pain combined with a chuckle, because he knew sometimes humor was the only thing that kept them from stating the serious issues in their lives. Packard considered it better to harbor his secrets, and his job, from his family to save them the pain he withstood.

Sorrow built within him for the destroyed families he saw every day of his life, whether it was from loved ones going to jail, dying from drug overdoses, or simply disappearing off the face of the planet. He never wanted his family to wonder why he hadn't come home, and he never wanted to trouble them with his own misery.

"I thought I was supposed to be the grumpy one," he said as Sarah sat up beside him.

"I can show you grumpy if you want."

Packard flashed a mischievous grin.

"I can think of another mood I'd rather see," he said as his eyes looked to the direction of their bedroom.

✱   ✱   ✱   ✱

Clay wasn't entirely happy with the situation Packard had put them in. Granted, the new hiding place for the Thailand guests was wired with sound and video, but that didn't ensure the Koda was incapable of putting something over on the officers.

As he sat beside his cousin and Sorrell in a local sports bar at a corner table, he wondered why they hadn't moved to attain the money the second they knew the location. He wanted a piece of Khumpa so badly, little else entered his mind.

He numbly agreed to follow Mitch to the bar because he had little else to do that evening.

"You're not acting right," Sorrell said, disturbing Clay from his train of thought.

"Yeah, you need to be thinking about getting laid and keeping Packard off our backs, not dwelling on what happened tonight."

Clay felt a bit disturbed about the insensitive nature of his two counterparts, but they had no idea about what he confessed to Packard about his past. At least he doubted they did.

"I'm not sure you two have your heads in the right places," Clay finally stated. "We're nowhere near done with the Koda, and I'm reasonably sure they have plans to destroy more of our city before they leave."

"Yeah, but Sarge said to take the night off," Sorrell said defensively.

"And he told you two to stay low and play dead so no one saw you. And where are we?" Clay asked with sarcasm, looking around him.

"In an inconspicuous public place," Mitch replied.

"That's an awful long word for you, cuz," Clay said.

Sorrell took a quick drink from the beer bottle set before him.

"You're pretty negative tonight, Clay. What gives?"

"I've got a lot on my mind, Ed. I shouldn't even be here."

"Sure you should," Mitch said, his eyes a bit glassy after several beers. "We've got to forget our troubles for one night."

In no mood to forget his troubles, and not one to drink alcohol, Clay looked to the glass of water before him. His friends often teased him about never drinking soda or beer, but a need to stay in phenomenal shape overtook personal preferences.

"You've been acting weird ever since that Punnim guy got killed."

"Yeah, what's up with that?" Mitch asked, probably getting too liquored up to do anything except mimic Sorrell at this point.

Clay rubbed his head in frustration.

"He said some things that shook me up before he was murdered, okay?"

"What kinds of things?" Sorrell asked, being the more sober of the two.

"Nothing," Clay said in short.

He stood up, pushing his seat back.

"Look, I've gotta get some fresh air."

Even as he walked outside his two colleagues followed him. He suspected they were more curious than concerned for his well-being. Walking over to a mesh fence, he spied a man tossing a plastic bottle to the ground just before he entered the bar for a good time.

Mitch noticed it too.

"Shit," Clay muttered as Mitch whirled around to confront the man.

"Hey," Mitch called, gaining the man's attention.

Probably not quite their ages, the young man likely had no idea he was being observed by three cops, or that he had truly broken a law. His potential good time was about to be ruined by an environmental fanatic.

"What's up?" the man asked casually, probably expecting Mitch to ask a piece of information.

"You just littered back there."

The man's face showed his exasperation. He probably wondered why anyone cared about a plastic bottle being tossed to the ground, but Clay had been around his cousin for years, tolerating Mitch's constant lectures. He knew by heart about how the Earth was decimated by everyone who threw away anything that didn't break down naturally in the environment.

Fortunately Clay learned years before to never throw anything except paper to the ground, or face his cousin's verbal wrath.

"What's the matter?" the man asked, looking to Sorrell and Clay for some sort of explanation, or possibly some sane help.

"You can't just throw bottles away like that," Mitch insisted. "That's littering."

"What are you?" the man retorted. "The litter police or something?"

"Hey, I'm-"

Sorrell cleared his throat, stepping in front of Mitch, who was about to obliterate their orders from Packard to lay low and play dead. Ordinarily Mitch told any and everyone who listened that he worked for the city police department, but this was not the time to be enforcing laws or making a public scene.

Though Packard and other officers had a lack of respect for Sorrell, Clay noticed the man thought of things other people never noticed. He was especially careful around children, probably because he had two of his own. Sorrell never did a thing to intimidate them, because children often shy from police officers. He knelt to their level, spoke softly, and treated them as equals, rather than inferiors.

His quick thinking, while Clay's mind remained muddled with his own problems, saved the three from a situation Packard would surely frown upon. Sorrell often thought of the little things, and for all of his bad luck and lack of dexterity on the job, he owned several powerful qualities. Two important qualities were uncanny powers of observation and raw strength the other officers wanted helping them out in a scuffle.

Now, without a word, he simply stared into Mitch's eyes, letting his usual beat partner know with the expression on his face that speaking was not wise.

"Sorry, man," Sorrell quickly said to the litterer. "Our buddy's had a bit too much to drink."

"I have not," Mitch protested, trying to play along.

"I think you have," Sorrell said, turning Mitch away from the man.

Clay simply gave the man a nod and a flat wave, trying to dismiss the incident as a drunken error of judgment.

"Smooth move," he chastised Mitch when they were a few steps further from the bar.

"He littered," Mitch stated, as though they might not have noticed.

"Yeah, well, the best move for you two is to get home."

"He's staying at my place tonight," Sorrell said. "Just in case that bitch comes back."

Clay smirked.

"I think she got what she wanted. But it's a wise move anyway."

"See ya tomorrow," Sorrell said as the two walked toward their vehicles, leaving Clay in the crisp night air by himself.

He started toward his own car when his cellular phone rang at his waistline, where it remained clipped to his jeans.

Plucking it from its clip, he looked at the phone number across its small screen, thinking it looked familiar, but uncertain who was calling.

"Hello?" he answered anyway.

"Clay, it's Emily."

His aunt by marriage, she sounded worried.

"What's wrong?" he asked.

"Your Uncle Bill hasn't come home from work yet."

Clay looked to his watch, which read just after nine o'clock.

"What time does he usually get out of there?"

"By five at the latest."

"Well, maybe he got held up."

"He always calls if he's going to work late, and we had dinner reservations at seven across town. I've called, I've paged, and I'm not getting any answer."

Clay stood silently a moment.

"I called your father, but he said he was tied up with some kind of overtime assignment pulling cars over. He suggested I call you. I know I sound paranoid, but it's not like Bill to disappear for hours at a time."

Clay mentally agreed.

Ball Memorial Hospital wasn't far out of his way on the way home, so he decided a quick stop wouldn't delay him from a good night's sleep too long.

"Yeah, I can check with security, but I'll look for his car first. What's he driving?"

*   *   *   *

Clay found himself at the hospital about ten minutes later. He considered calling his cousin, but decided against it, since his uncle was probably heavily involved in some kind of project, forgetting to check in with Emily.

Venturing into the basement first, he didn't see a soul as he walked the long hallway to his uncle's office, finding it dark and locked up. He looked around the area, seeing every door closed, and locked, when he tried each one.

He had obtained the car's make, model, and license plate number from his aunt, but with a parking garage six levels in height, each level holding dozens of vehicles, his time was better spent checking other avenues. The hospital police were more familiar with the garage, so they could check for his uncle's car faster than he was able to.

A few minutes later he found himself knocking on the hospital security office, then face to face with one of the officers as the door opened.

Looking him up and down, the officer apparently didn't recognize him, even though some of the city officers worked part-time at the hospital. Clay had hoped to find one of them around, but this man was a regular part of the hospital police staff by the look of the patch on his uniform's sleeve.

"Can I help you?" the man asked with some skepticism.

"I certainly hope so," Clay replied.

A few minutes later Clay stood by as the man typed away at a computer system set in the back partition of the security office. Clay had quickly explained why he was there, which sent the officer, who was the shift's captain, to ordering his outside officer in the security vehicle to check for Bill Branson's vehicle among the diminishing number of cars. With the morning shift long gone, the search was sure to be easier.

Raising Branson on the radio failed, but the security officer noted it might be on the charger, turned off, or set aside somewhere.

"If his car's out there, it shouldn't take long to find," the captain said as he typed something into the computer.

"What are you looking for?" Clay asked curiously.

"We've been on a higher alert with these terrorists around, so I'm checking where your uncle's swipe card has been used today. He has complete access to this building, so we wouldn't want his card falling into the wrong hands if something has happened to him."

Clay felt numb, suddenly wondering if Khumpa had something to do with this. It made complete sense, because his uncle was very organized, followed a strict routine, and made responsibility a number one priority in his life. With a hospital depending on his abilities, and a crew constantly picking at his brain, Bill needed to be accessible.

In some ways Clay resembled his uncle more than his father, because Bill was always reserved, usually calm, and intelligent in ways other men were not. He looked more like his uncle too, but Bill had a knack with numbers and formulas Clay never expected to comprehend during his lifetime.

After a minute or so, an index appeared on the computer screen, displaying locations and some sort of sector numbers Clay didn't understand.

"Nothing unusual here," the captain said, looking at the top portion of the screen. "I don't think he usually works past five."

Clay glanced to the bottom of the screen, noticing a few of the card entries took place up to two hours after five o'clock.

"Where's that?" he asked, looking to the first.

"That's odd," the captain said, staring at the log. "That entry is from the time clock leading into the garage."

"I could be wrong, but isn't Bill salary?"

"Yeah. So there would be no need for him to clock in…or out."

Both stood silently a moment.

"You think he was kidnapped or something?" the captain asked.

"Not necessarily," Clay said slowly, thinking the worst. "Has your man found his car yet?"

Placing a quick call over the radio, the captain received a response that the officer had indeed found Bill's car. He was beginning an assessment of the vehicle to see if there were any clues about the supervisor's whereabouts.

"The engine's cold," the officer's voice stated over the radio.

"So he hasn't left lately," Clay surmised, looking for any optimism in the captain's face.

Instead, he received a neutral, yet concerned, stare.

"You seem a bit more edgy about this than you probably should be," the captain noted a few seconds later.

Clay didn't have time to explain the full truth to the man.

Nor did he care to.

"We have reason to believe the terrorists may have the hospital cited as a potential target," Clay revealed a half-truth. "If I were a terrorist looking for full access to this building, I certainly wouldn't risk abducting a security officer when there are a few other people with at least as much access to every room, who don't wield guns."

"True," the captain said thoughtfully. "Then what do you suggest?"

"I want to look for my uncle discreetly with every man you have available. And come to think of it, every man who works for my uncle, too."

Nodding, the captain appeared to think it was a reasonable request, especially since he was basically in charge of protecting the entire hospital at the moment.

"Okay," he said. "You're sticking with me."

*   *   *   *

Ten minutes later Clay found himself searching hallways along the first floor with the captain. Other officers were assigned to the upper floors, five in total, leaving one man behind to monitor the emergency center within an enclosed room.

Considered the most volatile and active area in the hospital, the emergency department required a security officer around the clock to monitor unruly patients and observe who entered and exited the hospital. From early evening until the next morning the emergency department became the only means of entering the building for non employees.

Clay discovered the captain's name, which was Gerald Schilling. He had worked at the hospital over a two-decade span, and had retirement in his sights.

"This is going to take forever going room to room," Clay complained as they finished the last locked room on the first floor. "But if someone has my uncle's swipe card, they could get almost anywhere, right?"

"They *could* be anywhere," Schilling said, leading the way to the basement down a set of stairs that put them near the security office. "And worse yet, they could stuff him anywhere."

Clay shot daggers with his stare, and Schilling immediately caught it.

"I didn't mean it like that," the captain said. "I'm sure your uncle is alive and well wherever he is. We're probably both overreacting to this whole thing."

"I hope."

Without making a scene, the two quickly checked out the nearly vacant cafeteria, then looked through a few janitorial closets, the pharmacy, and the security office itself, since no one was around to guard it.

Cutting through the cafeteria once more, Schilling led the way back to the lower depths of the basement where Bill's office and the various shops were housed.

"I don't know why we didn't check back here first," Schilling thought aloud.

"Well, you're leading the way," Clay noted, hinting the thought had crossed his mind.

Clay warily followed the captain into his uncle's office as the man drew his firearm. Without his own gun, Clay hardly felt defenseless. In close quarters he was quick enough to use most anything as a weapon effectively. Able to hurl most any small object as a projectile with deadly accuracy, he hardly felt worried for himself.

Still, a tingle ran through his spine with the thought of finding his uncle's corpse around any corner.

Schilling flipped on the lights, cautiously looking around. Desks and cabinets impeded their search, but the captain quickly looked around and under every piece of furniture, then in the small closet, finding nothing.

In the meantime, Clay looked in his uncle's office, finding no keys, no briefcase, and nothing to indicate his uncle left the hospital hastily. The only odd thing he found was the computer left on. He moved the mouse, bringing it out of its sleep mode to reveal a map of the hospital.

Though his uncle was particular about certain things, he had no idea if Bill religiously shut down his computer or not.

He looked behind the door, finding no jacket or personal belongings. Only the hard hat his uncle sometimes wore in the construction areas hung on a hook. Clay knew that was something that remained in the office at all times.

Rubbing his chin, he began to wonder if they were jumping to conclusions about Bill's whereabouts. He looked up, finding the captain waiting at the main door.

"One down," Schilling said, turning out the lights and locking the door before they walked to the wood shop.

One by one they examined the shops, finding no clues in any of the rooms.

After they finished with the last room, Clay plucked his cellular phone from his side, dialing his uncle's home number. The signal was terribly weak, but he heard ringing between crackles of static. He remembered his uncle saying to never use a cell phone inside the hospital, but he failed to recall the reasoning.

At this point Clay didn't much care.

"Hello?" his aunt answered on the other end.

"Emily? This is Clay."

"Anything yet?"

"That's what I wanted to ask you. Have you heard from him?"

"No."

Silence filled both ends of the line a moment.

"I'm still looking on my end," Clay said. "I'll call you back when I find something."

"Okay. Thank you."

Clay ended the call as he collapsed the phone, replacing it along his hip.

"Where to now?" he asked Schilling.

"There are some rooms along these hallways, then the tunnel leads back into another section of the hospital we haven't checked yet."

Exhaling a sigh, Clay wanted results one way or another, hoping to salvage part of his evening plans if things turned out for the best.

"Okay," he said. "Let's get to it."

He followed Schilling down the hallway toward a pair of doors opposite one another in the middle of the long corridor. A dingy white, they had no sign or markings to indicate they were offices or any kind of shops. They were far removed from his uncle's office, so Clay figured they had to be broom closets or storage.

Schilling tried the lock before using the key, but found it locked.

"These are both mechanical rooms," he said, thumbing back toward the other door. "Half the time the staff leaves them unlocked."

Sounds of motors running and belts rapidly whirling around their pulleys filled his ears as he followed Schilling inside. As the captain pulled out his flashlight and service weapon, Clay flipped on the light switch, looking around the corner first as Schilling climbed over a large water main and a pile of necessary parts.

"I've always heard this place has rats the size of shoe boxes," Schilling revealed, raising his voice over the hum of the machines. "It's always given me the creeps."

Clay ignored the man's soliloquy a moment, snatching a flashlight from the ground to shine under the maze of waterlines encompassed by darkness. He shined the beam to the far wall, then back toward him, startled when he found a pair of eyes reflecting in the light.

Aiming the beam to reveal a man bound to the pipes, he discovered the identity of the captive, thankful the man was alive.

"Bill?" he called, scurrying under the pipes to join his uncle, drawing the attention of Schilling as he did so.

"Clay, thank God," Bill said as his nephew drew close to him on the dusty concrete floor, examining the handcuffs.

Reaching into his pocket, Clay pulled out a set of keys, searching for the key to his own set of handcuffs.

"What the hell happened to you?" Clay asked.

"Some terrorist ordered me to show him the hospital's layout and give him access to the whole place. He threatened me at gunpoint, and said he'd kill anyone who tried to rescue me. That's why I didn't yell out."

"It's okay," Clay replied, freeing his uncle's wrists from the cuffs.

Schilling observed from a distance, then led the way to the hallway where the three could better hold a discussion, away from the noise, once Bill and Clay were free of the steel pipe maze.

"You sure you're okay?" Clay asked.

"I'm fine," Bill quickly reassured him, though he was soaked from head to toe from his own sweat.

His usually neat hair looked scattered, as though someone had opened a pressure hose on him.

"We don't have time to horse around," Bill stated. "He planted a bomb in that room."

"*That* room?" Schilling asked, the color leaving his face as he swallowed hard.

"And I suspect he's planted at least two or three more to disable the hospital's main systems," Bill revealed. "I think he wants to take out the oxygen supply and the power."

Schilling turned to radio his men to meet him upstairs. He then switched frequencies on his radio to call the county police dispatcher. Their department typically dealt with any bomb threats.

Clay watched this, then turned his attention to his uncle.

"How much time do we have?"

"I don't know. He never showed me any of the explosives."

Wondering what needed to be done, Clay suspected this was part of the master plan Packard and Perry had spoken of when they were still on good terms.

"I know he planted that one last," Bill said, nodding toward the machine room. "But if they aren't set to detonate at the same time, who knows how much time we have?"

Clay looked into the open door of the machine room, knowing what had to be done, even if it was suicide.

"Stay with Captain Schilling until I meet up with you. I'm going to check it out."

"But-"

"Hey, I'm the cop. I get paid to do this shit."

Clay refused to reveal his primary concern that Khumpa was cold-hearted, willing to murder anyone to get revenge against him. His uncle gave him a strange look, as though there was something he needed to tell him.

"What is it?" Clay asked, softening his tone.

"I'll tell you later," Bill said, his eyes wandering toward a bulge the size of a folded sheet of paper in his shirt pocket.

He looked discontent, his blue eyes looking to his nephew with concern, and probably several questions.

"There will *be* a later," Clay promised, putting an assuring hand on his uncle's shoulder.

"Okay," Bill said, patting him on the arm.

Clay scrambled down the ramp of the machine room, then under the pipes once more after grabbing the flashlight. He noticed where it rounded a corner, following the pipes back toward a shaft with an unusual shape, as though it helped support or house something.

"Elevator?" he wondered under his breath.

A dim red glow, like that of an alarm clock, caught his attention in the far corner, only because it was the darkest part of the entire shaft.

He maneuvered his way past the last of the pipes, finding himself face to face with the bomb, reading the time remaining as it counted down.

00:05:37.

"Oh, shit," he muttered, quickly examining the bomb, a sickening feeling creeping into the pit of his stomach.

If the times were staggered, there was little or no chance of disarming the other bombs. With his extremely limited expertise in bombs, there was an equal chance of disarming this one in time.

Clay stared at the make of the bomb, realizing there were far too many wires for him to decipher which ones did what and cut them before it detonated. Instead, he looked at the housing, noticing it was fastened with a simple velcro device.

"Sweet," he commented to himself as he examined it for a trip wire of some kind.

Khumpa shared one trait with his uncle. They were both very anal-retentive when it came to doing a job correctly. Khumpa, however, was often overconfident.

That was his downfall in their clan, when they were both in Japan.

Clay looked from top to bottom on the housing, finding no loose wires or stray connections leading him to think there was any sort of booby-trap connected to it.

"Here goes," he muttered to himself, reaching behind it to undo the velcro straps.

He slowly removed the first, finding its two straps parted easily like slit pieces of rope. His hands started on the last strap, slowing pulling them apart until he heard a clicking noise from somewhere behind the device.

"Uh oh."

✳   ✳   ✳   ✳

Bill Branson had followed the captain about as far as he planned to. The man sent his officers scrambling to find the bombs without much of a plan. Granted, there was little time to plan without knowing how long they had before the bombs detonated.

Though he had no concrete proof there were other bombs, Bill had to believe Khumpa planned to use them to cripple the hospital's operations. After all, Khumpa never showed him any other devices, and he never specifically stated how he planned to carry out his scheme.

"I've got to get in touch with dispatchers to make sure the bomb guys are on the way," Schilling reasoned aloud as Bill followed him into the security office.

"By the time they get here it's going to be too late," the maintenance supervisor stated as the door shut behind him.

He deeply suspected Schilling was afraid to search for the bombs, fearing one might blow up in his face. Bill feared it too, but his nephew was laying his life on the line, so he wasn't about to stand around and do nothing. Hundreds of lives were at stake, and it was partially his responsibility to stop the monster he accidentally helped unleash. He also felt a deep sense of duty to everyone in the building because he was one of the few people who knew the layout by heart.

"We need manpower to search for those bombs," Bill said emphatically.

"And we need someone to dispose of them if they're found," Schilling said. "I've got my men doing a search as we speak."

"Goddamn it," Bill muttered to himself, snatching an extra set of building keys from a hook behind the door, and a radio programmed to hospital frequencies from a charger across the room, since his own were still missing. He presumed Khumpa had them, or might have dumped them in the trash somewhere on his way out of the building.

Schilling stared at him in awe as Bill crossed the room on his way out.

"You're to stay with me," the captain said in vain, as though wanting someone to testify later he was doing something at the moment of crisis.

"If you'd get off your ass and start looking for those bombs, I wouldn't have to go off on my own, now would I?" Bill asked, yanking the door open.

Schilling hung up the phone, probably cutting off a dispatcher on the other end.

"Who the fuck do you think you are?" Schilling demanded. "I don't have time for this bullshit, Bill. Unlike you, I know how to conduct myself in a crisis."

Fighting the urge to strike the man for being as stubborn as a mule, even if he thought he was doing right, Bill simply clenched his fist, shook his head, and walked out. Whatever Schilling hollered next went unheard as Bill darted down the hall, having a few ideas where some unseen bombs might be.

He looked at his watch, wondering how much time remained before the bombs detonated. The note in his pocket felt like it burned a hole in his chest, but the curiosity of what it said was the only pain he knew.

Reaching the first floor, Bill heard the officers over the radio speaking to Schilling. They reported they had found both the oxygen tank and electrical power station bombs.

"They have less than two minutes until detonation," one officer reported.

"Same here," the second said.

Silence filled the air a moment.

"Get everyone out of the area," Schilling ordered, satisfying Bill that he made the right decision.

"They're barely attached," one officer said. "We might be able to pull them free and detonate them somewhere else."

"Clear the areas," Schilling insisted. "If we take them somewhere else, we won't be able to protect the areas around them, and we don't know how far the blast radius will be."

"Yes, sir," both answered as Bill sifted through the key ring for the correct key to the cancer center to make certain no one lingered behind.

Though the center maintained regular business hours, janitors and other staff sometimes had business in the area after hours, and the new wing sat less than the length of two cars from the electrical station.

Bill let himself in, finding the area completely dark.

"Hello?" he called, receiving no initial answer.

Everywhere chairs and sofas sat in the waiting lounge, placed neatly between coffee tables. The fireplace at the head of this scene was unusually dark because a gas-powered fire burned in there during the daytime hours, providing artificial warmth, and some comfort, to those who visited.

A cathedral ceiling loomed above him, high and slanted. Two skylights were centered on either side of the ceiling, giving it a getaway cabin feel. It was the one part of the hospital that didn't look and feel sterilized.

Just outside the new wing sat six standpipes for fire department use in case of a disastrous fire. With a limited water supply, most fire engines were incapable of handling large-scale fires without hooking up to a water supply of some sort. Down the hall sat new equipment valued in the millions, so it seemed appropriate that such measures were taken when the wing was built the year before.

Windows were everywhere in the new wing, letting daylight stream in from the sides, and above in the skylight during the day. On a clear night a person might see the stars above, and the lights from the hospital's other buildings along the sides, but it was unusually dark this evening.

Except for a slight red glow from one corner.

Bill darted over to it, noticing a final bomb, likely meant to destroy the fire department's couplings outside, and act as a secondary device if someone found the primary bomb outside, attached to the electrical power source.

He read the digital display to himself.

00:00:22.

"Shit."

About to let himself out the front door to sprint as fast as possibly from the detonation area, he heard a voice from one of the back rooms.

"Someone in here?" one of the female custodians replied to his initial inquest, peeking her head out of a restroom she had been cleaning.

"Move!" Bill ordered, physically urging her toward a wing further into the hospital without being too rough.

"What's wrong?" she questioned.

"Bomb," he answered in short, pushing the door open, virtually dragging her along.

"Is this some kind of drill?"

"No!" he answered in frustration, desperately trying to get to safety. "There is a bomb back there and it's going off in a few seconds."

He rounded a hallway with the custodian in tow as the bomb did just that, hurling them both to the floor as windows shattered in the room behind them after a deafening boom sounded.

As the glass shattered, the doors flew open from the blast, bringing heat and debris toward the two hospital employees sprawled along the hallway floor. Bill covered the woman the best he could, getting pelted and stung by metal and plastic scraps along his backside for his trouble.

Like an earthquake was all around them, the ground shook and rumbled several seconds as sounds of the glass crashing and breaking entered Bill's ears. He heard thunderous crashes from the room behind him, and the outside. His best guess was some of the ceiling, roof, and chunks of concrete from the building itself, were plummeting to the ground.

His thoughts went to everyone else in the building. He hoped and prayed no one was killed, or even injured, during the explosions.

Slowly standing, he checked his body over for injuries, finding scrap pieces of metal and plastic sticking to his shirt, a few poking into his back. He plucked them out as the custodial woman stood up, surveying the damage from beside him.

"Thank you," she said numbly. "I didn't realize...what was happening."

"It's okay," he replied. "There just wasn't time to warn you."

Assured his back was intact without severe damage, he walked toward the cancer center, looking inside at the wreckage of what was once a virtual work of art. The entire skylight had fallen in, and chunks of the ceiling were missing. The entrance doors and most of the south wall were missing, leaving a huge gap where sliding glass doors once led to the parking lot outside.

Little fire existed because the explosion had blown out any flames as quickly as they came. A few tiny flames the size of campfires dotted the floor, but they were little threat to Bill, or the already decimated room.

Almost afraid to look, he made his way through the charred cinders piled throughout the room, toward the front. Smoldering sofas and designer chairs sizzled like they were bacon, impeding his path, but he kicked them aside, finally reaching the former entrance.

"Dear God," he muttered, realizing there was nothing left of the switch gear outside.

He looked around the area, seeing nothing except dim lights in several of the hospital rooms where the generator had kicked in, providing just enough light for egress, and to keep essential systems running. Several life-support systems and machines needed to keep running at all costs, so the generator put out just enough power to keep those functioning, and barely enough light to help everyone escape from the hospital.

"Leave the hospital?" he thought aloud.

It sounded odd to him, but perhaps the terrorists weren't so much trying to shut down hospital operations, but attempting to get everyone outside the safety of the large structure instead. He quickly put the thought aside as his radio sounded with activity from the security officers, reporting the damage to the hospital from the bombs.

Bill learned the oxygen tank, the electrical power supply, and the old emergency room, where several ambulances had been parked all day for training purposes, had been targeted. He assumed Khumpa had figured he was going to cripple the emergency room, but instead he had bombed a non functioning part of the hospital, by placing bombs along the outside in the bushes.

"Thank God for small miracles," the maintenance supervisor said under his breath, ready to find his nephew.

A crackle from the radio kept him from turning to begin his new objective.

"Sir, the basement bomb detonated before the others," he heard an officer say. "The visitor elevator shafts have been compromised."

"Compromised?" Schilling questioned over the air.

"At least one of the elevator cars is lying in the basement," the security officer stated, sinking Bill's heart to a new low. "We're getting a crew down there to check for survivors now."

"Detonated before the others," he repeated the words to himself, feeling a mist in one eye, refusing to believe anything bad happened to his nephew.

He stood numbly a moment, trying to decide whether or not he wanted to help in the search. The few men he had on duty were the people who would search the elevator and look for survivors. If he dared join them, he might not like the results, and he knew it.

Clutching the radio in one hand, he hung his head, wondering how he would find the words to tell his brother that Clay was dead, if that was indeed the case.

"You okay?" the woman asked, coming up behind him.

"No," he answered, turning to her. "Not at all."

Without a word, he started toward the basement, ready to see what hand fate dealt him after sparing his own life.

CHAPTER 14

▼

Jennifer Daly stopped at the Tillotson Avenue McDonald's restaurant beside the railroad tracks for a bite to eat before heading back to work.

Her shift at the hospital was due to end in a few hours, and cafeteria food didn't sound the least bit good. Besides, anything left in the serving lines was stale or cold after the dinner rush.

A six-year veteran of the hospital, she worked in the emergency room by choice, because none of the other departments appealed to her. In her spare time, she dated a county cop who had been through a rough week with two funerals and terrorists reportedly running free through the city.

He worked a few days a week at the hospital doing security, which was how they originally met. During his afternoon shifts he often stopped by to see her, but tonight was not one of those nights.

Not that her department had been busy, but he apparently had been. Friday nights were always good for traffic wrecks, drunks driving home, and domestic disturbances. She planned on seeing a share of it before her shift ended.

Standing in line for what seemed an eternity, she finally got a sandwich and fries before heading out to her car. She spied a tractor trailer parked parallel to the train tracks, and a familiar Ball State University police officer examining it from the side.

"Hi, Barry," she said to her father's best friend, Barry Irvin.

"Well, hi there, Jen," he answered, producing a quick smile. "You escape the hospital for the night?"

"Temporarily," she sighed. "So how are you?"

"Pretty good."

"And Kathy?"

"She's doing fine. Been itching to plant that garden of hers, so she finally started it today."

"When are you retiring to help her out?" Jennifer teased.

"That's the reason I *don't* retire, dear," Irvin replied with a crooked grin, indicating he knew better.

Jennifer looked to the bag in her hand, seeing steam escape in the cool night air. She decided to make the remainder of their conversation brief.

"So what are you doing here?" she asked curiously.

"Management said this truck has been parked here a few hours now," Irvin replied. "No owner around, and no one recalls seeing anyone get in or out of it."

"Strange," Jennifer reasoned aloud.

"Yeah. So I'm giving it a quick look to see if I need to have it towed, or if the owner might come back."

Jennifer looked the truck over, spying hazardous material placards along the side. Several times a year her staff drilled on hazardous spill incidents, and their roles at the hospital.

"Well, good luck," she said to the officer, giving him a quick wave goodbye.

"Take care, Jen," he called, returning to his work.

She hopped in her car, turned it on, and carefully edged her way toward the street from the parking lot. A train whistle moaned in the distance as the safety bars lowered on both sides of the tracks, cutting off the traffic. Luckily someone let her into traffic, since they were stuck, waiting for the train to pass.

Jennifer pulled away from the restaurant as the train's engine pulled across the tracks. Even from the distance of the closest stoplight she spied Irvin walking around the semi and its trailer. She began pulling away from the light when it turned green, reaching into her bag for a few fries to munch during the trip back.

With work basically three city blocks from the railroad tracks and the restaurant, she could count on a quick trip, but fast foot never stayed hot very long.

As her fingers clasped a few fries, Jennifer heard a thunderous boom from behind her. A glance into the mirror revealed three train cars buckling as they were lifted off the tracks, into the air, like a caterpillar in mid-crawl. A fireball rose from the tractor trailer and one of the cargo cars. Her mouth agape, she knew Irvin had been standing at the scene just seconds prior, and probably had no time to escape the tragedy unfolding before her eyes.

Stunned, she continued to look in the mirror as people stood from their cars to see the horrific accident firsthand. Jennifer watched as one person near the train exited his car, then grasped his throat, as though choking, and fell to the ground in a heap.

"Oh my God," she stammered.

She watched helplessly as more people fled their vehicles, only to be overcome by an invisible killer, and the image of hazardous material placards raced through her mind.

Irvin was certainly among the dead she decided as she threw her car into drive, flooring the gas in a desperate attempt to remove her car from the deadly gas coming her way. People fell like dominos as they escaped their vehicles, only to choke on the noxious gas, then fall to the ground.

Jennifer had no idea what the gas was, and she did not care at this point. She had to get back to the hospital where there would surely be a shelter the employees and patients could use.

If no one survived to alert everyone else, the results were potentially deadly to hundreds, maybe thousands. The hospital's air handlers alone were capable of sucking enough hazardous air to kill everyone in the north building, which housed most of the hospital's important functions.

And patients.

Her tires squealed as she zipped past a few cars, despite having a red light. Horns honked, and she saw a middle finger from the corner of her eye, but did not care. One car pulled in front of her, and despite her best effort to avoid a collision, she clipped the front of the vehicle, but didn't slow for one second.

Slowing meant potentially dying, and Jennifer had no intention of taking that risk as she reached for the cellular phone in her purse.

*   *   *   *

Bill had nearly reached the basement to join in the search when an urgent message came over his borrowed radio unit.

"This is Unit 43 to all units," Schilling's voice said over the air. "We just received word from dispatch that a serious hazmat situation just occurred down the road at the railroad tracks on Tillotson. We need to assist the emergency department in a mass casualty staging area."

Horrified for two reasons, Bill remembered seeing scores of people exiting the hospital on his way through. If a chemical spill, or whatever it was, reached them, they were certain to fall victim to it. Even worse, if they were gathered into the hospital in time and the air handlers sucked in the toxic air, they were equally doomed.

A recent upgrade ensured the air handlers ran on generator power, in case operations or other lifesaving procedures were underway when the power was cut to the hospital. Bill personally argued against the upgrade, mostly because it was a cost the hospital board might have been wiser to place in other areas.

Now it created a liability.

Deciding he was close enough to his men in the basement to do some good, he darted down the hallway, finding them sifting through the rubble by hand, and with machines, near the collapsed elevator shaft.

All eyes fell on him when he stepped foot in the area.

"I need you all to stop what you're doing," he stated calmly. "We just had a report that a hazmat situation occurred down the street, so I need you all to spread out and shut down the systems in the north building first, then the east wing, and the basement."

He found only four men standing before him, because the fifth had called in sick just before he intended to go home for the afternoon.

"Kelly, you're in charge," he told the senior maintenance man.

"Where are you going, boss?" the man asked, as though wondering if Bill was bailing out before the danger came.

"There are people who went outside because of the power outage," Bill replied. "I've got to get them inside before the gas gets here. You guys just make sure they have a safe environment to breathe once they're inside, because I'll be herding them into the north building."

Everyone nodded in understanding, their jobs suddenly much more important than ever before. For men accustomed to fixing things, they took their new role as heroes in stride.

"Okay," Bill said. "Get going and I'll meet you when I can."

Taking a deep breath, Bill felt unaccustomed to being a man of action, like his maintenance personnel. He was spared from a fiery death of a bomb's detonation for a reason. Not one to dwell on religion or higher powers, he found himself wondering if divine intervention spared him. He also wondered where his nephew might be, and if Clay was alive.

$$*\qquad*\qquad*\qquad*$$

Under ordinary circumstances Clay would have been within an earshot of his uncle's words, but the premature explosion, caused by him tampering with the bomb's harness, set it off earlier than expected.

Minutes to detonation became seconds after the click the young officer heard. He saw the clock speed up in sequence, leaving him precious seconds to escape the fireball created by the explosion.

Escaping the confines of the elaborate piping system, however, proved more difficult than expected, and with only a few seconds remaining, Clay dove on a nearby creeper system with a running start. He rode it like a bobsled down the smooth concrete floor. Narrowly missing the overhead pipes, Clay took the ride as far as it offered, distancing himself from the shaft and the main blast completely.

Despite the distance he quickly gained through his athletic nature and pure luck, it failed to keep him completely safe from the blast's wrath. The collapse of the elevator shaft compromised parts of the basement ceiling, bringing down concrete and materials everywhere around him.

Clay now found himself attempting to dig his way out of the debris lying everywhere around him, closed off from the rest of the basement by mangled pipes that leaked water and steam, and heavier chunks of materials he was incapable of moving by hand.

"Damn it," he said with a sigh, realizing his chances of escape were few.

His arms were raw where the creeper ride and the eventual fall of the ceiling chafed his skin. Blood streaks, some fresh, some dried, ran along his arms and torso, but he ignored the pain, considering himself extremely fortunate to be alive.

Giving Khumpa credit, he never expected the bomb to have a booby-trap set behind it. A lesser man would have been consumed by the bomb because of its location. Escape was by no means easy, but Clay had maneuvered his way out of the tangled piping system with no time to spare.

He hoped no one else had tried to remove the bombs if they ever found them. A secondary rumble told him at least one of them detonated, but he was detached from everyone and everything else in the building.

A single light source gave him just enough light to see the debris around him. Apparently a string of bulbs, about twenty feet apart, were lit after everything went black for a few seconds. Clay had one of the bulbs in his proximity, but it was housed behind a large chunk of concrete, so its light barely crept around the edges of the fallen rock.

"This stinks," Clay muttered, climbing over some of the smaller concrete blocks and broken piping, trying to find an escape route.

Jagged pieces of the metal pipes cut into his hands because he failed to see them in the dim lighting, but he pressed forward.

He thought he heard voices momentarily, but they disappeared as quickly as they came. About to disregard the sounds as his imagination, he heard them again, coming almost like a whisper, or perhaps muffled by something thick.

"Hello?" he called.

No reply.

"Hello?" he yelled louder this time.

A few seconds passed before he heard definite cries for help ahead of him.

He quickly, but cautiously crawled over the debris, receiving steam burns from a loose pipe he failed to notice in the darkness. Groaning in moderate pain, he carried on, wishing he had snatched the flashlight before making a dash to escape the bomb.

Then again, such an action might have cost him precious seconds.

"Keep yelling," he called through the darkness, thinking he finally saw a dim light ahead, other than the single bulb now behind him.

He followed the pleas for help, stumbling over the scraps along the ground until the lighting grew much brighter than before, and he found himself in a safe portion of the basement, but back to the area he originally ran from.

The elevator shaft.

Laying almost sideways on the ground, but supported by a concrete chunk to a leaning position, Clay found one of the elevator cars very close to where the bomb was located.

Voices came from inside the car, and he wondered why no one was here to rescue these poor souls. Then again, he figured, the rest of the hospital staff probably had its own problems at the moment.

Finding a loose pipe along the ground, close to the size of a pry bar, Clay used it as such, struggling with the door a few minutes until it finally began to open, revealing two relieved faces inside.

"Thank you so much," an elderly woman said, her back leaned against the portion of the car supported by the concrete debris.

"You're welcome," he said, spying a man beside her that he figured was old enough to be her husband, and probably was. "Give me a few more seconds and I'll have this door open."

He tugged on the pipe a bit more, feeling the door slowly give.

"Are you both alright?" he questioned as he used the pipe to secure the doors permanently open.

"I think so," the man answered. "We were on our way up to the third floor when we heard a boom from below us."

Clay assumed the cables gave way, sending the car to the bottom. He figured they were lucky to be alive, much less unscathed by the elevator car's collapse. Positive the elevators had safety features beyond their cables, he suspected his nemesis had neutralized any safety devices to ensure the car reached the basement.

"I won't promise the upstairs is going to look much better," he informed them, "but I'll certainly do my best to get you there."

He flashed a quick smile as he began helping them out, drawing stares from the couple toward his injured arms. Ignoring the stares and the various levels of pain his body felt, he hoped no one had died in Khumpa's evil attempt to further terrorize the city.

He also hoped his uncle hadn't done anything rash to get himself hurt or killed.

*   *   *   *

To almost everyone else gathered outside the emergency department, Bill probably looked like an escapee from the psychiatric ward, with his arms flailing as he screamed at the top of his lungs for everyone to get inside.

Thanks to the radio traffic, he now knew a little bit about the incident down the road. A few surviving witnesses gave statements to dispatchers, and from their descriptions, it sounded as though a gas was traveling through the air, killing every living thing in its path.

He emerged from the main lobby's sliding glass doors in the tail end of a desperate sprint to find people gathered around the centerpiece water fountain, sitting on benches, and some heading toward their vehicles.

"Stop!" he yelled out, realizing no one from the group of dozens would recognize him, except perhaps a few of the veteran hospital staff.

His job was typically discreet, considering he dealt with management most of the time, and found his office located in the basement where few hospital employees ventured, aside from his own staff.

"I know policy dictates we head outside when the main power is offline, but we have a chemical spill down the road that may be drifting this way," he said, pointing toward the site of the incident.

As everyone stared at him blankly, he envisioned his men desperately racing from floor to floor, pulling the large levers that shut down the air handlers by severing the power to each junction box.

"Everyone needs to proceed calmly into the lobby," he said, now pointing behind the large water fountain toward a few sets of double sliding doors.

"What makes you think it'll get all the way up here?" one person from the bunch dared ask the maintenance supervisor.

"Because it's three blocks away and the winds have been swirling," Bill replied heatedly. "Do you know how fast ammonia gas travels in the air?"

He had picked out the first gas that came to mind.

"Well, no," the person stammered.

"Neither do I, and I'm not waiting out here to find out," Bill said, slowly walking backward toward the door, waiting to see if anyone was listening to him.

Everyone looked to the person beside them for a moment, as though questioning if this many bad things could happen in a day, then the group moved toward the lobby like a herd of cattle.

In the distance, Bill heard the wails of sirens and air horns from fire trucks racing toward the scene. He hoped no one was foolhardy enough to get in the middle of it, since no one truly knew what toxic chemicals were released.

He knew this was no accident, and everything from the hazmat incident to the sabotage of the hospital was orchestrated by Khumpa and his group. It infuriated him that hospital security and himself knew about the bombs, but ultimately found themselves powerless to stop them from detonating.

Knowing the north tower was the one place his men were in the process of making safe, Bill led the people through the lobby area, down to an intersection of four hallways. He looked to the elevator shafts, seeing chunks of the floor missing, and heavy damage to the exterior walls of the shaft.

Cracks and missing pieces of building material in the walls led him to believe the damage was heavier than he originally anticipated, but by no means did he think the north tower was compromised.

He knew some gases were less dense than air, allowing them to drift upward. Still, he figured it was better to get the people upstairs to the tenth floor than to leave them in the lower levels where the various explosions may have left critical damage to the walls of the hospital.

If gases traveled upward, there was a good chance they would disperse outward, instead of penetrating the walls and windows of the hospital. Once he was up there, a clean sweep of the floor, closing all doors and windows, was almost certain to make the area safe.

If he was lucky, the deadly gas would never reach the hospital at all.

Luck, however, was one attribute missing from his life so far on this day.

CHAPTER 15

▼

A quick quarantine of the area, about a mile in any direction, kept the death toll from the chemical disaster to a minimum.

Over the course of the night Clay listened to the radio for news of the spill, learning it was definitely created intentionally, and the tractor trailer and train cargo car each held dangerous chemicals, that when put together, created a deadly mix.

Through documents provided by the trucking company and the railroad, the police learned a mix of Phosgene and anhydrous ammonia had killed nearly four-hundred people before the area was contained.

Clay knew both chemicals were irritants to the eyes, burning a person's throat, down to the lungs. No one who breathed the mix at close proximity was able to live more than a few seconds, and some residents down the road from the explosion had a taste of the chemicals firsthand, a few making it to the hospital for treatment.

While others never made it at all.

Clay spent part of his night finding his way out of the basement, assisting the elderly couple he found in the elevator shaft, then returning to see if the second elevator had fallen through, perhaps hidden behind the first.

He later learned it was stuck at the second floor, held by its cable or the metallic safety arms that braced against the shaft walls in case of accidents. He suspected Khumpa had tampered with the safety device on the other elevator, causing it to fall through the destroyed basement concrete.

No one was aboard the second elevator when the explosion from below disabled the shafts. Now it sat with yellow security tape around the doors on each level, waiting for repairs or the safety measures to fail so it might finish its descent.

All evening, Clay had spent time with various groups, including the security officers in the emergency department, waiting to see how many survivors came from down the street.

Fewer than he expected survived.

Most patients experienced the chemicals secondhand, unable to escape the path of the deadly mix before they breathed it.

Now he walked the staircase toward the top floor of the north tower, where he heard his uncle had taken a group of employees and patients earlier that evening.

One of the maintenance men informed Clay where his uncle was, and what a good job the man had done, saving dozens of people who might have died standing outside. He felt the hospital staff had acted brilliantly in their attempts to save people in ways they were definitely unaccustomed to.

He heard Bill had left the group long enough to help shut down the air handlers in the important areas of the hospital's buildings with his men. After that, he returned upstairs to check on the people, then stayed until it was safe.

Reaching the tenth floor, Clay opened the door, then looked both ways before entering the hallway. He instantly heard voices down the hall, assuming his uncle was ready to bring them downstairs now that the main crisis had passed.

It only took a moment for Clay to pass various rooms, following the echo of the voices, which sounded hushed. He wasn't certain what the tenth floor housed, but it probably had patients of some kind, he assumed.

He rounded a corner, coming face to face with the man he was searching for, unable to find the words when he saw Bill for the first time since they had parted in the basement. This was the man who had taken him fishing as a kid when his father was too busy doing police work. More like a big brother than an uncle at times, Bill was the one who helped straighten him out in high school before Clay did anything terribly stupid.

Granted, joining the martial arts clan helped Clay more than anything, but Bill had kept him sane long enough to get him there.

Drawing a crooked grin, Bill said nothing, but gave his nephew a quick hug while no one was looking. Keeping his hands locked on Clay's shoulders, he continued to examine him from head to toe as they stood silently a moment.

"You look terrible," Bill finally said.

"Thanks."

"God, I was worried about you," his uncle confessed. "They said a bomb went off early down there."

Clay smiled, shaking his head. The incident seemed fresh in his mind.
"It did."

Bill seemed to catch his apprehension to speak about it.

"You jacked with it, didn't you?"

"Yeah. I tripped a wire in the back and it went off early."

Sighing, his uncle seemed relieved he came away with only scratches and minor burns.

"Then I'm glad the security guys didn't mess with the other bombs."

Clay looked beyond his uncle to the scores of people milling about in the open room beyond. Some were chatting, others sat quietly, and a few were staring out windows on the far side of the room, on the opposite side of where the chemical spills would have drifted to.

"I hear you're quite the hero," Clay noted.

"I didn't do anything," Bill replied, as modest as ever.

Clay learned early to adopt that trait from his uncle.

"These people probably don't think it's nothing."

Looking to the people behind him, Bill stared a moment, then returned his attention to Clay, the same worried expression crossing his face as before, when they parted in the basement.

"What is it?" Clay asked, looking to the sheet of paper still tucked in his uncle's shirt pocket.

"It's addressed to you," Bill said, reaching for it.

He pulled out a folded sheet of paper, bound by a single piece of tape along one edge. Clay's first and last names were written neatly across the outside.

"You were to find this on my carcass after the bomb went off."

"How touching," Clay said sarcastically, knowing exactly what its purpose was, and who meant for him to receive it.

He looked to it, read it, then folded it up, not surprised in the least.

"You know about this man, don't you?"

"Yes."

"When you were in Japan?"

"Yes."

Bill looked exasperated.

"Why does he hate you so much?"

"Because I stole his pride," Clay answered in short.

"He doesn't have any shame, but I don't know about pride," Bill said. "He wanted to kill hundreds of people for no reason at all, didn't he?"

Bill knew about Clay's four years in Japan, but he didn't know the details. He had no idea Clay had been robbed of his wife and son at the hands of Khumpa.

"He wanted me to feel useless as a protector of the city," Clay finally said. "Half the reason he's here is to settle an old score with me."

Everyone in the room had seemed to notice Clay, so they grew restless. If he was able to come up and visit, why couldn't they leave?

Bill quickly ushered them to the stairwell, ordering them to begin the descent without him in a single file. Clay thought he was treating them like elementary school kids, but he supposed Bill needed to maintain some level of safety.

Finally alone with his nephew, Bill gave Clay a serious look.

"If he wants revenge on you so badly, why take it out on so many innocent people?"

"He wants to rile me up. He needs to belittle me before I confront him."

"Confront him?" Bill asked in shock. "You need to find him and put a bullet in his head, Clay."

In response, Clay shook his head negatively.

"It doesn't work like that."

"Like hell it doesn't."

"You don't understand, Bill. Our code requires us to end a blood feud through traditional means."

Bill raised his eyebrow inquisitively.

"Traditional? Code?"

"No guns. No modern weapons. We finish it with our hands and bladed weapons."

"I still say you take a gun and blow the mother fucker away."

Clay let a grin slip.

"That's not bad advice, but I'm afraid I can't take it."

Putting his hand against the wall, Bill looked to the floor, then back to his nephew with grave concern in his eyes.

"If you go through with this crazy-ass grudge of yours, can you beat the son-of-a-bitch?"

Clay turned away from his uncle, knowing the answer inside his mind and heart. Khumpa had succeeded in bringing out every emotion he had struggled to bury the past ten years.

"I guess that answers that," Bill said. "Does your dad know about all of this?"

"No," Clay answered softly. "When I came back, he never really questioned me about much of anything."

"If you don't think you can finish it, why try at all?" Bill pushed.

"There's an old saying you can only kill a snake by cutting off its head," Clay replied. "If I *can* beat him, other countries, other families won't have to go through the same pain we have."

Still not satisfied, Bill looked to his nephew with the same blue eyes they inherited down their family line.

"But if you don't think you can beat him, isn't that suicide?"

"I never said I couldn't beat him," Clay said. "The man has incredible skill, but he's arrogant, and he tends to make careless mistakes when he doesn't have to. That's why I was favored over him in our clan."

"I still don't understand all of this."

Clay forced a smirk.

"You don't have to. Just know if I don't make it back after tomorrow…I did it for the right reasons."

Bill's eyes shifted toward the note still clutched in Clay's right hand.

"Is that what that says?"

"It's implied."

"And I'm supposed to just let you go off to face this creep by yourself? Without telling anyone?"

"Yes," Clay said evenly.

His uncle was torn, and he knew it. Clay never intended to put Bill in such a predicament, but his uncle pushed the issue.

"Then okay. Your secret's safe with me."

"I know you don't understand any of this, but Khumpa took something very dear to me at a time in my life when things couldn't be any better. You don't have kids, so maybe you wouldn't understand what I went through."

"Oh, God," Bill said with realization.

Stunned, he was only able to breathe deeply a moment, looking to Clay, then toward the wall.

"I never knew."

"No one did. It's been my burden for all these years, but tomorrow, one way or another, it's over for me."

Bill looked him squarely in the eyes.

"I know we haven't been as close since we both got back to Muncie, but I don't want to lose you, Clay. Not this way. Can't you stay out of it and let the police handle it?"

"No," Clay said, turning toward the stairwell door. "And everything we just talked about stays between us."

As the door shut behind him, Clay was already a flight of stairs down, leaving his uncle confused on the top floor, alone. He explained everything to Bill because he owed the man that, after Khumpa endangered his life, but he needed his uncle to maintain his secrets.

At least for one more day.

Clay opened the note, reading it one last time.

You and I finish this tomorrow. I'll be in touch. Sato.

CHAPTER 16

▼

Nearing the end of his fitful sleep, Clay began dreaming about his past, only half realizing it wasn't real.

In a hazy setting, he found himself at age eighteen on a small boat with Bill, fishing in the late afternoon sun. He was about to embark to Japan with his father's friend, which his father fully endorsed.

"It'll do you some good," his father had said. "You'll finally grow up."

Clay took the statement to mean his father had failed in raising him correctly, but accepted no blame.

In some ways, his father had failed, because he always spent time with the boys from work, or at a neighborhood function that didn't require his attention specifically. Clay spent his entire life getting out from the shadow of a city police officer, only to wind up in the wrong crowd time after time.

"I can't believe you're going through with this," Bill commented as he threw out his fishing line.

It made a buzzing noise as the spool rapidly deployed from the weighted hook taking flight.

"I can," Clay replied sourly. "Dad doesn't want me around, and I'm certainly not going to college. It's not like I have a whole lot of options in my life."

Bill stared at the water, seeming to think of the right words to say.

"I just hope you don't stay gone forever."

"You don't have much room to talk, Bill. You moved away."

Shrugging helplessly, Bill began turning the reel in his hand.

"I plan on coming back once the right job opens up. And as you can see, I come back to visit."

He paused a moment, sneezed off to the side from his allergies, and sighed.

"Japan is just, well, so far away."

"I'll be fine," Clay assured him. "It's only going to be a year at the most, and I'll be back. By then maybe everyone will miss me."

Bill smirked.

"Mitch is going to miss you. He's got that mall security job all by his lonesome, so he'll have nothing to do except chase shoplifters and little kids."

"He'll be fine. I think he and I have completely different careers in mind."

From there, Clay's mind drifted to the extensive, sometimes torturous training overseas. He recalled sitting in a kneeling position for a full day, never moving a muscle as his mind relaxed and his thoughts focused on his inner karma and the complex move sets he had learned.

Farming during the day and training at night were the only things he knew. Seldom did he go to town, or even meet new people outside of his *dojo*, but the love of his life, Eri Funaki, lived right next door.

Clay lost himself in her, hardly ever taking the time to call or write home anymore. They spent what little free time they had together. She worked in town at a computer software company while he learned more of the Japanese language, moving up the ladder of the agriculture industry for his mentor.

One night Clay watched the sun set behind his master's house. He never heard the footsteps of Ryo Nosagi from behind. Accustomed to his master's silent approaches, Clay was not startled when the man sat beside him.

"You and Eri belong together," he said.

By this time, Clay had spent just over a year in Japan, deciding to stay longer than his original intent.

"I've never felt so right with someone before," Clay admitted, staring at the sun as it peeked through several distant mountaintops and trees.

"It's not quite like it used to be," Nosagi said. "Marriages are no longer arranged as they were in days of old. Eri's father has taken a liking to you."

Clay looked to his master, knowing he looked both bewildered and overjoyed. "Really?"

"Yes. He says you have grown past the rest of my class in work ethic and ability."

He felt proud of his accomplishments, but his hard work was as much for his personal growth as they were to make Nosagi proud of him. After all, the man had volunteered to bring him to Japan, paying for everything.

"So," Clay said, hesitating on purpose. "If I was to ask for Eri's hand in marriage, what would I need to do first?"

Nosagi stared at him a moment, then broke out in laughter. He was not laughing at the question, but rather why it took Clay so long to take the hint and ask it.

Beginning to realize he was dreaming in his subconscious, Clay subconsciously refused to wake up because he wanted to continue to see his family once more, even if it wasn't real.

It felt as though he was there as he lay on the couch, holding his son two months after Joe was born. He and Eri decided on Joe because there was a Japanese spelling of Jo, which was a male name.

Clay explained to her that in America 'Jo' was typically the female spelling of the name.

"But we won't be going to America, will we?" she asked, knowing they had discussed it many times.

"Not to live," Clay said with a smile. "Maybe just to visit."

Eri knelt behind the couch a moment, only her head visible to her husband.

"Do you ever miss it?" she asked.

Clay shrugged lightly.

"Sometimes. But I was never happy over there."

His wife gave him a kiss, then left to do some work in the kitchen.

Holding his son against his chest, Clay let Joe play with his fingers. His son wanted something to grasp, since his mouth held a pacifier in place. Such a good boy, Clay thought. Hardly ever fussy, sleeps through most of the night, and seldom cries, except when he's hungry.

Joe moaned and groaned lightly in his sleep, which Clay mimicked as he turned over in his bed, pulling the covers with him. He felt himself whining like a dog having a bad dream, because he knew the moment wasn't destined to last forever. The most dreaded part of his life was still on the way.

"Even your grandfather would like you," Clay commented quietly to his son. "I guess I was too much hassle for him."

By now Clay had his own house, which his father-in-law provided. He earned it by paying back the money it took to purchase the land, even though the man insisted against it. Clay was trying to do the right things for the right reasons. Never before in his life had he took responsibility, but Nosagi instilled a responsible nature into him, like it was instinct.

His mind raced ahead a year. Nosagi had just announced Clay was the heir to instructing his classes, which was anywhere from a few years to a decade away, but basically meant Clay was the apple of his instructor's eye.

After Clay made the commitment to stay in Japan and raise a family, Nosagi had a long talk with him about his future. His instructor commented about things they had never discussed before, and Clay never brought up because he respected the man so much.

"Sato is far too aggressive," Nosagi said one day as they walked a path surrounded by flowers and shrubs in Clay's back yard. "I think he plans to use the training for the wrong reasons."

"Master," Clay said softly. "You adopted him the same as me. If you wish to, you have the power to expel him from the class."

"I do, but I am too much of an idealist. He said he was quitting after I announced you as my successor."

"I've never complained to you before, but he's never shown me respect. When we're in class, he never pulls his punches. For some reason he's never liked me."

"You've never complained, and that's why you are my heir," Nosagi said, pointing a finger at Clay. "He has a cold heart, Sato does. I thought I could change him, but after so many years, I realize his path will never waver."

Already, Sato had threatened Clay more directly than he stated, but he felt the threats were empty, and just Sato's way of venting frustration. He had never shown any indication of being murderous, despite his cruel actions. On several occasions he had challenged Clay to duels with unlimited rules, meaning participants might be harmed, or killed in some cases.

With nothing to prove, and much more than his reputation at stake, Clay declined. He wanted to remain a family man, simple and clean.

Clay's mind ventured to his sword practice, hour after hour, alone in his training room. He worked with his sword and other weapons, then ran through each of the eighty-one mystic hand symbols used by the ninja in old Japan. Nosagi never told them exactly what they were training to be in so many words, but it was understood they were learning the art of assassination.

Like his classmates, Clay understood their learning was for traditional purposes only, to carry on the bloodline of the ancient art. They were never to abuse their abilities, harm innocent people, or murder.

He learned to do things he never thought humanly possible. A chain-link fence with barbed wire along the top was no longer an obstacle. Clay knew how to scale trees, even buildings, with ease.

One day he went to town for a meeting on behalf of Nosagi, to arrange for pickup of bulk vegetables a week later. He returned home, finding his front door wide-open, despite the chill in the morning air.

Isolated from town, the house had no neighbors nearby. Pleasant odors from the white blooming flowers in his front yard entered Clay's nostrils, but he ignored them, wondering why his door was open.

Stepping inside, he sensed danger, because his house was entirely too quiet, especially since his wife and son were home. When they were sleeping, he heard their exhales with his trained ears, but he heard nothing this time.

"Eri?" he called cautiously.

No answer.

He stepped through the living room, taking up a bladed fork, about half the length of his arm, from the wall as he passed. Stepping defensively around a corner, he saw nothing down the hallway.

Making his way into the kitchen, Clay spied the open back door, and a small pool of blood beside it. There, he found his wife on the ground, face up, no longer breathing. A few feet away, he saw the body of Joe. Both had their throats slit, but with intentionally small cuts so they bled out slowly.

Clay felt his body numb as he dropped to his knees beside them, taking Eri into his arms as he reached for his son. He fought back the tears because his life had been so perfectly happy with his family. They were his rock, his escape from the perils and disagreements that plagued his *dojo*.

He caressed Eri's silk gown, feeling dried blood in several spots. Sobbing to himself, he looked out the back door with tearful, almost blinded, eyes.

"I'll find you Sato," he vowed between sobs. "If it's the last thing I do, I'll find you, and murder you like the dog you are."

Waking suddenly, Clay found himself almost crying in bed. He stood before realizing he had done so, then walked across the room to a small picture book. Flipping it open, he found pictures of his past in the form of his wife and son.

A look at his alarm clock and outside the window indicated he had several hours before the sun came up. He took a seat beside his dresser where the photo album was located, then began flipping through the book to kill some time and recall better days.

"You better pray I don't find you, Sato," he vowed, unable to think of a day he hadn't trained for the moment, or thought of his slain family.

With the new developments, Clay's primary objective was hunting Sato, no matter what Packard wanted to do.

It was in everyone's best interest for Clay to work alone.

At least he thought so.

*   *   *   *

Perry knew little about his surroundings since he had been blindfolded shortly after leaving Muncie. He knew they were heading south from his office, and he consciously monitored which direction the car headed, and how often it turned, to make an educated guess where they were taking him.

Instinct told him it was late morning because he recalled hearing crickets, which were usually associated with daybreak. They also indicated he was outside city limits, because they were in abundance.

His blindfold had been taken off once he was securely inside the building he assumed the Koda had housed themselves in for at least a week's time. Now his confines consisted of a barren room about the size of a hotel room, with dusty floors, walls stripped down to bare wood, and no windows to speak of.

Even the walls looked hurried, as though put there to create some sort of makeshift office when the building was used for something.

With his hands tied behind his back, and his feet bound together, he was incapable of moving the heavy metal legs of the chair without giving himself away. Centered in the middle of the room, with no means of cutting the ropes visible to him, Perry had relegated himself to listening for any kind of activity in the main portion of the building where the Thailand natives housed themselves.

For close to an hour the group conducted heavy conversation in their native tongue, making the agent wish he had Saunders around.

Over the course of the night he had learned a few things about their plans he hadn't discovered before.

He now knew the diamond heist was orchestrated by the Koda, although carried out by a group of professional thieves who were later murdered by the group. He also knew they were stolen from a conglomerate of businessmen who meant to sell them at an auction. One of these men in particular was a rumored mafia boss just outside of Chicago, which was another reason the Koda were laying low.

It also explained who murdered Punnim during the shakedown where the Asian man escaped, nearly secured by Clay Branson before a tall man in a black suit showed up and murdered the fugitive.

He also knew Muncie was targeted, partly because Zhang was easily accessible there, and because Khumpa had some sort of beef with Clay. Things were coming to a messy head, and unless Perry escaped to warn someone, his city was in peril, because he overheard plans much graver than those surrounding the hospital, about to be carried out.

Eventually Perry heard footsteps in bulk, then a door close. He wondered if they were off to carry out another devious plan. Khumpa gave him a few details about the chemical spill and the hospital bombs the evening before.

Perry felt sickened by the actions of the group, wishing he wasn't powerless to stop them. He knew nothing of their future plans, which made him feel worse. With the sounds of several vehicles starting, then pulling away, he decided it was time to take action in whatever form possible.

No noise whatsoever came from the other room, but Perry was not naive enough to believe he was left to his own devices. He began scooting the chair across the concrete floor, creating a horrific screeching noise, sure to attract anyone in the next room.

He needed to know who was left in the building, and felt certain he was about to.

Apparently his restlessness attracted the lone sentry left in the building, who burst through the door with a purpose. Perry guessed him to be another imported college student the Koda somehow hired, because he didn't look nearly as dangerous as he tried to act.

Loosely holding a revolver, his stare burned a hole through the agent, who barely suppressed a grin, figuring it was only a matter of time before he found an opening to escape.

"You...be making too much noise," the Asian man said with broken, slow English.

"These ropes are too tight."

"You sit and shut up."

"Why don't you make me?"

Perry wanted to get some questions answered, but he felt provoking the young man was easier than trying to reason with him.

If he got his way, the answers would be forthcoming.

Taking offense to the agent's statement, the young man drew closer to Perry, as though to taunt him.

"Where the fuck did they find you?" Perry asked to further antagonize his sentry. "The gutters along campus?"

"You...shut up," the man said, struggling to remember the appropriate English words.

"They paying you big money? They're just going to kill you when this is over, so they don't have any witnesses left."

"No," the man said, defiantly shaking his head.

Khumpa had obviously brainwashed him into believing he was part of their group, contributing to a larger cause. Perry hadn't lied when he said they planned to execute him. Part of their usual method of operations was to murder anyone not already in their group. They stayed in small numbers for a reason, and when they found a need to expand, the recruiting process was often very secretive, and sometimes lethal to those who failed to meet their criteria.

"You really think they're going to let you live after everything you've seen?"

"Yes. You Americans are sneaking, and…"

"Conniving?"

He paused.

"Yes."

Perry decided conversation was getting him nowhere.

"Maybe you should grow a set and teach me some manners."

"Grow…a set?" the man asked curiously.

"I'm calling you a coward," Perry stated without hesitation. "You're a big man holding that gun in your hand, being a lapdog to Khumpa."

Perry knew he sparked something in the young man with his last statement, because now he was being confronted with a gun barrel turned toward his head as the young man began walking toward him.

Waiting until the Asian man was within striking distance, Perry used his pre-conceived plan in one fluid motion, bolting to his feet, despite them being tied together, bringing the chair up with him. His arms tied helplessly behind him, and less than a second to carry out his plan, Perry used the one offensive weapon he had, ramming his head squarely into the forehead of the younger man, driving him back.

Much to his chagrin, the gun remained in the young man's hands, but Perry whirled himself toward the stunned Oriental man, battering him with the chair, back and forth. He turned, finding his guard attempting to turn the gun to a ready position, but Perry used his head again, hearing a thud as it connected with his sentry's noggin.

This action floored the younger man, but the gun remained in his hand, and he maintained enough presence of mind to trip Perry by sweeping his feet outward. Perry landed hard, but made certain the chair took the shock for him, breaking one of the wooden legs in the process.

Perry quickly assessed the situation, seeing the groggy young man still trying to ready the firearm. In just the right position for one last defensive stand, Perry put his knees together, his back facing the younger man, and gave a forceful mule kick into the groin area that ended their skirmish once and for all.

A steady groan emitted from the younger man's vocal chords as the gun fell to the floor, allowing Perry to kick it aside and begin the process of freeing himself.

He questioned where he was, and exactly how he wanted to handle the situation. If he called for backup, every officer in the county was bound to show up. Scaring the Koda off did the police little good, and he knew the sheriff was just zealous and careless enough to pull such a stunt for the sake of publicity.

Without him present, their presumed escape route was forfeit, meaning nothing held them back from fleeing the city. Looking to the helpless former guard, Perry decided what needed to be done, even if he risked his own career and life to do so.

*   *   *   *

Most of the night had been miserable for Tom Lyons.

It was his first mass-casualty incident, but the scene before him was unlike anything in the movies, or even holocaust films.

As daylight crept over the horizon, a horrible revelation came to the police officers, emergency medical technicians, firefighters, and government officials witnessing the death and destruction up close for the first time.

Luckily the fire from the train and tractor trailer explosion burnt itself out in little time, but the gases loomed dangerously overnight. The only benefit had been low winds, allowing officials to warn residents and call in the government to take over the operation.

No one was allowed within a mile of the scene, except those traveling to, or leaving the hospital. Not even the fire department or local hazmat team from Anderson dared get near the disaster until the chemicals were dissipated by the air.

From experience, Lyons knew there was nothing more frustrating to a firefighter than having to sit and wait. He watched his brother firemen pace, stare, and cuss as they witnessed the aftermath of the explosion.

Being on standby was the worst feeling of all.

They were trained to *do*.

To *save*.

Walking up to the scene looked like something from films depicting the end of the world. Cars were lining the streets, some still running, a few of those with headlights on. Bodies were lying everywhere.

Some were sprawled in the middle of the street, a few on the sidewalks, several slumped against the drug store or the fast food restaurants. Several hung limply from their open car windows, failing to escape the noxious gases poisoning the air.

They looked a bit like manikins or actors, as though they might spring up any second. After all, there was no blood anywhere, and no visible injuries. At first glance, they just didn't look dead.

Most appeared covered with a thin layer of dust, which was probably produced by the explosion itself.

Lyons swallowed hard, taking in the scene and the lingering odors from the tankers and the mass of dead bodies. He had seen enough dead bodies to know people expelled urine and feces when they died from total muscular relaxation. Before him, hundreds of bodies assumed lifeless poses, each beginning to rot and decay from the inside.

He was new to his position as the arson investigator, forced to be at the scene because the bugles on his shirt collar demanded it. Wondering what kind of warped mind wanted to murder hundreds of innocent people, Lyons followed the lead of the Army officials, carrying several new, folded body bags like everyone else.

About thirty men were dressed and equipped to actually handle the bodies, which were going to be placed near the Tillotson fire station, because it remained surrounded by a fence. That made it secure from every angle, and easily guarded by campus and hospital police.

Overhead, helicopters had circled all night until the military showed up, ordering them away. Still, the media remained a safe distance away from the scene, their cameras rolling and their reporters interviewing anyone with half a brain they found walking by.

To Lyons, they were still too close.

He neared several bodies, seeing lesions along the skin of most of them. Oddly-colored patches of white, black, and red appeared, giving him a chill. Several bodies had their eyes open, staring directly at him like the fish in his aquarium sometimes did.

Except the fish were alive.

Lyons had trouble convincing himself all of these people were dead.

On the street corner he saw a boy lying face-down on the concrete, the remains of an ice cream cone melted by his side. His red hair looked like a patch of wild grass, blown by the gentle breeze. Everything else about him appeared stiff and unmoving, like a statue.

Next to him, a leashed puppy lay awkwardly on its side, like a dead spider with its legs sprawled to different lengths. Its mouth was crookedly agape, gasping for its last breath that entered its lungs like a ball of fire.

Beside one car he spied a mother on the ground with a child in each arm. Her husband laid beside her with his arm draped over her, and his other hand clasped around his throat. His last few breaths had to be excruciating, Lyons figured.

He closed his eyes, drawing a deep breath, as his brain took in the realization that everything around him was real.

Lyons had never been down Tillotson Avenue without there being a line of cars, smoggy air, and noise enough to prevent a person from hearing his own thoughts. Seeing it this quiet felt eerie, almost to the point that he never wanted to travel the street again.

It took several hours, but the departments came to realize Phosgene and anhydrous ammonia were the culprits. They did superficial damage to external skin, but together, they devoured the moist tissue inside anyone's throat, eyes, or lungs they found their way into.

Lyons wanted some kind of miracle, like discovering they had been stunned or paralyzed by the chemicals, but his wishful thinking was disrupted by the military officials ordering everyone to drop their bags in a pile, then leave the area the way they came.

He did so, thinking of the dozens of survivors being treated in the hospital's basement area beneath the new emergency department. Limited power allowed doctors and nurses to treat patients as the oxygen supplier, by contract, brought new oxygen bottles to replace the main system destroyed by the terrorists.

Much to his surprise, every agency worked well together. The coroner's office and city police didn't butt heads as usual, and the mortuaries supplied the number of body bags necessary to clean up.

Everyone from the county police to the nearby volunteer fire departments had pitched in until the government arrived. Lyons suspected most of the chiefs felt much like he did about the government stepping in.

He was relieved, knowing professionals who had dealt with such things before were in the city. Seldom did the departments drill mass casually disasters, because they truly never expected one so huge to occur.

In its defense, his department trained for medical purposes of saving a single or handful of lives at a time. They also trained to put out fires, operate aerial equipment, and perform search and rescue activities. Training for something they used every day they worked seemed much more practical, and Lyons would still argue that point.

Standing still a moment, the investigator turned for one last look at the scene as the military men, coated in protective plastic, treated the bodies as hazardous materials. They moved the bodies like cold, stiff meat to the body bags, callously tossing them into the black bags, then zipping them.

They're nameless, Lyons thought. Until the mess was sorted out at the temporary morgue, hundreds of families would wonder where their loved ones were.

He questioned what kinds of bastards were capable of such terror, then turned to find his chiefs. There were still lots of little tasks that needed completing.

*   *   *   *

Packard had dreamed about a vacation in Florida he had wanted for the longest time, making love to his wife on a sandy beach as the tide rolled past them, then returned to sea, licking the sand from their bodies each time.

He awoke from the incessant beeping of his pager to find it wasn't at all real, although certain parts of his anatomy below his waist seemed to think otherwise.

"Shit," he had commented, realizing it wasn't real, and the page was from his department.

Now he found himself trying to wake up as he sat in the passenger's seat of his unmarked departmental car.

He was informed by the deputy chief that the two officers guarding the Thailand guests were murdered, and the two guests he had a particular interest in were now presumed hostages of the evil group. Packard knew better, which was why he and his three officers were now on their way to Indianapolis International Airport.

Packard had covered for Mitch and Sorrell, stating he had no idea where they were. He assumed they were hung over from bar-hopping, which angered him, because they didn't follow his orders to lay low.

In reality, he fibbed because he wanted them with him, not answering bullshit questions from the brass. They wanted to interrogate the two officers about anything suspicious in the move to the new hiding location. Someone had compromised the safe house, and an internal investigation was being launched.

He wanted to conduct his own interview with the two officers, except it was destined to be less formal.

Packard was amazed the Koda let the other Thailand guests survive, but suspected it was simply because they were fellow countrymen. Khumpa hated Americans and anyone from countries that allowed the same freedoms as the United States.

"Do you two have any idea how those bastards might have discovered the safe house location?" he asked Sorrell, who was driving, and Mitch in the back seat, beside his cousin.

Mitch shrugged helplessly, so Packard turned his attention to Sorrell, who tended to talk more loosely about things.

"I didn't talk to anyone except those two last night," Sorrell said, motioning his head toward the back seat without taking his eyes off the road.

"Then it didn't come from us," the sergeant surmised aloud. "Were you followed?"

"I don't think so," Sorrell said.

Packard knew if someone had observed their actions from a distance, everything they had worked so hard to accomplish was in peril. For once he had felt a step ahead of the Koda, but his lack of action the night before, due to their exhausting evening, might have made his one ace in the hole null and void.

"There's two ways we can play this," Packard said as the airport came into view from the exit ramp. "I can phone the airport security and tell a small fib so we can carry our firearms past the first checkpoint, or we simply go without guns."

"We'd be on an even playing field if the Koda can't bring weapons in," Mitch stated.

"Not exactly even," Clay pointed out. "They're accomplished fighters."

"We're bigger," Sorrell said.

"Yeah, and I'm sure you remember how well you two handled yourselves against a woman much smaller than yourselves."

Uncomfortable silence filled the car.

"Hey," Packard said like a father breaking up a skirmish between his children. "We're going in without guns, we're getting the cash, and we're getting the fuck out of Dodge."

"If they're still there," Clay said. "How long after the murders did you get that call?"

"Fifteen minutes, maybe."

He knew what Clay was thinking. If they were too late, there was no stopping the Koda from completing every objective they had set out to accomplish. He suspected Perry was somehow involved, probably to use his credentials to remove Zhang from the jail.

As Sorrell pulled into the drive that led directly to the check-in area of the airport, Packard decided on a new plan of action. He directed his officer to pull up to the drop off point, then turned to Clay.

"You and I are going inside, unarmed. Ed and Mitch, you two stay out here in case they somehow slip past us. Leave the car over there," he said with a pointed finger, "and if anyone gives you any trouble, just flash your badges and say you're here for a prisoner transport."

"Don't they have records of that stuff?" Mitch asked.

"Yeah, but by the time they check everything out, we'll be out of here, one way or the other."

Checking his clothes over for anything metallic, Clay pulled out his gun and two spare magazines before stepping out of the car to join his sergeant. Packard felt a spare set of keys in his pocket. He tossed them into the car, wanting nothing to slow him down through the various checkpoints.

"I feel defenseless," Packard admitted as he and his officer walked through the front door, immediately encountering the first checkpoint.

"I don't," Clay said plainly.

"Yeah, but your hands and feet are weapons."

Clay replied nothing, but set to monitoring the area around them like a hawk. Packard focused on getting them through the first checkpoint, which they did with no trouble.

From there, they were free to move on, toward the storage lockers. He hoped perhaps the security guards were suspicious of Asian people, perhaps slowing the Koda down a bit at one of the metal detectors.

"See anything?" Packard asked.

"Nothing unusual," Clay replied, his eyes panning the area all around them.

Packard had the key from the two Thailand natives, which the Koda did not. Unlike a bank, the airport lockers had no security perimeter around them, and no armed escort inside a vault. They were mostly in the open, which meant the Koda would have to watch their backs at all times if they attempted to unlock the metal security box. After all, the airport was growing more crowded by the minute.

"Where are we going?" Clay asked, barely following his sergeant's lead as he scanned the area constantly.

"Almost there," Packard said, reaching into his pocket for the key which he was thankful hadn't held him up at the checkpoints.

If anything, the guards knew what it was for, and probably let the two officers through more quickly than usual.

Packard rounded a corner where the lockers were located, feeling his eyes grow to the size of small saucers as he spied two Oriental men at a locker. He quickly shoved Clay back the way they had just come, before the two men took notice from their attempted picking of the lock.

"What?" Clay demanded of the shove, his attention obviously diverted from Packard's discovery.

"Two Asian men around the corner working on a locker," Packard said.

"*Our* locker?"

"I think so. I can't read the numbers from here."

Clay seemed to think a moment, as Packard decided what course of action to take.

"Let me go over there," Clay said, holding his hand out for the key.

"By yourself?"

Clay peeked around the corner, spying on the two men a moment before returning his attention to Packard.

"They aren't the main players," he said. "They're henchmen sent by Khumpa, which means the others are probably around here somewhere."

Packard looked around him quickly, seeing no other Oriental people anywhere.

"I don't know about this."

"We have one chance," Clay stated. "If they get the money, they win."

"And if we start a major scene around here, we're fucked."

"What's the locker number?" Clay asked without hesitation.

"Fifty-six," Packard, said, placing the key in his officer's hand, giving a concerned look intentionally. "You be careful."

Clay forced a grin.

"Just watch my back, and when I come out of there, we're going to have to make a fairly quick escape."

"Okay," Packard said, moving to the center of the hallway leading to the lockers as Clay began walking toward the locker behind him.

*   *   *   *

As he approached the two men, it quickly became apparent they were amateurs, and had no idea danger was heading their way. Probably two more students conned by Khumpa's lies and treachery, they worked feverishly to pick the lock to the storage locker.

Clay learned long ago to never underestimate any opponent, so he studied them, but didn't picture them as fighters. Walking calmly toward them, with no one else down the same corridor, Clay wasn't discovered until he was about a step from both Oriental men, and by then it was too late for them.

One swift motion with both of his hands to the sides of their necks in a precisely aimed spot rendered both unconscious before they truly spied the danger they were in.

Looking behind him, Clay saw his sergeant standing guard at the end of the hallway as people milled by toward their flights, never giving the isolated hallway a thought. Good, Clay thought as he placed the key in the lock, turning it to find a briefcase inside.

He shook it, receiving little sound, but the weight indicated there was something inside, and spread throughout the case. Without taking the time to open the case, he started toward Packard, sensing a greater danger holding the case than he had before.

"I don't like this," Clay said as his sergeant began walking side by side with him toward the exit.

"What are you talking about?" Packard asked, his voice a cross between bewilderment and anger that likely stemmed from his impatience with Clay's behavior lately.

"This isn't over by a long shot," Clay answered. "Khumpa will not rest until he has this in his possession."

Packard scowled a bit as they approached the security checkpoint.

"As soon as we get out these doors and get back to Muncie, this case is going into lockup and we're done with this mess."

Clay wondered how such a fiasco had begun. Khumpa was capable of murdering the Thailand guests several times over, and likely could have possessed the money from the beginning. Perhaps there was something the group had to wait for, but Clay knew from experience the terrorist was never satisfied until he had everything he wanted.

This time, that included Clay's own head on a platter.

Easily passing the checkpoint without incident, the two cops walked outside, finding Mitch and Sorrell standing guard at the vehicle with arms crossed, as though bodyguards for someone important inside. Clay's eyes met those of his cousin, but the stare was brief, because both knew there was business to finish.

"Is that what I think it is?" Sorrell asked.

"Yes," Packard replied in short.

Sorrell assumed the driver's seat once again, wasting little time in pulling away from the airport's busy drop off area.

"Check it," Packard ordered Clay, speaking of the cash inside the briefcase.

"This was too easy," Clay said, looking behind him, expecting to see a car following them.

"Was there any sign of the terrorists?" Mitch asked.

"Yeah, briefly," Clay replied without going into detail.

Now Mitch took to periodically looking behind him as Clay carefully opened the briefcase, finding even bundles of cash. Taking a bundle out for inspection, Clay stared a moment, realizing he had never seen such an abundance of money before.

"Uh, those real?" Sorrell asked, his eyes visible in the rearview mirror.

"Keep your eyes on the road," Packard ordered.

Clay looked the cash over, holding a hundred-dollar bill up to the light, verifying it had the security strip inside it.

"I can't imagine they're fake because no one else should have touched them," he said. "Still, if they're the real deal, why aren't they busting ass to find us?"

"We're cops," Sorrell said. "How many places are we really going to go?"

As Packard looked back to Clay, the younger officer suspected his sergeant shared the same vision with him. In his mind he pictured the Koda gunning down innocent civilians and police officers to get their loot.

He was about to dwell on the situation more when Packard's cellular phone rang.

"Hello?" the sergeant answered.

A moment passed as he listened to whoever spoke on the other end.

"And why should I believe you?"

Several seconds passed.

"Fine. But if you're lying to me, I'll put a bullet in your head myself."

From the tone of Packard's voice, Clay knew he was not particularly happy about talking to this person, much less believing him or her.

"Change of plans," Packard told Sorrell. "We need to swing over and hit Highway 35."

"Okay," Sorrell answered.

Clay remained silent a moment before speaking his mind about something.

"If those two at the airport were Koda hirelings, there's no telling how many more they've got under their wing."

"You said it yourself. Khumpa will dispose of his own people when he's done with them," Packard replied.

"Yeah, but they're all still alive at this point. Something tells me you're about to lead us into the belly of the beast, Tim, so I'm just making a casual observation."

Mitch turned to look behind him once more, which he had periodically done throughout the trip. Surrounded by cars on either side, it was too hard to tell if they were really being followed or not, so Clay gave up looking.

"That was Perry," Packard explained. "It seemed the Koda left him in the hands of a lone henchman, he overpowered him, and is now at their hideout alone. He says he got some information from the guard, including the fact that the terrorists were heading to Indianapolis. So, we're heading toward their base of operations to check on him, and if the bastards are following us, we'll deal with them."

"How's that?" Mitch questioned. "We have pea shooters compared to the fire-power they've got. As I recall, we've already been through that once, and barely escaped with our lives."

"I'm not so sure about getting on 35," Sorrell said of the highway. "You can, uh, go for miles and not see a car sometimes."

"We'd be isolated, and fucked if they follow us," Clay clarified.

"Better us than everyone at city hall if we try dropping the cash off," Packard reasoned. "If they want a piece of us, they're going to find us no matter what. You know they aren't afraid of opening fire in public places, so it's better we keep it away from city limits."

"And just maybe they aren't following us at all," Clay said doubtfully, his anticipation of confronting Khumpa eating his insides away.

"Just maybe," Packard echoed his words, though not sounding very optimistic.

CHAPTER 17

▼

When the officers finally found themselves on Highway 35, it seemed deserted. Granted, travel along the state highway was usually light, but traffic was incredibly slow.

Several times Mitch had looked behind him, seeing nothing, but that didn't mean the Koda weren't somewhere lurking, lying in wait.

"How do you know Perry isn't part of this?" Mitch questioned Packard.

"I don't. You didn't see me exchanging pleasantries with him on the phone, did you?"

Clay sat back, meditating on the situation while the others conversed. He wondered what to expect of the Koda, and if his destiny was to confront Sato at long last. Many times he pictured how the day he confronted Khumpa might look, but he never expected a gunfight like the Old West with his colleagues at his side.

His enemy had brought the conflict home, and killed without reason or remorse. At this point Clay truly didn't care how it ended. If it took his own life to kill Khumpa, he planned to die.

Staring out the window momentarily, the view went from fields, to country houses, to wooded areas. A few small towns, virtually villages, stood between several linking highways and Muncie. A gas station with a handful of groceries was the largest business for most of the towns, but the people likely enjoyed peace and serenity Clay guessed he would never know.

Mitch turned to look behind them once more, but he stared more intently this time. Clay noticed they were nowhere near a town at the moment, with fields on either side of the car.

"Oh, shit," his cousin muttered, still staring like a cat eyeing a bird trespassing on his yard.

"What?" Clay asked, turning around to see a car quickly gaining distance on them with two men who looked like they meant business.

"They aren't Oriental," Mitch noted.

"No," Clay said. "Mafia, like the guy who killed Punnim."

Packard seemed to take notice as well, then reached inside his jacket for his firearm.

"Ed, step on it," he ordered. "You two get your guns ready. They're going to try and take us before we reach Losantville."

By no means a metropolis, the town a few miles ahead of them had several businesses, including a bank, a gas station, and a carpet outlet. Clay watched as the passenger pulled out a long rifle from the floorboard, which he came to recognize as an M-16. Rather bulky for shooting from a car, the automatic assault rifle had more than enough firepower to make the metal and fiberglass of their own car look like Swiss cheese.

"Roll down your window for a clear shot," Clay told Mitch.

"*My* window? You crazy?"

"It's going to get shot out anyway," Packard reasoned, siding with Clay.

Though he looked reluctant, Mitch complied, then took aim with his semiautomatic at the passenger, since the driver was still concentrating on closing the gap between the two cars.

A momentary lucky break came their way in the form of an oncoming pickup truck, forcing the pursuing vehicle to swerve back to its own lane. Sorrell kept his eyes on the road from what Clay noticed as he readied his own weapon.

He rolled down his own window in case the car stayed directly behind them. As luck had it, the truck quickly passed, and the men in black suits were quickly over in the other lane again.

Clay looked to the front, reading the speedometer at over seventy miles-per-hour. He felt the car surge forth, knowing the speed was climbing, but their pursuers refused to give up.

As the opposing sedan crept up toward their own vehicle, the front bumper grazed their rear bumper. Clay knew one wrong tap, and their vehicle would hurl into an uncontrolled tailspin. Sorrell seemed to notice it as well, because he sped up, then wove in front of the other car, not letting it get close enough to do damage.

Clay noticed the passenger had his rifle readied with barely enough time to pull Mitch down to the seat as bullets sprayed the inside of their car from the strange angle behind them. Feeling no damage to himself, Clay peeked up, noticing the man was waiting for a clearer shot at them.

He was not out of ammunition yet.

"Everyone okay?" he heard Packard ask.

"Yeah," all three answered almost casually.

For the most part, their car seemed intact. Clay saw no holes on the inside, despite the power of the assault rifle. Still protectively pushing Mitch down against the seat, Clay felt his cousin trying to maneuver his pistol to a useful position while rising from the seat.

"Hey," Mitch complained. "I can't breathe down there."

"Just trying to keep you alive," Clay explained, seeing the opposing car draw closer for another volley of rounds.

Mitch took notice of the car creeping up as well, firing two shots into the windshield, both missing either man.

"Shit," he muttered.

"Step on it, Ed," Clay said with as much agitation as he felt.

"I can't push it any faster," Sorrell replied. "We're coming up on the next town."

An idea struck Clay, but he needed the right set of circumstances to place the other car directly behind them. If the passenger ran out of ammunition, that was another advantage to keep him safe if he chose to carry out his crazy idea.

"Ed, can you cut them off?" he asked.

Sorrell grunted to himself, looking in the rearview mirror, then to the side mirror. Their car cut over suddenly, but the pursuing vehicle refused to move. Instead, more bullets came their way, forcing everyone to duck. At that particular moment, Clay heard the worst noise possible from the front seat as Sorrell cried out in pain when the last few bullets struck.

Their car swerved back and forth along the road, finally sending the other car directly behind them in line. Clay took a quick glance to the front seat where Packard examined Sorrell, who was holding his left shoulder with his right hand while steering erratically with his damaged left arm.

He grimaced in pain while Packard attempted to help control the car. Sorrell was probably having enough trouble controlling the bleeding from his shoulder.

"He's reloading," Mitch noted, since he had been staring out the back the entire time.

Clay raised his firearm, then took deliberate aim, but found his actions caused the driver of the other vehicle to begin swerving. Attempting to time the driver's motions, Clay fired several shots when he believed the car was going to pass before him, like a hunter in a video game, waiting for ducks to fly past.

His shots missed their intended target because the driver was more talented than Clay anticipated. He was likely compensated well for his skills by his employer.

"Cover me," Clay told his cousin, rolling himself through the shattered back window, onto the trunk of the car.

"What the fuck are you doing?" Mitch asked in obvious surprise as Clay clutched the bottom of where the glass would be, to hold himself steady.

"Just cover me," Clay said, knowing they were quickly approaching the town.

He refused to let their battle endanger anyone at the intersection the two cars were nearing. To anyone else, what he was about to try was suicide, but if Mitch kept the two men occupied, Clay planned to end their conflict quickly. And if everything went according to plan, no lives would be lost.

Keeping a strong grip on the car's frame, Clay slowly gained his footing on the trunk, even as the unmarked police car swerved. Momentarily finding both of his feet steadied on the trunk, Clay began to stand up when the car jutted wildly into the left lane. Falling to his back, Clay barely maintained his grip on the window's frame.

He caught a glimpse of the M-16 making its way toward the outside of the car behind him, ready to spray him with bullets if he failed to make a move soon.

"Keep it steady!" he yelled to no one in particular in the front of his own vehicle. "Shoot at him, Mitch," he added sternly, nodding toward the man with the assault rifle.

To this point Mitch had refused to fire any shots, but Clay suspected it was because he was in the firing line. His cousin was sensitive about certain issues, including hurting innocent people. If he clipped Clay with a bullet, he would likely spend some time in the hospital's psychiatric ward after grieving to the point of a breakdown.

Even if it was just a flesh wound.

Mitch took a quick aim, then fired three shots into the windshield of the car pursuing them, creating multiple cracks along the window. This made it difficult for the driver and passenger to see, but also opened up Clay's plan to a more feasible conclusion.

With both cars riding steadily in a straight line, and the assault rifle temporarily out of sight, Clay stood, mentally measured the speed of both vehicles, then leapt subtly into the air. Putting his feet straight out in front of him, Clay let momentum sail him through the air, and feet-first into the windshield of the pursuing car.

His feet impacted with the chest of the passenger, who failed to turn the weapon on Clay fast enough. Clay felt the man jar against the back of the seat, then collapse from a lack of oxygen to his lungs. In the same motion, he used the back of his hand to chop the driver in the side of the neck, rendering him unconscious as he cut the flow of the carotid artery to that side of the neck. The man gave a quick cry of pain as he began raising his hand to his neck, but fell limp before aiding himself.

Still lying with his back to the dash, Clay realized he had just basically lost complete control of the vehicle by knocking the driver cold.

Taking hold of the steering wheel, he flipped himself over in one motion, setting himself atop the driver's lap as his foot searched frantically for the brake pedal.

Heaved breaths came from beside him as the passenger clasped his chest, which likely had Clay's footprints stamped across it in reddish flesh. Reaching over, the officer took hold of the assault rifle, tossing it to the back seat before the man regained any of his senses.

As Sorrell pulled the car to the side of the road ahead of him, Clay followed suit. He stepped out of the car hurriedly, his primary concern being Sorrell's health.

"He's okay," Mitch said, intercepting Clay between the two cars, clasping his right arm. "How are those two?"

"Alive. For now."

"I can't believe you just did that," Mitch said, his expression turning from serious to a cracked grin.

"I wasn't letting them take it to city limits. No matter what."

Packard stepped from the vehicle momentarily as Mitch went back to secure any loose weapons before the two henchmen realized their criminal careers were coming to an end.

"That wasn't very bright," the sergeant chastised. "You could have been killed."

"Or all of you could have," Clay countered. "I'm not going to allow that."

"You can't play guardian angel forever."

"I shouldn't have to, but these assholes keep coming after us. I'll deal with Khumpa and end this."

Packard gave a sour look.

"We started this together, and we're going to end it together," he said. "I'll help you kill that son-of-a-bitch if that's what it takes."

Clay sighed aloud.

"Right now we'd better find out exactly who these two are, and what they want."

"I think we know that," Packard noted.

Clay looked to their unmarked car, now riddled with bullets. Sorrell opened the door, clasping his left shoulder as he slowly stood. His face expressed the pain he felt as his right hand held a cloth to the shoulder, slowing the bleeding.

"How bad is it?" Clay asked.

"Bullet went clean through."

"He has to be the luckiest guy on the planet."

Packard smirked.

"After the week he's had, I'm not sure just how lucky he really is."

"His nine lives are about up."

Slapping Clay on the back, Packard started toward the car as passers by slowed to look at the two damaged vehicles.

"We'd better get this over with," the sergeant said, taking notice of the growing traffic. "Let's see what these two know about us and the Koda before we take them into custody."

In other words, Packard wanted to torture them if necessary before letting the two men fall into the regular judicial system.

"Whatever you say, boss," Clay said, following Packard's lead.

*   *   *   *

Perry felt a lump in his throat as he sat in the chair, ropes around his hands in the same room the Koda had left him in.

He heard noises outside, and if it wasn't Packard and his crew, Perry figured he was destined to regret his decision to remain at the headquarters to lure the Koda back.

His restraints were actually not holding him at all. He had loosely tied the ropes around his hands after hogtying his former captor, then leaving him a half mile down the road. Now he had a gun tucked along his backside, and little hope of using it if the Koda returned in full force.

For the next thirty seconds he watched several men of foreign birth walk through the front door, ending in four total. None of them were the figureheads of Khumpa's group, however, leading the agent to believe these men were sent to clean up the warehouse.

And any loose ends.

Now Perry hoped Packard believed him and came straight to the location. Perry still had no idea exactly where he was, but he recognized a few surroundings as those on Highway 35. Sometimes during the summer he traveled the road on long trips.

All four men seemed a bit too jovial for the agent's taste. They were cutting up, telling jokes, and occasionally looking his way. Two were holding guns, and the agent felt unsure if he was capable of shooting them both before one fired back.

Seeing no one from the leadership group present disturbed him, because he knew they were off to sabotage something or kill someone. He inched his finger toward the gun tucked into his belt as two of the henchmen walked slowly toward him, the smirks disappearing from their faces like dandelion seeds in the wind.

These two were the ones without guns, putting Perry's mind in a panic mode.

He suddenly had an idea of how Custer's last stand probably ended. His finger slid its way across his belt until it touched something cold and metallic. About to grab the weapon completely and fire away, Perry retained his composure, waiting for the last, desperate second before opening fire defensively.

As the two foreigners drew within grabbing range, one of the others posed a question, looking around the wide-open area of the warehouse. They finally realized their colleague was missing, and not anywhere around the premises.

One of the men with guns stepped outside to explore the grounds while the three remaining henchmen shot Perry dirty stares. He simply shrugged, putting forth a face devoid of any guilt, knowing full well they were not going to find their fifth man.

When the sound of a car pulling into the gravel drive outside entered Perry's ears and the fourth henchmen dashed inside, the agent knew Packard and his crew had arrived.

Eyes darted wildly as the four men argued about their plan of action.

From what Perry saw, they had no plan, and no time to create one.

Until their eyes all looked his way.

Their designated leader, one of the two with a firearm, said something quickly. The same two started toward him again, but he wasn't about to be held hostage while Packard and his men were placed in harm's way.

His right hand clasped the loaded weapon behind him, pulling it forward with a deliberate aim as his left hand helped steady the firearm.

Eyes wide with fear, the two men stopped dead in their tracks, then the leader took notice, aiming his submachine gun toward Perry and the two aggressors.

Rolling back from the chair, Perry took cover behind a plasterboard wall as the bullets flew by, clipping the other two men in the process. Fear made men dangerous to everyone in their vicinity when they were consumed by it. His background in psychology told him this Thailand native was as scared as a trapped rattlesnake, making it nearly impossible to take him alive.

Perry needed him alive because he wanted some answers. The last thing he wanted was Packard charging inside, shooting everyone.

"Perry?" he heard someone call from outside, directly through the wall where he was trapped.

"I'm in here," the agent shouted back to let the officers know. "There are two down, and two still standing with firearms."

"You okay?"

He recognized the voice as Packard's this time.

"Yeah. I'm trapped behind a wall, and I have the gun of my former warden."

"You suppose they speak English?"

"Doubtful."

Silence filled the air a few seconds.

Perry guessed the sergeant was sending his men around the building to flank the Koda's lackeys.

One of the fallen thugs began crawling toward Perry, threatening to expose the agent by pulling him out of cover, but the agent quickly kicked the man in the face, flooring him once more. He overheard the two remaining hirelings talking between themselves in their native tongue rapidly, as though they were extremely worried for their lives.

With Packard around, they'd better be, Perry thought.

Aside from three overhead doors, the warehouse only had one real entrance in front, and another door in back, which the agent knew was still locked.

He wondered how far he dared trust the sergeant, but Packard hadn't shot him through the wall.

Yet.

While Packard distrusted him for his leadership role in the task force, despite not knowing all the facts due to Furnett's deception, he considered the sergeant a cowboy in the modern world. Police were supposed to have checks and balances to keep them from violating rights and running corrupt task forces.

"Can you and your men shoot at both the front and back doors at the same time?" Perry found himself asking the sergeant through the wall.

"Yeah. In ten seconds, do what you're going to do," Packard replied.

"That would be ducking," Perry commented uneasily to himself.

Packard called out a command for all of his men to fire when he ordered them to do so toward the north end of the building. This prevented them from accidentally firing upon each other through the building itself.

Counting down the ten seconds, the agent safely viewed the two nervous men in the other room, then heard gunshots ring out as bullets came from both long sides of the building. Covering their eyes as they indecisively scrambled for cover, the two men looked as though they were dancing in the center of the warehouse floor.

Perry deliberately stepped around the corner of his cover, aiming the gun straight ahead. The two thugs were too preoccupied to see him coming their way until he fired a shot into one's kneecap, flooring him. Though the other seemed to have an idea of returning fire, he found the agent had already beaten him to the draw. He dropped the firearm as Perry called out for Packard.

"It's clear, Tim."

All at once both the front and back doors burst in, followed by four police officers. Perry noticed one of them was bleeding from his shoulder, but carried on as though nothing was the matter.

Packard looked to the two men, now beginning to cower because they were not true soldiers, then gazed at Perry.

"We had a little delay on the way here," the sergeant explained as his officers secured the two remaining terrorists in training. "It seems we came across the cash everyone is looking for."

"Everyone?"

"Well, the guy who lost his diamonds. I guess he's determined to get something for his troubles."

"This is sounding familiar."

Packard nodded.

"The guy who murdered Punnim is apparently part of a faction sent to recover diamonds, money, or both."

"So I take it you're trusting me if you're telling me all this."

"Can you prove you're on my side?" Packard requested.

"My partner had the terrorists furnished in every way, from weapons to their hiding place. He was being vague about Zhang's whereabouts for a reason. And he was conveniently on vacation when this whole mess started."

"Where is he now?"

"Dead. They killed him because they didn't want any loose ends."

Packard raised an openly skeptical eyebrow.

"And they brought you instead?"

"To get them out of the country when they were done. They apparently thought I could drum up extradition papers on a whim to get them out of the country."

An awkward silence filled the room a moment.

"Doesn't he need medical assistance?" Perry questioned, nodding toward Sorrell, who leaned against a wall for support, his blue eyes monitoring the prisoners cautiously.

"Probably," Packard answered, "but we can't afford to be rooted to any one spot for too long because of the money."

"Take them to city hall, or even the jail," Perry suggested.

"I thought about that, but city hall is by no means a fortress, and there aren't very many places to lock such a thing down at the jail. Prying eyes might find out what we've got here, then it's back to square one."

Perry thought a moment. He knew the group was in serious danger if they held on to the cash, especially with two merciless forces pursuing them.

"You can't keep running," he finally said.

"Actually, I have an idea that might solve all of our problems," Packard said with a sly grin, giving the agent an uneasy feeling.

CHAPTER 18

▼

After learning everything the group could from the two captured mafia thugs and the two Koda guards, the task force moved forward, knowing where Khumpa and the remainder of his thugs were hiding.

Packard left Perry behind to call the county police. From there the agent would handle the arrests and make certain the paperwork was started.

"You can't be serious about this?" Clay asked as Packard drove toward a bank.

Mitch had taken Sorrell to the hospital, while Perry dealt with the mess before the second phase of Packard's plan went into motion.

Clay was uncertain about Packard's aggressive tactics in this particular situation.

"If these puppies aren't safe in a bank vault, where will they be safe?" Packard asked in return.

"I'm not talking about that. I'm talking about hitting the Koda head-on. It's going to be dangerous for everyone involved."

Packard sighed aloud.

"I called in the SWAT team, and if the information is right, this should be an easy sting. They won't know what hit them."

"Assuming they aren't already tailing us."

"What's got you so wired? You afraid I'll shoot your buddy before you get your hands on him?"

Clay sat quietly a moment.

"I don't think you're grasping just how dangerous he is, or what lengths he'll go to just to get his way. He's not going to lie down and let you cuff him. Sato is a killing machine who knows no emotions, and has no remorse for anything he's done."

"So how did you two wind up going through this ninja training anyway?"

Clay forced a smirk with a brief chuckle.

"I told you before-"

"You're not a ninja," Packard finished. "I know damn well you're a lot more dangerous than you pretend to be, especially after the way you subdued those two punks at the airport. I just want to know how you and Khumpa wound up in the same training camp."

"It's called a *dojo*, and Khumpa was basically a mutt, just like me. A kid with no direction, no life to speak of. The master found him overseas before he ever came to America, and started training him with several other students."

"I thought these types of things were very secretive, and difficult to join."

"They are, but the old ways are dying out. I guess the master figured it was one way he could keep the traditions alive, by teaching students of different nationalities."

Packard made a turn onto a different street, cautiously looking into the rear-view mirror. He evidently saw nothing unusual because he dove into their conversation without hesitation.

"I seem to recall a tactical training session we had where Cooper wore the protective armor," the sergeant noted. "He beat everyone into the ground with that plastic club until you came along."

"So?"

"You had him down on the ground before anyone knew what was happening, tapping out and crying for his mama."

"What are you trying to say, Tim?"

"That you're definitely more than you let on to be."

"And I'm banned from tactical training sessions by our training officer."

Packard chuckled, apparently recalling the written order.

"Only because you refused when they asked you to teach some of that stuff."

Clay did so, but only because even the most basic moves and techniques took hours to practice and master. Western culture bred people with limited patience, so he knew his time would be wasted teaching his fellow officers anything from his past.

"So you can throw those pointy stars and climb buildings with metal claws and stuff?"

"Yes."

Packard gave a stunned look, as though he expected a different answer, or his officer to conceal his past further.

"And you could kill a man with your bare hands?"

"Yes."

Clay felt uncomfortable talking about his past, particularly since he worked for years to leave his memories of Japan overseas where they belonged. In truth, he knew what he was capable of, and what was necessary to stop Khumpa. Like himself, the man had uncanny abilities to sense danger, and a ruthless nature that forbid him from killing no one.

Even a SWAT team stood in harm's way with a man like that.

"And those pointy star thingies are called *shuriken*, Tim."

"Does the sword have a cool name too?"

"Not particularly. What I went through over there is almost a religion. You have to believe in what you're doing, and respect life, the world around you, and death. I've heard it said that if you die without realizing your intention, you die uselessly."

"And you haven't realized that intention?"

"Not until I see Sato dead. Only then will I think about living a normal life again."

"All these years I worried about you never having much of a social life. I guess now I know why."

Clay tapped his fingers against the leather arm rest on the door, while Packard simply gripped the steering wheel, looking forward as he drove.

"Maybe I dwelled on it too long, or just gave up on life because of the guilt I felt, but I missed out on some good opportunities."

Packard made another turn, hesitating before he spoke again.

"I'm not going to pretend to know what you went through, so I'm no critic. You have an amazing gift most any man, woman, or child would give almost anything to have. I just wish you would let the rest of us inside your head sometimes to help you out."

"I don't need help. There's only one form of therapy that's going to make me better."

"It's no coincidence he's here, is it?"

"Not in the least."

"Why would he seek you out after what he did?"

"Because he thinks I ruined his life."

Packard pulled into the parking lot of the bank, stopped the car, then stared at Clay momentarily.

"I'm not going to ask for details, because it's none of my business, but I need to know one thing before I condone you getting anywhere near him."

"If I spot him, you're not going to have time to condone anything."

"But...can you beat him?"

Understanding fully what Packard asked him, Clay had no real answer. In the world he and Khumpa trained in, life and death came swiftly. One wrong move, or the quicker of two cuts, made all the difference.

"I can kill him, yes."

"In the frame of mind you're in?"

Though somewhat comforted his sergeant cared enough to prod into his past, Clay didn't like where the line of questioning was going.

"You don't understand the warrior mind set we're trained in," he said, making certain his tone came across as upset. "When it comes time for the two of us to finish our business, we're not going to dick around, there isn't going to be small talk about who wronged who, and one of us is going to be left in a bloody heap."

Packard looked at him briefly, then turned his attention to the briefcase in the back seat.

"I just don't want that bloody heap to be you."

Clay refused to lighten his tone.

"I'm not making any promises, and if I don't come back alive, don't worry. I have no regrets, because I don't have much left to live for. Sato killed me years ago, and he knows it."

"Listen to yourself, kid. This isn't the same Clay who jokes around with his cousin and makes fun of Sorrell when the four of us are together. I realize I'm no saint, but you're starting to scare me a little bit."

"Don't go thinking I'm perfect either," Clay said, sensing something wrong with their situation.

He looked out his window, seeing plenty of cars in the parking lot of the bank. Taking a look in the other direction, he saw a van pull out from a spot, and several people walking toward the entrance doors.

"What is it?" Packard asked.

"Hold up a second," Clay said, slowly opening his door, then stepping out.

What he sensed as local danger initially formed something different in his mind as he realized Khumpa had played him, and the task force, for fools.

Pacing a moment with his hand cupped to his forehead, Clay knew, to some extent, what was unfolding.

"Clay? You okay?" Packard asked, cautiously stepping from the car.

"Tim, you might as well forget putting those in storage," Clay said.

"Why?" Packard questioned hesitantly.

Pacing the parking lot a moment more, Clay let his thoughts catch up with his sudden hypothesis.

"We never stopped to wonder where Khumpa and his group were, did we?" Clay asked his sergeant almost accusingly, as though they were negligent.

"I guess not."

"While we've been busy getting their precious money, they've been busy getting something more important."

Packard looked worried, and from what Clay had just figured out, he had every right to be.

"Clay, I don't like where you're going with this," the sergeant said, possibly getting the gist of what Clay had figured out.

"While we were busy getting their retirement fund, they've been busy collecting insurance," Clay deduced aloud. "So everything we've done is about to be in vain."

It all made sense. Khumpa's objective was partly to make Clay feel inadequate about defending his city's people from terrorists, while providing residents with distrust, possibly hatred, toward the police force.

"What time is it?" Clay asked.

"Mid-afternoon. Why?"

"Call your house."

Packard looked stunned, then worried beyond any sense Clay had ever seen from the man.

He fumbled for his cellular phone, then nervously pressed the button for his home number in its memory.

Several seconds passed with no answer, Packard's eyes shifting from his hand holding the phone to Clay's direction.

Finally, he hung up, starting for the car.

"We've got to get over there," Packard said with evident fear in his voice.

Clay jumped in the car, ready to assist however he could.

If they weren't too late.

In the meantime, Clay pulled out his own phone, deciding to make sure everyone in his family was safe.

*   *   *   *

Mitch sat in the emergency room area that treated blunt trauma, stab wounds, and gunshots, among other ailments.

He flipped through a magazine as the physician examined Sorrell's shoulder. With mock indifference, he stared as the man numbed the wounded area, then set to running stitches through the broken skin.

Very little in the room warranted a second look around. Mitch had visited enough hospital rooms to feel acquainted with their equipment. He hated the sterile feeling of hospitals, but felt some relief in how the management wasted no time beginning the repairs from the terrorist activities. By the look of every entrance he saw, the changes included more security.

"I'll be back in a minute," the physician said after several passes with the needle.

Mitch waited until the man left before saying anything to Sorrell.

"I don't even see why we're here," he commented.

Sorrell shot him a questioning stare.

"You should have your own room by now."

"Very funny," Sorrell retorted. "I'm surprised your fat head doesn't take some of these wounds for me."

Mitch gave a look of surprise because Sorrell actually had a reasonable comeback.

"He probably had to get more thread because he realized he needed to zip your mouth shut," Mitch chided.

"Uh, no, he needed to close yours. Especially since you're reading *Woman's Day* there."

"Huh?" Mitch asked, looking to make certain it was the science magazine he had picked up.

It was, and Sorrell had pulled a fast one on him.

"That does it," Mitch said, feigning anger. "I'm telling him to sew your dick to your pants."

"At least he wouldn't have trouble finding mine."

"Keep it up and I'll tell your wife about the time you puked after riding the Ferris wheel at the fair."

Sorrell put a finger in the air as he pretended to think a moment.

"As I recall, you had two beers less than myself, and, uh, blew chunks right beside me."

Both were forced to shut up and act professionally the next five minutes after the physician returned to finish the stitches in Sorrell's shoulder area.

"The nurses said you were in here earlier this week for a crushing injury to your forearm," the doctor noted.

"Yeah," Sorrell said. "It's not been my week."

"He's a black cat," Mitch said. "Don't let him cross your path."

Chuckling, the doctor examined his finished product a moment.

"That may be impossible, considering how often he's in here."

Sorrell didn't find the comment funny, but Mitch shot his fellow officer a sinister grin.

"I'll be back in a minute with a prescription for you," the doctor said. "I know it's a flesh wound, but you'll want to take a few days off work to let it heal."

"Try telling my boss that," Sorrell countered.

Shrugging, the doctor left them alone once more.

"Quit your whining so we can get out of here," Mitch said with a tone he knew Sorrell wouldn't take as serious.

He picked up a magazine once more, but Sorrell kicked it from his hands.

"If I wasn't afraid of using up your nine lives, I'd flip you off that examination table right now."

"You don't have the muscle or the balls."

Mitch grabbed hold of Sorrell's left foot, but Sorrell swung a pretend punch his way, backing him off.

"You're lucky the doc's back," Mitch said, pointing a finger at his fellow officer.

Sorrell just returned a smirk as the doctor handed him a few slips of paper, verbally giving some instructions.

Mitch heard the distinct tone of his cellular phone, indicating his cousin was calling him.

"What's up, cuz?" he answered.

"Mitch, I think the Koda are going to kidnap someone from one of our families as insurance to make sure they get the money and a clean escape."

"Whoa, whoa. Take it down about a hundred miles-per-hour and run that by me again."

Clay sounded rattled, which was very uncharacteristic of his cousin.

"We're heading to Tim's house right now. Ed needs to call home and make sure everyone is there."

"Holy shit," Mitch muttered slowly. "So that's where they were?"

"Yeah, and we were busy collecting their loot for them."

"Okay. I'll tell Ed right away."

Mitch was about to turn around, but Clay kept him on the line.

"After that, check on Bill."

"Uncle Bill?"

"Yeah. I called Emily and she said he went into his office to get started on the reconstruction of the hospital."

A realization struck Mitch like a pile of bricks upside the head. Of course Bill was going to be an integral part of rebuilding the hospital, since he filled out work orders, contracted companies for construction, and signed virtually every invoice that had anything to do with maintenance or repair.

"Fuck," Mitch commented under his breath. "Okay, I'm on it, Clay."

He looked to Sorrell, who already wore an expression as though sensing something wasn't quite right.

"What?"

"We need to call your house real quick, buddy."

*   *   *   *

Packard's breaths came in light heaves as he opened the door to his house, then stepped inside to find it empty. He frantically looked around a moment, then looked to the clock on the wall.

A quarter to four.

"Does Sarah have a cell phone?" Clay asked.

"No. She hates the things."

Usually she was already home with the kids, unless she stopped off for supper, or a few groceries. Her job allowed her to pick the kids up, so when the terrorist threat came to town, Packard insisted she do so, despite objections from his son and daughter.

He started into the house, looking through the kitchen and living room for any signs of a note, or a red flashing light on the answering machine.

Nothing.

"God, I hope you're wrong about this, Clay," Packard said.

"Me too."

Packard leaned against the kitchen counter, rubbing both hands against the sides of his head in frustration. He was accustomed to being in control of situations, but lately things had gotten out of hand. In the world of drug dealers and gang members, he controlled the right amount of people like a chess game. With terrorists, however, he was a fish out of water.

Khumpa was unlike any criminal he had ever seen or heard of. The man simply did as he pleased, and sometimes without obvious motives.

Only Clay seemed to have a grasp on the situation, and even he remained one step behind his nemesis.

Opening the refrigerator, Packard took out a beer and offered it to Clay. Naturally Clay refused with a shake of his head, so the sergeant opened it and guzzled it a moment. Technically they weren't on duty, but Clay didn't appear approving of him consuming alcohol.

"I'm coping," Packard said.

"From one vice to another?"

"This one's not habit," the sergeant replied, taking another sip. "I wish Sarah would get home already."

He wandered to the couch, unsure of what to do with himself. Usually by this time, if he was fortunate enough to be home at such an early hour, he spent time with the kids or watched the news.

Clay failed to offer words of encouragement, but that was only because the younger officer probably suspected more with each passing moment his guess was accurate. Packard's nature was never to sit around and wait for something, but it seemed more logical than cruising around a city of several square miles, hoping to find his wife.

"The money safe?" Packard asked his officer, wanting to make certain the one piece of collateral they possessed remained in their possession.

"Right here," Clay answered, patting the briefcase on the table beside him.

"I feel like I'm being held for ransom and I don't even know if they've got anything yet."

"Same here."

Packard shifted his thoughts toward Clay. He knew the younger man had been through an ordeal the past few days, barely escaping the explosion under the hospital, then nearly losing his uncle.

"Surely Khumpa figures your uncle blew up, tied to that pipe, doesn't he?" Packard asked.

"I hope so. The news has been focusing on the hundreds dead at the railroad tracks, so the hospital incident was overlooked. I can't believe Bill went back to work already."

"He probably didn't have much choice with all the structural damage to the hospital. They can't waste time when the power and oxygen are knocked out. You've got to figure there's hundreds of patients there at any given time, and they can't turn away people for very long. He's probably a key figure in getting that place back to standard operating procedure."

Clay forced a weak smirk.

"I *know* he is. That's what worries me."

"They must have restored the power if Ed was admitted to the emergency room."

"Sounds like it. That basement was a mess. I don't know about the structural integrity, but there was water and steam everywhere. It'll take weeks to get it all straightened out."

Packard didn't feel like conducting small talk, but it beat staring at the walls. He wanted answers, and the waiting game was killing him.

Clay perked as a noise came from outside the house. A few seconds later Packard heard a car pull into his driveway, momentarily curious how Clay sensed and perceived things so much better than other people.

Looking out the window, Packard saw his wife's car. He started for the front door, anxious for a report.

"Finally."

*   *   *   *

Mitch led the way through the basement hallways, surprised how little damage showed. Every pipe, whether carrying water or steam, seemed intact, and no cracks or discoloration were visible along the walls themselves.

He held his firearm in front of him, down along his waist defensively. Sorrell followed him closely behind, unable to draw his own weapon because of his compounded shoulder injuries.

"You gonna draw my gun for me?" Sorrell asked for the third time since they first entered the hall.

"No. I'm a better shot, and you'd probably use your good arm to shoot yourself in the foot."

"I feel naked without it."

"Shut up," Mitch warned. "My fat head is going to block any projectiles, remember?"

Sorrell said nothing, apparently recognizing the negative connotation of his earlier words.

Trying to be cautious, but anxious to reach his uncle's office, Mitch walked along the hallway, carefully crossing any intersections where terrorists might be lurking. He doubted Khumpa had enough nerve to return to the hospital, but if he wanted Bill dead, or as a hostage, there was little stopping him from entering the facility.

Even the guards were able to do only so much with visitors and patients flooding the hospital after the events of the past few days.

He rounded the corner, stopping suddenly as a maintenance man crossed his path. Sorrell bumped him from behind, then backed off. Wide eyes from the hospital employee stared at Mitch, who wore no uniform and displayed no badge.

"Muncie Police," Mitch quickly said. "Is Bill Branson around?"

"I have no idea," the man answered uneasily, not readily trusting the two cops.

Mitch wanted to question him further, but he wanted to find his uncle even more.

"Okay, go," he told the man, who wasted little time scurrying down the hall with a small toolbox in hand.

Continuing down the hall, Mitch felt a bit more at ease since he saw a living person milling about. He suspected everyone was busy repairing the hospital, or at least keeping it functioning properly. If Bill was around, he probably went unnoticed, making calls or inspecting various areas of the north tower to make certain it was safe for habitation.

Noise came from almost everywhere in the form of hums and running motors. Mitch felt somewhat unsafe because no one would ever hear noise above the machines, and Sorrell was basically a cripple in any kind of skirmish.

"Don't bump me again," Mitch said. "I'm holding a gun."

"Well don't, uh, stop like that."

Shaking his head, Mitch simply continued to the end of the hall, making a right turn toward his uncle's office. He had only visited Bill's office once, but the hallway was easily navigated. A wrong turn led into a main part of the hallway, so there only one realistic way to go. Eventually the hall led to the shops and the maintenance office, then a back exit.

Mitch rounded the last corner, seeing a light on within his uncle's office. He approached with caution, stepping to the blind side of the door. Turning to Sorrell, he pulled the officer's firearm from his left side, then handed it to his right hand.

"You shoot me and I kill you," Mitch warned.

"I used this hand to shoot at the academy," Sorrell said in his own defense.

"You whack off with that hand?"

"No."

"Then you don't really use it, do you?"

No answer.

"Stay put," Mitch said, sliding across the front of the door, which was mostly glass on the top half, looking inside as he moved.

He saw no one in the secretarial room, but a glimpse of someone in the back room where his uncle's office was located.

Suspecting the person was Bill, Mitch wanted to enter, but felt uncertain whether his uncle was alone or not.

"Back me up, but don't come inside," Mitch told Sorrell before turning the knob to the door.

He gave a nod, then pushed the door inside, unable to see inside the back office once he rounded the door. Bill probably enjoyed the privacy his office gave him, but this time the low visibility around the corner proved more of a hindrance than a benefit to Mitch.

"Uncle Bill?" he called.

"Mitch?" he heard from around the corner.

"You alone?" he asked in return, slowly making his way around the large desk seated right inside the doorway.

"Yes. To what do I owe the visit?"

Mitch rounded the desk, his gun held before him, then peered into his uncle's office warily, sticking his head inside to make sure nothing lurked behind the door or his uncle's desk. From behind the desk, Bill eyed him as though he was reaching a new level of insanity.

"You sweeping the building for terrorists or something?"

"No. Clay says the bastards are after one of our family members, so he wanted me to check on you, since you're idiotic enough to come back here after what already happened."

By now, Sorrell had entered the front door, apparently curious what he was missing.

"Well pardon me for having a job to do," Bill said defensively, adding a touch of irritation to his tone. "I had a hospital without power, without an oxygen supply, and damaged structurally in its most important building. I've solved two of the problems, and I'm making sure the third problem doesn't cave in, killing hundreds of people working and healing up there. If this bothers you or your cousin, that's too bad."

"Clay's worried Khumpa might target you."

"Why would he?" Bill asked, sitting back with an audible sigh.

"Maybe he knows you aren't dead."

"How would he?"

Mitch took one of the two open seats beside his uncle's desk.

"He could be watching your house. Maybe he's even watching Emily."

Bill sat back in thought a moment, a perplexed look crossing his face, then turning to frustration as his cheeks reddened.

"Damn you two. I can't be calling home every five minutes, checking on my wife. I about had myself talked out of constantly worrying, but you had to stroll in here and remind me, didn't you?"

"It's for your own good," Mitch said. "If you're not going to look out for yourself, we're going to keep watch over you."

Bill looked from Mitch to Sorrell, but the left-handed officer simply shrugged defensively, trying helplessly to replace his gun to its holster by reaching across his body. His paunch kept his hand from cleanly reaching around.

The maintenance director seemed unimpressed by the visit, and perhaps disturbed that the two officers lingered in his office, despite his relationship to one.

"I'd feel better if you were at home," Mitch finally said. "Or better yet, somewhere Khumpa wouldn't think to find you."

Bill reached behind him, pulled out a revolver, then set it atop the desk with a thump.

"I've already taken some precautions," he admitted. "And he won't be getting any assistance from me a second time if he comes around."

"Still, you'd be better off away from here."

"No," Bill said sternly. "And if you two don't leave, I'll have to call security."

Mitch smirked, then chuckled. They all knew it was an empty threat, and simply Bill's way of stating he wanted to be left alone.

"Yeah, right. At least do me a favor and lock your door."

"I will."

"Promise?"

Bill held his hand over his heart.

"Fine. I had it locked earlier, but all my people kept knocking and getting frustrated when they couldn't get inside."

"Maybe they need to be more cautious too."

Mitch stood from the chair, then motioned for Sorrell to follow him out.

"Hey," Bill called.

"Yeah?"

"Is Clay right on this?"

"Probably," Mitch replied. "We've called Ed's house, and everyone was fine," he said, thumbing toward his partner. "If it's no one in our family, that leaves our sergeant, and I haven't heard anything back from him or Clay yet."

"Who does he have?"

"A wife, son, daughter," Mitch answered slowly, feeling uneasy.

Bill nodded, looking to the family photos lining his desk.

"I hope everything comes out okay."

He seemed a bit more accepting than before, perhaps glad deep down that family members cared enough to check on him.

"Take care, Uncle Bill," Mitch said, leading the way for Sorrell as they left the office. "And lock that damn door," he called back.

*   *   *   *

Clay watched through the window, but divided his attention between the car outside and his sergeant's expression. He had a bad feeling about the entire situation, and when Sarah stepped from the car with a worried expression, and only her daughter, his heart sank.

"No," Packard muttered, flinging the door open.

Sarah stepped inside, immediately clasping her husband's arm.

"The school said someone picked Ryan up," she said, "but it wasn't a vehicle I was familiar with. What's going on, Tim?"

Packard said nothing as his face flushed and he rubbed his head in frustration. Removing a kid from school was no easy task, so the terrorists must have created a brilliant plan to evade any questions Ryan, or the school faculty, might have had about taking him.

Clay knew Khumpa had outsmarted them, but he wondered what the next step was as Packard took his wife aside, explaining the situation to her.

"How could you let this happen?" she demanded when he finished.

Clay wanted to take Nicole aside, but he was no good with kids, and she was old enough to understand her brother was abducted. Nothing he said was going to sway her opinion otherwise.

"I've been doing my job," Packard insisted. "I had no idea they were going to target any of you."

"Can you get him back?"

"Yes," Clay answered before his sergeant said anything regrettable. "They only want their loot, then we can get Ryan back."

"Oh, just like the several hundred people they let go at the railroad tracks? Or the dozen office workers they shot in the head so mercifully? You think they're just going to let Ryan waltz right back into our arms?"

"Sarah, you're upset," Packard said, taking her hand, trying to be reasonable.

"You're damn right I'm upset. My baby boy has been kidnapped and you're standing around thinking everything is going to fall right into place."

"We *will* get him back," Packard promised.

"How? You don't even know who took him, or where he is."

"They want what we have," Clay stated. "They aren't going to hurt him until they get it back."

Packard shot a glare as though it was the wrong thing to say to his already hysterical wife.

Nicole simply slumped on the couch, unable to comprehend exactly why everything was happening this way.

As Clay debated what to do next, Sarah began sobbing on the couch. Packard pulled her close, but he was able to provide little support for what they all knew had happened.

"Damn this task force," she muttered between sobs. "I wish you had never gotten involved with this mess."

Khumpa was ruthless, and certainly not above murdering a child for sport, or simply to add to his infamous terrorist group's name.

Startling everyone in the room, the phone rang from an end table beside the couch. Packard looked to Clay with questioning eyes, then slowly reached for the device after a small shrug from his officer.

"Hello?" Packard asked slowly.

Clay observed the sergeant listen a moment. Packard's eyes grew narrow as he breathed heavily, angrily, through his nose. Part of Clay's training overseas was to read emotions, to better defeat an enemy. Right now he considered Packard an easy target if he chose to confront the man.

Of course, he had no intention of ever doing so.

"You son-of-a-bitch," Packard stammered into the phone. "I want him back."

Khumpa obviously said something threatening, because Packard shut up and said nothing more. He listened a few seconds longer, then offered the phone to Clay.

"He wants to talk to you."

Now Clay felt awkward. He never expected to speak with Khumpa, or to have anything except a violent confrontation with the man the next time they crossed paths.

"Yes?" he asked, unsure of how to even greet his arch nemesis.

"Good to hear from you, Clay," Khumpa's voice clearly said over the line. "You and I have some unfinished business to take care of."

Clay said nothing.

"I'll keep everyone else busy tonight while you and I conduct our business downtown."

"Where?" Clay demanded evenly.

"There's no need to be hasty. I'll let you know the time and place later. Just come prepared."

Clay closed his eyes, exhaling heavily as his body shuddered at the prospect of confronting Khumpa.

"There's no need to harm the boy. This is between you and I."

"You know I would never kill an innocent being. If I get my retirement fund back, there will be no need for any bloodshed. Except yours."

Saying nothing, Clay clenched the phone. Khumpa lied blatantly about never killing innocent people, considering he performed such acts daily.

"You have no answer to that, do you, Clay? I always was better, and it'll take someone better than you to stop me. You can't even protect this pitiful city of yours from me. Tonight will mark the highlight of your failures, and the beginning of my destiny."

"What is your destiny, exactly? To rape, maim, and murder as many people as possible?"

"After what you've done to me, you have no right to question my intent."

"I've done nothing to you that you haven't done to yourself."

Clay looked to the Packard family, who listened with bated breath to every word he said. Their eyes were unblinking, wide with anticipation that perhaps he might deliver news, good or bad, to them momentarily.

"You robbed me of my position, my dignity, and my life as I knew it. I had no choice but to enact some form of revenge for those wrongs."

Clay felt rage shoot through his body, and a bit of moisture in one eye as the memory of his slain wife and child entered his mind. He let it pass, calming himself before he spoke again.

"You bastard. What you did cannot be forgiven, by me or God himself. I'll play your sick game, Sato. Tonight, we end this once and for all."

"You're more right than you know. As I said, come prepared. I'll call you with instructions later."

Clay heard a click over the line, then hung up the phone.

"What did he say?" Sarah pleaded.

"Nothing much concerning Ryan. I'm sorry."

"Will he let him go?"

Clay looked to the floor, then to his sergeant.

"I don't know."

"He wants me to bring the others to the Cowan Elementary School back parking lot at six-thirty," Packard revealed. "No SWAT team, no one else. He said his people would exchange Ryan for the money."

Clay refused to believe the exchange was destined to be so simple. He foresaw death and bullet rounds being exchanged.

"I can't trust him, can I?" Packard asked.

"No."

"And I don't have you coming along on this exchange, do I?"

Clay hesitated, knowing he needed to speak the truth to avoid raising his sergeant's hopes.

"Probably not."

Packard glanced from the floor, to a wall, then back to Clay.

"I'd feel a lot better if you were there."

"So would I, but he seems to have other plans for me."

Taking a step toward the door, Packard motioned for Clay to follow him outside. Clay did so, following his sergeant onto the porch as Packard closed the front door.

"What if I break the rules and take a whole team with me?"

"They'll kill Ryan, knowing full well they're going to be executed for terrorist crimes if you take them alive."

"What can I do?"

Clay thought a second, then an idea came to him.

"I have an idea, Tim. And it might just bring all of you out alive."

CHAPTER 19

▼

Packard still had no idea what exactly Clay was doing to help him as he let Sorrell pull their vehicle into the parking lot. He knew the Cowan high school and elementary school areas to some extent, but refused to scout the area beforehand. If the Koda caught him snooping around, it jeopardized their plan.

"What are we doing exactly?" Mitch asked one last time for clarification from the back seat.

"We meet Khumpa's sister and Zhang here for an exchange. We're supposed to come alone with this," Packard said, patting the briefcase full of cash.

"Why'd they take Ryan?" Sorrell asked.

Mitch cleared his throat before giving an answer.

"Because they knew we would follow Tim without question, and if it was anyone except his kid, he might be inclined to do things differently."

"But it *is* my kid, so let's do as they say," Packard said sharply.

Silence filled the car until Packard shifted in his seat. His leather jacket creaked a bit as it rubbed against the car seat.

Sorrell pulled around the main building of the school, allowing all three a view of the parking lot, several industrial trash bins, and a playground in the distance. Aside from a car parked in the center of the parking lot, Packard saw nothing unusual.

"You'd better hope Perry is a team player," Mitch said. "If not, we may be gunned down like we're mafia lackeys done wrong."

They had dropped the agent off half a mile back at a four-way stop sign. Perry rolled out of the car quickly enough that anyone watching probably never noticed anything odd. An embankment into a ditch concealed his initial drop point, and he said he planned to find the most discreet, quick way to the parking lot.

He was their only backup unless Clay managed to make the trip before he was summoned by Khumpa.

Dusk began settling across the fields around the school, though there was light enough to see details in most everything around the three officers.

Packard made certain there were firearms tucked into each of the car's four doors, and that each officer had a secondary weapon concealed in his ankle area. He suspected the terrorists meant to disarm them, but he refused to become defenseless prey for them to murder at will.

"Tell me again why my cousin isn't here," Mitch requested.

"I'm not sure he isn't," Packard said. "But he's going to confront Khumpa tonight, no matter what happens."

"And how do we know Khumpa isn't here?"

"We don't."

Packard knew he left no reassurance in the hearts of his officers, but he questioned his own judgment for going against standard departmental procedure. Officers never went into situations like this without a foolproof plan and lots of firepower.

He had neither.

In case he was unable to assist in any other way, Clay gave Packard three small, metallic-coated balls about the size of ping pong balls. He instructed the sergeant about what they were, and how they needed to be used. Their purpose was distraction or escape if things went bad.

Even if Clay guessed correctly, and the Koda were truly down to their two leaders, without any henchmen left at their disposal, they had a strategic advantage. Even if the three cops outnumbered their adversaries, they faced the possibility of being disarmed to get Ryan back. At that point it was up to Perry to save them, because Packard planned to comply and let the terrorists think they had won.

Clay's destiny hinged on a phone call, and the sergeant realized that. In the officer's mind, he had one opportunity to stop Khumpa, and those who might follow his lead, from spreading their evil across the world.

If Khumpa called, he was bound by duty and honor to confront the man.

"I hope Clay knows what he's doing," Packard muttered.

"I hope we know what *we're* doing," Sorrell said uneasily.

Still restrained by his sling, Sorrell was of little use in a firefight, Packard surmised. His entire body had taken a beating the past week, but he never complained about contributing. Packard had new respect for the man, especially since it took nothing more than the mention of Ryan's abduction to hear "I'm in" from his lips.

"If things get bad, you're going to have to whip us out of here quick," Packard told Sorrell, who was the best trained of any of them behind the wheel.

"Okay."

Sorrell pulled the car to a stop as Packard swallowed hard, unsure of what to expect from the situation. He knew he wanted his son alive, no matter the cost, but he felt guilty dragging his task force into his problem. It was his fault they were stuck in this dangerous web to begin with, little more than fodder for the terrorists to pick apart.

He saw two adults sitting in the other vehicle, and recognized them instantly as Zhang and Issaree Khumpa. Though he struggled to look behind them, he did not see his son in the back seat. He was going to be furious if they had stuffed his son in the trunk.

Or worse.

For a moment everyone sat in their respective vehicles and stared coldly. Packard took a deep breath, then opened his door, ready to see what cards fate dealt him.

*   *   *   *

So far, Perry had accomplished his part of the plan perfectly. He managed to skirt along the road without being detected, and at the same time monitored the area for any signs of additional terrorists.

Seeing none through his trained eyes, he felt confident they were about to surprise the Koda and overtake the confident murderers.

Getting Packard's son back was his priority, but after the business of dealing with the terrorists ended, he planned to investigate Packard and his task force thoroughly. It went against his better judgment helping the man this way, but if he didn't agree, Packard planned to leave him out completely.

Now he crawled along the ground leading up to the school's front yard, still searching for lingering thugs. Dressed down from his usual attire, Perry wore sweat pants and an old college sweatshirt, now stained with grass and mud.

His primary firearm was nestled beneath his armpit in a shoulder holster, while another rested along his ankle. With dusk came cooler temperatures, making the ground wet and slick. Perry felt relieved when he finally reached the building.

Taking a careful look around, he spotted no one along the front of the building, and nothing across the street. There were no places to hide out front, so he began sneaking along the wall, staying close to the brick structure to make certain he wasn't spotted.

If memory served him correctly, around the corner was a large dumpster, and a jutting corner that led to one of the school's back entrances. He saw headlights from the car, but they were further back in the lot, allowing him plenty of space to sneak around the corner. From there he could set himself in place to act when necessary.

Preservation of Ryan's life was his motivation, and the only reason he truly agreed to help Packard. Whether he was willing to admit it or not, Packard needed all the manpower available, against trained terrorists.

Perry listened a moment as car doors finally opened, drawing his firearm from the shoulder holster, readying himself for action. As he stepped around the corner, however, a pair of arms crashed down upon his forearms, knocking his firearm to the soft ground.

No one heard his trouble as an imposing man, taller and more muscular than himself loomed over him. Perry had no time to react or think of strategy before a hand slapped itself around his throat, hurling him against the brick wall, knocking the wind from him.

A groan emitted from his throat as every muscle in his back ached. He felt even worse when a fist rammed into his stomach, but he refused to yell out for fear of compromising Packard's operation. This man was not one of the terrorists, and if he guessed correctly, this was the man Clay confronted when Punnim was murdered. Extremely powerful, knowledgeable, and quick for such a tall man, he had the agent fearing for his own life.

He was intelligent enough to keep Perry from mounting any offense, and quiet enough to avoid disturbing the transaction about to take place.

Perry assumed he wanted the money to compensate his employer, or for himself. If he wasn't stopped, Packard and his officers might be killed from behind with no chance of defending themselves.

His caution led the man to hold up an imposing open hand, giving the agent some warning that it was coming his way. Perry ducked as the hand grasped for his throat, probably to cut off his breathing on a permanent basis.

Ramming his right fist into the larger man's stomach, Perry felt an instant ache in his wrist from the impact, assuming he had caused little damage to his enemy. Backing away, he found himself close to the metallic dumping bin, worried he might collide with it, creating a noise that might distract everyone around.

As he waited for his attacker to regroup, Perry tried listening to the conversation down the hill in the parking lot, but heard nothing yet.

His opponent seemed to sense his need for silence, so he charged suddenly, launching one fist across Perry's face before the agent could react. Stunned, Perry felt another ram him in the gut, then both of the man's forearms crash down upon his back when he hunched over.

Groaning lightly to himself, he felt himself picked up by the sweatshirt before a large hand clasped his throat. From there, he felt his feet leave the ground as the larger man hoisted him in the air, slamming him down to the unforgiving earth below. Rolling to one side, Perry saw the man reach inside his coat, probably for a silenced weapon.

Through the cobwebs in his mind, he knew he needed to act, or die at the hands of a heartless killer, bent on retrieving material goods for his master.

CHAPTER 20

▼

Clay had planned on backing his sergeant and Perry at the school, but a disturbing call kept him from carrying through on his trip to the school.

Khumpa phoned, stating he was at city hall, and there would be a sign of where to go when Clay arrived.

With his gear in the back of his car, Clay felt ready for the confrontation, though not entirely thrilled about the games his nemesis played with him. That was vintage Sato, playing mind games to gain an advantage.

As Clay pulled into the parking lot of city hall, dressed in his police uniform for the time being, he decided to look past the games and underlying messages Sato sent him. He had dressed in his uniform for reasons of access.

If Sato chose a private area to finish their business, Clay needed a way in. He wasn't about to scale walls and leap fences, only to fall into traps set by his enemy.

A conventional entrance served to keep him safe.

Stepping from his car, Clay looked around the parking lot, finding nothing unusual. A patrol car was parked near the main entrance doors of the three-story building, meaning someone was probably downstairs filling out a report. He wondered what Sato meant about finding a sign at city hall about their next meeting place.

He felt the gun belt along his side, carrying his firearm, handcuffs, pepper spray, and an ASP baton, among other things. His tools of the trade were different in Japan, and he often preferred the tradition of toting a sword as men did hundreds of years ago before him.

Of course in Japan, he never carried his weapons in town. They were used and worn exclusively around the *dojo*, but he lived and breathed the traditional way of life.

As he neared the entrance doors, Clay felt uneasy, as though he was being watched. A sixth sense was developed by members of his clan, and he certainly felt uneasy at the moment. Nonetheless, he opened the first set of tinted glass doors, then used his swipe key to turn the red light on the magnetic lock to the second set of doors green.

Now unlocked, the doors let him pull them open to step inside.

Strangely, no one sat at the information desk in the center of the four-way intersection on the first floor. Sometimes called the penalty box because officers not in the chief's good graces were stuck there for duty, it provided a way for citizens to see a police officer any time of day.

Even officers monitoring the desk needed restroom breaks, but he felt uneasy as he passed the stairwell door and the elevators, hearing nothing except silence. The usual hum from the water fountain to his right entered his ears, but he was listening for footsteps or any kind of unusual sound.

Nothing came.

Stepping forward, only the noise from his duty boots echoed through the vacant hallway intersection, where district court was held during the day and people came to pay their city bills.

He reached the desk, noticing a glow from the television mounted inside the large enclosed desk where the officers usually sat. Someone was monitoring the desk, but no one was there at the moment.

Drawing closer, he peered over the top of the desk, which came just over his waist in height, finding a disturbing sight on the floor below.

Beside the rolling office chair, huddled into a fetal position, lay a body with blood streaming from the throat area. From the look of the sergeant who was murdered, Sato had done it recently. None of the blood had dried, and as Clay stepped inside the centralized desk, he touched the body, finding it warm.

He knew Gerald Fyke as one of his father's friends on the department, so this felt somewhat personal. Whether Sato knew it or not, it hurt Clay deeply to see the officer dead. The attack was unnecessary, but designed purely to make Clay feel inferior and powerless.

Fyke was the man who first showed Clay around the police division in city hall as a kid. He and several other officers were ultimately responsible for helping him do well on the test, and in the interview, to make the department. Their advice made the difference. They were the same officers who kept him from getting in worse trouble as a kid, and scared him straight a few times.

His decision to travel to Japan with his mentor was partly because of their advice to find himself and grow up right. Now, one of the men he idolized as a child lay in a heap, atop his own blood on the floor. Training told him not to touch the body because he might contaminate evidence, but he decided not to roll the body over, fearing he might see the man's blank death stare looking through him.

Clay bowed his head a moment, then cleared his head to look for a note or some sort of sign about what he was to do next.

He found an open cellular phone atop the man's pants with a phone number already typed in. Pressing the talk button would call the number, so Clay assumed that was exactly what Khumpa wanted.

Scooping up the phone, he walked to a secondary entrance point of the building to avoid being seen by any incoming fellow officers. He stepped outside, pressed the button, then listened as it rang twice on his end before being picked up.

"So nice of you to join me, Clay," Sato answered.

"You murdering bastard," Clay said softly enough that no one around the front parking lot might hear. "You've proven your point. Let's cut to the chase."

"There's one piece of unfinished business to take care of," Sato replied coldly. "It seems Vincent Panelli has stuck his nose in our business too many times this week."

What is he talking about? Clay questioned inside his head.

"He's the man who wants the diamonds back, or a healthy amount of cash for compensation, and he's holed up downtown in the new apartment complex your downtown development committee just helped rebuild. He's heavily guarded, but that's half the fun. We can't have any loose ends running around, can we?"

"Don't do this," Clay stated, knowing many of his bodyguards were probably family men, possibly ex-cops.

He wanted no part in murdering anyone, especially people trying to make a living.

After being chased that afternoon by two of them, he questioned their moral fiber, but he was not about to play God, regardless.

"It's too late. I'm already outside the building, waiting to strike. You're welcome to stop me if you like, but you'll have to be quick. I want it to be just you and me when I'm done. Just follow the trail of blood and you'll find me."

"No," Clay said under his breath in a distraught tone as a click reached his ears through the phone.

He closed his eyes, took a deep breath, and prepared to do the unexpected. Falling into Sato's sick games was bad enough, but now he was about to be implicated in murder if he failed to stop the man. He wanted no part of this secondary fight, but that was Sato's strategy. If Clay hesitated or questioned his own actions for a second, it gave the Thailand native a distinct advantage.

Taking the phone with him, he headed for his car, prepared to do what he could to stop Sato from murdering more people.

✽   ✽   ✽   ✽

Khumpa had already scaled the building beside the new apartment complex when he phoned Clay with the invitation. From his vantage point, he saw most everything he needed to prepare a strike against a dozen or more men.

Panelli, like most men in his position with wealth and power, figured he could buy his protection, even in a smaller city. Importing his goons from Chicago was going to be of no help to him, Khumpa figured, because he had no other advantages. He was holed up inside a building with too many windows to be defensible, and no active alarm system that Khumpa had seen.

Though the building was finished aesthetically, it didn't have the final touches necessary to allow it to be rented. Panelli had to know someone politically in the city to have attained the building, but Khumpa didn't care about minor details at this point.

He had a job to complete, in order to secure his own retirement.

Most of the buildings in the area were three stories in height. Both the building he was perched on the roof of, and the renovated apartment building were typical brick buildings, fitting the standard mold.

With barely any sunlight remaining, Khumpa felt safe from being spotted. Several guards were posted at the front door, virtually daring anyone to cross their path. They carried no visible weapons, but he detected they were armed to the teeth from the lumps in their sport coats. He wanted no attention drawn to himself, so they were destined to be the lucky ones.

For the past five minutes, the same man dressed in a black suit had walked the second floor hallway facing Khumpa. He seemed attentive, looking out the windows periodically, methodically taking his time during his walk to inspect every door he came across, and every noise his ears detected.

He also carried a radio, but Khumpa had yet to see him use it, meaning he probably didn't have to check in periodically with his colleagues. Even so, Khumpa planned on wasting little time dispatching of the guards dressed in dark suits once he gained access to the building.

As the guard walked to the end of the hallway, he readied his bow with a specially-devised arrow that had a flexible, light wire cord attached to the back of it. Coiled behind him like a cobra, the rest of the wire cord was designed to unwind easily once the arrow took flight, following the shaft wherever it landed.

The arrow head itself had a four-sided, thick blade that pierced most any material, then screwed itself into the surface from momentum alone. This allowed the cord behind the arrow to be pulled snug.

Khumpa had studied the man's patterns enough to know he was due to return in about a minute, so he prepared himself on the rooftop, using his feet to push the bow outside as he maintained a grip on the bow's cord and the arrow. Assured the wire would not cut him when it followed the arrow, Khumpa breathed deep and slow, ready for the ensuing battle.

He had studied this man enough to know he wore a wedding band, appeared former military from his stance and rigid walking style, and had a firearm tucked beneath his sport coat in addition to the automatic weapon strapped around his shoulder.

If anyone made a worthy first target, it was this man. He posed enough threat to warrant his execution before any of the other guards Khumpa had spied.

As the man crossed the window during his rounds, Khumpa timed the guard's gait, then let the arrow soar through the air at a frenzied pace.

The entire incident took only seconds to unfold and end as the arrow bore through the window with little more than the sound a of pebble tapping the glass. Following its path, it pierced the guard's throat through the side, killing him within the second it took his body to realize it was doomed. His hand reached up defensively to his throat, but fell limply to his side before it ever touched the wound.

From sheer momentum, the arrow pierced the man's throat, then continued into the wall behind him, screwing itself into the building materials. Luckily for Khumpa the entire window had not shattered. The arrow pierced so quickly it only cobwebbed a bit from the impact hole.

Dead weight from the body tugged downward on the wire, but Khumpa had expected no less. He had killed two birds with one stone, so to speak. Tugging the wire tight, he wrapped his end around an exhaust system behind him, leaving a downward descent to the second floor of the opposite building.

If the building were farther away, he might have used a pulley wheel attached to a handle to slide down the rope for quicker access, but it was only about the length of two vehicles away. He took hold of the rope, tested it with his weight while still above his initial building, then started down the rope, hand over hand, creeping closer to the second story of the mobster's hiding place each second.

In less than a minute Khumpa stood readily on the second floor, after carefully lifting the window beside his entry point. He found himself face to face with a mirror along the hallway after examining the dead body. He stared at himself, dressed in black, wearing the traditional ninja outfit called the *shinobi shozoku*, including the scarf that served as a combination mask and hood, concealing his identity in case someone saw him from a distance.

Only his eyes were visible through the face piece.

He thought about disposing of the dead guard, but it seemed simpler to jam one set of doors shut, then exit through the opposite doors, killing everything in his path.

Khumpa quickly jammed the doors with a wedge normally used to keep them open, then silently opened the opposite door, finding a universal lobby devoid of people. Several unpacked boxes containing television sets, furniture, and lamps sat across the spacious area. They were no doubt part of the building's next phase of life, an apartment building for residents wanting a downtown apartment and the trinkets that came with the high price they would pay.

With only three floors, there were going to be guards spread out seemingly everywhere. He assumed the mafia boss was shielded on the third floor, so Khumpa planned to make his way there after ensuring no one interfered with his intentions.

The lobby he stood within had doors behind him and to his left. Both were shut, which he assumed was a security measure for the henchmen to know if an intruder had carelessly left the door open.

Grinning to himself beneath the mask, Khumpa turned the knob, deciding to leave the door ajar just enough for someone to notice.

*   *   *   *

Clay drove past the apartment building once to make certain he knew which area Khumpa had spoken about on the phone. Seeing three guards posted at the front door, he decided not to approach in his police uniform. If Khumpa went on a successful killing spree, which Clay had every indication he would, Clay served only to implicate himself if he let someone see his face.

Particularly in a recognizable uniform.

After parking his car a few blocks away at the Radisson Hotel, to make certain it wasn't obviously isolated, he opened his trunk, taking a large duffel bag out.

He found an alley, changed to the traditional *shinobi shozoku*, with mask and hood, and went about picking which weapons suited him best from the bag. He tucked them into pockets, loops, or the sheaths along his back, then carefully placed the bag in a dumping bin where he planned to recover it later.

If he died, his weapons went out with the trash, doing no harm to anyone else.

Dying was something he had long since come to terms with, especially if it meant ridding the world of Khumpa.

Clay made his way up the alley with silent steps, drawing dangerously close to the three men guarding the door.

Dangerous for them.

Taking out a short bamboo shaft, he reached into a pouch, carefully plucking a tiny dart from its casing before loading it into the weapon. He carefully measured the distance in his head, accounted for the slight breeze, and waited for one to round the corner for an inspection of the building's side.

With one powerful blow from the gun, Clay downed the man almost instantly as the dart struck his neck at the jugular vein, rendering him unconscious. He slumped to the ground, unheard by the other two guards, both dressed in dark suits.

Leaving his position for the corner the first guard had just rounded, Clay took out another dart, loaded it, and decided to wait until one of the men turned or left before firing it. With only one left, and no one observing from the inside of the building so far as he was able to tell, the third man would be easily dealt with by any number of means.

A few seconds later, the third turned to light a cigarette, leaving Clay an opportunity to strike his partner with a dart. Making a slight, brief groan, the second man fell to the ground.

"Hey," the man said, bending over to check his partner as though he might have passed out for some standard reason, shaking him slightly at the shoulder.

Clay rounded the corner in a flash, striking him with a short, wooden staff in the head, leaving him unconscious as well.

To avoid taking more time than necessary, he searched the men for keys, finding a set to unlock the front door with, rather than picking the lock. He let himself inside, then dropped the keys to the side, locking the door to ensure the men did not interfere if they were to wake up.

His blue eyes peered through the open area of the mask, allowing him to see inside the second set of doors, spying two more men sitting in the lounge area. There was no good way to surprise them, and he knew for certain Khumpa had entered through an elevated position because his wire remained snug between the two neighboring buildings.

Waiting meant creating a greater chance of Khumpa successfully killing everyone else, so Clay had no desire to create any more delays than necessary. If he waited, one of them would probably come to check on the other three anyway, so he decided to open the door and take his chances.

*   *   *   *

After Packard opened his door, his officers followed suit. All three men stood outside the car a moment, the sergeant holding the briefcase for the two terrorists to see. He felt absolutely dirty handing over a fortune to a group that deserved nothing less than the death penalty.

He spied his son in the back seat of their car, letting him know his decision was right, and would be a hundred times over if he had to decide.

Warily, the two terrorists opened their doors, pulling guns out with them. Packard made no sudden moves because he, Sorrell, and Mitch were shielded by their own car doors, and he hoped Perry was in position to help in some way. A distraction of some sort, or a wounding of one of the terrorists was Packard's best hope.

Both Mitch and Sorrell had drawn their firearms, but Packard kept his hands on the briefcase and his eyes straight ahead. Neither of his men held their weapons in a ready position, because Packard had instructed them to maintain a defensive posture, to avoid gunplay if possible.

"I want to see the money," Issaree said, nodding toward the briefcase the sergeant held.

"Let me see my son," he asked, rather than immediately complying.

A sour look crossed the woman's face, but she opened the back door, yanking Ryan from the back seat. His hands were bound in front of him, but he appeared completely unharmed. His face bore a look of pessimism, as though he didn't expect his father to rescue him from the two monsters holding him captive.

"The money," Issaree demanded again, holding Ryan in front of her.

With the moment of truth at hand, Packard fumbled for the correct action to take. If Perry was in position, he was supposed to fire a shot, or make some sort of noise by now. Suddenly Packard's mind filled with doubt.

What if a third terrorist killed the agent?

Was Perry on their side after all?

If he moved from his spot, was Packard destined to be gunned down?

Instead of moving anywhere, he simply opened the briefcase, displaying the contents to Issaree from the short distance between their two vehicles.

"It's all there," Packard stated.

"Bring it to me," she ordered.

"I'll meet you halfway," he countered. "When I hand them to you, I want you to let him go."

"I do not negotiate with police," she sneered.

"And I don't negotiate with cowardly terrorists."

Issaree pulled Ryan close, putting the gun up to his head. The look on Ryan's face sunk his father's heart, because he never wanted his boy to be so terrified of anything. Now he had little choice except to comply with her wishes.

"Bring it now," she said.

Sighing to himself, thinking the end of his life drew near, Packard stepped away from the car door. He took one step forward when an echoing metallic noise reached everyone's ears, causing them to freeze momentarily in place.

Packard knew instantly it came from the industrial dumping bin, but he wasn't sure from what. His eyes met with Issaree's as Ryan backed away from her, while she was momentarily distracted. She seemed to sense Packard had something to do with the noise as her eyebrows lowered with anger.

"Run, Ryan!" Packard shouted to his son, who was already several steps behind the terrorist.

She spun around to take action against Ryan, but a gunshot rang out from Mitch's firearm, clipping her in the shoulder. Caught in the middle, Packard dove behind the door as Zhang fired an automatic weapon in his direction.

"Fuck!" Packard said to himself, hitting the concrete hard, quickly checking himself for any projectile damage.

His jacket had protected him from serious scrapes and scratches, but his left elbow jarred against the concrete. Though not broken his funny bone struck the pavement, leaving it momentarily numb.

He heard shots from his officers, and automatic gunfire simultaneously as he drew his own weapon. Reaching into the car, he groped for the shotgun, pulling it to him as he observed things from the ground.

Both Mitch and Sorrell were standing, but that quickly changed as Sorrell took a bullet to the shin. A splatter of red liquid spewed from the leg, then it gave way, collapsing Sorrell to the ground in a heap. His face appeared agonized, and for a moment he seemed to forget exactly how much danger he was in, so Packard crawled halfway under the car, pulling the officer under the vehicle with him.

"Stay here," he ordered Sorrell, who had little chance in any kind of fight with his injuries.

Sorrell's only reply was a groan from the pain as he clutched his leg, temporarily forgetting about the gunfight around him.

Packard regretted leaving Mitch alone momentarily, but he quickly scanned the area again from under the car, firing a shotgun blast into Zhang's kneecap to return the favor for Sorrell. Zhang hobbled on one leg, which kept him from firing the automatic weapon at Mitch.

Deciding to avoid a cumbersome situation by racking the shotgun with no available space under the car, Packard set it down, scooping up his service weapon, which was temporarily laid by his side.

Taking careful aim, Packard watched the man's good leg, then fired again, clipping Zhang's healthy calf muscle, bringing him down like a chopped tree.

As he slid to the other side of the car to finish off Zhang, he heard a shriek from Issaree, who had likely been hit by Mitch. He regained his footing on the other side of the car, found Zhang reloading his weapon, and aimed at the terrorist just as the magazine clasped itself into the Mac-10 the terrorist had been firing.

Propped with his back against the car, Zhang spied Packard, then whirled his weapon toward the sergeant, who had already stood from a kneeling position. Packard fired first, hitting the terrorist in the chest, sending spurts of blood into the air because the bullet hit so close to the heart.

A loopy look crossed Zhang's eyes, then he slumped fully to the ground. A small stream of blood trickled to the ground from his chest, then stopped, because his heart had stopped.

While this had been occurring, Packard missed everything else on the other side of the vehicle. No sign of Issaree or Mitch was evident from the driver's side of the vehicle, so he quickly, but cautiously, rounded the back of the car, finding his other officer on the ground.

"What the hell happened to you?" Packard asked Mitch, taking his side.

He saw Issaree laid out by the driver's side door of her own vehicle, a small pool of blood by her side. Packard assumed she was dead, but his primary concern was keeping Mitch from joining her in the morgue.

Mitch's breaths came in heaves, and one look at the man's side told Packard why. A bullet had pierced the side of his armored vest where the velcro pieces kept it together. How a bullet had reached that area was a mystery to Packard, because he had an entire car door acting as a barricade, and no reason to expose that side to Issaree during the gunfight.

Zhang never left his post, so that only left one explanation.

Perry had aligned himself with the terrorists and shot Mitch from somewhere out of sight.

"Don't you leave me," Packard ordered Mitch, pulling out his cellular phone.

He glanced behind the other vehicle, seeing no sign of his son, which was exactly what he wanted.

"Getting cold," Mitch mumbled through labored breaths.

Reaching into the car, Packard snatched a towel he sometimes used to clean his weapons, placing it against his officer's side with pressure to control the bleeding.

"Ed, you okay?" he asked, dialing 911 on his phone to get an ambulance started their way.

Packard heard no answer from Sorrell as he placed the phone to his ear. He heard it ring once, then something tugged him from behind, by his jacket's collar, with enough force to throw him two parking spaces from where he was.

After tumbling end over end several times, Packard came to a stop, then looked at an ominous figure looming over him, dressed in black.

"God, no," he muttered as two large hands reached down for him like the God of Thunder, Thor, selecting an ox to devour.

CHAPTER 21

▼

Khumpa waited less than a minute for his prey to show up. It came in the form of an older guard, probably close to middle-age, with peppered, parted hair, who looked suspiciously at the door as he entered the lobby.

He failed to notice the figure above him like a spider, braced in the corner of the ceiling by arm and leg strength alone. Looking around the room, the man seemed to be curious where his colleague might be, but not overly concerned, as though the man might commonly disappear for short intervals.

Or perhaps Khumpa guessed correctly, and the initial guard was one of the better employees, so good that the others didn't need to keep track of him.

Khumpa preferred to think he was correct.

Hearing no other voices or footsteps in the distance, the master of *ninjutsu* decided to end this conflict before it began.

In one swift motion, he released his position from the ceiling, pulling his sword from its sheath along his waist before his feet landed on the floor.

"What the?" the man asked, startled by the visitor who had swooped upon him.

He reached for his gun, but Khumpa simply waited until he had the weapon halfway drawn, severing the man's hand at the wrist with a clean cut from the sword. A cry of pain from the sentry was quickly silenced as Khumpa ran the sharp edge of the blade across the man's jugular vein, creating a gurgling that replaced any other vocal sounds.

The man's hand clasped his throat, but he fell to the floor in a heap before any of the injury could be attended to.

Khumpa examined the body a moment, hearing a set of footsteps from the hallway behind him. He decided not to hide, because he knew Clay was coming to confront him. A need to make his adversary feel further inferior drove Khumpa to continue his murderous ways without hesitation.

He silently darted to the end of the hallway, waiting for the next guard to round the corner. Khumpa drew his *kusari-fundo*, a short chain with small weights at each end, and waited for the steps to draw closer.

For far too long he had used modern means of weaponry and treachery to maim and murder his prey, but nothing felt as rewarding as the traditional means. Feeling a man's life slip away in his hands was an almost orgasmic experience compared to the distant kill, using a sniper rifle or automatic weapon.

As a bearded guard rounded the corner, Khumpa held the weapon in one hand, letting one weighted end fly upward toward the man's throat. He followed the path of the weapon by swinging around the side of the guard, prepared to catch the opposite end of the chain. This would put him in position to strangle the man with ease, but the unexpected happened.

Already holding an automatic weapon with a long barrel, the man simply raised the gun with quick reflexes, catching the *kusari-fundo* long enough to deflect it and duck out of the weapon's original path.

His next move was predictable to Khumpa as he placed the gun in a ready position to fire, but the warrior kicked the gun uselessly away from the guard. Reacting quickly, the man took a defensive martial arts position, unprepared for Khumpa's next use of the chained weapon.

In one swift move, Khumpa swung the chain around the man's arm, which locked itself into place. Khumpa then tugged downward, flipping the guard hard onto the ground, back first.

Khumpa kept hold of the chain, and the man's arm, following him to the ground with a front roll. He landed perfectly with the guard's arm extended helplessly in his grasp. Any number of choices were his for the taking, including breaking the man's arm at the elbow, locking his head with his legs to snap the man's neck, or using any number of his other weapons to kill the man instantly.

With the wind knocked from his lungs, the guard had grunted upon the landing, now stunned several seconds while Khumpa decided his fate. He seemed a worthy adversary in the normal world, but against someone of Khumpa's training level, he was simply a training dummy.

One of the first lessons Khumpa learned from his master in Japan was to never uselessly expend time or energy. He always had a difficult time listening to that piece of advice because it took the fun away.

Knowing the automatic weapon was far enough away that it could not be picked up, Khumpa released the arm lock, letting the man roll to one side, then regain his footing. He appeared perplexed, as though he knew he was outmatched, but forced to continue fighting in futility.

In Japan's warring days, the samurai often used dead bodies for sword testing, where they checked the sharpness of their blades. It also served to help them learn the most vulnerable parts of the body, so their swords cut the most effective areas.

Khumpa rather enjoyed this technique, though it was commonly outlawed centuries ago overseas. In his adopted method, he tested his weapons on victims of his own wars, but he preferred them to be alive when he did so.

He had already decided this man was to be spared for such testing, because he had managed to avoid certain death once.

Khumpa felt somewhat embarrassed his attack had failed, so this man was to die slowly and painfully once all matters were settled with the only man in the city capable of giving Khumpa any real fight.

Wasting little time, the guard swung at Khumpa, but the terrorist simply ducked the punch, kicking the guard in the abdomen, leg, and shoulder area with a single leg before the man fell to the ground.

Wounded, but with nothing broken, the man hesitantly rose to his feet, took a martial arts stance, and kicked at Khumpa, but the terrorist ducked, sweeping the man's other leg out from under him. Landing hard on his back, the guard grunted in pain, but Khumpa gave him one more opportunity to regain his footing and strike.

Instead, the man remained in a lying position, then reached for his radio, prompting Khumpa to attack before he transmitted any vital information.

Kicking the radio from the man's hand, Khumpa dropped down to the man's torso, forcefully thrusting the back of the guard's head on the floor, rendering him unconscious. Khumpa shunned himself again for being careless, but this man was destined to pay dearly, after Clay Branson was gone forever.

A voice came over the radio unit, then another, drawing Khumpa's attention because they were questioning where some of the guards were.

Quickly gathering and replacing his weapons, the terrorist darted down the hallway on his toes, barely making a sound through the split-toed footwear adorning his feet.

He checked the remainder of the second floor, finding one of the guards missing. From his initial scouting of the area, he knew one guard was positioned near the elevator at all times. With this man missing, Khumpa wondered if he had gone upstairs, or went in search of the missing guards.

From a nearby door, Khumpa heard the flushing of a toilet, then looked from side to side, formulating a plan of attack.

Only one prisoner was allowed to survive for sword testing, so this man had to die for Khumpa to ascend the building and complete his objective.

He found a place to hide as the door from the restroom opened.

*   *   *   *

An odor of fried fish and some sort of vegetable reached Clay's nostrils as he remained outside the second set of doors momentarily. He observed one of the guards radioing something, then looking confused, likely because there was no response.

After saying something to the other guard, he walked toward a visible stairwell, allowing Clay to sneak into the front lobby while the second man went to tend to their supper.

Now the sounds of frying fish and boiling water entered his sensitive ears, along with the sounds of stirring, like a wooden spoon scraping along the bottom of a pan.

Deciding to waste as little precious time as possible, Clay waited around the corner for the man to stir his components on the stove. As the man returned to the lobby, Clay immediately struck him in the arm at a nerve point, rendering the man's right arm useless for about fifteen seconds, if he was lucky.

Immediately on the attack, the man wildly swung his left arm, but Clay countered by swinging his leg around, into the man's ribs. Neither Clay, nor Khumpa, were trained expertly in bone breaking, but they were both powerful enough to crack ribs and snap smaller bones through holds. Clay was incapable of breaking a femur with a kick to the thigh, because such training needed to be taught from childhood.

As the man clutched his ribs, reaching for a gun or his radio, Clay took a *shinobi-zue* from the pack attached to his back. A cane of sorts, the *shinobi-zue* traditionally conceals daggers, full swords, an embedded spear, or chain with a weighted end. This particular model housed a chain on one end, and a small sickle on the other, which was easily activated when Clay pressed a small switch.

Refusing to kill any of the guards, Clay simply used the blunt end of the weapon to jab at the man's injured ribs, creating further pain for the guard. He quickly forgot about reaching for whatever weapon he meant to grab, then swung his right fist at the disguised police officer.

Clay dodged the blow, striking the man in the kneecap with his staff, creating a new painful area for the guard. Not waiting for the man to recover, Clay kicked the knee again, sending the man crashing down on both knees. He then spun a roundhouse kick toward the man's head, rendering him unconscious with the blow.

Without hesitation, he reached the stove, shutting off two burners before moving the two pots to the cold burners on the back. The last thing he needed was a fire alarm going off in the middle of his one chance to stop Khumpa.

He eyed the stairwell, hearing footsteps come down.

"Mark! Come quick!" a man's voice echoed from the nearby stairwell before the second guard returned to view. "I can't find anyone up there!"

Clay replaced his weapon to the pack on his back, then darted silently to the staircase, waiting until the man appeared before kicking him solidly in the sternum. The blow sent his back against the wall, allowing Clay to throw an open-handed punch into the sternum, stunning the large guard.

Like most of the guards, he appeared to be in great physical condition, but a punch aimed at Clay's face was easily deflected as Clay took hold of the man's arm in a braced position, launching him into an opposing wall.

He struck face-first, breaking his nose, which caused blood to ooze down his face. Flushing red with anger, the man swung wildly at Clay again, but the officer easily anticipated the move, catching the arm as he threw the man to the ground, following him down with a punch to the nose once again.

Striking the already broken bone, Clay observed the man clutch his nose in obvious pain, then pulled a short staff from his side. He raised the man helplessly to his knees before striking him in the side of the head with the staff, ending his misery.

At least until he regained consciousness.

Again, Clay looked to the stairs, knowing what waited for him a story or two above was the event that would change, or end, his life.

With catlike silence and quickness, he darted up the stairs, determined to find his nemesis before more damage was done.

*   *   *   *

With everyone else around him dead or critically injured, Packard found himself in a fight for his own life. Yanked to his feet by a man almost a foot taller than himself, he was hurled across the parking lot, trying to land with his arms tucked to prevent him from tumbling, or breaking any bones.

He hit the ground hard, bouncing like a discarded piece of furniture until he came to a stop, his body feeling like it had been beaten with a stick across every square inch.

His mind raced for a solution to avoid being hammered to death by two huge fists.

The man was not Perry, and he was likely the reason the agent was missing. Wearing a suit of black, with a face chiseled from stone, the man was obviously a cold killer, sent there with one objective in mind.

He briefly considered snatching the snub-nose .38 holstered around his ankle, but the two hands forcibly wrapped themselves around his jacket collar, pulling him once again. He felt himself launched shoulder-first into the back of his own vehicle, barely able to shift his weight enough that his collar bone didn't snap like a twig.

Regardless of his efforts, his shoulder and arm muscles felt like someone had used them for baseball practice with a metal bat. He groaned audibly, falling to the ground like a discarded sack of potatoes.

Packard had dropped the briefcase near the passenger side of the car, but this man meant to ensure no witnesses were left when he took back his boss's prize.

"Where are the diamonds?" the man asked as Packard scrambled to get any kind of defensible position on the concrete.

Apparently acquiring the money wasn't satisfactory.

Packard sat on the ground with knees bent and arms behind him, somewhat like a fiddler crab, looking up to the ominous man.

"The Asians have them. The money is near the car."

As the man turned to look, Packard charged him with every bit of strength he had left. By no means a small man himself, the sergeant's thick shoulders plowed into his adversary's abdomen, but the move had little effect.

For all intents and purposes, he bounced off the man like a pebble thrown against a wall, tumbling backwards, yet prepared to defend himself when the man threw a fist in his direction.

Packard ducked the blow, ramming his own fist into the man's stomach, determined to do damage there, since reaching the man's head was impossible until he brought him down to his own height.

Finally he felt some give to the man's rock-hard stomach, hearing an audible exhale of forced air with a painful groan. Packard swung an elbow into the man's temple as his head hung momentarily from the last punch.

His assault was short-lived, however, as the man pushed him away defensively, then clocked him with a jab that came and went with speed and power Packard had never seen before.

Falling straight back, the sergeant felt blood ooze from his nose as his head felt like it was spinning. He tried collecting his thoughts before the next onslaught, but a foot propped against his upper chest, just below his throat, pinning him to the ground.

Packard struggled to remove the appendage from his throat before his windpipe was crushed, but there was enough weight behind it to keep him from doing so. With a cocky, sinister grin, the man looked down to him. Feeling more weight applied to his throat, Packard felt dizzy as he began seeing flashing orbs around his head. Lack of oxygen was putting him close to passing out.

"It's just business," the henchman said evenly, applying more pressure to the sergeant's throat, even as Packard tried kicking at his hind leg to trip him up, or at least release the hold. "Don't struggle. I'll make it quick and painless for you."

"Like hell," Packard said between labored breaths, snatching a glass shard that brushed against his left hand, stabbing it into the man's calve muscle, cutting his own hand in the process.

The pain was welcome, because it allowed him to breathe again.

He rolled back from his assailant as the man pried the glass from his leg. As he placed himself in a kneeling position, Packard reached for the small caliber gun at his ankle, undoing the latch, then wrapping his fingers accordingly around it as the large man charged him once more.

Without adequate time to draw the weapon, Packard found his face receiving a hard knee from the man, sending him tumbling back once again. His firearm took several bounces away from him before landing between the two men.

Looking into the man's eyes, Packard saw desperation and fear for the first time in a split-second before both leapt toward the weapon.

Quicker and lighter, the sergeant gained his footing just long enough to literally dive for the weapon. He snatched it, landed hard on the ground, and found time to roll away from his adversary before the man clutched him again.

Without hesitation, Packard aimed the weapon upward at the man. Even kneeling on the ground, the man seemed huge. No longer did he seem arrogant, but he wasn't giving in, either. He stood, then took two deliberate steps toward the sergeant, who was still reeling from the earlier scuffle.

"Don't come any closer," Packard warned.

Another step.

"Stop."

Another step.

"Stop, damn it," he said with considerably more emphasis.

Packard wanted this man alive for questioning. If the two terrorists were confirmed dead, he needed someone to piece together the facts. His story would have more holes than a strainer, otherwise. Now less than a car length from him, the man seemed determined to somehow take the sergeant with him if he had to die.

Another step.

A gunshot rang out, echoing through the barren fields around the school, as a stunned look etched itself across the man's face. Blood dripped from his mouth as he fell to one knee, gave Packard an awkward stare, then collapsed completely.

Along his back, a small pool of red formed from a bullet wound, which gave the sergeant every indication of where the shot originated.

He looked to the garbage bin where the noise had come from earlier, finding Perry lying stomach down on the ground, his hands limply dangling along the ground. His semiautomatic pistol laid before him, but he looked to be in no condition to use it beyond the shot he had just fired.

Packard evaluated the damage around him, finding no one capable of movement, except Sorrell, who had taken Mitch's side, trying to keep him alive.

Both of the terrorists lay dead beside their vehicle, while Perry appeared to be unmoving, possibly even dead.

In the distance, Packard heard some form of sirens, and another look to Sorrell indicated the officer had completed Packard's original 911 call.

He felt numb, being the only person left in decent physical condition. Though he wanted to check on everyone's condition, he needed to find his reason for being there first.

"Ryan?" he called through the night air, hoping his son heard him. "Ryan? Come here!" he shouted.

Sirens continued coming his way, and by now he recognized the blaring air horn as that of a fire engine.

With no sign of his son, he began crossing the parking lot, continuing to call his son's name. Fears that a stray bullet had clipped his boy crept into his mind, but Packard fought the notion, refusing to give up hope.

His heart sank as the sirens drew closer. Torn between his son and the men he endangered to get Ryan back, Packard decided to tend to the others and ask the incoming firefighters to help him search when a figure appeared at the opposite end of the parking lot.

"Ryan?" Packard asked himself, stepping forward.

CHAPTER 22

▼

When the man emerged from the restroom, waving a newspaper in front of his nose to mask the smell that followed him, Khumpa waited patiently from the corner behind the man's chair.

A big-screen television took up most of the wall, hiding the thin Khumpa behind its dark form perfectly. He blended with the shadows, leaving little indication he was there, unless someone made a point to look around the side of the electronic device.

Stationed beside a window, and near a door, the chair was in a perfect position for someone to monitor every entry area of the room that led to the third floor via staircase or elevator.

Entirely concealed behind the wicker chair, Khumpa observed the man glance around the room, then sit in the chair, never looking behind it.

Careless, Khumpa thought.

He realized he had little room to criticize others, after allowing the hospital to remain standing, and functioning. With his face plastered across every newspaper and television station, he dared not return to the scene of the crime. He had observed the destruction at the railroad crossing from a distance the morning after the explosion.

If he had religion, he might have felt remorse for the hundreds of bodies lying in the street, beside stores, cars, and gas pumps.

Having religion meant practicing mercy.

Therefore, he had neither.

Waiting patiently, hardly breathing a bit, Khumpa almost felt guilty about murdering the guard, but in a cat toying with a mouse sort of way. His carelessness had left him open to attack, but most conventional military men and police officers never checked every corner, or every piece of furniture, unless their purpose was to search.

This man's objective seemed to be returning to the article in his magazine.

Silently reaching into the black cloth of his uniform, Khumpa retrieved a *kyoketsu-shogei*, which basically is a medium-length rope with an unusual small sickle at one end. The sickle itself looks like half a spade with a curved point, and another sharp point extending upward from the center.

As the guard engrossed himself in the article, Khumpa carefully moved from behind the television, careful to make no shadows within the man's peripheral vision.

Surprised when the rope draped around his neck in two quick loops, the guard reacted as Khumpa figured he would, groping for the object cutting off his oxygen, rather than turning on his assailant. He flailed to and fro, trying to loosen the strands cutting into his throat, but Khumpa kept moderate pressure on the choke hold, toying with the guard.

After a few seconds of struggling, the man reached inside his sport coat for what Khumpa assumed was a firearm. He despised that Clay had sold himself out to his old American lifestyle, becoming a police officer. In doing so, he abandoned his traditional ways, carrying firearms as his primary source of defense.

Khumpa doubted Clay even bothered to hide his traditional weapons inside his belt buckles, or his shoes, for fear his fellow officers might discover his past. Khumpa had no shame about his past, and that was why he knew he was destined to kill his adversary.

Clay was soft, weak, because he gave up his tradition, and his will to live, when he returned to America.

In the meantime, Khumpa imagined the man struggling in his grip was his true adversary, taking up the bladed end of the weapon. Raising it above his head, he struck swiftly, lodging it in the man's skull, killing him instantly, painlessly. There was no blood, no mess. It was perfect, as it would be when Clay died at his hand.

He decided it was time for more trickery, so he pushed the button for the elevator, which was sure to attract the attention of someone.

As the car rose from the first floor, Khumpa heard the man's radio sound as the remaining guards questioned aloud who was operating the elevator, and for what purpose. He chuckled maniacally to himself, watching the elevator doors open.

He stepped inside, quickly scouting the cramped space for the best way to fulfill the next phase of his plan. The breadcrumb trail was already in place for Clay, but he wanted a larger than life finale to shock the officer even more.

Clay was about to learn why, deep down, he never wanted to find Khumpa in Japan. If he had tried hard enough, he would have found the man named Sato. Though Clay was the apple of their master's eye, he was no match for the skill and experience of the slightly older Khumpa.

He was about to find that out.

$$*\qquad*\qquad*\qquad*$$

What Packard thought might be his son turned out to be a concerned neighbor who crossed a secondary parking lot and the school's playground to check on the commotion.

"Everything okay?" the short woman asked as she drew near Packard.

"Not exactly," he replied. "Have you seen a small boy around by chance?"

She shook her head negatively.

"Do you need me to call the police?"

"We are the police," Packard answered almost distantly. "It's been taken care of. Could you do me a favor and call for the missing boy? His name is Ryan."

"Sure," the woman replied.

"He ran off that way," Packard said with a pointed finger.

He wanted to look for his son more than he cared for his own life, but he was ultimately responsible for three other men with him, all of whom suffered wounds.

Walking toward his own vehicle, he took a moment to check for a pulse on either of the terrorists, just to make sure no surprises came his way. He looked at Zhang's wounds, knowing he had done the job right the first time.

Issaree Khumpa, however, he needed to verify. As he knelt beside her body, he stared at a wound in her lower shoulder, near the heart. A large amount of blood appeared across her throat, which he assumed was the fatal wound. He could not distinctly see a wound, but there were coarse pieces of what he thought appeared to be fleshy chunks embedded within the blood. The lack of lighting kept him from seeing much detail.

She was not breathing, and he felt no pulse, so he walked over to Sorrell, who was putting pressure on Mitch's gunshot wound.

"How is he?" Packard inquired.

"Not good," Sorrell answered, his own wound causing him to grimace as he spoke. "I hope the ambulance gets here soon."

"Me too," Packard answered. "I'll be right back."

Sorrell nodded.

As he approached the FBI agent, Packard felt certain he was already dead. Wet blood glimmered from the man's back as he lay face-down on the ground. Kneeling beside the man, Packard felt for a pulse, finding none. He spied a gunshot wound that went clear through Perry's stomach, out his backside, leaving a mess of blood and dangling flesh in its wake.

"Thank you," Packard said silently, feeling remorse for the man who had no family, and little left to live for toward the end of his life.

Perry must have fought agonizing pain just to survive long enough to kill his own murderer, Packard deduced. If the man's dying shot was that accurate, Packard hated to imagine how precise he was on a regular basis.

He guessed the man shot Perry with a silenced pistol, probably after a struggle, but the agent fell or stumbled against the dumping bin. That likely created the noise that triggered the shootout between Packard's men and the two terrorists.

It also gave the henchman opportunity to take a clear shot at Mitch.

He knew the departments would form a task force, and the ballistics experts might piece together a scenario from all the recovered bullets and trajectories.

Packard returned to Mitch's side, since he was the only person left to save. Sorrell maintained pressure on the wound, but the towel appeared to have significantly more blood on it. Dropping to his knees, he touched his officer's skin along the neck, which felt cold and clammy. By no means was the sergeant an expert in medical science, but his limited first responder training told him Mitch was in serious trouble.

"Don't you leave me," Packard said, unsure if Mitch was able to hear, since his eyelids were fluttering.

"That an order?" he asked weakly, confirming he was still conscious.

"Yes."

"Fight it, Mitch," Sorrell said. "Keep talking to me."

Packard heard the fire trucks draw near the school. He looked to Sorrell.

"You tell them exactly where we were?"

"Uh, yeah," he said with a second or two of hesitation.

Packard quickly stood up, grabbed the briefcase, and tossed it into the trunk for safekeeping. As the first pumper truck pulled into the back lot, he waved it down, then approached the first man stepping from the truck to ask for blankets and any medical supplies they had.

"You're lucky we were all at the station for a meeting," the officer in charge said once Packard briefly explained the situation.

He wanted to stay with Mitch, but he wanted to find his son more. There was nothing he could do to help his officer, because the firefighters were better trained in emergency medical techniques. Besides, Packard was always a bit squeamish around blood and death when it concerned someone close to him.

As several of the firefighters tended to Mitch, with Sorrell keeping close vigil, Packard turned to the fire department officer in charge.

"Thanks for getting here so quick."

"No problem. That's what we're here for."

Packard hesitated a moment before asking his next question.

"Say, can I get a few of your guys to help me look for someone?"

*   *   *   *

As the elevator car reached the third level, Khumpa listened carefully, standing atop the car itself, while two armed guards spoke between themselves, as the elevator car doors opened.

"I can't reach anyone down there," the first said, pressing a button to keep the doors forced open.

From the emergency hatch in the car's top, he spied both men through the tiny crack he had left between the hatch and the opening. The first had a full goatee of black, with his hair buzzed about half an inch from his scalp. He seemed serious, but not very attentive. Khumpa figured him former military, because he was impatient and rash. Already he saw the man wanted to dash downstairs to see the problem, not realizing he was endangering himself by not comprehending the danger first.

The second man, dressed in a dark suit, held an Uzi submachine gun at his side, appearing more calm and collected. He kept his chocolate-colored hair parted, with a thick mustache just above his lips. Closer to middle-age, he seemed in no hurry to investigate, his focus remaining on their employer, as it needed to be.

"If we go down there, it leaves Kyle by himself," the second man said, revealing exactly what Khumpa wanted to hear. "We stay here and wait it out. It's probably just a radio malfunction of some sort."

Spying something along the floor, the first man knelt to investigate. Khumpa had purposely spilled blood droplets on the otherwise tan floor with the intent of distracting whoever checked the elevator first.

He was about to get a two-for-one special.

"What's this?" the first guard asked, swiping up a sample of the blood with his thumb and forefinger. "Blood."

"That's not good," the second said, losing a bit of his poise.

Standing, the first guard seemed to be lost in thought a moment.

"We need to tell the boss."

"You kidding? He's about to lose his top as it is, with Clark gone so long."

Khumpa pulled two short spears from his pack, about nine inches each, readying himself for an attack. Each end of the weapons had sharpened points, capable of penetrating flesh, muscle, and bone with the correct force behind them.

"He'd better get those diamonds back or the boss'll be pissed."

Hearing the words, Khumpa hesitated. Suddenly he knew who they spoke of, and wondered if the man was endangering the plans he and his sister worked out to eliminate the cops and retrieve their retirement funds.

Deciding it didn't matter, he quickly wrapped his legs around a stable part of the elevator, armed each hand with a short spear, and tossed open the hatch without so much as a sound.

His torso appeared from above like a fish born into the water, wriggling its way from the womb, except his movement was smooth. Both guards looked up simultaneously, trapped within the elevator car, hypnotized by the object in black seemingly hovering above them.

Wasting no time or movement, Khumpa twirled the spears in his hands effortlessly, like a cheerleader might spin a baton. With both guards watching his hands, he studied the puzzled looks on their faces.

Sheep following a shepherd to the cliff's end, he thought, stopping the twirling momentarily.

"What the hell?" the first guard asked as the second man looked at him with a confused stare, then returned his gaze to Khumpa.

As he effortlessly twirled the spears in his hands once more, Khumpa had any number of places to inevitably stab the weapons, but he decided he wanted discretion. As both men turned their heads his way for the last time, apparently incapable of moving or making a decision because of the bizarre nature of his attack, he let the spears find their marks.

If he had chosen to stab them anywhere in the cheeks or throats, and missed his mark, there was a very good chance the men would have screamed in agony before dying. Ordinarily Khumpa had no trouble hitting precise marks, but with two targets, and the potential for either moving, he decided to avoid any mishaps by simply plunging the spears into the corner of their eye sockets. Such an action allowed the spears to penetrate their brains for an instant kill.

Neither fresh corpse remained standing for more than a few seconds, and no noise was uttered from either victim. If time had permitted, he might have collected one of them for sword testing, because he liked multiple victims.

And he had lots of swords to test.

Time barely permitted him time to kill the remaining henchman and Panelli before Clay caught up with him. He had little doubt the last guard was holed up with the mafia boss in some room, which he suspected was at the end of the hallway.

Khumpa kicked the two fresh bodies entirely inside the elevator, allowing the car to travel to the lower floors in case Clay preferred avoiding the stairways.

If he had noisily murdered the two guards, he might have drawn out the last man, but risked allowing Panelli an opportunity to phone the police. A door was no object for a man of Khumpa's skill to overcome, but he wanted to invoke fear into Panelli before the man died at his hands.

He needed to lead the last man out, to allow Panelli to witness his death firsthand. Only then would the mafia overlord realize what a tragic mistake he made in coming after his diamonds.

Khumpa hoped his sister was able to dispose of the last henchman before he complicated things. He had faith in Issaree, because she shared his black heart. She had no second thoughts about putting bullets in people, particularly Americans, when business was at hand.

On his toes, Khumpa darted down the hallway, scouting each door he passed, convinced the last door was his target. He heard voices inside, indicating he was correct, which brought a devious smile to his face, still concealed beneath a veil of black cloth.

*   *   *   *

Clay assessed the damage on the second floor, realizing from the bodies he discovered, the men guarding Panelli never had a chance of defending themselves.

Vintage Sato, he thought.

Khumpa was all about tricks and deception. He also took advantage of the weak and unprepared. Only someone of his own skill level could stop him, but he killed with no regard or respect for his power.

Or his tradition.

Clay found the first man with the thin cable ran through his neck from where the arrow had pierced his flesh to lodge itself in the wall.

He found the second man with bloody injuries to his throat and wrist, which had bled out severely, despite his heart stopping seconds after the attack began.

Last, he found the guard rendered helpless, bound with a roped weapon. Clay knew he was the fly to Khumpa's spider, meant to be murdered later when Khumpa's appetite for death returned. He knew of the man's sword testing techniques, shaking his head to himself as he undid the bonds, despite the man remaining unconscious.

If he died during the battle with Khumpa, at least one victim might escape the man's torturous methods.

Clay decided not to rouse the man because the last thing he wanted was for fellow police officers to arrive while he battled Khumpa. He had no wish for his secret to be discovered, or to battle his colleagues while trying to escape.

Moving silently along the second floor, Clay found an elevator and staircase separated by different hallways. Knowing Khumpa might leave traps in either, he decided to call for the elevator first, stepping aside when it arrived, the doors separating to reveal a ghastly sight.

"Damn it," he muttered to himself, realizing the two men lying with spears jutting from their heads were beyond his help.

He tried the stairwell door, finding it jammed shut from the other side. Fighting with the door was an option, as was breaking the glass to see what held it shut, considering it opened his way.

Deciding against it, Clay stepped into the elevator, careful to avoid the small pools of blood from the bodies. He pushed the button for the third floor, allowed the elevator to ascend, and listened carefully for any noises that seemed unusual. His ears were trained, and sensitive enough, to detect flying insects, projectiles, and movement along the ground from far greater distances than the normal person.

If Khumpa was nearby, and moved, he would know it.

The first noise to reach Clay's ears was not that of his enemy moving, but the sound of death. When the doors opened, he spied the last of Panelli's henchmen falling to the ground with a short sickle lodged across his throat, leaving a bloody mess everywhere around the weapon.

Khumpa had already advanced into the room where Panelli was begging for mercy.

Darting down the hall at top speed, Clay reached the room as Khumpa thrust his *katana* through the mobster's abdomen, leaving a blank stare across Panelli's face that came with inevitable death.

Panelli slumped to his knees, holding the area where the wound had been inflicted as Khumpa withdrew his sword cleanly.

Through the black mask, his eyes met with Clay's. Squinting sinisterly, the eyes distracted Clay just long enough for Khumpa to withdraw a small metallic ball from his uniform. He raised his arm, then let it fly toward the ground, creating a smoke bomb that quickly filled most of the room, leaving Clay blind and oblivious to his opponent's whereabouts.

Waving his arms before him as though he was wiping down a car, Clay cleared the haze from the air around him, realizing Khumpa had slipped out a back door. He obviously had his battlefield chosen, again leaving the officer at a disadvantage.

As Panelli lay groaning, about to die, Clay paid him little attention, knowing there was nothing he could do, even if he wanted to. The sword had severed a few major organs with one clean cut, meaning even immediate medical attention was not enough to spare the man.

Internal bleeding was due to take him any moment.

Making his way through the office, which was filled with a large table and a dozen chairs, Clay darted through the back door, finding another hallway. It led to another stairwell, which he guessed led to the roof of the building.

Deciding time was of the essence, he took a deep breath, then headed toward his final destiny.

CHAPTER 23

▼

Packard finally found his son in a nearby field after calling his name repeatedly. With half a dozen firefighters close by, the sergeant felt confident he was going to find his boy, but he questioned in what condition until Ryan emerged from a bush.

Dropping to one knee, Packard hugged his son when Ryan reached him, thankful the ordeal was finally over.

"My God, are you okay, Ryan?"

"Yeah."

"I was so worried."

"So was I. Did you get the bad men?"

He looked his son squarely in the eyes.

"Yeah. They won't be bothering us anymore."

Picking his son up, Packard quickly thanked the firefighters all around him before they headed back to the scene.

"I knew you'd get me back, Dad," Ryan said, bobbing in his father's strong arms as Packard carried him back.

His ribs ached from the earlier scuffle, but he gladly toted his son along, just to make certain nothing else happened to Ryan.

"I'm glad you did, because I wasn't real sure."

"Is Ed okay?"

"Ed's fine."

"How about Mitch?"

Packard balked.

"I'm…I'm not real sure, kiddo. We're gonna find out here in a sec."

He felt a lump in his throat as the group emerged from the edge of the field and the ambulance rushed off, sirens blaring and strobe lights whirling. Sorrell remained behind, appearing dejected.

Packard had seen hundreds of various accidents and house fires result in people being carted to the hospital. The medical technicians always allowed someone to ride in back with the patient, which would have been Sorrell in this case, unless something was seriously wrong.

Setting Ryan down when he reached Sorrell, he put a hand on the officer's shoulder because it appeared Sorrell was wiping away some moisture from his eye. He also seemed a bit choked up.

"You okay?"

Sorrell nodded, now wiping his nose dry with his sleeve. He kept his head turned so Packard couldn't read his emotions, though the sergeant sensed Sorrell was hurting, almost like a puppy missing his young human companion.

"Mitch said he couldn't feel his legs," Sorrell managed to say after a few seconds. "He lost a lot of blood."

Packard's eyes followed those of his officer toward the pool of blood left atop the pavement, partly soaked into the blacktop. It shimmered red and white from the strobe lights of the remaining fire trucks.

"You want to go to the hospital?" he asked Sorrell.

An affirmative nod was his reply.

"I'll drive, Ed."

Packard checked with the fire chief a moment, wanting to see if there was anything else he needed to do before checking on Mitch.

"Anything you need from me, Luke?"

Luke Salyer was a gruff man with a secret tender side. Packard knew how to work with his type, which was why Salyer took to him.

Near retirement age, the Cowan Fire Department Chief had seen everything during his three decades on the fire department. Packard had worked with him several times, and nothing seemed to shock the man. He had an unwavering sense of duty, and the men and women who worked on his department worked with him for years or a matter of days.

There was no in between.

"I radioed the county police," Salyer said. "I'm pretty sure they're going to want to have a talk with you."

"Then they can come to the hospital."

"What about the bodies?" the chief asked.

"That's what the coroner's office is for. If Scotty Hahn comes out here, give him my regards. I bet he hasn't slept a wink this week."

Letting a grin slip, the chief nodded his head, then motioned with his hand for Packard to leave while he still could.

"I'll mop this up. Go check on your officer."

"I appreciate it."

"You won't after the county boys track you down. I won't be able to hold them off for long."

Packard gave a quick wave, then asked Ryan to jump in the back seat as he slid behind the wheel. He started the car, seeing red and blue lights in the distance, guessing the county boys had been eating on the north end of town. If so, that explained why it took so long for them to arrive.

Scooping his cellular phone from the dash, he steered the car toward the opposite end of the parking lot to escape undetected. He reached the main road, then hit the speed dial for his home phone. Sarah would have to meet him at the hospital if she wanted to see Ryan anytime soon, because checking on Mitch was Packard's new priority.

*   *   *   *

Clay dashed up the final flight of stairs, springing through the partly open door that led onto the roof. Housed by four tiny walls, the entrance to the roof was easily accessible with good reason.

As he landed atop the roof, his toes sternly holding him upright, Clay scouted the area, finding crates of lounge furniture, a volleyball goal, a basketball goal lying on its side, and several small tables lining the rooftop. Obviously meant to be a recreational lounge to residents, the roof had an incomplete mesh fence around it, which reminded Clay of the jail, where workouts and sporting events took place behind the fence atop the building.

Like most of the building, this had yet to be finished, which created hazards with so many boxes and pieces of furniture in the way.

They posed nowhere near the threat of the man standing across the lengthy rooftop, holding a sword at his side, waiting patiently for Clay to make the first move.

Each stared intently into the other's eyes, but Khumpa waited until Clay began settling into a kneeling position before doing the same.

Both knew the tradition they were about to follow, because to do otherwise meant betraying their faith, and everything they had learned in Japan. Even

Khumpa, who had strayed from the way of the modern ninja, knew better than to forego his tradition, because the *kuji-in* were the strength of the warrior.

Nine primary hand symbols, known as the *kuji-in*, evoked different powers in a warrior, which were used before combat such as this.

Kneeling completely, both men stared across the roof to one another, placing their fisted hands in front of them, leaning forward to respectfully bow. Khumpa had laid his sword to his side, while Clay kept his sheathed along his back.

Clay went first, forming his fingers into a shape quite unusual to anyone else. Nothing like a gang sign, his fingers virtually meshed together, forming a shape he had memorized years before. He held them to the left side of his chest, near the heart, for his adversary to see.

"*Rin,*" he said aloud, his eyes never wavering from Khumpa.

Rin is used to bring strength to the mind and body.

"*Retsu,*" Khumpa countered, forming his fingers into a sword-like symbol.

He wriggled the symbol like a slithering snake, down from above his head, then thrust the imaginary sword forcefully toward Clay.

Retsu enables telekinetic powers in a ninja, allowing him to stun an opponent with a touch or shout.

"*Toh,*" Clay countered, which allowed the warrior to reach a balance between liquid and solid states of the body.

His decision to invoke the symbol had nothing to do with the hot tub several feet behind him.

"*Hei,*" Khumpa said appropriately, considering the symbol was used psychically to mask one's presence to another.

He formed the symbol before him with both hands.

"*Zen,*" Clay finished, hoping to bring enlightenment and understanding to himself about his opponent and their tradition before the battle had opportunity to kill him.

Khumpa reached for his sword, indicating he was done conjuring any further assistance from within, so Clay's fingers touched the grip of his sword instinctively. He unsheathed it with considerable ease, considering the memories flooding his mind.

His wife, his son, his uncle whom Khumpa tried to murder. Officer Frye, his fellow task force members, and Packard's son. The thought of hundreds lying dead near a railroad intersection came and went, then his mind focused on the work ahead of him.

Masterfully twirling the sword by his side a moment, Clay watched Khumpa do a similar move with his *katana*, then raise it to his chest, poised to charge and strike.

Clay raised his sword, then the two men charged one another, their weapons clashing with a metallic scraping sound as they gracefully sailed through the air, landing on opposite sides of the roof. Aggressively striking, Clay felt each of his assaults blocked by Khumpa as he tried for an opening with slashing attacks.

Khumpa's body was fresh, his mind still strong, allowing him to parry. Backing away after the initial attack, Clay found himself distanced from Khumpa by nearly a car's length. Instead of attacking in return, Khumpa immediately went to his bag of tricks, pulling out a small spear meant for throwing.

Clay spied the weapon, but found himself barely able to dodge it as the spear missed his face by inches.

As Clay avoided the first attack, Khumpa set to using a small weighted rope, twirling it in midair a few seconds before letting it fly toward Clay's sword. It wrapped itself around the handle of the sword, allowing the weapon to wrest itself free when Khumpa tugged his end of the rope.

Having nothing except his bare hands to defend himself, Clay monitored where his sword landed for future reference. At one point in his life, Clay would have been deathly afraid of having no ready weapons against a *katana*.

Experience had taught him well, because now he felt no fear, even as Khumpa jabbed at him with his sword.

Clay leaned from side to side, avoiding the sharp blade, then jumped as Khumpa swept at his feet with the weapon. He landed easily, finding the sword lunged at him once again.

Dodging once more, he performed a handspring to distance himself from Khumpa. Instead of waiting, Khumpa charged, leaving Clay little choice except to do the same. If he turned, he limited his options, because a fence was the only thing behind him.

As the sword sliced through the air where Clay's abdomen would have been, the officer dove forward, over the blade, rolling forward until he regained his footing. Clay sensed Khumpa was about to charge again, so he pulled a small metallic ball from inside his outfit. Throwing the *metsubushi* to the ground, Clay created a large puff of smoke that prevented Khumpa from seeing him as he retrieved his *katana*, then ducked behind one of the crates.

He decided to play a game with Khumpa to turn the tables.

Reaching into his outfit, he pulled out a star shuriken, waited until Khumpa turned toward him, then hurled it toward his adversary's eye socket.

To his dismay, Khumpa deflected the bladed weapon with his sword handle, which sent it harmlessly flying against the mesh fence. Realizing his concealment was hardly defensible, Clay jumped atop the crate, waited for Khumpa to charge him, then flipped effortlessly to one side as the blade cut nothing except the air.

Aggressively attacking, Khumpa forced Clay into a parlay the officer wanted anyway. Tiring Khumpa was his primary objective, since the terrorist had likely missed workouts, and neglected his studies of *ninjutsu*.

Clay wasn't perfect, but he built his own training facility inside his house with the intent of continuing his training, doing so on a regular basis. He was younger, equally quick, and probably a bit more powerful, but he lacked the extra years of training Khumpa had received.

Blocking powerful cuts and slashes, Clay found himself forced several feet back. He neared the hot tub, which was filled with water he assumed had to be cold, simply because the tub was not running, and summer had not yet arrived.

As he stepped on one edge of the tub, he felt one foot slide along the wet surface, despite his caution. From the corner of his eye he spied Khumpa's sword coming downward to sever his arm, but a quick retraction of the sword blocked the crippling blow, costing him his *katana* as it fell into the dark water.

This time there was no opportunity to recover his sword, and little precious time to evade Khumpa's attack as his adversary stabbed at his torso and head several times, forcing Clay to bob and weave.

Backed into the mesh fence, Clay waited until Khumpa thrust the sword directly at him before leaping several feet into the air, clutching the fence as he did so. Using Khumpa's shoulders as a prop, he kicked his enemy in the face before Khumpa was able to recover his sword, then kicked him away.

Clay dropped to the ground, getting a running start before performing several handsprings away from Khumpa. As Khumpa retrieved his sword from the fence's grip, Clay pulled a staff nearly two feet in length from inside the black cotton of his outfit, releasing the weighted chain from one end of the weapon.

He whirled the chain in the air momentarily, then whipped it toward Khumpa's arm, catching the man off-guard. Khumpa likely thought the intended target was the sword he held, but Clay took advantage of his surprise, yanking the chain toward him, bringing Khumpa in tow.

Though Khumpa stumbled a step, he recovered, using his arms to spring him back to a standing position.

He sliced at Clay with the sword, but Clay deflected the blow with the chain, using the slack in the chain to his advantage by swinging it around Khumpa's hands, binding them within its unrelenting grasp.

Much to Clay's surprise, he let the sword go without a fight, freeing his hands to withdraw two small blades from within his uniform quickly. In the same motion, he knelt, slicing the officer across the front of both thighs. Bloody streaks formed instantly where the cloth had been cleanly cut, but they were mere flesh wounds, meant to slow Clay's attack.

Recovering quickly, Clay took up the other end of the staff, releasing a lever that let a small sickle emerge from the opposite end of the chain. He took up the chain's slack in the other hand, swinging the weapon toward Khumpa's head and torso with precision speed and force.

While he was dodging Clay's assault, Khumpa failed to realize his adversary whirled the chain once more in his opposite hand, letting it fly once more toward Khumpa's right ankle. It wrapped around the appendage like it was meant to be there, allowing Clay to give the chain a quick tug, pulling Khumpa to the ground.

With one quick swing, Clay figured he had Khumpa's torso, at worst, in the range of the sickle, but Khumpa pulled his short sword, the *wakizashi*, from his side to block the attack.

Once again he slashed at Clay's thighs, but the officer was wary of the attack, performing a handspring to one side to distance himself from his enemy.

Using one of his few remaining smoke bombs, Clay threw it to the ground, finding it to be nothing more than a dud as it fizzled and sparked, producing little more smoke than a child's Fourth of July firework.

Shit, he thought.

Changing the tide of the battle once more, Khumpa pulled out his own metallic ball, launching it to the ground. Smoke immediately billowed upward as though the lid had been lifted from a burning trash barrel.

Unable to see anything through the smoky haze, Clay brushed the cloudy air away, listening and looking for any sign of Khumpa. Everywhere the crates and furniture blocked a complete view of the building, so he began a cautious exploration of the rooftop, determined to end the games once and for all.

*   *   *   *

Packard pulled into the back lot of the hospital, taking Ryan with him as he and Sorrell entered the sliding door of the emergency department. The ambulance had been pulling into the front bay on the other side of the building as they passed.

Sorrell limped badly, with blood still oozing from his wounded leg. Waiting for a second ambulance would have served only to delay their arrival at the hospital. Sorrell had more endurance than Packard had ever witnessed from any police officer.

Since the county police were involved with the entire mess, they had called Mitch's parents, sparing Packard that painful ordeal. He hated telling anyone their loved one was injured or dead. People were always shocked and devastated, and when he told people these things, there was nowhere to hide, and certainly no way to avoid it.

He nodded to a nurse at the front desk, then proceeded into the department itself, familiar with the hospital after babysitting drunk or beaten prisoners so many times. Several of his friends worked security at the hospital, but he didn't recognize anyone inside the security room as he passed by.

As they waited at the central desk to see where Mitch was about to be admitted, Packard looked to Sorrell's face. Looking as though he had already lost his best friend, the officer's eyes were flushed red. He trembled slightly in anticipation, biting his bottom lip absently to the point that it bled.

Packard took hold of his son's hand, wishing Ryan didn't have to witness the spectacle of them unloading Mitch from the ambulance. If Sarah arrived soon enough, Ryan might be spared the bad news Packard himself didn't want to hear.

Looking as badly as any victim Packard recalled ever seeing, Mitch had a ventilation bag, coupled with an oxygen tube, strapped around his head. His shirt was torn off, allowing two defibrillator pads to stick cleanly against his chest and side. Blood marred the sheet the emergency medical technicians used to cover him.

Monitoring his chest carefully, Packard saw a rise and fall, indicating Mitch was still breathing on his own.

At least for the moment.

Unconscious, he looked helpless. His head simply bobbed against the pillow as they removed him from the ambulance, wheeling him inside to the first room on the left where the hospital staff quickly took over.

Packard nudged Sorrell, who had little more than a blank look when he turned to see what Packard wanted.

"Put your badge on your belt," Packard said, doing so himself.

Sorrell shot him a quizzical look.

"Otherwise they'll kick us out."

"Oh," Sorrell replied vacantly, complying.

With room enough for a dozen or more personnel, the hospital staff usually let the technicians, security, and police remain to see the proceedings, unless the situation called for privacy.

Packard felt extremely uncomfortable bringing his son into such an adult situation, but no one was free to take him elsewhere, and he certainly didn't want Ryan with a stranger after everything the boy had endured. To this point, Ryan had remained exceptionally quiet, possibly stunned by his own traumatic events, compounded with the man he regarded as an uncle bleeding on a cot before his eyes.

As they transferred Mitch from the medical cot to the ER table, Ryan finally looked up to his father.

"Is Mitch going to be okay?"

"I don't know, Ryan," Packard answered.

At least they haven't used the defibrillator, he thought. It was likely hooked up as a precaution, but he suspected it might be used any second.

He heard the door open behind him, only because he stood so close to it. Turning, he spied his wife, who immediately dropped to one knee, pulling Ryan close. She looked up to him, already understanding the situation. Though Sarah worked in the trauma unit, her visit to the hospital was strictly personal on this occasion.

She stood, gave Packard a quick kiss on the cheek, then ushered Ryan and Nicole out of the room.

"Thanks," the sergeant said quietly to his wife.

Looking to Mitch with a concerned look, she nodded, then followed the kids outside.

Packard listened to bits of the conversation across the room.

He heard them discussing the preparation of a surgical table, the staff surgeon who would do the surgery, and how difficult it was to stabilize Mitch because of the blood loss.

"What are they waiting for?" Sorrell asked impatiently.

"If he's not stable, they can't operate," Packard whispered back. "They need to put blood and fluids back in him before they cut."

Sarah had told him some of these things before. He wasn't even positive he was telling Sorrell accurately how emergency surgery went, but his primary goal was to keep his officer from thinking negatively, or saying something that might get them kicked out of the room.

By now the medical personnel had Mitch hooked up to several machines, but they continued to monitor several things manually.

"He's stopped breathing," one team member said after a moment.

Packard felt numb all over, unable to move or comprehend what was about to happen next.

Making matters worse, the rhythmic beats from the EKG monitor that measured Mitch's heartbeats, suddenly became a continuous high-pitched wail. This could only mean his heartbeats had stopped, indicating there was a flatline.

"No, no, God, no," Packard muttered to himself as the crew scrambled to bring Mitch back.

CHAPTER 24

▼

With his weapon defensively outstretched beside him, Clay monitored the entire roof as he cautiously stepped between crates and bundles. He found no indication of Khumpa anywhere around, so he decided to see if his adversary might have hidden over the edge of the roof.

One edge had no fencing at all, so he drew near the hot tub, briefly considering retrieving his sword from the murky water. Sensing a trap, he warily kept a distance from the tub, still turning his body with the weapon leading him, in case he was attacked from any side.

Reaching into his uniform for a *kaginawa* in case of a sudden fall, Clay took hold of the thirty feet of thin rope with a four-pronged grappling hook at the end just in time.

As he peered over the edge of the roof, Khumpa suddenly lurched upward with the blunt end of his sword, striking Clay in the ribs. The move stunned Clay enough that Khumpa took hold of the material around his shoulder, throwing him off the rooftop.

Dropping the staff for full use of both hands, Clay tossed the hook of the *kaginawa* toward a steel post he had spied before looking over the edge. If it didn't take hold, he was destined for a hard landing from three stories up, onto solid concrete.

He had practiced for years on his throws and grappling with the tool, so he wasn't surprised it clasped the steel bar, then held his weight as his fall was abruptly stopped. Looking up, he noticed Khumpa had already scaled the rooftop and left, likely preparing his next surprise for Clay.

Berating himself for letting Khumpa outsmart him, Clay began ascending the rope. Even Khumpa wasn't evil enough to slit the rope. There was no honor in that, and he certainly hadn't waited so many years to murder Clay with a technique used only by cowardly gangsters and thieves.

Reaching the top of the roof, Clay pulled himself onto the flat surface, standing above the hot tub, seeing no sign of Khumpa. He watched the water on the tub, seeing no bubbles, or signs of anyone beneath the surface. Why it wasn't covered eluded him, but he stayed clear of the luxury machine, knowing Khumpa might be lurking beneath the water's surface.

Clay was capable of holding his breath several minutes. He remembered Khumpa once holding his breath five minutes, so he reached to his side, pulling out a metallic black staff. It housed a sword, which he planned to use in due time, since he dared not retrieve his own from the bottom of the filled tub.

Keeping watch in all directions, he backed himself toward the sickle he let fall when Khumpa tossed him over the side. Taking up the weapon, he withdrew the chain, setting the black staff aside momentarily.

Whirling the chain above his head, Clay finally let it fly toward a patio table. It wrapped itself around the base of the table, allowing Clay to give it one swift tug. He watched it fall into the hot tub, confirming what he suspected as Khumpa shot up through the water surface, now holding two swords.

One of which was Clay's.

He sliced through the table's shade covering with ease, landing beside the hot tub, poised for action.

Letting the sickle drop to the ground once more, Clay charged Khumpa with the staff, fighting off both blades at once.

Ducking, weaving to each side, and blocking with the metallic staff, Clay avoided more nagging injuries until Khumpa extended one arm too far with Clay's old sword. This mistake allowed the younger fighter to knock the sword free by whipping Khumpa's arm with the solid staff.

A quick cry of pain emitted from Khumpa as the staff likely cracked a bone in his forearm.

He jabbed at Clay with his remaining sword, missing the head twice, then the torso once as Clay ducked before rolling out of the way. Landing several feet away, Clay sensed danger upon him as Khumpa slashed downward with the sword.

Clay deflected the sword once with the staff, but Khumpa kicked it free from his hands, leaving him without a ready weapon. Lying flat on his back for defensive vision, Clay saw the sword tip come toward his head. He moved his head to avoid the piercing blade, then rolled, avoiding two more stabs in the process.

A clanking sound filled the air each time the sword connected with the concrete surface of the roof.

Drawing dangerously close to a cluster of furniture and boxes, Clay stopped rolling, finding the sword coming straight for his face.

He instinctively raised both hands, catching the sword on its blunt sides between his palms, preventing the killing strike.

As Khumpa pressed downward, Clay used every ounce of strength to keep the point of the sword, now inches from his skull, aimed between his eyes, to finish the job. He fought to turn the blade sideways, which might have reflected sun into his enemy's eyes on a bright day, but this was dusk, with barely enough light to see anything.

Still, the move put Khumpa off-balance, allowing Clay to withdraw his *wakizashi*, slashing Khumpa in one thigh. As the older warrior withdrew to assess the damage, Clay regained his footing, then his *katana* with a short walk to where Khumpa had dropped it.

Apparently not ready to finish their battle with swords, Khumpa used another sneaky tactic, throwing three consecutive stars at Clay. Deflecting the first two with his sword, Clay had no time to react to the third star *shuriken*, except to duck.

The star flew harmlessly over his head, but as he stood, Clay failed to react before a short knife with a thick, rounded handle, struck him in the right shoulder, its blade nesting in his muscle tissue.

Instinctively, he pulled it out smoothly with his left hand, firing it back toward Khumpa, who was more than ready. He caught it in midair, holding it for Clay to see with his own blood staining the blade.

Khumpa gave an evil laugh simply to enhance the mind games he played, then tossed the blade to one side. Both men knew Clay would not fail to catch it a second time.

Both combatants were growing tired, they were wounded, and each was losing a fair amount of blood. Clay had fared better than he expected, but only because Khumpa was not as sharp as he once was with weaponry. Either he let his practice go to the wayside, or he was toying with Clay, luring him into a false sense of security.

Either way, the time to end their conflict had come.

Khumpa held his sword out to one side, raising his other arm. He left it raised, indicating he was ready to do battle once more, and that it was now Clay's move.

Standing in a ready position, Clay held his sword out in front, with both hands, stared a moment, then charged his adversary with a clear run across the rooftop.

*   *   *   *

Packard found himself literally pushed outside the trauma room by the medical technicians and extra hospital staff with Sorrell when the crash cart came into view.

"No!" Sorrell cried, trying to push his way back inside.

Several members of the medical staff equaled his size, but looked reluctant to physically restrain him.

"Ed, we've got to let them do their jobs," Packard said at the door, trying to reason with his officer. "Come on," he added sternly. "If we're in there, they can't do their jobs."

Sorrell looked absolutely torn, like he was condemning his best friend to death if he left, but he followed Packard, rubbing his forehead in distress as he breathed in heaves.

Packard suspected he was about to break down completely, but felt that was better than having Sorrell in the room, potentially interfering with lifesaving efforts.

Both men made their way to the ambulance bay, which held the Delaware County ambulance that brought Mitch, and another ambulance from Eaton. No one was in the bay, so Packard let the double doors close behind them. If he didn't distance Sorrell from the trauma ward, the officer might be tempted to peek through the windows.

Sorrell limped to a wall where he could support his injured leg. Several times he had refused medical treatment when it was offered, and Packard learned the bullet went through the side of his calve muscle. Though not life-threatening, the injury needed serious medical attention, and soon.

"It's not fair," Sorrell said, obviously fighting the urge to cry, or completely break down.

"I know," Packard said in a softer tone than usual.

Sorrell slumped against a nearby wall, letting himself slide to the ground, where he sat complacently to worry about Mitch in his own way. Packard never showed his emotions very well, but felt at least as concerned about his officer's condition, because it was entirely his fault Mitch was injured at all.

He took a nervous breath, cupping his mouth with his right hand, letting his worries catch up with him. There were consequences if Mitch died. Clay would likely hate him, the force would probably demote or fire him, and the internal investigation would probably be headed by a young, zealous officer in their internal affairs department.

If that happened, Packard might see jail time from all the angry young officers destined to turn on him because he caused the murder of their colleague.

He knew he was thinking the worst, so he let his thoughts return to Mitch, rather than his own bad luck.

"God, I would give anything if you let him live," Packard vowed silently.

The double doors opened, startling him, while drawing Sorrell's attention. An EMT walked into the bay, opening one of the large doors meant for the ambulances to enter. He stepped outside a moment, so Packard decided to see if the man knew anything about Mitch's condition.

A tall, thick man with thinning dark hair, the EMT look haggard, as though he had already been through a rough day. He reached into his tan uniform shirt's front pocket, pulling out a pack of cigarettes. Lighting one for himself within seconds, he noticed Packard, offering one to the officer.

Packard started to refuse, then thought of the stress killing him from within, far quicker than tobacco ever could.

"Thanks," he said, taking one, then allowing the EMT to light it for him.

Packard vowed to quit again in the morning.

"I'm sorry about your friend, man."

"What can you tell me?"

Taking a drag from his cigarette, the man thought a moment, then exhaled into the night sky.

"He was shot from the side, obviously, but I think the vest did more damage than it helped."

Packard gave a confused look.

"It kept the bullet bouncing around his insides," the man explained.

"I saw blood on your blanket. Did the bullet come out?"

"No. That's half the trouble. If they stabilize him, they'll need x-rays or a C/T to find the stinkin' thing. It's still lodged in there somewhere, and he has internal bleeding."

The man paused, giving a sympathetic look.

"*Bad.*"

"You've seen this stuff before," Packard said, realizing his tone was a bit more pleading than he intended it to sound. "What are his chances?"

Saying nothing, the EMT simply shook his head negatively.

"You never know in these cases," he finally replied.

Packard took a few drags from the cigarette, which no longer seemed as appealing as it originally had. He flicked it onto the concrete drive, returning to the garage bay as he exhaled smoke in front of him.

Sorrell was no longer in sight, so he quickly made his way into the emergency department through the double doors, finding the officer beside an open trauma room door, no longer able to control his emotions as tears flowed freely. His left hand masked his face, but the sergeant knew from the scene around him exactly what he missed.

As though he had been stunned with a paralyzing toxin, Packard felt rooted to the floor, forced to take in every tragic image around him.

The open trauma room door.

Sullen faces on every staff member.

The EKG monitor turned off beside the bed.

A sheet speckled with blood, covering the man he once knew as an officer, a friend, and a compassionate human being.

He stood frozen in place, breathing through his nose, hearing nothing except his own breaths and the flood of thoughts crowding his head.

Closing his eyes, Packard felt emotionally overwhelmed. He wanted to hole up in a dark corner alone to mourn, but several pairs of arms wrapped around him. Opening his eyes, he found Sarah and the kids there to comfort him as the staff closed the trauma room door.

Again, the coroner's office was about to be called. Packard had no desire to stay at the hospital, but he wasn't about to leave Sorrell alone.

"Come on, Ed," he urged, leading the hobbling officer toward the lobby area.

He wasn't particularly thrilled about confronting Mitch's parents, but it needed to be done. Packard had several things to answer for, so he decided to start there.

After that, he was on his own.

*   *   *   *

With no crates or furniture left between them, Clay and Khumpa had a wide-open rooftop on which to duel. Clay felt blood oozing from several open wounds, but he wasn't quitting until he received a fatal blow, or Khumpa was dead without question.

Raising his sword over his head, then bringing it down close to the center of his torso, Clay charged as Khumpa darted toward him. They leapt in the air, each having a similar idea, their swords clashing, deflecting each other's blow harmlessly.

Each hit the ground, then leapt again simultaneously, displaying their similar training. Again the swords deflected one another, leading them into close-quarters combat.

Khumpa acted as the aggressor this time, swinging his sword with ease, looking for an opening in Clay's defenses. Blocking each slash with a counter, Clay maintained a safe distance, waiting for Khumpa to commit himself too aggressively.

When Khumpa did so, bringing a large swing to one side, Clay countered the move, blocking the swing as he knocked Khumpa's sword effectively out of the way. He then thrust the handle of his own sword at his enemy's head. Khumpa ducked, so Clay tried the move again, then again, keeping his blade between himself and Khumpa for defense.

While he was busy ducking the sword handle, Khumpa refused to initiate a sloppy offensive attack, because avoiding the handle was his primary concern.

If Clay stunned him with a strike to the head, their battle was certain to be over with a clean cut through his torso.

He dodged, however, forcing Clay to use a new strategy. Instead of thrusting the sword handle once more, Clay held it perpendicular to Khumpa's throat, forcing the man to defensively put his hand up to clasp Clay's hand.

Clay's idea worked perfectly, allowing him to use his own momentum, forcing Khumpa back several steps before tripping him with a foot sweep. Khumpa hit hard, finding less than a second to react as Clay's blade thrust toward his head like a sewing machine needle in action. Coming down straight, with great force, the blade hit nothing except the rooftop as Khumpa rolled evasively.

Stabbing downward a few more times, Clay missed as Khumpa barely evaded the tip of his blade. As he reached the edge of the roof where a mesh fence blocked further evasion, Khumpa stabbed his shorter sword toward Clay's feet, forcing Clay to jump, then handspring out of the way, all while holding his own sword.

Khumpa reached for something under one of the tipped patio tables, then threw his arm out toward Clay. Receiving fine sand to both eyes, Clay whirled to escape more punishment. Another trick had gotten him, even though he knew sand was used to weight down the umbrella stands to the tables. He cursed himself for falling prey to the deception, sensing danger coming up from behind.

Instinctively holding his sword flat above his head, he prevented a killing blow as Khumpa swung downward at his shoulder blade. Rolling to one side, Clay now had his vision restored, so he caught Khumpa at another swing of the blade, punching his adversary in the sternum to distance himself.

Khumpa stumbled back, but took another aggressive charge at Clay, his sword over his head, poised to strike Clay down. Instead of merely blocking the strike with his own weapon, Clay held his sword in front of his chest for protection, letting his shoulder strike Khumpa in the sternum. He heard a painful groan, and a forced exhale from his adversary, but Khumpa continued desperately to kill Clay by turning his sword downward, toward Clay's abdomen.

Keeping his right arm raised with his own sword to block Khumpa's weapon, Clay used his left hand to withdraw the *wakizashi* sheathed at his waist. Using one swift movement, his fingers twirled the blade into a useful position. With its blade facing his own abdomen, Clay thrust his left arm toward his side, sending the blade dangerously close to his guts.

At the last second he moved it just millimeters away from his flesh along his stomach. The blade plunged into Khumpa's chest, directly beneath the chest cavity, near the heart. Blood spurted out in rhythmic streaks each time Khumpa's heart beat. Though the blade didn't instantly kill him, the blow was fatal as blood pumped from his body.

Khumpa's face registered shock as Clay pulled his mask away. Khumpa reached for the blade in his chest, as though thinking he might be able to reverse the killing blow in some way. Staggering, he had no arrogance, no tricks left.

In no mood to prolong the battle, or watch Khumpa suffer as his adversary might have with the roles reversed, Clay readied the *katana* at his side, then lifted it.

One clean cut severed Khumpa's head from the neck, letting the body slump to the ground in a heap.

He replaced his sword to its sheath, then removed his own mask, staring at the body of his greatest enemy. Blood soaked into the rooftop as Clay considered what a waste of humanity Khumpa truly was. Almost a dozen bodies below him proved that fact, because ultimately Khumpa failed, taking hundreds of innocent lives with him beforehand.

"I hope you burn in hell," Clay said under his breath, deciding to leave before anyone else entered the building.

He heard no sirens, but knew from personal experience his colleagues stealthily came to such scenes with lights off and no sirens, hoping to catch a burglar or killer before the criminal escaped. Reaching the edge of the roof, he spied a patrol car in the distance. Clay decided to use Khumpa's method of entry as an escape route, so he replaced his mask, then darted for the opposite end of the roof.

They might find Khumpa's fingerprints, but Clay was careful from the onset to never touch anything aside from his weapons. He planned to gather any remaining weapons he found if time permitted, then leave the premises before anyone he knew spotted him.

As things were, Khumpa's murder would remain unsolved, and no one in their right mind was ever going to care.

CHAPTER 25

▼

When the next morning arrived, Packard felt worse than he had the night before. Even the beating he took didn't compare with the sore muscles and fatigue he suffered after a night of only two hours of sleep at best.

Deciding to avoid any media attention, or the wrath of his supervisors for the time being, he rented a motel room just outside the city limits. Unable to sleep, he told Sarah he was making an errand to their house while lying beside her in bed.

"If you wait, we can go when the kids get up," she said in response.

"I have to stop by city hall, too. I'll have my cell phone with me if you need anything."

"Okay," she said, letting him kiss her forehead.

"Love you," he said, suddenly realizing he said the words too infrequently.

She gave a clam-shaped wave with her hand, then closed her eyes, probably exhausted from the night's activities.

Buildings and streets blurred past Packard as he drove toward their house, wondering how Clay fared. He dared not call the officer, because he felt certain Clay knew about Mitch's death. Packard had no words to console the Branson family, and he felt worst of all for letting Clay down.

Packard really wanted time to himself, but he needed to stop by city hall at some point to face the music, although he didn't want to put his family through any more trauma. He decided to stop by the house to pick up a few supplies, and some files from work.

Perry's death allowed him the luxury of placing the blame on the agent's shoulders if he chose to. After all, Perry was the head of the task force, so it was his call. No one else could dispute the claim except Sorrell, and he trusted the man to keep quiet.

Sorrell was shook up by Mitch's death, leaving Packard to question if he planned to remain with the task force, if the force even existed in the wake of the terrorist aftermath.

After all, Packard was unable to take credit for anything leading to the deaths of the terrorists if he let everyone believe Perry was in control of the situation. It seemed fair to let Perry have the glory after the heroic sacrifice the man made to save Ryan. Packard felt bad about laying the blame on the man for getting Mitch killed through an operation he never actually led, but Packard didn't want his career to end. He wanted to keep things the way they were, if that was at all possible.

As he passed a factory, the smells of smog and molten metal entered his nose. Their unpleasant industrial odors displaced the scents of flowers and fresh-cut grass. May was right around the corner, leaving Packard to wonder how his summer might be spent.

He hoped it wasn't spent looking for a new job.

A few minutes later, he pulled into his quaint suburban driveway, seeing none of his neighbors outside. Morning dew covered the green grass along his yard as he left footprints in their fragile blades, trudging toward his front door.

He unlocked it, let himself inside, and felt somewhat naked, leaving his jacket, badge, and holster in the car. Usually, he arrived home, having to pluck several items from his body before truly settling in.

There was no need to get comfortable, because he was only staying a moment.

Leaving the front door open, he crossed the living room, knowing exactly what he needed, and where to find it.

He snatched the files from the top of the desk in the study, then ventured upstairs momentarily to use the restroom, planning to snag his portable radio after that. Sorrell and Mitch had brought their own radios the night before, so he left his at home, considering the unmarked car also had a radio unit.

Now he wanted to know everything he was missing before marching into city hall.

As he quickly descended the stairs, he heard the living room door shut hard. Packard dismissed it as the wind at first, but saw it open once more, slowly swinging inside. From the look of the shrubs in his front yard, there was no breeze.

And no reason for his door to shut.

"Clay?" he called cautiously. "That you?"

*   *   *   *

After spending part of his night dressing his wounds, Clay called his cousin's cellular phone, receiving no answer. He called Sorrell after that, discovering the truth about the entire incident at the school.

Sorrell had a difficult time narrating the saga because he sounded distraught. Between broken thoughts and sentences, he finally got to the part about Mitch dying at the hospital.

Now sitting near family and friends at his Uncle David's house, Clay blamed no one except himself for what happened to Mitch. Everyone around him wanted to blame Packard or Perry for the fiasco, but Mitch knew the consequences as well as anyone, Clay figured. He was destined to be labeled a hero, with a portrait and plaque in city hall for every police officer to see every day those men and women came to work.

Clay felt terrible about his cousin, one of his best friends, dying in such a way, but Mitch had truly saved countless lives by helping take down Zhang and Issaree Khumpa. He always pictured himself growing old with his cousin, retiring with him around the same time. They had years to plan a retirement spot, buy some land for a fishing lodge, and take their families on vacations together.

Everything was hypothetical, based on each getting married and having kids first.

Clay now questioned if he wanted to continue with police work. It was Mitch, and his charismatic speeches, who lured Clay into his career. Now his past had caught up with him, and might continue to do so. Everyone around him was in jeopardy if he stayed where he was, becoming complacent.

"You holding up okay?" Bill asked, venturing from the rest of the family to seek Clay at the staircase beside the entry door.

"I suppose," Clay answered.

Clay moved over, allowing his uncle to sit beside him.

"You're not blaming yourself for this, are you?"

"Partly," Clay answered.

"Khumpa was going to do what he did to some other country, and to other people, if he didn't do it here."

Clay nodded.

"I know that."

He paused, looking straight ahead to his aunts, who were all crying beside his mother. Everyone missed his cousin. Anyone who didn't had to be heartless in Clay's opinion.

"Khumpa's dead," Clay said quietly enough that only his uncle heard.

"I figured that, or you wouldn't be sitting here."

Bill looked to the full wrap around Clay's arm.

"I see you didn't escape unscathed."

"Not hardly," Clay answered, looking to his shoulder and legs.

He then looked to his uncle.

"I wasn't there for Mitch and the others last night, because I confronted Khumpa on his terms."

"You said it yourself. It had to be done."

"But at what cost? What did I risk if I stayed to help the others, Bill? I could have taken out all three people they faced in the parking lot within seconds. An FBI agent and my cousin would still be alive if I had."

Bill said nothing.

What could he possibly say to make his nephew feel better?

"He was my best friend in the whole world, and I can't even bring myself to cry," Clay chastised himself aloud.

"You're hardened after all the bullshit you've been through," Bill said. "You'll mourn Mitch in your own way. In time."

Clay bobbed his head affirmatively, knowing he had the rest of his life to question his choices. Dwelling on the past, or moving on to make his cousin's death something used as a positive to save other cops, was another choice he needed to make.

His cellular phone rang at his side. Plucking it from its clip, he found an unfamiliar number, but decided to answer it, just to take his mind off the moment at hand.

Standing, he motioned to his uncle he would only be a moment as he stepped outside.

"Hello?"

"This Clay?" a voice asked from the other end.

"Yeah. Who's this?"

"This is Pat Maddox from the coroner's office. I wanted to reach your sergeant because we've had a little problem over here, but they said he was indisposed. They gave me your number because they thought you might be able to reach him."

Clay didn't doubt the sincerity or authenticity of the call, but questioned what the coroner's office needed with Packard.

"What *sort* of problem?"

"Well, one of the bodies from last night came up missing. We had it bagged and tagged, but now it's gone."

"There was a shitload of bodies from the hazmat scene. Could there have been a mixup or something?"

"Uh, *no*," Maddox said as though the thought was incomprehensible. "This came up missing from the morgue itself, and the bag was left on the floor."

"Body theft?"

A momentary pause.

"Well, the morgue has pretty strict access. That's why we wanted to talk to your sergeant."

Clay wondered why they wanted to question Packard about a body. He probably had much larger concerns at the moment.

"Can I ask what body?"

"Last name is Khumpa."

"Male or female?"

He heard the rustling of papers as the deputy coroner looked through files on the other end of the phone line.

"Female."

"Ah, *shit*," Clay said before realizing it.

"What is it?"

"Nothing. Thanks for the info."

Before Maddox was able to question him further, Clay ended the call, peeking his head inside the door. His uncle was still seated on the stairway bottom.

"Bill, tell everyone I had to go," he said quietly, not wanting to gain everyone's attention.

His uncle started to ask something, then thought better of it, waving Clay away instead without saying a word.

Clay made his way around the dozen or more cars, looking like they were plopped in an arena for a demolition derby the way they all faced different directions.

He knew exactly what had happened, and where Issaree was going. Clay tried Packard's mobile and home phone, but there were no answers to either. As he started his car, he prayed he wasn't too late.

*   *   *   *

Packard reached the bottom of the stairs, confronted by a walking corpse.

Her clothes tattered, filthy, and bloody, her stare somewhat vacant like one might expect a zombie to look, and the rigid way in which she stood gave him the idea he was facing an animated corpse.

"It can't be," he stammered. "They pronounced you dead last night."

Wiping the small chunks away from the dried blood along her neck, she showed no degree of pain, indicating the injury was fake. An evil sneer crossed her lips as she pulled a small throwing knife from her belt, launching it at Packard within a second's time.

His reaction failed to save him from the blade as it dug into his shoulder, just above the chest, sending him crashing onto the stairs.

He had no idea how she faked death well enough to fool the coroner's office and medical personnel, and he didn't care. With all of their problems, perhaps they did an overly quick check of her vitals.

Like a cat, she pounced on Packard, kneeing him repeatedly in the thighs, then once in the groin. She reached for the knife in his chest, but Packard snatched her hand, punching her in one eye with his free hand.

Rolling back, she tumbled herself to a ready crouch as Packard pulled the knife from his shoulder, discarding it up the stairs where it could do no more harm. He felt inept using a blade, while she was a master with sharp objects, so he decided to leave neither of them with a weapon.

He felt the pain from the fresh wound as blood oozed out.

She feigned a charge until she drew close, then swung a kick toward his head, which he ducked. Before her foot had a chance to touch the ground, she swung it toward his knee, buckling it, sending him to the ground.

Packard cried in pain as her hand chopped the side of his throat, then his ribs, and finally into his abdomen. Throwing him headfirst to the ground, she stomped on his kidney, drawing another painful groan from him.

For a woman much smaller than himself in stature, Issaree knew how to use her hands and feet effectively. Every blow hurt because it was delivered with force, in just the right spot.

He rolled away from another hard kick, then regained his footing, reaching into his pants pocket. She looked stunned when he pulled out a small metallic ball, then hurled it to the ground, creating a smoky living room as he darted for a way out, or perhaps the phone.

Packard had no firearms stored anyplace readily, because of the kids, so his only chance of defending himself was hand-to-hand combat, which he felt extremely insecure about.

"I'll never make fun of the boys again," Packard mumbled, remembering how Mitch and Sorrell were both battered by the woman.

He crawled his way into the kitchen, hoping to reach the phone with enough time to dial 911, but Issaree found him before he reached the counter.

Standing, Packard caught her leg as it swung toward his head, launching a fist into her nose, drawing blood. His kidney burned, as though he was going to piss blood, but he didn't care.

Nor did he have time to.

He threw her leg upward, expecting to trip her up, but she used the momentum, doing a flip instead. Landing on her feet, she blocked his egress from the kitchen, throwing punch after punch at his face and torso.

Packard blocked several, but kicks started coming his way, creating more damage to his side, then his kidneys when he turned to avoid the barrage. He dropped to his knees as he turned, firing a fist with his weight behind it into her abdomen, forcing the air from her as she doubled back.

Heavily injured, but infuriated, Packard stalked her as she landed heavily on the ground, mounting her chest before laying several fists into her already bruised face. She took each with a cry of pain, but after the fourth punch, brought her legs up to knock him from her chest.

She drew a knife from the dispenser in the kitchen, quickly bringing herself closer to him. Packard had little chance of defending himself because his damaged shoulder prevented him from raising his right arm, and his left arm was battered to the point it could barely move.

Apparently realizing this, Issaree charged him from across the room, but Packard heard a hard footstep to his right, then the sound of a gun discharging.

Issaree flailed in mid-step, dropping the knife as her arms flew limply at her sides. A fresh, red wound appeared on the chest where her heart was located. Her eyes rolled toward the ceiling with a blank look as her body fell limp to the floor. Her rage had prevented her from ever seeing her death coming, but she likely would have tried killing Packard anyway.

"Thank you," Packard said, finding Clay standing there with his service weapon in hand.

"You're welcome," Clay answered neutrally.

"I'm sorry about Mitch," Packard decided to say quickly.

Clay shook his head from side to side.

"It's my fault. I never should have left your side."

Packard looked to Issaree's body, seeing the knife by her side. In horror movies they always came back, but she wasn't about to twitch.

"How did you know?" he asked Clay, sensing his officer's sixth sense had kicked in.

"It's a ninja trick. You can slow your heartbeat down to the point of near-death through deep meditation. If someone gets proficient, they can hold their breath for minutes at a time, and conventional medical devices in the field won't catch it."

Packard let a grin slip.

"So you're admitting it."

"What?"

"That you're, well, you know?"

Clay forced a smirk, turning toward the front door.

"I'm not admitting anything," he said as he stepped into Packard's front yard.

A neighbor stepped outside from the house next door.

"Should I call the police?" she asked, apparently worried about the fired gun.

"Yes," Clay answered without hesitation.

"Why didn't you just lop her head off like you did her brother's?" Packard asked.

Clay mocked a confused stare.

"I have no idea what you're talking about."

Rolling his eyes from disbelief of Clay's denial, Packard peeked inside to make sure the body wasn't moving.

It wasn't.

"For what it's worth, thanks again," he said. "If that asshole hadn't followed us there, your cousin would still be with us."

Several other neighbors had cautiously wandered outside to see what was happening. Most stared at Clay, dressed in civilian attire, holding a gun in his left hand.

"You realize Ed is going to be your responsibility now, right?" Clay said more than asked.

Packard thought a moment about how close Mitch and Sorrell had been for years. If he didn't step up to keep Sorrell in his task force, assuming the inquisitions went well, the officer might never recover from the traumatic incident.

"I'll take care of it," Packard said. "Does that mean you're going to bat for me?"

Clay looked him in the eye a few seconds, then gave an affirmative nod.

"I think we both have some skeletons that need to be moved from the closet to the back yard, Tim. Once all this is over, we'll grab Ed and work out the details."

"Yeah," Packard said without showing any enthusiasm. "We'll do that."

Although he felt thrilled Clay was on his side, Packard still had concerns about losing an officer under his command. Of all people, he thought, I would lose one of my favorites. Mitch was going to be missed by everyone. Their police department hadn't lost any officers in the line of duty in over a decade.

It sometimes took the most unexpected casualties to remind officers how dangerous and unpredictable their job was. Packard peeked inside one last time, thankful to be alive, and more thankful Clay remained by his side.

He never promised to be the most ethical supervisor in the world, but he promised results. Packard wanted to be known as someone who got the job done, because his primary goal was always going to be clearing the streets of the criminal element that affected his city's people, and especially their children.

When he did that, he slept with a clear conscience every night.

Epilogue

▼

Three months later

Packard sat in a veranda connected to a steakhouse in the center of the city, watching trees rustle in the distance as storm winds blew past. Overhead, the skies grayed, warning of an incoming July thunderstorm.

Safely tucked away with a wooden privacy fence beside him and an overhang that covered every table from above, Packard decided to chance his luck by remaining outside.

Several plastic trees were potted around the six round tables. Smells of cut grass and flowers intertwined with the grilled food from inside, leaving pleasant aromas everywhere around the sergeant. Music played lightly from overhead speakers, while a server made his way around the three occupied tables, asking anyone if they needed refills.

Beside him, Sorrell studied the menu, but glanced up every so often at the clouds, which glided at a heated pace across the sky.

No longer did cravings for nicotine plague Packard, but humidity was about to agitate everyone, once the storm passed through.

He put down his last patch two weeks prior, able to function without thinking about a cigarette every ten minutes. He still had bad habits, but those were between him and his officers.

And the occasional criminal his task force used questionable tactics on to extract information.

"You worried there, Ed?" Packard finally asked, still looking at his own menu.

"I hate getting wet."

Sorrell had grown significantly the past three months. Clay and Packard adopted him as their own, giving him equal status in everything they did. No longer did he stutter as he had, because he felt much more confident as an officer around criminals *and* his peers.

It was taking some time, but other officers began showing him respect. Packard and Clay said nothing except good things about him, and he made strides in his workload. He interrogated suspects, made arrests, and even dropped several pounds in his efforts to get himself in shape. Packard figured he was tired of chasing drug dealers around, getting winded after running a city block.

"So who's this new member we're getting?" Sorrell asked, putting down his menu.

"Hamilton," Packard answered. "I don't know much about him, but Clay highly recommends him."

"Then it can't be good."

Chuckling to himself, Packard took a sip from his lemonade.

"He's not that bad," Sorrell added. "I worked with him in patrol awhile when he started."

Packard took a deep breath, wishing Clay would arrive. He was absolutely thankful Clay and Sorrell stuck up for him, giving a slanted version of the truth to investigators. They made Perry both a goat and a hero because he allegedly ordered the mission to meet the terrorists, but killed Panelli's henchman in the process.

He kept his task force, and they continued to take drugs and guns off the streets, even though it always seemed there was someone to take every dealer or seller's place.

"Is the new guy going to slow us down?" Packard asked casually.

Sorrell looked at him a moment, then shifted his eyes toward the table.

"I don't think so. He'll play ball."

"Clay seems to think so, too."

With a beer in front of him, Sorrell was setting an immediate example of how things weren't always done by the book. Without set hours, the task force members didn't have to worry about drinking on the job.

Packard didn't ask his officers to do anything the criminals didn't do. He leveled the playing field, bending and breaking laws to get what he wanted.

And needed.

If they roughed up a dealer, he didn't go to jail as long as he talked.

Packard wanted the bigger fish, and he made sure he left his bait in place to avoid disrupting the big pond of drugs and arms.

When Clay finally pulled up, he stepped from his car, holding a folded newspaper in one hand. He wore sunglasses, though they were unnecessary with the overcast sky. Instead of entering the restaurant and walking through, he leapt over the short mesh fence on one side of the veranda, seating himself beside Sorrell.

He laid the Chicago newspaper before Packard, who instantly noticed the headline.

Suspected Drug Dealer Found Dead in Apartment.

"What is it?" Sorrell asked, trying to stretch his neck for a better look.

"Apparently our friend Salas was murdered overnight in his apartment," Packard replied, still reading the subtitle and article to himself. "Both of his hands were severed clean, leaving him to bleed to death."

"Yuck," Sorrell commented, making a sickened face. "Can't say I'm gonna miss him though, after the prick shot me."

Both looked to Clay, who shrugged.

"I'm not going to miss him."

Packard gave his officer an odd smirk, indicating he knew how Salas came to his death, but Clay remained as casual as ever.

Salas had pushed the issue the past month, stating within his ranks, that he wanted Packard and the task force dead. With the FBI hounding him, it seemed unlikely Salas was going to make any risky moves, but apparently Clay had decided to make certain the drug pusher never followed through on his promise.

Deciding not to push the issue in front of Sorrell, Packard slid the paper aside.

"Water, please," Clay said as the server returned, removing his sunglasses before placing them in his shirt pocket.

"Your buddy getting here soon?" Packard inquired.

"I told him to be about ten minutes late, just like you asked."

Folding his hands on the table, Packard looked to Clay a moment.

"Before we get down to the usual business, I just came from the chief's office."

"Uh oh," Clay said, giving a concerned look.

"Nothing like that, Clay. It seems they're going to grant your request of a memorial for Mitch in the basement, across the street at the park, and in several major police magazines across the nation. The university is going to offer a scholarship funded by the FOP, and get this."

Packard opened both hands, tapping his fingers against the table for effect.

"They nominated Mitch posthumously for a heroism award in our national newsletter, and the results came in this morning."

All of this likely came as a shock to Clay, because he seemed stunned by most of what Packard had said so far.

"Don't keep me in suspense," Clay said. "And?"

"And he *won* the thing," Packard said, smiling broadly, as were both his officers when they heard the news.

"Fuck yeah," Sorrell said before realizing they were surrounded by several people who took offense to such language in public.

Clay seemed overwhelmed, and the happiest Packard had seen him since Mitch died.

"I can't believe it," he said. "How on earth did his name get tossed into all these things?"

Packard lifted his head skyward, looking up as he did so, bobbing just a bit.

"I might have sent off a few nominations."

"Outstanding," Clay said, still looking awestruck.

"I've got something better for you," Packard revealed. "The chief has been asked to send someone to Washington to give a speech on Mitch's behalf at a national conference. With a little persuasion from me, he came to the realization there was no one better than you to do it."

Balking a bit, Clay seemed reluctant to commit to public speaking.

"I don't know if I could."

"You're his cousin," Sorrell chimed in. "His best buddy. Who better?"

Clay thought about it a few seconds, probably coming to the realization Packard had that morning. There was no one better to represent his cousin than himself, because they lived and worked together their entire lives.

"Yeah," Clay said. "I'll do it."

He raised his water glass.

"To old friends and the jobs left to do."

Each tapped their glasses together. It was a new beginning for each of them, and a chance to move on with their lives. Packard was thankful for his second chance, deciding to make every moment count.

He spent more time with his family, realizing he wasn't going to solve the world's problems in a day. Now he was seated beside two officers he considered his brothers. They too were his family, and he knew he couldn't request two better people to take his side than them.

Even if he wanted to.

About the Author

Patrick O'Brian is a professional firefighter in Muncie, Indiana. He has published several books, including arson mysteries and suspense thrillers. During the summer months the author enjoys roller coasters and theme parks. He also enjoys photography and bidding on internet auctions.

0-595-33099-1

Printed in the United States
22154LVS00003B/109-126